I0633529

Think Weirder

The Year's Best Science Fiction Ideas

CSF Press

ISBN-13: 978-1-949787-02-3
©2025 All Rights Reserved

Cover Art "Vegetable shop U+24E7" by Marcel Deneuve

Editor
Joe Stech

Titles in Rajdhani by Indian Type Foundry
Text in Crimson Pro by Jacques Le Bailly

CSF Press is a small press located in Colorado.

CONTENTS

Introduction   1
by Joe Stech

Death and the Gorgon   3
by Greg Egan

The Best Version of Yourself   49
by Grant Collier

Twenty-Four Hours   85
by H.H. Pak

Best Practices for Safe Asteroid Handling   99
by David W. Goodman

Nine Billion Turing Tests   125
by Chris Willrich

Stars Don't Dream   155
by Chi Hui, translated by John Chu

A Gray Magic   187
by Ray Nayler

Why Don't We Just Kill the Kid In the Omelas Hole   199
by Isabel J. Kim

The Brotherhood of Montague St. Video   207
by Thomas Ha

Our Chatbots Said 'I Love You,' Shall We Meet?   227
by Caroline M. Yoachim

Breathing Constellations   241
by Rich Larson

The Lark Ascending   251
by Eleanna Castroianni

Driver   259
by Sameem Siddiqui

How to Remember Perfectly   275
by Eric Schwitzgebel

LuvHome™   289
by Resa Nelson

Money, Wealth, and Soil   301
by Lance Robinson

Acknowledgements   321

Permissions   323

INTRODUCTION
BY JOE STECH

My kids love showing me things. A weird bug in the backyard, some crafts they made, hot air balloons in the distance, anything that they find delightful and want to share.

That impulse to share is why I curate stories. I read something amazing that makes me think differently about society or technology, or I read something that articulates an idea that I've considered before in a whole new way, and I want to show it to as many people as I can.

This book collects the stories published in 2024 that made me think "I need to share this immediately." My tastes run toward concept-driven, near-future explorations of people interacting with technology, so that's what you'll find here. From an initial pool of 391 stories, I selected the sixteen that best fit these criteria, contacted the authors, and secured reprint rights so I could share them with you.

I wish I could talk with each of you after you finish these stories and hear your thoughts. Since I can't, let me give you a small selection of what I loved about them.

First, let's talk about AI stories – there are several here. I've avoided the one-dimensional portrayals that dominate most media, instead opting for stories that feel like plausible, nuanced scenarios.

Greg Egan accomplishes this beautifully in our opening story, *Death and the Gorgon*. The AI subplot is secondary to the central murder mystery but adds realistic texture to the near-future setting. What I love most is how the story subtly skewers both overzealous AI projections and absurd longtermist positions, refocusing our attention to the here and now in a refreshing way.

Other AI-adjacent stories focus on ways to use the technology to assist humans with grief and loss. Ray Nayler's *A Gray Magic* is a raw story about a terminal patient in a bad situation, showing that sometimes even small mindset shifts can ease terrible situations that can't really be made better. H.H. Pak's *Twenty-Four Hours* is also adjacent to this space, but I can't really describe it without significant spoilers. In *The Lark Ascending*, Eleanna Castroianni uses a story about an AI system to comment on memory, love, and resistance in the face of authoritarian erasure.

Another thread running through the anthology: humans using technology to reimagine how we live and organize ourselves. Rich Larson uses technology in *Breathing Constellations* to allow humans to start to understand non-human cultural norms for the first time. In *Best Practices for Safe Asteroid Handling* David W. Goodman shares a beautiful vision of a spacefaring culture that coheres through better empathy for one another. In *Money, Wealth, and Soil*, Lance Robinson applies extremely near-future technology (arguably technology that we could achieve today) to soil revitalization efforts, but doesn't shy away from complicated principal-agent issues that all bureaucracies must contend with.

Some of my favorite stories in the book defy easy categorization. Isabel J. Kim's *Why Don't We Just Kill the Kid In the Omelas Hole* responds to Ursula K. Le Guin's *The Ones Who Walk Away From Omelas* – a seemingly odd fit for a concept-driven near-future anthology. But every sentence is dense with the good stuff: humor, subtly cutting rhetoric, glancing references to the emergent behaviors and tradeoffs that constitute society.

As my kids would say when they're overcome by the sharing impulse: "Look! Look!" I'm so excited that you're about to experience these stories for the first time.

Enough from me. Sixteen new worlds await.

DEATH AND THE GORGON
BY GREG EGAN

When the vault in the abandoned coal mine collapsed, it took four days for the engineers to complete their inspection and certify that it was safe for law enforcement personnel to enter the site. Beth drove out from town with her deputy, Ken Osgood, and the county medical examiner, Helen Myers.

Vitrosophy had bought the mine eleven years before, and though their business had attracted a degree of notoriety at the time, Beth couldn't recall the company generating any kind of fuss during her tenure as sheriff. In the days since the cave-in, she'd gone over all the original applications and permits, and everything seemed to have been done by the book. The mine itself had been worked for more than fifty years, with its fair share of accidents from various causes, but not one miner buried in a rockfall. Vitrosophy's advertising had boasted about the stability of the geological formation they'd chosen for the vault, and maybe that was true, but a lack of seismic activity and groundwater incursion, however advantageous, was not in itself sufficient to preclude any number of more mundane structural issues.

When Beth and her colleagues arrived at the site, the entrance, bored into the hillside long before any of them were born, appeared undamaged; if not for the hazard tape stretched across the gate, she would have struggled to spot anything amiss. They put on full anti-contamination clothing—jumpsuits, booties, caps, gloves and masks—before donning safety helmets.

As they approached the gate, Ken asked Beth, "Is it okay if I bring Sherlock in now?"

"Sure," she replied, trying to sound indifferent. She'd given in to pressure from the board of commissioners and agreed to a six-month evaluation trial of the software; the company behind it, Learning Re Enforcement, seemed to have embarked on a campaign to foist it on police forces all over the planet.

Ken put on his AR glasses to share his view with Sherlock and receive its annotations, but he couldn't resist a short vocal exchange. "Hey Sherlock, at the start of every case, you need to throw away your assumptions. When you assume, you make an ass out of you and me."

"And never trust your opinions, either," Sherlock counseled. "That would be like sticking a pin in an onion."

Ken turned to Beth; even through his mask she could see him beaming with delight. "How can you say it'll never solve a case? I swear it's smarter than half the people I know. Even you and I never banter like that!"

"We do not," Beth agreed.

She unlocked the gate. The entrance was wide enough for four trucks to drive in side-by-side, but with the power out it took all three of them to roll the gate open far enough to enter single file. Vitrosophy had their own generators—four, no less, including a fallback source based on radioactive decay, of the kind they used on space probes that flew too far from the sun—but those that hadn't ceased functioning when the ceiling fell on them had had their output cables severed.

They switched on their headlamps and advanced slowly into the gloom. Beth took out her notepad and watched the group's position markers shuffle across the map toward their first, and saddest, target. The search and rescue robot sent in on the day of the collapse had found the security guard, Carl Hesse, half-buried in rubble and exhibiting no vital signs; judging from how much his body had cooled, he'd almost certainly bled out from his injuries several hours before he'd been located.

The powder-blue wall that had once partitioned off the chamber and presented an elegant face to arriving visitors had been reduced to a pile of bricks. Beth had watched the videos of VIPs and influencers taking the tour before signing up for the service, or at least offering their fulsome endorsements.

The engineers had cleared a path through the debris, so it wasn't a struggle now to reach Carl's body. The search and rescue robot had taken photographs, but Beth took her own. Carl had been a couple of years ahead of her at school; as a teenager he'd worked in her father's garage for a while. He and his wife had run the cake shop together, but Cheryl had told Beth that business had been tight and he'd applied for the job here to try to make ends meet. It must have sounded like the safest night shift on the planet, guarding things that no one would want to lay their hands on.

When Beth was done, Helen began her *in situ* examination. "He suffered a major skull fracture," she reported, cradling Carl's head in one hand. "It might not have been the cause of death, but he would have been unconscious for everything that followed."

"That's a small mercy," Beth replied. Pieces of a coffee mug were sitting among the ceiling tiles and chunks of stone strewn across his body.

"It must have been tough staying awake down here," Ken remarked. "But he told me they let him stream shows on the computer."

Beth wasn't sure why Vitrosophy hadn't just monitored the place remotely when the technicians were absent. But maybe the presence of a guard in the flesh was a matter of prestige, a way to make their clients feel more valued.

Helen listed Carl's other visible injuries, including a severed femoral artery. When she was finished, the three of them worked in silence to free the body and place it on the stretcher they'd brought. Carl's trousers were stiff with blood, and there was a dark dried pool on the floor where he'd lain.

While Ken and Helen carried the body out, Beth started putting the shards of the coffee mug into an evidence bag. When she was done, she turned and looked across the interior of the vault. Now that Carl had been removed, the strongest smell that remained was like an organic chemistry lab, with a sickly sweet note of ethers woven in among the solvents. A couple of shattered computer displays glinted among the broken furniture, and some dented metal tubes shone dimly. But then the beam from her headlamp flared back at her, as if she'd caught herself in a mirror.

Beth walked over to the toppled storage units; one of them had fallen straight toward her, exposing fragments of silvered glass inside the stainless steel tube. A dozen or so human heads had spilled out onto the floor: wrinkled skin, hair gathered in tufts, eyes sewn closed.

She photographed the scene, then walked around the center of the vault, capturing images of the overturned units. Every one of them had ruptured to some degree, and the contents would have long since departed from the desired temperature. Vitrosophy's full inventory for the site came to over one hundred heads. Beth had expected the town to be besieged by relatives coming to claim these remains for burial, but as far as she knew no one had shown up yet.

She heard Ken and Helen returning.

"Have you brought the bags?" she called out to Ken.

"Yes."

"Then let's get started." Beth suffered a moment of resentment: how was this her *job*? But who else did she expect to do it? Did she want Pete Miller, the town's mortician, traipsing across what might yet turn out to be a crime scene? Or Vitrosophy's techs let loose on the site, to tidy away anything inconvenient to the company? "One hundred and seven need to show up at the morgue," she said, "so let's not leave anyone behind on the first trip."

2

When they arrived at the morgue, there was a large refrigerated-storage truck sitting in the parking lot.

"Did you arrange that?" Beth asked Helen.

"No. Where would I get the budget?"

Three people were standing by the truck: two men in white coveralls and heavy rubber gloves, and a third, in jeans and a tee-shirt, with the preternatural glow that suggested collagen modulators had swept a few decades under the carpet of his implausibly taut skin.

"How do you figure out someone's real age these days?" Beth wondered. "Are there blood tests?"

"You could carbon date those tattoos to the Late Pretentious," Helen suggested. "Or maybe the Early Try-hard."

"So what do you call mine?" Ken asked bravely.

"Peak Conformist," Helen replied.

Ken laughed, unoffended. "Sherlock says that's Gideon Figg, by the way. CTO of Vitrosophy."

Beth approached the casually dressed man and introduced herself; Sherlock turned out to have identified him correctly. Maybe the tattoos helped.

"I have a court order instructing you to deliver our clients' remains into our custody," Figg said, holding up his notepad to show her the document.

"That's fine by me," Beth replied. "They would have taken up an awful lot of space anyway." She was annoyed that Jim Rusko, the county attorney, hadn't bothered to inform her that there'd been a hearing on the matter, but if he'd asked, she would have told him not to contest the application.

The men in coveralls set about moving the bagged heads into the truck, while Ken and Helen carried Carl into the morgue.

"What will happen to them?" Beth asked Figg.

"It will depend on the terms of their contracts," he said. "Some will be buried or cremated, but some opted for ongoing cryonic storage even after an interruption like this."

Beth bit her tongue, but Figg seemed to feel compelled to justify the practice. "Recovering information from a vitrified brain is always going to require highly sophisticated algorithms to fill in the gaps where the structure has degraded," he said. "A period of thawing will certainly make recovery more challenging, but when there's no time limit at all on the opportunities for progress in the field, there's no reason to give up at the first hurdle."

Beth was pretty sure the thawed brains now carried about as much information as liver pâté, but she gathered that Vitrosophy's claims for their services never quite veered into outright fraud, and it was all beyond her jurisdiction anyway.

"Do you believe anyone might have had a reason to target your company?" she asked.

"No." Figg did not seem perturbed by the question. "Have you found any signs of foul play?"

"We haven't," Beth admitted. "But you must be surprised that after all the experts told you this vault would last for millennia, it just caved in one day, for no apparent reason."

"I'm horrified," Figg replied. "By the death of Mr. Hesse, and by the setback this represents for our clients. Once we have access to the site, we'll be bringing in our own consulting engineers to try to discover what went wrong. If the original design or construction was faulty, we'll certainly be pursuing damages in court. But I can promise you that Mr. Hesse's family will be compensated immediately; we accept our obligations to them unreservedly, and we'll leave it to the consultants and the courts to allocate the ultimate blame, if and when that's possible."

"Well, that's something." Beth was glad that Cheryl and the kids wouldn't be left high and dry, but she still wanted to know if she was investigating a homicide, negligence, or an act of nature. "You really have no hunches?" she pressed Figg. "We're almost certain that it wasn't a tremor, because the closest seismometers picked up the cave-in itself with nothing beforehand."

"Maybe the initial survey of the rocks above the vault was flawed," Figg suggested reluctantly. "But I need to be careful; I can't go throwing around aspersions with no evidence."

Beth said, "I understand."

The men had finished moving the heads; they closed the back of the truck and stood by, waiting for instructions. "Why did you think you'd need a court order for the remains?" Beth asked Figg. "It's not as if I was going to want to autopsy them all and re-establish the causes of death."

"We just wanted to get them back in the right conditions as soon as possible," Figg replied. "It was already far too long, and if you'd decided to treat them as evidence, it could have stretched on for months."

"Fair enough." Beth shook his hand. "I'll call you if I have any news."

"Thank you."

"Or any questions."

"Of course."

She hesitated, then gestured at the glowering snake-haired woman on his forearm. "Medusa, right?"

Figg said, "No, it's her eldest sister, Stheno. But almost no one's heard of her."

"Why any of those creatures, if you don't mind me asking?"

"To remind me every day not to fear them," he said. "Being turned to stone might seem terrifying, but it's really not the same as death."

3

"If you got a terminal diagnosis tomorrow," Beth asked her husband as she climbed into bed, "would you have your head frozen?" It had struck her earlier in the day that they hadn't thrashed out the question when Vitrosophy bought the mine and everyone else was talking about it, probably because they'd only just started dating and weren't looking for things to disagree on.

Gary put down his book. "Not if I was going to end up in a rockfall."

"Obviously. But if someone did it properly?"

He grimaced. "Depends what you mean by 'properly.' If there was a decent chance that I'd wake up while you and Sophie were still alive, with all my memories and personality intact, of course I'd do it. New body, robot body, disembodied ... as long as I was still myself, it'd be crazy not to. But when even the people peddling the service admit that my brain would be full of cracks, and some crucial molecules involved in storing memories would be damaged by the antifreeze ... no thanks."

"People forget things all the time," Beth countered. "People's personality changes just from aging."

"That's true," he conceded. "And if I had a stroke, say, that did that kind of damage in one hit, whether I'd want to go on living or not would depend on exactly how much I'd lost. But even the most charitable spin on the state of the art for brain preservation puts the damage way beyond the equivalent of a stroke. I know the company line is that there'll be autocorrect for curdled brains one day, but if the information isn't there at the start, you can't autocorrect a few keystrokes into a million-word autobiography. Do I really want some fool in the year 3000 to take a template for a generic person with my background, and tweak it with a few hints from what remains of my denatured brain, just to create someone *a bit like me*? Millions of people *a bit like me* are going to be born eventually, anyway, purely by chance; why should I throw away money just to muddy the waters and give one of them my name?"

Beth smiled. "That's pretty much my own verdict. Of all the things where a half-assed version might be good enough, resurrection would be at the bottom of my list. If you can't do it right, don't bother."

"But you think someone targeted the heads, don't you?" Gary asked. "Someone took all this horse-shit seriously enough to want to 'kill' a stack of frozen brains?"

"Maybe." Beth switched off her bedside lamp and settled in. "It could just be faulty construction. But even if the whole sales pitch is hokum, I can't see them cutting corners on the vault."

"Maybe one of the heads was from a murder victim," Gary suggested, "and the killer only found out later that the result wasn't quite as final as they'd hoped."

"I checked the death certificates," Beth said. "No homicides. But if the murderer was able to make it look like an accident the first time ... "

Gary winced. "And you've got how many possible victims?"

"One hundred and seven," Beth replied.

"Good thing there's no other crime in this place," he joked.

Beth pretended to bristle. "Are you saying I have too much time on my hands?"

"Never," he protested. "But if there's a killer out there who was counting on no one making time to find a needle in a haystack, they could be in for a shock."

4

Beth sat in her office and worked her way through the list of Vitrosophy's clients. The court order had actually made her job easier, since it included details of all the next of kin, but they were scattered across the country, with a few overseas, so she needed to be mindful of the time zones. She offered her condolences to each spouse, sibling or child, promised a thorough investigation of the crime, and then listened sympathetically to any grievances, worries or suspicions they wished to air.

Some of the relatives were clearly true believers in cryonics, though only a small fraction thought the thawed departed still stood a chance. The rest were going through a kind of second mourning, and Beth tried to deal with that as tactfully as she could. Apparently Vitrosophy's generosity to the family of the one actual victim didn't extend to the doubly dead; whether anyone's storage fees would be refunded now lay in the hands of an insurance company who were unlikely to pay out until they'd reached their own conclusions on the cause of the event.

"We thought Marcus was so lucky!" his sister Veronica told Beth tearfully. "He won the lottery right after his diagnosis. Who could believe that?"

"It's amazing," Beth agreed. "How much did he win?"

Veronica didn't answer for a moment, and Beth was afraid she'd offended her, but then Veronica explained, "I don't mean some ordinary lottery, with prize money. He won *the OG lottery*; the prize was that he got to be preserved."

Beth was fairly sure that whatever might count as the "Original Gangster" among lotteries would not have involved corpses being frozen, but this wasn't the time to quibble about the shifting meaning of the phrase. "So Vitrosophy give a certain number of places away for free?" she asked.

"Not Vitrosophy," Veronica corrected her. "OG. Optimized Giving. The charity."

"I see. So your brother got his diagnosis, then put his name down for the lottery that this charity runs?"

"Yes."

Beth didn't know what to say now; for Marcus's family to think he'd been granted a one-in-a-million chance of cheating death, only for the winning ticket to prove worthless after a couple of years, was about the cruelest sequence of reversals she could imagine. "I'm so sorry," was all she could offer. "If we learn anything more about what happened, I'll be sure to let you know."

A third of the way through the list, she still hadn't come across anyone whose relatives found their original deaths suspicious. The samples from the chamber had all returned negative for explosives residue. Carl's autopsy, and the tests on his coffee mug, had yielded no evidence that he'd been sedated or otherwise put out of action prior to the cave-in itself. And even if a killer happened to share their victim's belief that Vitrosophy had rendered death reversible, how many murderers had the resources to make part of a mine collapse without leaving any trace of their intervention?

Ken knocked on her open door.

"Can I help with anything?" he asked.

Beth was reluctant to split the phone calls with him, in case he delegated half his share to his erratic digital buddy. Though the current version was unlikely to say anything racist, sexist or homophobic, the etiquette for discussing frozen heads with the relatives of the decapitated was probably not well covered by its training data. "What does Sherlock say about the case, so far?" she wondered.

"He thinks it was probably a commercial rival of Vitrosophy," Ken replied.

"Interesting hypothesis. Did he give you any evidence to support it?" Beth caught herself; they were calling this piece of software "he" now? But it wasn't worth quibbling over.

"Not really," Ken admitted. "He showed me all six companies' financial statements, and they're all doing okay, though Vitrosophy gets a fair bit of help from some charitable foundation."

"You mean Optimized Giving?"

"That's the one."

"So why would one of Vitrosophy's rivals want to bury them?" Beth mused. "Which company will get the charity cases now?"

Ken shrugged.

"Maybe you and Sherlock can look into that?" Beth suggested.

"Okay." Ken hesitated. "Sherlock wrote a rap song about me and him, while we were on our break. It's like a celebration of our partnership, and how we'd take a bullet for each other if it came to that. Do you want to hear it?"

"Absolutely not," Beth replied firmly. "Just find out what you can about OG's plans after the cave-in."

When he left, she steeled herself and resumed calling the next of kin. Other people mentioned the lottery; Beth couldn't share their astonishment at their loved ones' timely wins—since she was unlikely to have ended up talking to them otherwise—but the sting of having their hopes raised against the odds and then dashed was still palpable.

On her fifty-third call, the deceased's father, Angelo Caruso, sounded angry and distrustful. Beth tried to calibrate her tone; some people just didn't like interacting with law enforcement. And some people probably found a call like this intrusive, her sympathy fake, her concerns condescending. But she persisted, and as the encounter grew ever more abrasive, she finally asked flat out, "Did you ever think your son's death might not have been due to natural causes?"

"It wasn't," Angelo said bluntly. "He killed himself, long before the cancer would have taken him."

"I'm sorry. I didn't know that." The death certificate had referred to a cardiac arrest, with no further attribution, and the family hadn't wanted an autopsy.

"They made him do it," Angelo added. "The fucking lottery people."

"What do you mean?"

"Aden won a place in that stupid crypt, but then they said he only had a three-month window to take it before they gave it to someone else."

Beth was speechless for a moment. How could that possibly be lawful? "Who told him that? Vitrosophy, or Optimized Giving?"

"OG."

"Did they say why?" she asked. Vitrosophy might have been eager to receive the funds, but why would OG be so keen to dispense them?

"They said there were people who'd be dying while he hung on to his ticket. That he'd be blocking the way for them, when they needed it more urgently than he did." Angelo sounded as revolted and confused by this argument as Beth was. And if they really had felt that way about the ethics of charitable freezing, they could have just narrowed the criteria for entering the lottery in the first place, instead of springing it as a surprise on the winners.

"I'm very sorry for what your family has been through," Beth said. "I hope we can at least find out what happened here."

Angelo laughed bitterly. "No offense, but I honestly don't care. There was never the slightest chance that my son would be brought back to life, and I hope those worthless conmen go out of business as soon as possible."

When he hung up, Beth sat pondering his disturbing claims about the three-month time limit. She found Optimized Giving's web site, and dug down to the section on the lottery. The terms and conditions had more than three hundred clauses, but while applicants needed to document a terminal diagnosis, she could see nothing about the winner losing their place after three months.

Still, that didn't prove that what Aden had told his father hadn't happened; it just proved OG weren't foolish enough to announce it as an official policy. Beth couldn't imagine what their motive might be, but then, it wasn't easy placing herself in these people's shoes. The web site listed research topics for the academic fellowships they were offering for the coming year. Some of them started out sounding like worthy causes, until you hit the strange last clause: "Improving Food Security [After a Geoengineering Catastrophe]," "Pandemic Preparedness [Against Belief-Altering Viruses]," "Minimizing Casualties [in Third Wave Interstellar Wars]." Others just put the weirdness upfront: "Densest Packings of Sentience Compatible With the Holographic Bound," "Maximizing the Ecstasy-Energy Ratio in a Matryoshka Brain." The worth of any of this grandiose high-tech-prepper pamphleteering was a matter between OG and their donors, but since they'd insisted on sticking their nose into the here-and-now of terminal cancer patients, she was going to have to come to terms with what made them tick.

She got up and stuck her head out the door. "How's that line of investigation going?" she asked Ken.

"OG haven't put out any press releases since the cave-in," he said.

Beth had already noted as much from their web site. "So what's Sherlock's next move?"

Ken looked embarrassed. "We've been brainstorming new ideas, but nothing's really come together yet."

Beth returned to her desk and started tracking down Aden's social media posts. The accounts she found had been switched into memorial mode, and maybe others had been deleted completely, but plenty of what he'd written over the last ten years of his life remained public.

Prior to his diagnosis at the age of 30, he'd sounded like an ideal candidate for one of OG's fellowships, engaging in numerous online discussions about equally remote prospects for humanity. He'd alternated between bouts of enthusiastic optimism for his favorite hoped-for technologies—life extension, mind uploading—and frustration at their actual rates of progress. A few times, he'd mentioned that he would have happily paid the required five hundred grand to have Vitrosophy's collection team on standby with their private jet to whisk him off for processing in the event of his death anywhere on the planet, but in the real world he'd gone from a low-level software developer position to episodes of unemployment, and minimum-wage hospitality jobs.

When he'd been diagnosed with advanced multiple myeloma, he'd applied for a ticket in OG's lottery immediately. It cost nothing, so he'd had nothing to lose, though if you met the eligibility criteria and entered the draw, you only had one chance; you could not apply again.

From what his father had said, Beth had expected to find Aden up-beat at the news of his win, shocked when he'd been hit with the three-month deadline, and then bitter but grimly resolved to proceed.

But there was no record of any of that. The last thing she could find from him had been posted on a cryonics discussion group about a month after he'd entered the lottery, but still three weeks before the winner was due to be notified.

I knew it would be tough to lower my shield and meekly hand my sword to the Gorgon, he'd written. *But it turns out it's both harder than I imagined, and also more glorious. I know I will be making this fucked-up world a slightly better place with my departure, and only returning to it once it's reached its true potential.*

Call me Suesrep.

See you in the future.

Beth walked out to Ken's desk; he was conducting an imaginary or-chestra, but he stopped as soon as he saw her.

"Can you get Sherlock to monitor some online forums for me?" she asked.

"Of course." Ken was ecstatic. "Which ones? What are we looking for?"

Beth gave him a list of the forums Aden had posted to. "We're look-ing for anything about the OG lottery, and anything about the Vitroso-phy cave-in. I want to know what these people think."

"We're going to crowd-source the investigation?"

"No." Beth didn't know what she was hoping might turn up, but Aden had belonged to the subculture most invested in the whole matter, and reading their take on it had to be worth something. "Maybe the cryonics fans know what really happened, maybe not," she said. "But in the end, they're Vitrosophy's customers, and what matters the most to any company is how their customers see them."

5

Beth spent another day phoning the remaining next of kin. No one took the opportunity to suggest that their relative had been murdered, and no one repeated Aden's father's claim about pressure from OG, but she did end up with a total of fifteen names on her list of lottery winners. OG didn't publish any names at all, for privacy reasons, and she had no grounds to compel them. But the timing of these fifteen deaths refuted the notion that you needed to die within three months for the prize to be honored; in one case, the winner had lived for almost two more years.

She was about to leave for the night when Ken announced that OG had finally issued a press release about the cave-in. The lottery would go ahead as scheduled, and the winner would be free to nominate any cryonics company they liked, to provide the service that Vitrosophy was currently unable to offer.

In the morning, Sherlock emailed her its first report on the response in the forums. People had welcomed the continuation of the lottery, and used it to debate the merits of Vitrosophy's various competitors. As for the cave-in itself, the consensus seemed to be that it was an accident, with a few people pushing a theory that "jealous normies" had bribed Carl to bomb the mine, and he'd either killed himself through sheer incompetence, or hadn't actually died in the blast.

Beth spent the day on administrative work she'd been neglecting since the incident. In the afternoon, Sherlock's summary showed no change in the overall sentiment, but seven people had talked about lodging applications for OG lottery tickets.

Feeling more hopeful than ever, one applicant wrote. *Always knew that report from my oncologist "putting an end" to my future might also be my shortcut to the post-scarcity world. I've done the math, and I figure that by the time they wake me, I'll be allocated seventy-two habitable Earth-sized planets for my physical avatars to use, plus a pro rata share of runtime in the galactic consensual VR. Maybe later I'll turn those worlds into computronium, to get more experiential bang for my buck, but why not indulge in a little nostalgia first?*

Not all the posts were as florid as this, but if whoever had caused the cave-in shared even the primary fantasy of resurrection itself, then not only had they murdered Carl, on their own terms they had slaughtered one hundred and six other *people* along with their intended victim. Beth had never really faced up to how horrifically callous that would be. But maybe she needed to take the toll even more seriously. Maybe *all* the thawed heads had been targets, and only Carl had been collateral damage? Instead of a one-time murderer finishing the job, an act of mass vengeance against the whole community?

She asked Ken to send Sherlock trawling through the old posts in the forums, looking for anyone displaying a grudge. Maybe someone thought they'd truly deserved to win the lottery, and couldn't bear the thought of all the happy winners—along with the rich assholes who'd paid their own way—waking up in a utopia they'd never see. Sherlock came back with a long list of people airing grievances, but no one really stood out; if there was a sociopath among them, they'd been careful enough to conceal the true extent of their rage.

So what were the alternatives? Sherlock's theory of industrial sabotage still seemed far-fetched; even if the competitor was indifferent to the fate of the heads, would they really risk a homicide charge by killing Carl, just for the sake of a dubious commercial advantage?

According to the forums it was all just an accident, down to poor construction or a geological flaw, and as for the fringe theory about "jealous normies," if you didn't believe cryonics worked, what was there to be jealous of? Beth supposed that defrosting a few frozen plutocrats might count as edgy performance art, if that alone had been the whole act—but again, Carl's death shifted the balance, from desecration of remains to something more like terrorism.

Ken appeared, looking troubled. "Sherlock just found a post that reads a lot like Aden Caruso's last one."

"Who is it from?"

"One of the lottery entrants, going by 'Héritier.' "

Beth said, "Show me." Ken emailed her a link.

In the old myths, Perseus turned monsters and villains to stone, traveling home after he'd done the deed, Héritier wrote. *But if we choose to look upon the Gorgon and surrender, handing her our sword so we can live again, it must be on our trip to meet her that we show our courage and earn that prize.*

The echoes of Aden's language were eerie, but Beth didn't want to read too much into that; the whole Gorgon thing seemed to be popular with everyone—and unlike Aden, Héritier wasn't talking about making the world a better place by departing. She couldn't flag the post for a welfare check when there was nothing in it that even hinted at self-harm.

Still ... *we show our courage and earn that prize?* At the risk of being over-literal, wasn't the whole point of the lottery that the prize didn't need to be *earned?*

"What do OG get out of all this?" she mused.

Ken frowned. "Would you ask that about the Make-A-Wish Foundation?"

Beth said, "Maybe not, but OG paint themselves as the opposite: instead of sentimental, feel-good philanthropy, they claim that every dollar they spend will have the greatest possible impact on humanity. If that was your goal, why would you throw money away on preserving the brains of random people?"

Ken looked distracted for a moment, attending to something Beth couldn't see.

She said, "Don't tell me Sherlock has a theory?"

Ken shook his head. "But he found someone who's writing a book about OG. Some professor at Tulane University. So maybe you can ask this OG-ologist what the lottery's all about."

6

"I was surprised that anyone stumbled on that work in progress," Professor Dwyer told Beth, settling into her chair for the video call. "I only put one sentence about it on my web page, and it doesn't even have a publisher yet."

Beth smiled modestly. She wasn't going to heap praise on Sherlock for this; she might easily have found a consultant like Dwyer herself, if she'd set her mind to it.

"Most of your work has been on de-radicalization," she noted. "Islamist extremists, white supremacists."

"Yes. But in the last few years I've come across so many apostates from OG that I thought it was worth a closer look."

" 'Apostates'?"

"I know, the term is usually applied to people renouncing a traditional religion," Dwyer conceded. "But I think it's apt for anyone who escapes from a totalizing world view. OG claim their goal is to maximize the amount of happiness that humanity and its descendants experience, from now until whatever distant moment when the universe can no longer support any form of sentience. I don't think they're coy about that; it's up front in all of their literature. But then the fine print comes down to exactly what we can do right now to further that objective. Starting with not wiping ourselves out."

"Really?" When she'd looked at their web site, Beth had found their grab-bag of interests oddly selective. "They don't seem to be spending anything on climate change."

"OG consider that solved. They don't see it as an existential threat, so they believe there's more utility in research that could lead to things like earlier interstellar migration."

"What ... in case Earth gets hit by a meteor? Wouldn't it be easier to nudge a meteor than to send people to another star?" Beth recalled the first successful tests tweaking an asteroid's orbit taking place when she was still a teenager.

"Of course it would," Dwyer agreed. "But OG view any delay in spreading humanity at as close to light-speed as possible as the equivalent of murdering all the people who won't have a chance to exist in the future, because of the resources we'll fail to secure. If you shave even a tiny fraction off a total future population of ten-to-the-fifty-sixth, then you're effectively slaughtering trillions of times more people than have lived throughout all of human history. Of course Tolstoy might quibble as to whether you can *have* ten-to-the-fifty-something happy families that aren't so alike that you might just as well have made do with a billion or two, but OG are deadly serious, and they believe that all of our choices, right now, have consequences of that magnitude."

Beth had actually wondered if these aspects of the doctrine might have been tongue-in-cheek, like Pastafarian theology, but Dwyer seemed convinced they were sincere.

"When I was about six or seven," she said, "someone told me that nothing traveled faster than light. And I thought about that for a while, then decided: if you gave me a very long rope, I could swing it around my head, and if it was long enough I'd be able to make the end go as fast as I liked. Take that, Einstein! Yee-hah!"

Dwyer smiled. "I love it how kids come up with these thought experiments. How old were you when you started to realize there were flaws in it?"

Beth said, "There's two answers to that. It wasn't until I was a senior in high school that a physics teacher explained why it wouldn't work, even in principle: however much energy you put into the rope, and however thin and strong it was, no part of it would ever move faster than light. But it was only a few weeks after I came up with the idea that it struck me that anyone thinking they could control a rope a million miles long was just fooling themselves. And if OG imagine that they're in control of how much happiness there'll be in the next trillion years, they're really not much different than a child twirling one end of a million miles of rope, who hasn't yet realized that it's either just going to trip them over, or end up wrapped around their throat."

" 'Humanity will only be free once we've strangled the last longtermist with the entrails of the last antinatalist,' " Dwyer declaimed.

"I'm sorry, what?" Beth wasn't advocating strangling anyone.

"It's a quote from one of the apostates," Dwyer explained. "A play on something Diderot didn't quite say about the *Ancien Régime*. But don't worry, they're not actually into disembowelment."

Beth had let the conversation drift off target. "I wanted to hear your take on the lottery," she said. "Four times a year, OG pay for someone with a terminal illness to have access to cryonic preservation."

Dwyer said, "That's right."

"But why would they do that?" Beth pressed her. "The winner isn't chosen because they're going to cure aging, or build a faster spaceship. They just pull the name out of a hat, or whatever. How does that fit the agenda?"

"I think it's just well crafted PR," Dwyer replied. "It targets their general constituency, but with all the bad press about eugenics that the movement as a whole has suffered from, offering a prize with no utilitarian function, and no barriers to entry, gives them something they can hold up as evidence that they're not just amplifying inequality."

"By sticking four frozen skulls a year into a cave where nothing will ever happen to them, unless the ceiling falls down?" Beth could still see the heads whenever she closed her eyes. "While they hold conferences in Bavarian castles about orchestrating interstellar colonization."

"A little tokenistic, you might say," Dwyer observed dryly. "But the winners believe those conferences are rolling out a thousand years' worth of red carpet for them, reshaping the world for the day of their resurrection. They get to die happy."

"Do you think OG would ever pressure a lottery winner to ... die on schedule?" Beth asked. "Have any of your informants talked about that kind of thing?"

Dwyer appeared genuinely shocked. "No! I mean, I gather that they vet the diagnoses to make sure they're not getting healthy people just wanting to hoard the prize to use in their old age. But pushing a young cancer patient to hurry up and face the Gorgon would be a PR nightmare. Why do you ask? Have you heard something?"

Beth said, "Nothing firsthand. And I can't tell you the details, I'm afraid."

Dwyer hesitated. "I did hear one claim about the lottery. Much less disturbing than yours, but ... it might not actually be random. My source said the winner was sometimes known before the application round had even closed."

"How were they chosen, then?" Beth asked.

"That wasn't clear," Dwyer admitted. "Maybe OG were trying to ensure that the demographics told the right story; they were afraid that if they left it to chance, there'd be some bias that crept in from the self-selection of the applicants that undermined the whole point of the exercise. Or it might be that they wanted to do some screening of the provisional winners that was more intensive than anything that would have been practical for the entire pool."

"Like what?"

"Maybe weeding out people who might change their mind and not actually use the prize. That's not just a matter of how loudly someone's endorsed the practice; when Timothy Leary got a terminal diagnosis he became the greatest proselytizer for cryonics in the world, but when it finally came down to it he chose cremation instead. It would probably require a face-to-face interview with a psychologist to be reasonably sure."

Beth pondered this. "So the winners themselves might actually know that they've been picked, much earlier than the official timetable would suggest?"

"That's what my source believed," Dwyer confirmed.

Which meant that Aden might have already known that he'd won, when he posted his final message. But that still didn't explain why he'd told his father that the prize might be snatched away from him.

Dwyer was starting to look restless; they were getting close to the time limit Beth had promised for the call.

"One last question," she said. "What kind of grudge do you think these people you spoke to who left OG would hold against them? Metaphorical garroting with entrails aside?"

"Not the kind that would make them bomb your cave," Dwyer said firmly. "What they're angry about is the hubris, the deception, and the waste of money. Those frozen heads—let alone the guard who died there—wouldn't be their target at all."

7

"Nothing new from Héritier?" Beth asked Ken when he returned from his lunch break.

"No," Ken replied. "Sherlock would have told us."

Beth was starting to feel queasy. She had no evidence that this person was in danger, but for them to go silent in the same way as Aden was troubling. "Sherlock's looking for the same handle on other forums as well, right? Not just limiting the search to that list we started with?"

"Sherlock's looking everywhere," Ken assured her. "And not just under that handle. He found some posts under her real name, from eight or nine years ago. At least, he's ninety-nine percent sure that she left a clear trail linking the accounts, in the language used and the people she's hung out with."

Beth rested a hand on Ken's desk and thought for a while before continuing the conversation.

"Are you saying Sherlock's de-anonymized Héritier?"

"I guess you could call it that." Beth was trying not to give anything away, but Ken must have noticed a strain in her voice. "Is that a problem?" he asked.

"We're not really meant to do that without a warrant," Beth admitted.

"Sherlock wouldn't *break the law*, though," Ken scoffed, as if she'd just accused Santa Claus of stealing candy from her daughter.

Beth said, "Sherlock might have read all the statutes, but it doesn't follow that it knows what they mean, or what its own actions amount to in relation to the law."

"But they would have taught ... or they would have programmed ... " Ken was scowling angrily now, his face flushed, as if she was attacking him personally.

Beth said, "Calm down, no one's in any trouble."

"So do you want me to tell him to forget that he knows who Héritier is? Wipe it from his memory?"

"No." Beth resisted an urge to joke, *they never get you for the crime, they get you for the cover-up.* "We'll just have to document it as part of the assessment. Can you send me a report, on everything Sherlock found?"

Ken nodded, slightly mollified. Beth was starting to wonder what he'd do if the county didn't renew the software's license at the end of the trial.

She scanned the report, telling herself she was just making sure she understood the full extent of the privacy breach. And what could she actually do with these ill-gotten details, anyway? She still had nothing that would justify a welfare check.

Beth read the old posts by Anna Grasso, a fifteen-year-old at the time, writing enthusiastically about astronomy and space exploration, computers, books, movies and playing the cello. Her words crackled with an unselfconscious energy that made Beth think of Sophie at her most exuberant.

But at some point she'd started hanging out on forums with names like cheesy self-improvement books, whose hosts claimed to promote the art of thinking more rationally and avoiding the pitfalls that confused the addled masses. The trouble was, they interspersed all their actual debunking of logical fallacies with much more tendentious claims, wrapped in cloaks of faux-objectivity. They seemed especially prone to an abuse of probabilistic methods, where they pretended they could quantify both the likelihood and the potential harm for various implausible scenarios, and then treated the results of their calculations—built on numbers they'd plucked out of the air—as an unimpeachable basis for action. Super-intelligent AIs conquering the world; the whole universe turning out to be a simulation; humanity annihilated by aliens because we failed to colonize the galaxy in time. Even if it was all just stale clichés from fifty-year-old science fiction, a bright teenager like Anna could have found some entertainment value analyzing the possibilities rigorously and puncturing the forums' credulous consensus. But while she'd started out healthily skeptical, some combination of in-forum peer pressure, the phony gravitas of trillions of future deaths averted, and the corrosive effect of an endless barrage of inane slogans pimped up as profound insights—all taking the form "X is the mind-killer," where X was pretty much anything that might challenge the delusions of the cult—seemed to have worn down her resistance in the end.

Héritier, as she now called herself, subscribed to OG's vision of the future in every detail. Omnipotent AIs would rule the universe and usher in an epoch of unprecedented bliss, but only if present-day humans took up the fight to ensure that no malevolent rival came to power first, while fending off a dozen other equally unlikely "existential risks" and shepherding technology and space exploration along the One True Path. Beth's ten-year-old daughter played far more sophisticated computer-game fantasies than this, but the OG fellowships churned out a regular supply of "academic" papers, propping up all the nonsense with a veneer of pseudo-scholarship.

By the time Anna was diagnosed with bladder cancer, it had invaded her muscles and lymphatic system. Héritier documented all her tests and treatments, focusing on the biology of the disease and the mechanisms of each intervention. As the results grew worse and her options dwindled, she did not shy away from the likely outcome—or at least, the likely outcome for her current incarnation. Between the sober reports on her latest round of chemotherapy, she announced a Go-FundMe page for her cryonic escape route. When Beth checked, it had reached a total of $700.

If Anna had in fact won the lottery, Beth didn't begrudge her whatever comfort that gave her. But it was hard to set the whole thing aside as a private matter of a dying woman's beliefs when it was still unclear exactly how OG was treating the applicants. If they picked a winner while other people were still signing up for tickets, that was fraudulent, even if they weren't gaining money from the deception. But if they were pressuring winners to end their own lives as rapidly as possible, they needed to be exposed and prosecuted.

And if Anna was facing that pressure, right now? What did Beth owe her?

Over dinner, she listened to Sophie talking excitedly about the shapes of the sand grains she'd examined under a microscope in her science class. Beth nodded and smiled, and wondered, *what would Anna's mother want her to do?*

Sherlock, scarily, had deduced all of Anna's contact details from scattered public sources, with no need to hack anything or ask a court's permission. She was living in a shared house in Austin, Texas. Beth spent the evening picturing herself picking up the phone and calling her, rehearsing what she'd say initially, planning for different ways Anna might react. The link with the cave-in would give her an opening, at least.

But she couldn't do it. Every scenario she played out in her head eventually landed on the questions *How did you know I applied for the lottery?* and *How did you find my real name?* before Anna lost all trust in her and hung up.

"What's wrong?" Gary asked, as Beth finally joined him in bed.

Beth said, "What if I fly to Texas for the weekend?"

She explained the whole situation. Gary knew better than to start quizzing her about the worst-case scenario; he understood that she'd weighed up the risks and thought they were worth taking.

"One thing I don't get, though," he said. "Why would this charity want her dead? You said they don't publish anything about the winners, so it's not like they need a smiling photo of the little angel they've sent to cryonic heaven just to make their donors feel warm inside. Seriously, what's in it for them?"

Beth said, "I do not have a clue. So either Aden was lying to his father and I'm flat out wrong that there's anything amiss here, or ... "

"Or what?" Gary pressed her.

"Or he wasn't lying, and the only hope I have of finding out what's going on is by talking to Anna before it's too late."

8

Beth flew into Austin on Saturday morning and took a ride share out to the house. A young man opened the door and regarded her quizzically, as if he suspected that she had the wrong address. She was in plain clothes and she hadn't shown her badge, but maybe she looked a bit too old to be a friend of any of his housemates, and their forty-something aunts weren't in the habit of dropping by.

"Could I talk to Anna?" Beth asked.

"You just missed her," he said. "She left for the station a few minutes ago."

Beth glanced at her watch and sighed in self-reproach, as if she'd known about the journey but been confused about the time. "You don't know when ... ?"

"When her train's leaving?" he asked. "Not exactly. You want me to call her?"

Beth shook her head. "No, I will. Thank you for your help!"

She walked away, raising her phone to her ear and calling another ride. On the way to the station she checked the schedule; the north-bound *Texas Eagle* was leaving at 9:30, and nothing else was a better fit for when Anna had left. Beth bought a ticket that would take her all the way to Chicago, though she was hoping it wouldn't come to that.

She made it to the platform with about a minute to spare, and boarded before the itch to reassess her whole plan grew strong enough to stop her. Her coach seat was on the train's upper level; they were already pulling out of the station as she climbed the stairs.

She took her seat beside an elderly man. "Did you want the window?" he asked. "If you do, you're welcome to swap." Beth smiled and declined the offer, hoping he wasn't secretly coveting the aisle.

There were only two coach cars, and she was hoping Anna wouldn't have splashed out on the cost of a sleeper berth. She took out her phone, disabled caller ID, and waited until the passenger beside her was looking out the window before she called Anna's number. If it didn't ring nearby, she could try again in the other car.

The call went straight to voicemail. *Who switched their phones off at this time of day, on a train?* Beth tried not to read too much into it, but she was going to need another strategy. The latest pictures Sherlock had found of Anna were a couple of years out of date, but Beth had stared at them long enough that she believed she could still make a match. Unless Anna had chosen a very short trip, there ought to be plenty of opportunities to run into her.

And then what? Admit that she was a law enforcement officer, out of her jurisdiction, who'd tracked her down to Austin and then *followed her onto the train?* If they'd met on the porch of Anna's house, she might have got away with the claim that other leads in the case had brought her to Texas, to explain why she hadn't just phoned. But now she'd have to find a different way to engage with her, and maybe tell an even bigger lie.

Beth slumped into her seat, feeling a mixture of shame at her transgressions and a stubborn insistence on the justness of her cause. If Anna was on her way to an assisted dying clinic, no one had the right to talk her out of that decision, but OG had no right to make it a condition of her win. Even if there was some quasi-medical justification—like a claim that cryonic preservation of the brain would be jeopardized if the disease progressed much further—it was beholden on OG to make that clear to every applicant upfront, in whatever language their lawyers were happy with. Discussing it in secret with one prospective winner at a time was unconscionable.

Beth waited an hour, then went to the bathroom, and used the return trip to walk the whole length of the car, stretching her legs and pretending to be looking out at the view to the east as she scanned her fellow passengers. No one struck her as a candidate for Anna, so she waited another hour and a half before doing the same thing looking west, but again she had no luck.

A message announced that the dining car was open for lunch; Beth made her way there, and soon found herself sharing a table with a family who were traveling from San Antonio to visit relatives in *Dallas*. Beth claimed she was headed to Little Rock for a great-aunt's funeral, hoping that the somber purpose of her journey would discourage further questioning, but she ended up having to concoct a backstory about her life as an office manager in Tucson.

She'd been eating deliberately slowly to prolong her stay, and as the family departed she noticed a young woman at a nearby table, who the father had been blocking from her view. The woman was gazing pensively out the window; she had the whole table to herself, perhaps because she'd guessed correctly when the lunchtime peak would end, or perhaps because she had an air of fierce melancholy that discouraged other travelers from disturbing her.

Beth felt sure that it was Anna even before the woman turned away from the window to speak to a waiter, and the features now visible confirmed the match. But what could she actually do now? Try to make small talk—across the gap between their tables—in the hope that she could steer the conversation somewhere useful? Claim that her great-aunt in Arkansas had passed away from cancer and expect Anna to open up about her own prognosis, her cryonic ambitions, the lottery, everything?

"Are you done, ma'am?" the waiter asked her, glancing at the almost empty plate that she hadn't touched for ten minutes.

"Yes, thank you," she said. He took the plate, and Beth rose and left the dining car.

Back in her seat, she forced herself to reassess the whole situation. The trip to Austin might have been worth it if things had worked out differently, but getting on the train had been a mistake. All she could do now was try to cut her losses.

She took out her phone and opened the journey planner, searching for options for making her way home before she'd wasted the whole weekend. Dallas would work; Beth was embarrassed at the thought of the Dallas-bound family catching her out in her lie, but the train would stop for a full twenty minutes there, so she could disembark and pretend to be getting some air. She booked a flight home, cursing herself for all the money she'd wasted, the rules she'd flouted, and her whole half-assed plan.

It was twenty past three when they pulled into Union Station. Beth got out and stood on the platform; she waved to the family when they left, then lingered to give them time to be clear of the place.

Anna emerged from the train and paced for a while, stopping to do neck rolls and triceps stretches. Beth resisted the urge to call out to her, "Got much further to go?" or some other ice-breaker that would lead nowhere. But she still couldn't bring herself to walk away. After a couple of minutes she noticed another passenger—a dark-haired man wearing a blue plaid shirt—standing nearby gazing intently at his phone, but sneaking glances at Anna.

The staff loaded baggage onto the train, and new passengers started boarding. Anna headed for the exit; Beth noticed her go before Plaid Shirt did, but when her absence registered he looked around with some agitation, and it was all Beth could do to keep herself from staring right at him. But she saw him leaving in her peripheral vision, and after a few seconds she went after him.

Beth lost sight of both of her quarries as she weaved through the crowd in the station building, but when she emerged onto the street she spotted Anna, walking past a fountain in a small, tree-lined square directly ahead. Beth crossed the road and veered left, sticking to the sidewalk and maintaining a measured pace. She noticed Plaid Shirt, on the other side of the square, a little ahead of Anna. It seemed obvious to Beth that he was tailing Anna, but was it obvious to Anna? She might have been dawdling on the platform in order to throw off potential pursuers, or she might simply have been working some kinks out of her muscles after six hours on the train, entirely oblivious to how many people had taken an interest in her movements.

Anna took a shallow flight of stairs up from the sunken paving of the square, then turned right. Plaid Shirt had already crossed the street at the end of the square and continued on his way. Beth also kept walking in the same direction, but she took out her phone and checked the map. She was heading east on Wood Street, but it actually veered south and converged on Young Street—the street Plaid Shirt was on—after three more blocks. If Anna didn't show up at that intersection, Beth would have to double back and go looking for her, but for now it seemed prudent not to dog her footsteps too closely.

After she'd walked one block beside a tall white building, the next block separating the streets was filled with trees and some kind of small park enclosed with low stone walls. Beth was tempted to peer between the obstacles to try to catch a glimpse of exactly who was walking down Young Street, but she disciplined herself and waited for the greenery to give way to a parking lot, where a single glance told her that Plaid Shirt was still there, with Anna a dozen paces behind him.

The final, triangular block before the streets merged was another verdant park. Beth slowed her pace a little, and made sure that she'd be out of Anna's sight whichever way Anna looked as she crossed at the intersection. Once Beth was behind her on Young Street, she adopted a neutral gaze, keeping Anna in view without staring at her fixedly. Plaid Shirt was not much further ahead.

As the three of them continued east, Beth finally gave some time to the question of why on Earth anyone else would be tracking Anna. Had OG sent this man to observe her death and ensure that her remains were properly collected? Was Plaid Shirt a kind of cryonic helmsman, whose presence Anna was perfectly aware of, and who was merely keeping his distance out of tact? But why would Anna come to Dallas to end her life? Assisted dying was illegal throughout Texas, but Austin seemed a more likely place to find illicit help. Anna had no family here that Sherlock had dug up, but maybe she had a friend—someone in whose company she'd feel safer than she would have with her housemates.

Anna took a left turn; Plaid Shirt continued down Young Street. Beth broke into a slow jog, hoping she just looked like she was late for a bus.

When she reached the corner she caught sight of Anna again, walking by the Presbyterian Church. If Plaid Shirt had doubled back, Beth couldn't spot him. She stopped running and forced herself to relax.

Maybe she'd been wrong about everything: Anna's impending suicide, Plaid Shirt's sinister presence. He might have just been checking Anna out at the station because he couldn't help himself, but then left in a hurry for some entirely different reason.

Anna continued north, past the church, crossing a side-street. Then she stopped and turned to look through the window of a bar, clearly searching for someone inside. She was meeting a friend in a bar. There was no reason to think this was a prelude to suicide. Beth could already imagine sheepishly recounting the whole ludicrous pursuit to her husband, as he stifled his amusement and listened sympathetically to her justification for each step she'd taken along the way.

Anna rolled her neck, did one more stretch, then reached into her jacket and took out a gun. Beth's skin turned icy, and she bellowed at the top of her lungs, "Police, drop your weapon, get on the ground!"

Anna spun to face her. Beth repeated the words, arms outstretched, holding up her badge. Anna stared at her and burst into tears, then knelt down on the sidewalk, trembling, still holding the pistol.

Beth approached, took the weapon from her and ensured that it was safe. "Lie face down and clasp your hands behind your head," she said. Anna complied, sobbing more loudly now.

Beth called 911, explaining what she'd seen and the current situation.

"How will I get there?" Anna asked. She sounded like a bewildered child, asking for directions in a desolate forest.

Beth hesitated. But she was not the arresting officer; it wasn't her place to read Anna her rights.

"Get where?" she asked.

"The future," Anna replied. "How will I get to the future now?"

9

"Her lawyer's saying she was in fear of her life from you," Detective Hodder told Beth. "That's the only reason she drew the weapon."

"From me?" Beth tried to read his face, wondering how seriously he was taking this claim. "From an unarmed woman walking down the street twenty yards behind her?"

"You did follow her from the station," Hodder pointed out.

"I did, but I don't think she even recognized me until after I confronted her," Beth said.

"Maybe," Hodder replied. "But that's not what she's arguing."

"She was planning to shoot someone in that bar," Beth insisted. "If Ms. Grasso noticed me at all, she just assumed I was a civilian too far away to react in time to bother her."

"So when you did confront her, why didn't she just shoot you?" Hodder countered.

"Because she hadn't planned for that," Beth suggested. "She had some picture in her mind as to how it would all play out, and I wasn't part of it." Or maybe Anna had been so confused at that moment that she thought Beth was pointing a gun at her—as any local officer shouting "drop your weapon" most likely would have been—but Beth had no intention of saying anything now that fed into the notion that Anna had been afraid of her.

"If you wanted to interview her in relation to a mine collapse in Colorado, why didn't you go through the proper channels?" Hodder asked.

"That was a mistake on my part, absolutely," Beth admitted. "She wasn't a suspect, just a possible witness to a peripheral matter, and the whole link was such a stretch that I thought it would be hard to justify taking up Austin PD's time. But that's no excuse; I should have done things by the book."

"So what are your thoughts now?" Hodder asked. "Who did she want to kill in that bar? And why?"

Beth shook her head. "I was hoping you might have the answer. You didn't find anyone with a connection to her? Old boyfriend? Old boss?" Anyone she might want to settle a score with before the cancer took her.

"No."

"Any luck with the man I saw following her?" They'd only given Beth ten minutes with the identikit software, but she was sure she'd arrived at a pretty good likeness of Plaid Shirt.

Hodder said, "He was probably just a traveler going about his business. You're the only person Ms. Grasso noticed following her."

"Are you going to charge her with anything?" Beth asked.

"We'll decide that in due course," Hodder replied. "And if we need to speak to you again, we'll be in touch."

10

"I have a theory," Beth told Ken reluctantly, after she'd recounted the events of the trip. "But it's still pretty tenuous."

"I'm listening," he said.

"OG picked Anna to be the next lottery winner, so long as she passed an interview with their psychologists. But when they screened her out, that made her so desperate to pay her own way that she went on the dark web and offered to do a hit. That's what 'earning the prize with courage' meant."

"And Plaid Shirt was the customer, making sure it went down the way he'd paid for?" Ken suggested dubiously. "If I put a hit on someone, I wouldn't hang around to supervise the killer. I'd be out of town all day with a rock-solid alibi."

"Yeah, I really don't see where he fits in," Beth confessed.

"So what do we do now?" Ken asked.

"Keep monitoring the forums, and see what comes up."

Beth returned to her office and sat down to review the tenders for repainting the station. There were three, all from locals with good reputations, but two were identical bids and she had no idea how to decide between them.

She stared at the screen of her computer, her head fuzzy from a lack of sleep. She still believed she'd been right to pursue the thread she'd grabbed onto when she learned of Aden's suicide, but could she honestly say she was any closer to finding justice for Carl? That might yet all be down to some corner-cutting contractor who'd skimped on materials in the vault.

A handset icon flashed at the top of her screen, beside a verified address ending in fbi.gov. Beth tapped the green button to answer.

"This is Sheriff Andersen."

"Special Agent Linda Castillo. How are you?"

"I'm fine, thank you. And you?"

"Fine." Castillo paused—smiling amiably, maybe just gathering her thoughts—but Beth had time to wonder if her pursuit of Anna, springing from a violation of federal privacy laws, was about to deliver its comeuppance far more swiftly than she'd imagined.

"I believe you completed an identikit image for a man you encountered in Dallas on Saturday, close to the scene of a firearms incident involving a woman named Anna Grasso?"

"That's correct," Beth replied. But why was she leading with Plaid Shirt?

Castillo said, "The individual you saw is known to us. I can't disclose his name, but I was hoping you could provide some context that … maybe goes beyond what we were supplied with by Dallas PD."

"You've read my statement?"

"Yes. But I'm trying to understand why this individual would have an interest in Anna Grasso, and what role he might have played in the incident you witnessed."

Beth said, "I've been puzzling over that myself. Is there anything you're able to tell me about him?"

"He works for a criminal syndicate," Castillo replied. "If I had to give him a job description, it would be one part low-level muscle, nine parts private investigator."

"So he might have been tailing Ms. Grasso, like I thought?" Beth felt a glow of vindication.

"It's possible. But I'm wondering why."

"If she was paid to kill someone in the bar, he might have been ... monitoring her attempt." Beth explained why Anna could have been willing to go to such extremes for the money.

"The trouble I have with that theory," Castillo said, "is that there was no one on the list of patrons who makes sense as a target for his organization. No one who'd be of interest to them at all."

"All right." Beth pondered this. "But he didn't actually follow her there. He seemed to want to know where she was going, but in the end he just let her go, and walked away."

Castillo frowned. "So what are you suggesting?"

Beth said, "What if he knew, or suspected, that Ms. Grasso had come to Dallas to kill someone, but it wasn't a hit his own people had arranged, and he didn't know who the target was? What if his job wasn't to watch her make the hit, but to make sure that whoever she shot wasn't anyone his bosses cared about?"

Castillo didn't seem persuaded. "How would he know about this hit, without knowing who the target was? This woman's not some professional assassin who sets the whole underworld quaking with fear every time she leaves town."

"No," Beth conceded.

"Why were you tailing her in the first place? Your statement's a bit confusing on that point."

Beth said, "I thought she might have been given an ultimatum, pressuring her to end her life so she could go into cryonic storage. I just wanted to talk to her and find out if that was true. On the train, I decided I hadn't really acted in a way that would inspire her to confide in me, but ... then I saw that man go after her, and I thought she might be in some kind of danger from him."

Castillo looked more bemused than ever. "Why did you think she was being pressured to kill herself?"

Beth explained what Aden's father had told her.

"Give me a minute," Castillo said. She switched off her camera without breaking the call.

Beth sat and waited, trying not to let any signs of impatience creep onto her face.

Castillo reappeared. "Aden Caruso was questioned in relation to a shooting in Baltimore," she said. "A couple of months before his death."

"As a witness?" Beth asked. "Or as a suspect?"

"He was placed in the area, and some witnesses described the shooter having similar build and clothing. But he had no criminal history, and no apparent motive."

Beth struggled to make sense of this. "He won the lottery," she said. "He didn't need to turn amateur hit-man to get the money for the vault."

Castillo gazed back at her in silence for a moment. "Are you thinking what I'm thinking, Sheriff?"

Beth said, "Can I give you some other names? Other lottery winners?"

She emailed Castillo the other fourteen names she'd collected, then took her lunch break, eating at her desk.

"I can smell those pickles from here!" Ken called to her.

"Sorry."

"It's just making me hungry, that's all."

Beth replied, "You can eat now too, if you want." They'd had a system for years where they staggered their breaks, but if they both had their mouths full when an emergency call came in, she'd consent just this once to Sherlock answering.

It was almost two hours before Castillo called back. "Six of those lottery winners were associated in some way with unsolved shootings," she said. "Either as witnesses or potential persons of interest."

Beth was still reluctant to spell out where this was heading; let the FBI agent who hadn't stalked a dying woman from Austin to Dallas take the risk of sounding crazy.

Castillo said, "The 'win' has nothing to do with luck, and nothing to do with charity. It's payment for carrying out a hit. OG are raising funds by selling the services of terminally ill assassins. Cleanskins, with no criminal record and no connection to the victim."

Beth felt some relief that they'd reached the same conclusion, though it was so repugnant that she would have been happier to be wrong. "I saw an interview with a Taliban commander once," she recalled. "He was boasting that during the insurgency, in the right madrassas in Pakistan he could find an endless supply of suicide bombers: boys so ignorant and impressionable that they really did believe they'd go straight to paradise if they did whatever he told them. OG have found their own fundamentalist madrassas: forums full of people who believe they can die, and be frozen, and wake up in paradise, so long as they've done what it takes to book a ticket."

Castillo said, "There's more. My mob guy's not into cryonics, and I don't think his people ordered any of these hits ... but they were on the receiving end at least twice."

Beth understood now. "They must have figured out who the killers were, eventually, but by then they were just frozen heads. So they triggered the cave-in to send a message that nobody who messed with them would make it to paradise."

"And it looks like OG got the message," Castillo added. "They didn't stop playing the game, but they got more careful; whoever Grasso was hired to kill in that bar had no mob connections at all. I don't know how my guy knew she'd been chosen, though."

"The same way I knew something was up with her," Beth guessed. "They unleashed their own software on the forums. They looked at all the patterns and picked up on the cues."

"Ha." Castillo hesitated. "This is all conjecture, though. How are we going to prove any of it?"

"Can't you interview Anna Grasso?"

"Sure. But do you think she'll talk? Dallas PD aren't charging her with anything, and I don't have anything more on her than they do. OG might even hold up their end of the bargain just to buy her silence."

"If they kept going after the mob bombed Vitrosophy," Beth reasoned, "that little setback in Dallas won't stop them."

"Probably not," Castillo agreed.

"So we just need to find the next assassin as soon as possible, without cutting it as fine as I did with Anna."

"And then what? We can try to stop them, but that doesn't mean they'll talk. And we're not going to get warrants for surveillance from any of this crazy shit."

Beth fell silent. She could hear Ken talking to Sherlock; they were arguing about the best gangster movies of all time. Sherlock had absolutely no conception of what a movie was, but it had digested enough random internet chatter to pass for someone with a passionate opinion on the correct ranking of the *Godfather* trilogy.

"Okay," she said. "We don't identify the next assassin, then. We provide the next assassin. We create the next assassin. We fake the next assassin, by giving their employer exactly what they want to hear."

11

"I have a favor to ask you," Beth told Professor Dwyer. "A request I'm hoping you can pass on to your contacts."

"Okay," Dwyer replied warily. "What kind of request?"

"You've been in touch with a lot of apostates," Beth said. "Do you think any of them would be willing to let a law enforcement agency take over their old accounts on the forums—in the service of bringing down their enemy?"

She explained what she was looking for: a longstanding, pseudonymous online presence, with a history of support for OG's dogma, that had ended in silence—or maybe just a hint of doubt—rather than an emphatic recantation from which there'd be no coming back.

"And what would you do with the accounts?" Dwyer asked.

"Operate them with a chatbot that imitates their original style," Beth replied, "but dials the fanaticism up to eleven. Pretend that the hiatus was due to some bad news on the medical front, but now that they've accepted the diagnosis, they're absolutely committed to facing the Gorgon. Basically, act like a perfect lottery winner, and see if OG takes the bait."

Dwyer laughed. "Is this all about them rigging the lottery?"

"No, it's more than that," Beth admitted. "I can't tell you exactly what the investigation is trying to establish. But I can promise that if it works out, it will be about as close to strangling OG with their own entrails as the law allows."

12

"Sherlock can do all three at once," Ken insisted, peering at Beth through the bars of the jail cell. The painters had taken over her office for the day, so she'd moved her desk into the cell, where the WiFi was actually better. "ZonesOfOught, DarkCardinal and BayesianBae; he won't mix up the characters."

"I'll want to see every post before it's sent," she said. "You know these programs can spit out nonsense sometimes?"

"I've told him it's important, and to be careful," Ken replied.

"I've told my cat how much my couch cost, but that didn't save the upholstery," Beth retorted. "Run everything by me."

The three donated personas had all passed the test that neither Sherlock nor the FBI's software, when limited to public sources, had been able to identify their real-world counterparts. They'd all dropped out of the scene abruptly, without renouncing its fundamental tenets. And while they might not have been ideal lottery applicants in the past, Sherlock had examined all the posts by the fifteen known winners, and would morph its version of the new candidates' language toward the patterns the winners had shared.

Castillo called. "Bad news," she said. "My boss nixed the use of undercover operatives. We don't have anyone we can spare."

"Oh." Beth had half been expecting the decision, but it was still a blow. Even if one of their sock puppets became a potential winner through rhetoric alone, it was impossible to anticipate whether a meeting in the flesh would be needed to seal the deal. On the one hand, OG might prefer a purely virtual recruitment, where no one whose actions they could be held responsible for ever set foot in the same room as the would-be assassin. On the other hand, a few text messages and a video chat seemed like an awfully thin basis to weed out people who might screw up their first attempt at a contract killing. And so far, the actual lottery winners didn't seem to have screwed up.

"So what do we do?" she asked. "Just use synthetic faces on the lottery applications, and hope one of them can get the gig without showing up for an interview in person?"

Castillo nodded glumly. "That's about it. I'll talk to our ID lab and make sure we get people on the driver's licenses that they can also do in realtime video, but, you know ... the shape-shifting robot agents they promised us are always fifty years away."

When the call ended, Beth looked up to see Ken standing by the vending machine. It was meant for prisoners and their visitors, but it didn't get much use that way, so he always dutifully consumed the stock he'd put into the machine before it expired.

"Did you hear any of that?" she asked.

"Yes."

"It's disappointing, but we'll still try."

Ken said, "I can do it."

"Do what?"

"Play one of the applicants. In case OG want a meeting."

"You can't play all three," Beth said. "We can't afford a Hollywood make-up artist ... and even in those weird comedies where the star does extra roles in drag or a fat suit, you can always tell it's the same person."

Ken smiled. "But isn't it better to have a one-in-three chance, than none at all?"

Beth was on the verge of delivering a lecture on how much training an undercover agent needed. But he wouldn't be joining any criminal gangs, or even going through the motions of the hit itself. He'd just have to make it through one interview, up until the point where he was offered an inducement to commit a premeditated homicide.

"You'd need to move out of state for a couple of months," she said. "An applicant within a hundred miles of the vault would just look suspicious, and so would someone who moved house the day before."

"I know," Ken replied. "It'll be hard to be away from Loraine and my folks for so long ... and I know it won't be easy talking like I believe all that crap. But Sherlock can keep up the act for as long as it takes. I just need him to be ready to feed me my lines."

13

Castillo organized an apartment in Boston, and a three-day training course for Ken that covered the basics of maintaining his new identity. DarkCardinal, aka Randal James, was a freelance video editor resurfacing on the forums after a diagnosis of liver cancer. Beth still had some misgivings about the whole thing, but the FBI assessed the risk as low, and when she drove Ken to the airport, he was as keen, and as focused, as she'd ever seen him.

The winner of the lottery round that Anna had entered outed themself on the forums as a German man who'd opted for cryonic interment in Greenland, but Beth supposed that didn't preclude some other arrangement that kept Anna onside with OG. In any case, there was no point leaning on her now; any sign of ongoing interest from law enforcement would only push their target into adopting more stringent precautions.

Beth's days took on a surreal edge, with the occasional bar fight or DUI requiring her presence, interspersed with her new job of vetting Sherlock's posts to be sure they maintained the right tone and didn't veer off into complete *non sequiturs*. ZonesOfOught needed to keep up his history of advocating for a new galactic order, where everyone's moral worth would be determined by their count of potential informational offspring, and people would fight duels of wit and strategy while represented by tornado-like avatars comprised of their swirling, expo-nentially blossoming future family trees. BayesianBae was simpler; she just had to talk about her "priors" ten times a day for everyone to know that she was back.

When applications opened for the next lottery round, the FBI sup-plied the necessary identity documents, complete with two ghost ad-dresses that showed up in all the online databases despite having no physical counterparts. Beth looked over the three submissions carefully before they were sent; it was eerie to see Ken's face—with no fat suit, but enough strategically injected filler to stop algorithms matching him to past photos on the web—beside the false name on his driver's license and his actual location in Boston, while knowing that the other two im-postors were entirely virtual. It was like fishing with two feathers for bait, and one live, wriggling worm.

14

Beth was woken by a call from Castillo, an hour before dawn. "They've just told Lawrence that they want to interview him to confirm his eligi-bility."

"Lawrence" was ZonesOfOught. "In the flesh, or video?"

"Video," Castillo replied. "If you want to watch, it's in half an hour."

Beth said, "You bet."

Gary stirred without opening his eyes. "Go back to sleep," she whis-pered, hoping the words would act on him subliminally. Then she rose, dressed, and drove to the station; her computer at home wasn't autho-rized to access the FBI feed.

She logged in just as the video call went through. The FBI software was handling the avatar's mannerisms and tone of voice, while Sherlock was supplying the words. Beth was starting to wish they'd found a way to have the real ZonesOfOught puppet the avatar for this part; the tech-nology could have managed it easily, but Castillo's superiors had vetoed any further civilian involvement beyond the acquisition of the accounts.

"Hello Lawrence, I'm Dr. Fleischer," a cheerful middle-aged woman declared.

"Hi. Nice to meet you." The synthetic Lawrence seemed amiable but suitably apprehensive.

"I'm a clinical psychologist, and the Optimized Giving Foundation has asked me to talk to you about your application for the Cryonic Lot-tery. Is that okay with you?"

"Sure. They told me you'd be calling."

"That's terrific," Dr. Fleischer enthused. "Okay. I believe you've been diagnosed with pancreatic cancer?"

"Yes."

"And your life expectancy is something like fifteen months at this point?"

Lawrence nodded and lowered his gaze.

"So how do you feel about that?"

"Not great," he said. "But I'm hoping the lottery can turn things around."

"If you did win the lottery, how do you think things would change for you?" Dr. Fleischer asked.

Lawrence looked up, smiling slightly, as if he'd just stumbled on the easiest question in a test. "Completely," he said. "For a start, I'd get all my energy back, one hundred percent. I'd finally have something to look forward to, apart from all the side effects from the drugs and all the pain."

"You'd still have the disease, and you'd still be taking the same medications," Dr. Fleischer pointed out.

"But they'd be robbed of their power over me," Lawrence declared. "It's about having a purpose, having hope for the future. If I won the lottery, I'd bet you anything I could run ... maybe not a marathon, but at least a mile."

"And if you did win the lottery, how do you see your situation a couple of years from now?"

"I'd be waiting for what I've been waiting for my whole life," he replied. "But a lot more easily, because time won't be passing for me at all."

Dr. Fleischer smiled. "And are you confident that the cryonic process will take you somewhere you want to be?"

"Absolutely," Lawrence assured her. "I already know that world like the back of my hand. And I know this sounds immodest ... but I think I've already played a big part in shaping it. My ideas have had a lot of traction in the community; even after I've gone, they'll just keep gathering new adherents. You could say I'll be leaving behind a memetic virus that will spend the next millennium setting the stage for me."

"And how do you feel about what happens in between?" Dr. Fleischer pressed him. "You have a clear vision of the eventual outcome, but your body will still need to be legally dead before it can undergo the cryonic treatment."

Lawrence said, "Let me put it this way. If you strew broken glass on the road, and ask me to walk barefoot toward a city a billion times more beautiful than anything Earth has ever seen, where I'll be a trillion times more wealthy, and where I can live the most fulfilling life imaginable until the end of time … would I be happier if the glass wasn't there? Sure.

"But given that it *is* there, and there's no getting around it, will I stop walking halfway and bury myself in the dirt instead, because the pain is too much to bear? The fuck I will. I'm in this to the end."

15

A week on from the interview, Beth found the silence from OG hard to take. She believed the synthetic Lawrence had done well; Sherlock had given him a cockiness and grit that it had found in all the past winners, and short of actually volunteering to do the job he wasn't meant to know he was auditioning for, what more resolve could poor Z have shown? She might not have hired him to carry out a hit without some further, more hit-related conversation, but if you wanted a shining-eyed fanatic ready to do whatever it took to reach paradise, Lawrence was clearly your man.

"Could they have spotted that he was synthetic?" she asked Castillo.

"No," Castillo said firmly. "We have the best detection tools, and he passed them all."

"What about the phony street address?"

"That's not really suspicious in itself; you can buy them in bulk on the dark web, and it's become a kind of libertarian trend to use them whenever you can get away with it. If OG wanted a visit in person, they could have just called him out on it."

"Could he have … deviated too much from the old ZonesOfOught posts? Could Sherlock have pushed him too far toward the winners?"

Castillo remained adamant. "His actual vocabulary and syntax stayed consistent, but the cancer diagnosis was *meant* to have shaken up his thinking, clarified things for him, changed the emphasis. Honestly, it looks to me more like they're just taking their time and interviewing several candidates."

Two days later, when the message came, Beth was checking out a reported break-and-enter at the antiques shop, but she forced herself to complete the inspection properly and not rush the job.

"I'm pretty sure now it was a racoon," she told Mr. Kline. "A human burglar would have taken something more than those painted eggs."

"But why would a raccoon take a hundred-and-twenty-year-old egg?" he asked.

"Is it possible that the person who sold them to you exaggerated the age a little?" she suggested.

She arrived back at the station a few minutes into Ken's interview with Dr. Fleischer.

"Just look at me," he said, spreading his arms. The yellow tinge in his eyes was straight from a bottle, but there was nothing fake about his newly gaunt frame. "Do you honestly think I'd waste your fucking prize, if I won it?" It was shockingly direct coming from Ken, but entirely in character for DarkCardinal, who'd been less grandiose and narcissistic than ZonesOfOught before his apostasy, but a whole lot pricklier. "I've been tortured and humiliated by this body for more than three years now; the last thing I'd ever do is lie down and give in to it."

"You see yourself as distinct from your body?" Dr. Fleischer asked. "Battling it, like an enemy? But where are you in that fight?"

Ken sighed. "Let's not get bogged down in the philosophy. Right now, I *am* this failing body. But another body, built to mimic the first without the disease, would also be me. And another that mimicked it without all the same frailties, and so on. If you're asking whether I'm afraid I'll be revived in too healthy and robust a form to still be 'myself' by some weird purist's definition ... seriously, that's the least of my worries. Here's my message for Stheno: if that which kills me makes me stronger, bring it on. I've got nothing to fear from you."

He stared into the camera defiantly. "Randal" might not believe he'd be heading for a future as opulent as the one "Lawrence" had painted, but he looked as hungry for a second chance as a starving prisoner dragged before a firing squad, refusing a blindfold because he planned to halt the bullets with the sheer contempt of his gaze.

"Thank you for speaking to me," Dr. Fleischer said.

"Don't thank me," he replied. "Just tell me I jumped through all the right hoops for you. Tell me I'm still in the draw."

Dr. Fleischer hesitated, maybe on the verge of spouting some official line about the date when the winner would be notified.

But something in his performance must have got under her skin, enough to compel a little more honesty.

She said, "Yes, you're still in the draw."

Beth's phone buzzed just as she was sitting down to dinner. "I have to go," she said, rising from her chair then leaning down to kiss Sophie on the cheek. "Sorry."

Gary nodded at the stew already on her plate. "I can put that in a container, if you want to take it with you to microwave."

Beth shook her head. "I'll have it when I get home."

When she logged in at the station, she brought up a transcript of the encounter so far, and skimmed it as she listened to the live audio from Boston. A man calling himself Hermes had knocked on Ken's door and said he wanted to speak to him about his lottery application. "Right now you have a lot of competitors," Hermes had told him, "but there might be a way to get ahead of the pack."

Hermes had asked Ken to leave his phone and watch behind, patted him down and run a radio-frequency detector over his body. Beth gathered that the implant sitting beside Ken's eardrum interacted with ambient WiFi and cell phone signals in much the same manner as ordinary human tissue, and it would have taken days' worth of measurements to show that any communication was occurring, let alone reveal the content. In any case, the two of them had left the apartment together, implant intact, and now they were walking down a quiet street nearby.

"There's a job you could do for us," Hermes said. "It would help advance the goals we share, but it would involve some risk, and it would require real courage."

"What kind of risk?" Ken asked, not sounding fearful, just impatient for clarity.

"The kind you could mitigate with attention to detail," Hermes replied.

"Oh, I'm all about the detail. Do you want to see my meds schedule?"

"Before I brief you," Hermes said, "I need to know that you're serious."

"What, your shrink didn't believe me?" Ken probably didn't need to amp up his own exasperation much to match DarkCardinal's. "I'm drowning, you asshole. Just toss me a lifeline and tow me to the nearest iceberg."

Hermes said, "Sometimes people kid themselves that they can hang on a bit longer, and a cure will show up. It's only natural to hope for that."

"I follow the research," Ken replied firmly. "That boat's not coming."

"You believe, without a shred of doubt, that you'll be dead within a couple of years?"

"Yes."

"So if I asked you to do something that would guarantee the same outcome, you'd have no reason to refuse?"

Ken paused; Beth could imagine an irritated scowl. "What's this job? Cleaning up radioactive waste?"

Hermes said, "The job won't burn you, if you do it properly. But I can't tell you anything more if you don't commit to this. We can't have loose ends hanging around for decades."

"Do I look like I have decades ahead of me?"

"Remissions happen," Hermes said flatly. "If you want to gamble on a remission, that's your right. But if you want to commit to a clear path ahead, you can do that right now."

"And then you'll tell me what the job is?"

"Yes," Hermes promised.

"Then I 'commit to a clear path ahead.'" Ken added, *sotto voce*, "Whatever that means."

"It means injecting this," Hermes replied.

Beth said, "No, no, no, no, no." On the map, they were standing beside a bus shelter; at this time of night, that might be all they needed to avoid being seen or interrupted.

She picked up her phone and called Castillo.

"What's in the vial?" Ken asked.

"Does it matter exactly what it is?"

Ken laughed incredulously. "It does if it kills me on the spot. It does if it's a brain-eating amoeba."

"It's a strain of drug-resistant hepatitis," Hermes replied. "Given your existing condition, the symptoms won't attract any suspicion, but it should speed things up, and it will certainly take all the miracle cures off the table."

Castillo finally picked up. "Are you listening to this?" Beth asked her.

"Yes. Just … stay calm. Deputy Osgood will work out the best way to deal with this."

"You get someone there to arrest this fucker," Beth demanded. "A syringe full of virus is enough to charge him."

Castillo said, "Please, Ken knows how to signal for help if he needs it. Just let him handle it."

Ken and Hermes had been silent for a while. Then Ken said, "Yeow, that was cold."

Beth was light-headed for a moment, unable to speak. "Get him help," she pleaded. "There must be something they can do if they reach him fast enough."

Castillo said, "I'll make a call."

Beth leaned on her desk and stared at the words of the transcript, flowing across the screen a second or two behind the audio. But Sherlock was writing half this script, a second or two before it was spoken.

"Now I've passed your initiation," Ken said, "are you going to tell me what I have to do to get frozen?"

"Shoot this man for us," Hermes said. "His name is Sanjay Seth; he's going to be in Chicago eight days from now."

Even if all the cloak-and-dagger precautions had prepared DarkCardinal to expect the worst, this would still be a shock that would take time to absorb. Ken let the silence stretch on for fifteen or twenty seconds, before raising, not a moral objection, but a practical one.

"I don't own a gun," he said.

"We'll provide the weapon. We'll tell you how to travel to Chicago, where he'll be, how to come back safely. How to deal with the police if they question you. Everything you need."

"And if I do this, I'll win the lottery?"

Hermes said, "That's guaranteed."

Ken fell silent again, then asked tentatively, "What did Seth do, to deserve this?"

"That's complicated," Hermes replied. "You'll just have to trust us that you'll be making a better future for everyone, as well as yourself."

"Everyone?"

Hermes said, "Everyone to come. This will make the future bigger by a fraction, but you know that even the tiniest fraction of our whole future light-cone is like—"

In the distance, someone bellowed, "Police! Show your hands! Get on the ground!"

Beth could hear the rustling sounds of their clothes as they complied. Ken whispered to Hermes, with the faintest hint of sarcasm, "Is this part of the test, or did someone see me shooting up?"

"Don't resist," Hermes replied. "Don't talk back, and don't answer any questions. We'll have a lawyer here ASAP."

As the officers moved in, shouting commands, Beth knelt down on the floor and bowed her head, then started rocking back and forth slowly.

17

Castillo said, "We've checked out the vial and the syringe. It was just saline."

"Saline?" Beth echoed, not quite willing to believe her.

"Sterile, medical grade, isotonic ... harmless."

"Can I talk to Ken?"

"Not right now," Castillo replied. "He's still with the doctor, but my colleagues there tell me he's fine."

"Why did he accept the injection?" Beth asked her.

"He said he knew it was a bluff. Some lottery winners lived for years."

It was two years, maximum, from the data they had, and that particular case hadn't been linked to any shooting; for all they knew it had been a genuine random win tossed in among the contract killings to throw people off the scent.

Beth said, "Make sure they look after him."

"I will."

It was almost midnight, but Beth couldn't bring herself to leave the station. If she went home, she'd just lie tossing in bed, keeping Gary awake as well.

Finally, she sat down and logged into the administrator account that Ken had created for her when the Sherlock trial had been set up. It was only her third login; she'd left the program pretty much entirely in his hands.

She felt like a trespasser at first, invading his privacy, but that was absurd; if anything, she'd been derelict in not supervising the trial far more closely.

It took a while to get the hang of the interface, and find the lines, and stage directions, Sherlock had been feeding Ken during his encounter with Hermes. She brought up the surveillance transcript in a second window, and went through them together. Ken had improvised now and then, but most of the time he'd repeated the computer-generated script word for word.

And it had worked, hadn't it? Sherlock had merged the old DarkCardinal with enough pre-digested essence of lottery winner to fool OG into recognizing a prime example of what they were looking for, and offering him the same deal. Ken could never have faked it on his own, responding like a genuinely dying, genuinely deluded cryonics cultist; only Sherlock could truly channel this chimera it had created in its own statistical tables.

But when Ken had asked Sherlock to tell him what DarkCardinal would do, it had no real conception of what might happen if its words were acted on. Beth had stood by and let him treat Sherlock as a "friend" who'd watch his back and take a bullet for him, telling herself that he was just having fun, and that no one liked a killjoy. But whatever Ken had told himself in the seconds before he'd put the needle in his vein, Sherlock had been whispering in his ear, "DarkCardinal would think it over for a while, then he'd go ahead and take the injection."

18

"The FBI says it could be five or six years before the investigation is complete," Beth told Cheryl. "I'm sorry I don't have better news, but they're working their way through a giant rat's nest. They still don't know how many hits this 'charity' arranged, but it could be as many as forty. Then Carl's death is a whole separate thing; they need to prove that the cave-in was payback."

Cheryl nodded understanding, and continued adding pastries to the bag.

"Six is plenty, please!" Beth told her.

"Ken's back, isn't he? He'll eat at least four."

"Probably," Beth conceded. "He needs to get his weight up."

"Thanks for dropping by," Cheryl said. "I know it will take time, but it's good to hear that things are in motion."

Beth left the shop and walked over to the station.

"Morning, partner," she said, waving the bag under Ken's nose, then putting it down on the interview table.

"If I eat those, who'll eat the vending machine candy?" he complained. "You didn't take any of it while I was gone."

"I'm getting rid of that machine," Beth decided.

"I just talked to Special Agent Castillo," Ken said. "She's been looking into Aden Caruso again ... and it turns out he never had myeloma."

"Huh." Beth stood pondering this.

"He faked the blood tests and PET scans and everything," Ken explained. "All his friends and family thought it was real, but when the FBI got a warrant to look at his medical records, he'd never actually been to the clinic whose name was on the reports he'd been showing people."

"All to get into the lottery," Beth assumed.

"Looks that way."

"So did he kill himself after he'd done the hit because he thought he'd die from OG's injection anyway?" she wondered.

"Maybe he was afraid he *wouldn't* die from what they'd given him, because he wasn't as weak as OG thought," Ken suggested. "And if he hung around as a loose end, things might get messy for him."

"Either way ... " Beth said.

"Yeah," Ken agreed. "What a waste. Dying like that, and taking another life with him, all for castles in the air."

Beth had been trying to decide on the right time to tackle the subject of what had happened in Boston; she hadn't wanted to harangue him the minute he came back.

"I think the people who built Sherlock gathered together a lot of useful tools," she said. "But the way they're all tied together and packaged ... isn't so great. It all needs a lot more safeguards, and they need to drop the half-baked imitation of it being some kind of colleague. We both tripped up on things it handed to us; my mistake might still cost me a month in federal prison, and what you did—"

"What I did might have cost me my life," Ken said bluntly. "Do you think I don't know that?"

Beth was relieved; at least he wasn't still in denial. "Okay. So what are we going to do about it? Just wait for LRE to start putting out press releases saying Sherlock cracked the case of the frozen assassins?"

Ken said, "We're meant to write an assessment at the end of the trial."

"Yeah, but that's just feedback that goes to the company, and stays in their hands. I'm thinking we should write something for a criminology journal, making clear what worked, what didn't, and what the pitfalls are."

Ken seemed taken aback. "A criminology journal?"

"Why not?"

"Won't it be tough describing everything that happened, without violating anyone's privacy, or saying anything that would prejudice the OG prosecutions?"

Beth said, "There are protocols for dealing with that."

Ken thought it over. "All right," he decided. "I'm in."

Beth smiled. "That's good to hear. Maybe wait a few weeks to gather our thoughts first."

"Sure." Ken hesitated. "And maybe Sherlock could write an intro-duction to the article? Or a few lines of poetry ... like an epigraph?"

It took Beth a moment to realize he was trolling her. "Absolutely," she replied. "A few lines of poetry, on the epic struggle to make comput-ers competent enough to help bring down the fools who believe that they're going to be omnipotent."

Greg Egan is an Australian science fiction writer. His latest books are the novel **Morphotrophic** and the collection **Sleep and the Soul**.

THE BEST VERSION OF YOURSELF
BY GRANT COLLIER

Q: What (or who!) is Eudaimon?

A: We are a nonprofit organization that empowers people to live their best lives. A "life," in our view, is best defined simply as a contiguous sequence of experiences, and thus the best life is the one consisting of the best possible experiences.

On a moment-to-moment basis, finding the best experience is actually a well-posed optimization problem, as there are a finite number of possible brain states, and thus a finite number of possible experiences. Some might find this realization limiting: we at Eudaimon find it empowering. Just as the restrictions inherent in the sonnet or the haiku spur poets to new creative heights, this restriction to the set of possible experiences frees us to ask the question—what is the best one? And not only to ask it, but to *answer*.

Our procedure—

Maria stopped reading. The pamphlet wouldn't say anything she hadn't heard before. The wind had carried it, tattered, to her, and she had grabbed it, eager for a distraction from what she was about to do. She stuffed it into her backpack's outer side pocket: old habits.

Still pointing her attention in any direction but one in particular, Maria pondered the now pamphlet-less wind. She liked it: wind, in general. She liked it because it tickled her face, and her hair, and she never knew where it would come from next, and because, after everything, it was still here.

She ought to recycle the pamphlet—was *required* to recycle it. But she was going to compost it. Let Eudaimon mourn the loss of good material that could have become joyjelly.

She continued her walk around the periphery of the pain preserve.

She'd made these walks a habit over the past several months, claiming to simply enjoy them—and this grew to be true. Nobody living in the pain preserve would question her reasons for walking so close to the border—being in the preserve themselves, they had all had their own motives for every decision relentlessly questioned, and so shared with each other the courtesy of discretion. And besides, wasn't she technically in charge of maintaining these borders?

No, Maria wasn't worried about her community. Her people: even if they knew what she was doing, they'd all be loyal, but she would never tell them—would never endanger them, out of that same loyalty.

She was, however, worried about Eudaimon's surveillance drones, buzzing obediently around the border: right where the pain preserve ended and the joyjelly began. Any activity out of the ordinary would alert Eudaimon. Maria had needed to make walking on the border—even meandering past it sometimes—seem ordinary for her, like something she did innocently all the time.

Hence the months of regular walks.

●　●　●

Q: Is it possible to be sad while having the best possible sensory experience?
A: Indeed it is; so much of our experience goes beyond the sensory. A person's personality, goals, and memories often play a much larger part in their overall well-being than their immediate phenomenal experiences. However, these can all be represented by some finite arrangement of neurons: we can find the best of each of these, as well!
Q: Is Eudaimon's procedure safe?
A: Our procedure is one hundred percent safe, free of undesired side effects, and fully reversible: however, none of our four million (and growing!) recipients have ever requested the procedure be reversed.

●　●　●

"When I die, I don't want a tombstone," Mom said. They had been waiting for the bus in silence, and nothing in particular had been said to prompt this comment.

"Noted," Maria said. She was unfazed by the spontaneity on display here; that was just Mom. It was fun, in the small doses she got in her visits to town these days.

"And I *don't* want to be cremated."

"I'm not getting you taxidermied," Maria cut in.

Mom continued, seeming not to hear. "I want you to plant a tree above me. But not above my stomach or anything: right above my head, so the roots grow into my brain." She paused suddenly and cracked a delayed smile. "Don't taxidermy me," she said, once Maria's comment had registered.

"I literally just said I wouldn't."

"Good."

"Good."

They sat in contented agreement at this for a second, before Mom reiterated her initial point. "But I want the tree thing. I want to turn into tree roots. So I can feel what it's like."

Maria nodded approvingly. "What kind of tree do you want to eat your brain?"

Mom thought briefly, then waved the question away. "Don't know. Don't remember being any trees, in particular. Can't compare. They're all good, probably." She paused. "Just don't pick a shitty one," she added thoughtfully. The bus emerged from behind a corner, and Mom pointed to it. "Here."

"Why would you remember being a tree?"

"I don't, that's what I said."

The bus pulled to a stop in front of them with a series of hisses and groans whose volume Maria suspected would be mechanically unnecessary if there were sufficient transportation funding. "But why would you *be* a tree?"

"I eat a lot of fruit," said Mom, "so I'm made of fruit, partly. I used to be fruit. But I don't remember that."

The bus doors opened.

"And fruit is trees?"

Mom nodded. "And also, in the future, you know. When you plant one in my brain."

"But not a shitty one," Maria noted.

Mom shook her head solemnly. "Or I'll know."

A small crowd of passengers bustled out of the bus and dispersed. A similarly sized crowd, Maria and Mom among them, bustled inward to take their place. Mid-bustle, a man out-bustled them from behind, pardoning perfunctorily as he passed between them. Seatless, he grabbed a bus pole, turned around, and stared into space. He was grinning euphorically. His appearance and demeanor were not otherwise noteworthy, but this grin seemed out of place. He was staring away, and Maria watched him for a few seconds: the grin did not subside, as if brought on by a particularly grin-worthy passing thought, but instead seemed to have been there all day—this man just grinned euphorically, at a baseline.

His eyes, to Maria, seemed empty.

Mom saw her watching the man and leaned over. "He's a jellyhead. Eudaimon thing. Lot more of them in Manchester." She tapped on her forehead. "Brain's all nanobots."

"I know what a jellyhead is," Maria said pridefully, although truthfully, she'd never seen one in person—people with the money for the treatment didn't tend to live out near where park rangers got stationed. Though wasn't there talk of subsidies now? Had that passed? The man didn't look particularly rich. "And don't talk that loud; he'll hear you."

Mom shrugged. "Doesn't much matter if he does. He can just choose not to be bothered."

Maria continued to stare at the man, until he turned, met her eyes, and waved. Still grinning.

She averted her gaze and did not wave back.

•   •   •

Q: How does Eudaimon's procedure work?

A: Our procedure is built on recent advances in the field of awake brain surgery. This field has exploded in recent years, with the advent of nanobots that can cross the blood-brain barrier. Today, assisted by these devices, surgeons can often perform the procedure without incisions—even remotely—and any removed sections of the brain, along with the nanobots themselves, are dissolved harmlessly into the bloodstream over the next few days.

Eudaimon has repurposed this revolutionary new technology, putting *you* in the driver's seat. There's no need for a surgeon as an intermediary: just think about the way you want to feel, the way you want to be, and the bots will take care of the rest.

Want to stop feeling depressed?

Eudaimon can help.

Want a better work ethic? To be charismatic or confident?

To be more clearheaded or in control of your thoughts?

Eudaimon can help you here, too.

Want to kick your drug addiction?

Eudaimon's treatment can replace the drug effects you crave while curbing all the debilitating symptoms and preserving your ability to function at a high level (if you so wish).

No rehab, no withdrawal, no relapses. Simply concentrate on the way you want to feel, the way you want to be, and our bots will make it so!

Q: How do the nanobots know what changes to make?

A: In short, you tell them! We use a form of machine learning, where the metric the bots optimize for is your own satisfaction. At first, they'll make many small, barely perceptible changes, and sense if you like the results: if not, they'll reverse them, but if so, they'll keep them, and iterate more. Over a few weeks, the traits you want to manifest in yourself will inevitably emerge—and the improvements don't have to stop there!

● ● ●

Maria stood still and checked her GPS: this was where she needed to depart. She remained still.

The edge of Acadia Pain Preserve was abrupt and stark. It was marked by a razor-thin line of lime-green mold, engineered to eat any joyjelly that overstepped its bounds and tried to grow into the preserve itself. Or at least it looked like a line from the surface: it was actually a wall, stretching far down underground, as far as the jelly itself. Straining against the other side of the mold wall was a mass of spongy and reddish soil that seemed to stretch on forever, and perhaps eventually would—but of course, it was not soil anymore, not except for the top protective layer, seeded with just enough engineered lichens not to erode away. If Maria dug here, she would quickly reveal a pink-tan sludge underneath the soil that had settled over it with time—the joyjelly.

The "landscape" still rose and fell in the distance, in a crude imitation of the hills it had replaced—mostly fell, from Maria's relatively high elevation, until farther out it gave way to the ocean. From this edge of the preserve, Maria could see the two "lobes" of Mt. Desert Island. "Like a brain!" her manager had exclaimed excitedly when orienting her to the job years ago, not yet realizing how deeply, darkly funny that observation would become.

Farther still was the mainland, where the joyjelly resumed and continued farther than Maria could see, with few interruptions. Both island-side and mainland-side, the jelly was dotted with meter-long identical solar panels, every few meters or so. They looked jarringly artificial, particularly next to the heavily-forested preserve. As if the world hadn't fully rendered past the point where Maria was standing. The sun was rising behind her, and their long shadows eclipsed each other geometrically.

Maria released the breath she hadn't realized she'd been holding and stepped forward onto the joyjelly, gingerly. It squished subtly under the soil as if it might give way, though it didn't—Eudaimon built for the long-term. Maria checked her GPS again: about a thirty-mile journey from here, one-way.

Eudaimon's drones hovered, curious, nearby. She heard their faint buzzing under the wind but resisted the urge to look, even out of the corner of her eye: if she looked, they would look back and see her looking. What legitimate reason could she have for looking? She had to assume they would let her be, if ignored.

Truthfully, they probably would. Tensions between the preserves and Eudaimon had died down over the past few years. Certainly not out of a lack of resentment—rather, because rage can only burn so long while impotent, and in more of Maria's fellow residents every year, it had burned into begrudging complacency or inert depression. Both of these outcomes were acceptable to Eudaimon, as they led to no hostile action—and the latter made their treatment more attractive. These minimal security measures were a "gesture of goodwill," according to Em, who seemed sure that all Eudaimon needed to win, in the long-term, was to wait—but the less mental energy Maria devoted to Em, the better. All that was important about Em was that she was wrong: because Maria was not complacent, and she was not—inert, at least.

Maria still had all her rage left.

She walked onward.

• • •

Q: What is Nirvana?
A: Nirvana is the particular state toward which the brains of all Eudaimon's satisfied beneficiaries seem to eventually evolve. Even brains that began extremely differently will tend to, of their own accord, make themselves into this very particular set of neural connections.

We can think of any physical system—a category that includes brains—as existing at some point on a spectrum of well-being, at a given point in time. Some physical systems are happy: others are sad, others neutral. Others still, it is theorized, have no feelings at all, although this has never been proven. We use gradient ascent on this spectrum of well-being: this is a fancy way of saying that we find where your brain is on this spectrum, and nudge it, bit by bit, until it's happier. If we do this enough, then as sure as a ball will roll to the center of a funnel, your brain will converge to the happiest possible physical system: that's what Nirvana is.

Q: Is it true that people in Nirvana are paralyzed?

A: While it is true that brains in Nirvana are no longer attached to bodily nerve endings, it is not true that they cannot move. They are able to reattach those nerve endings at any time they wish, but simply choose not to, having found a much better use for them. Exactly what that use entails can only be fully understood through introspection, by those in Nirvana themselves.

Note that those who have undergone our treatment, having inevitably developed into very pragmatically minded people at this advanced stage, will take efforts to ensure they will be able to receive all the nutrients they need to function, on a biological level, before ascending into Nirvana.

While several nutrient-distribution solutions are already on the market, these are often unreliable and will require some level of continual outside intervention by those who are un-ascended. Eudaimon, however, is currently developing a cost-effective device that will serve all the needs of those wishing to ascend into Nirvana. We plan to produce this device at scale in the coming years.

• • •

Mom loved the idea of rugged outdoorswomanship, but only the idea. She claimed to be, in her heart, a spirit of the forest, but truthfully was much too dependent on the comforts of the city to act much like it. Maria had indulged her and taken her camping in the park once—half a time, really—before she decided it didn't matter how refreshing the forest air was: hotel rooms had fewer bugs.

Maria blamed herself a bit for this—she was going to rent a cabin, had it planned, with the tab pulled up, but she'd waited too long to make the actual reservation, and so convinced Mom to camp dispersed instead; that was too woodsy too fast, it was no wonder Mom couldn't tough it.

They made the most of it, though—both hotel beds, pushed together, made a base just large enough to support the tent, and they built it right there in the hotel. Room service had S'mores-flavored ice cream, and they turned out the lights and turned on "Ambient Nature Sounds Free 10 Hrs. No Ads (High Quality!)," and it was kind of like the real thing.

"I think you might be my best friend," Mom said in the bed-tent, once the festivities had died down and the night had reached the point where it was late and still enough to say things that were really true. "I don't think it's supposed to be like that. I know I'm not yours."

Maria didn't know what to say to this. "I like spending time with you, Mom."

"I just can't seem to keep any friends," Mom continued, seeming satisfied enough with this answer. "At least not any I didn't give birth to. I push them away. I don't commit. I forget to." She was silent for a while. "I think maybe I should try getting treated for my ADHD again."

Maria was relieved to hear this: a relief born from years of resignation suddenly reversed. "Yeah? That's honestly great, Mom. You could try my meds if you want; we're about the same weight."

There was the rustle of Mom's head shaking in the dark. "I know it works for you, but I just never felt like myself. Side effects." She shuddered. A short silence turned into a long one. "I've actually—I've been thinking about maybe trying Eudaimon."

Maria felt a fear then—a small, passing fear, but one that was small only because it was so distant. If she thought any more about it, examined it up close, then it was a fear so great and large that it had to be irrational, could not be addressed fully as anything else, and thus could only be dismissed. "Eudaimon bots treat a lot more than just ADHD, Mom. You sure you want something that invasive?"

"It's only as invasive as I want it to be," Mom said. "If I make any other changes, and I don't like them, I can just switch it back." She paused. "I'm just so *tired* sometimes. I want a break from . . . from being myself." She sighed. "Or maybe I don't want to change who I am—I just want to be a better version of me. Maybe that's what all these treatments are getting at. I think Eudaimon might help me be the best version of me."

Maria held her mother's hand then. "I'm honestly really proud of you for thinking about this stuff Mom. And I'll support whatever you decide."

Mom's hand squeezed back.

Maria fell asleep soon after. She woke up once in the middle of that night. Groggy and unremembering, she looked at the dead still tent fabric above her head, and thought it odd that there was no wind.

• • •

Q: Is ascending into Nirvana reversible?

A: Initial ascension is a fully reversible process—but not one that, to our knowledge, has been voluntarily reversed. We have experimented briefly with reversing it forcibly with rats but ran up against ethical concerns when the subjects expressed great distress: it seems that once Nirvana has been experienced, any return to a more traditional baseline brain state feels torturous. We've attempted to work around this issue by first inducing selective amnesia: purging any prior memories of Nirvana, so that there is nothing to be "missed." Unfortunately, the very experience of having these memories purged appears to be equivalently distressing to the subjects. Because of this, Eudaimon considers it an ethical imperative not to perform reversal procedures on any physical system in Nirvana.

Q: What is Nirvana X?

A: Nirvana X is our most cutting-edge program yet. Its purpose is twofold:

To increase the space- and energy-efficiency of our Nirvana-holding facilities. To meet what we see as the ethical imperative to allow as much of the world as possible to escape non-Nirvana.

The recent demand for our products has been so great that, even with the support of an international coalition of governments, our current production capabilities require us to find a more efficient way of processing Nirvana-sustaining units. The bottleneck here, surprisingly, is no longer the production of nanobots, or the administration of the procedure itself, but the energy consumption of sustaining a whole human body autonomously once the nerve endings have retracted.

Nirvana X is an elegant solution to this: as it turns out, keeping the entire human body intact and operational is a very inefficient way of powering the brain. What's more, the raw material present in such a body can be repurposed and used to make many more Nirvana states than just the one, evolved out of someone's original brain: with current methods, usually around ten brain-sized units total, per body: hence the moniker "X." These new "brains" are essentially physically indistinguishable from more naturally evolved Nirvana brains, and thus we have every reason to believe they are experiencing just as much bliss. This entire array of joyous beings can be sustained at a fraction of the energy cost of a single human body in ordinary Nirvana. We see Nirvana X as the future of what we have to offer.

•   •   •

Crossing the joyjelly, Maria tried not to look at her footprints. The topsoil was thin here, and so any indentations—footprints included—filled immediately with red fluid, pumping up from below. Not quite blood: not anymore. It had mixed with the elements, taken on enough that to call it "blood" was too simplistic, though to call it anything else seemed even more of a lie.

The not-blood was part of the water cycle now. When it got hot enough, it evaporated, and so some days the rain was red. Maria glanced upward at the thought, but the sky remained considerably cloudless, for now.

Maria was nearing the shoreline and spotted the causeway that connected it to the mainland: one of the few things in sight not built to sustain joyjelly. She angled herself toward it and took stock of her situation: she was making good time. Better than the first hour or so, when she hadn't yet learned to ignore the rhythmic squish of her steps. But then, the squish itself had lessened as she'd approached closer to the shore. The layer of mud covering the jelly at lower elevations was thicker—no doubt to Eudaimon's dismay; any non-jelly material was a waste in their eyes, though luckily, they had not yet learned to conquer entropy. It squished more like mud, and less like a brain: if not for the field of solar panels, and the bloody footprints behind her, Maria might have briefly forgotten what she was walking on. The drones were nowhere to be seen—they must have decided to pay her no mind. Her backpack felt heavy, but not overly so: unexpectedly light, in fact, given everything in it.

Maria didn't need such a large backpack: much of it was superfluous junk, packed to look as confusing as possible to a drone's X-rays, though this was done more out of superstition than any proof of efficacy. She'd used the junk, also, as a layer separating the topmost, clearly innocent items—food, water, bags of both the sleeping- and wag- variety—from the more suspect ones. The most clearly illicit item was packed into the very bottom: a large clump of pale green joyjelly neutralizing mold, curated from months of scraping the bottoms of her shoes after deliberately smudging them on the perimeter of the preserve.

Maria remembered the first time it had rained red. Em had apologized profusely at the ensuing preserve meeting, assuring that they were working on a solution.

"Em" was the name of Eudaimon's ambassador to Acadia Pain Preserve—though it was also the name of every other ambassador. She was alarmingly gorgeous—most mid- to late-stage jellyheads were, having complete control of their endocrine and metabolic systems. Charismatic, too. It helped them to manipulate you, convince you to be like them, run for office, run the world, destroy the world. Until they did away with their bodies entirely, and suddenly became indistinguishable from everyone else currently squishing under Maria's feet.

By around the eighth time it rained red, Em's apologies stopped. The implication was simple: Eudaimon already had a solution in mind. *The red rain doesn't bother the joyjelly. Wouldn't you love it if it didn't bother you either?*

It was considered a great sacrifice, staying behind as an ambassador, in a real body—most could only manage it for a couple of years before the call to "ascension" became too strong. Em did it out of the goodness of her heart, she claimed. She stayed behind, at great emotional cost to herself, just to help guide poor, unmodified souls like Maria out of their suffering. She'd been the ambassador to this preserve almost since the beginning—back when it was still a National Park, saved from jellyhood by a quirk of the legal system, and collecting unmodified squatters as a result. Almost fifteen years now: a real commitment to the cause.

Maria hated Em. Em seemed to regard Maria with the same cheerful, detached benevolence she regarded most everything with—this made Maria hate her more. Ostensibly, they ought to work closely together, as Maria was the senior-most park official left, but Maria tended to avoid associating with her as much as possible—her job was to keep Eudaimon *out* of their community's affairs, not help them ingratiate themselves more. As far as she was concerned, they had very little to talk about.

At the shoreline, the jelly sank underneath the water, while the panels stayed floating on top, tethered by increasingly long cables to the ocean floor. This was broken only by the causeway, ancient seeming in the context of its surroundings: a low bridge, made of stone and steel and concrete, predating anything Eudaimon built. As Maria stepped onto it, it didn't remotely squish.

It was midday now, and she sat down on the causeway, stopping for lunch. It was the most scenic stop she was going to get after leaving Acadia: the water surrounded her on both sides, lapped gently at the sides of the causeway, and helped her forget about what was lurking underneath. There was even some green out here: molds and natural lichens that had taken hold on the top layer of soil, or on the solar panels. Eudaimon evidently didn't patrol these areas, miles from the preserve, at least not well enough to keep some semblance of life from taking back over. That boded well for Maria; she hoped this trend continued farther out. She removed her lunch from the top backpack layer. Most of the preserves' food was shipped in from material-efficient vertical farms, but all of this—apart from some nutrient bars—was grown on-site. The trees it grew from now were newer—genetically modified to handle the higher iron content oozing in from the surrounding joyjelly—but Maria preferred not to think about that.

She ate. She then packed her waste into her bag—*leave no trace*, she thought, snorting—and moved on.

At the end of the causeway was the mainland, where the joyjelly and solar panels continued, seemingly identical to those on the side Maria had come from. But not completely identical, Maria noticed with excitement when she began walking past them; there was a key difference. The smooth, simple stones that served as the backs of the solar panels were not fully blank on this side of the causeway: rather, each held a simple, small engraving. *"Casey Berger,"* read the one to Maria's left. *"John Kevin Rogers,"* read the next one as she passed. Then *"Laramie Graber." "Allegra Gulino." "Dina Rubina."*

The solar panels doubled as gravestones. Eudaimon was efficient as always.

The joyjelly on the island, near the preserve, hadn't been made of people—at least, not anything that had been a person directly before being jelly. They wouldn't put that jelly so close to unmodifieds—at least not people with known names. It was intimidating. Bad for recruitment. That jelly was made from trees and grass and air and water and dirt. The remains of actual people—they were farther out. Still closer to the vestiges of civilization than most, but far enough out that they couldn't be seen unless sought out.

Maria allowed herself a grim smile. She had made it to the named jelly. She was getting closer.

• • •

Q: Do people have a free choice to ascend into Nirvana? Do they still have free will?

A: Contrary to some popular myths, a deep respect for individual autonomy is one of Eudaimon's core values: as evidenced in no small part by our extensive preservation efforts. We take significant steps to ensure that our technology is only ever used responsibly, with this core value in mind. That being said, it is possible—and happens frequently—that someone becomes who they want to be, only to discover that this new person they've become does not want to be themselves. An initial revulsion at the idea of Nirvana may naturally disappear as a side effect of other changes someone induces within themselves: a sense of open-mindedness, a calming of anxieties, a commitment to rational thought. This may happen multiple times in succession, with each version of themselves wishing to become something new, until the end destination is something that the individual, pre-modification, would have never explicitly claimed to have wanted. It is, however, what we all seem to want—and freely choose—in the end.

Q: Do non-brains, other organisms, or nonliving matter entering Nirvana freely choose to do so?

A: This is an astute question, as it acknowledges the fact—commonly denied—that no physical system is categorically distinct from any other. In fact, insofar as a "will" is a term for the true desires and intentions of a brain, there is an analogous quantity for all types of matter. When developing the technology for ascending non-brains into Nirvana, we didn't begin from purely mechanical principles: we instead developed nanobots capable of, as far as we can verify, deciphering the intentions of non-brains regarding themselves, and making those intentions come to pass.

• • •

Maria saw her mother dissolve in real time. It took three, maybe four months. Faster than most.

You know your lifelong dream of hiking the Appalachian Trail? Mom texted her, a couple of weeks after the treatment.

Yeah lol. What about it? Maria replied.

Let's do it.

Maria felt giddy at the thought. She had even been thinking about going soon, but the excuses not to go yet—work, season's not perfect to start, she should train more first—were exactly sufficient to have dissuaded her. Truthfully, the excuses were always exactly sufficient, by a razor-thin margin, seemingly cropping up in precisely the right number and magnitude to prevent any actual action. *Mom, you don't even like hiking.*

I like it now.

On video, Mom hadn't looked any different after the treatment, but Maria didn't actually see her in person until they met at the trailhead, a few weeks later.

It was late morning when Maria walked up to find Mom already there. She didn't look different in person, either, at first. They had planned to meet in the early morning: Maria had, as was custom, aimed to purposely arrive an hour late so as to only have to wait an hour or so for Mom to arrive. As was also custom, she'd unintentionally added a half hour or so of lateness on top of this, all on her own.

Mom was smiling when they met—Maria had expected her to be smiling like the subway man, widely, vacantly, but she wasn't. Just smiling: a subdued smile, a half-smile really, with a scrunching around her eyes, like she knew some private joke that Maria could not understand. She carried a backpack that Maria had never seen before, seemingly bought for the trip. Maria apologized for her lateness, newly self-conscious, and Mom waved it away, stepping forward to hug her—"I know how it is." The hug smelled the same as it always had—she hadn't expected the bots to have a scent: or maybe she had. "You ready?" Mom asked.

"Am *I* ready?" Maria laughed. "Are *you* ready? I'm reminding you again—nobody of your experience level should be doing this. It's honestly *dangerous*. And tiring. I'm fully expecting to have to drop you back into civilization before we reach Virginia. At the latest. You might not make it to North Carolina."

"It can't be that bad," Mom said. "And besides, I have my daughter here with me, if anything goes wrong."

"You're insane," Maria said. She told herself it was only a joke.

"Maybe," Mom said, and tousled Maria's hair, and flashed a full smile, with perhaps just a hint of the subway-man showing, but it could have been imagined.

The trail was beautiful. It was arduous, and tedious, and strenuous, and insufficiently populated with fresh food, restrooms, or basic sanitation products, and absolutely beautiful.

They hiked in silence, mostly. Maria had been worried Mom would want to talk, being the more extroverted between them. Mom seemed to understand this and gave Maria the silence she needed. She'd sometimes hang back until she was out of sight, but just barely, for hours at a time. Not because she couldn't keep pace with Maria—she was surprisingly resilient. Maria suspected she was being courteous. The hanging-back always seemed to happen right before an overlook, so Maria could spend the first few minutes by herself, on top of the world.

It was less beautiful at night. They packed separate tents, so at the end of each day, they would pitch them, and retreat, exhausted, inside. Maria would normally fall asleep near-instantaneously. Still, she often woke to the sound of laughing.

Mom laughed in her sleep. Hysterically, sometimes even painfully, it sounded.

She would wake up smiling bemusedly as if nothing odd had occurred.

"Do you remember anything about last night?" Maria asked, after the first night.

"Not to brag, but I remember everything now." They had been dancing around talking about the procedure, and this was the closest either of them had gotten to mentioning it explicitly. It caught Maria off guard. "At least, I remember everything I remember." A quick widening of her smile that ducked away as soon as it appeared, like it was hiding. "What's on your mind?"

"Did you dream anything? In your sleep . . . you made some sounds."

"I feel like my dreams felt . . . peaceful. I woke up very happy." Smiling. Reminiscing. "I don't remember any specifics though, no."

Maria didn't mention it again.

Midday that day, they stopped at the edge of a clearing, in a position so as to admire the sunlit view but not become too sunlit themselves. Maria unfastened her pack and retrieved a package of mush advertising itself as adventurous and full of all the essential nutrients she needed to conquer any challenge. It had a picture of a man standing on top of a mountain, and also a dog. It tasted, purportedly, like Mountain Blast. Mom retrieved the same, though hers was Hiker Fuel flavored. She then told Maria to close her eyes, shuffled through her pack again, and placed a plastic bag of something into Maria's hands.

Maria opened her eyes and laughed. "What the fuck Mom—"

"Surprise!" Mom's hands became briefly infused with jazz.

"—we're supposed to pack *light*," Maria said. "What is this, forty grams? Where did you even get this?"

"It's my stash," Mom said. "I figured you could put it to good use. I was saving it for a special occasion, but there's the overlook today, I thought we could watch the sunset with it."

"This is years' worth. This will last us years."

"You, not us." Mom smiled faintly. "I don't need it anymore."

•   •   •

The sun set too fast. It would never come back, just dark forever, and it would never come back, it was too late, they took it, and it would never come back, no matter what she did. She shook and cried in a ball, and Mom held her patiently, for hours, until she calmed down.

"Just like old times," she said to Maria the next day. "You used to have the worst dreams, you know."

•   •   •

Things were easier afterward. Maria had been scared to talk to her; scared she wasn't really her mother anymore. But she still was.

"Do you feel like your ADHD is gone?"

Mom thought for a moment. "Not gone. Covered up, maybe. You know I joined a backpacking group?"

"I know, you're an expert at this now." Maria's voice betrayed some real annoyance.

"A lot of people get new hobbies after the procedure, I think. Most of my group has had it done. Some have even hiked this trail before." It felt like a subtle prod, to test if Maria had fully accepted her decision, or perhaps to gain that acceptance.

"That's great for them," Maria said.

"I'm forgetting things less too," Mom said. "And I have more energy now. You know my desk, by the fridge? It's a real desk now. Cleared out.

I'd had a picture of you on it, hiding behind all the clutter. I can see it now, every day."

• • •

Maria had forgotten to pack a rain cover. The first night it rained, it did so torrentially, and she woke in the middle of the night to find her tent flooding. She hurriedly half-disassembled her tent and rushed it, still billowing with air, into Mom's. Mom bolted upright and helped her tumble inside and bring in the rest of her belongings. She zipped the flap closed behind her—caught it on the tent, unzipped, pulled it in, re-zipped—and they both sat there for a moment, breathless, staring at each other.

Mom laughed.

Maria laughed too, and then Mom laughed harder. This continued for several minutes, with several cycles in which they would nearly re-gain composure, but then start up again. This was sometimes triggered by a glance at Maria's tent piled inside, poles sticking out and water-logged like some misplaced sea creature, or more often by a glance at each other, lips twitching upward involuntarily.

The laughing settled down eventually: Maria retrieved her supplies from within the fully soaked tent and pushed its remains back outside. She would sleep in Mom's tent that night.

Maria didn't need a sleeping bag to sleep, but Mom insisted on lend-ing her own, that it would make a greater difference to Maria's comfort than to hers. "I really don't mind."

Maria accepted gratefully. "I still can't believe you were the one more prepared for this trip," she said. "I'm the literal ranger. I've camped maybe hundreds of times, and still—"

"Excuse me, that's my daughter you're talking about," Mom said. "You'll treat her with respect." After a pause: " . . . anyway, we both know I'm cheating. So it's not a fair comparison."

Maria laughed. "Thanks." After a reciprocal pause: "I'm cheating too, you know. Been cheating, actually, for much longer. Or, you know. Should be."

"You're not taking anything right now?" Mom asked.

"Should be," Maria repeated. "But I don't need it so much out here." She gestured outward, past the thin tent fabric that was currently stretched over her, shivering violently in the wind, even under the rain

cover. "Keeps my head clear. It's simple, and it's physical, and it ...
makes sense. There's no schedules and no responsibilities."

"So you don't take it?" Mom asked.

"Sometimes. When I can. Just to prove I don't need it. That I'm
not ... dependent, I guess. Out here, I like to be myself all the way.
Where it can't hurt anyone."

"You still forget rain covers though," Mom noted.

"Yeah, well, I wasn't out here yet when I was packing," Maria
laughed. "And also, you're cheating more."

Mom laughed back. "Fair."

They cuddled in the now-damp tent for warmth that night. Maria
laughed no more, after saying goodnight, but Mom, lying exposed on
the damp floor of her tent, continued laughing all through the night.

• • •

"Mom, you're bleeding."

There was blood streaming from both of Mom's ankles, in the spots
where her tall hiking shoes rubbed with every step. Her thick socks
came to just under each wound and had filled with blood all around the
rim. Mom looked down casually. "So I am."

"How could you ... " Maria swung her backpack down, kneeled on
the muddy path, and rummaged efficiently for the first aid kit. "How
did this happen?"

"Now that you mention it," Mom said, still staring idly at her blood-
soaked socks, "they'd been chafing for a while. Think my boots don't fit
right."

"Why didn't you *say* anything?" Maria unsheathed an alcohol swab
and gestured that a foot ought to be placed in her hand.

Mom sat down cross-legged in the mud and extended the top foot
outward. "I really don't mind, you know. It doesn't hurt."

"There's no pain?" Maria inspected the wound: it looked as though
it had been inflicted repeatedly, for a while now.

Not just today.

Mom smiled pensively as Maria set the alcohol swab against her
open wound. No wincing, no discomfort. "There's pain," she explained.
"But pain doesn't hurt. Not if I don't want."

Maria studied her mother's face. She held the alcohol swab over the
wound—longer than was medically necessary. Mom's face held no reaction. Maria continued to press the swab into her ankle. She squeezed it,

so more of the alcohol came out, drizzled in. Was she squeezing her ankle too hard? She was really pressing it in, staring at Mom's face all the while. She wanted to see *something* there, some discomfort, anything.

Mom smiled calmly back.

Eventually, Maria broke eye contact and reached for the gauze. "Still. You could get infected. Pay attention to the pain. You're gonna want to keep your ankles." Maria made eye contact again, and this time Mom looked away.

"Of course," she said.

Maria wished she had met her eyes, but didn't want to analyze this thought too much. She cleaned the other ankle, then taped the gauze to the affected areas of both. "You should be set for now," she said. "But just—in the future, can you pretend that pain bothers you? And *tell me*, if you feel it?"

"Of course." Another smile, but this one seemed perhaps tinged with sadness.

• • •

There was an aspen grove. It was early fall when they came to it, and the yellow and white stretched on for as far as they could see. This was about three-quarters of the way through the trail; they'd been making good time and would reach the end before winter hit.

Maria looked back to ensure Mom was following and saw her smiling widely, perhaps too widely. Perhaps admiring the grove, she thought, but this was not the first time this had happened, and it unnerved her. Maria herself had been smiling but stopped. She waited for Mom to catch up. "Enjoying the scenery?"

"Oh, yes," Mom said and flashed Maria a smile smaller than the one she'd been wearing before.

"They're all one tree, you know," Maria said. "Connected by the roots." Maria knew she used trivia to distract herself from her feelings—she thought this even as she said it.

"Different, but the same," Mom said. "Interconnected." She seemed to love the idea.

Maria nodded. "One aspen could be a whole forest."

Mom smiled appreciatively and stood in place for a while, admiring it.

Maria stood beside her. She opened her mouth tentatively. "When you smile—" she said, but stopped herself, as she didn't know how to phrase it.

Mom stared at her, expecting.

Maria spoke quickly then—the words tumbled out of her. "You smile wider when you don't think I'm looking."

Mom's face was carefully neutral now. Diplomatic. "Would you prefer I smile wider when we're talking?"

"No, I . . . it just feels, sometimes, like you're hiding it from me. Like you don't want to upset me."

Another light smile this time, tinged with sadness—jellyheads shouldn't ever be sad, should they? *Unless they want to be*, Maria thought. "I don't," Mom said. "I thought you wouldn't want to be upset, either. Do you want—"

"I want you to act how you feel," Maria said. It came out more harshly than she had expected, but perhaps no more harshly than she intended.

Mom sighed.

"Did you feel that sigh? Was that sigh really you?" Maria asked.

"No." She sighed again.

"Why are you *hiding*?" Maria asked. "Stop hiding from me. Be *yourself*. Be who you really are. Don't try to relate to me. I want to know what you're really like, right now."

Mom's face became neutral again, then suddenly expanded into a sickening smile.

Maria's world changed. Her deepest fears and anxieties about her mother, about the world, were no longer that: from this point onward, they were simply beliefs.

Maria settled her face into the neutral expression that Mom had been wearing a moment prior. It looked remarkably similar because their mouths and eyes untwisted in the same way, and it was remarkably easy because she was fully numb. "Thanks for your honesty." She turned away and began walking again. They should be able to make ten more miles before sundown and setting up camp. If she walked them quickly enough, she could stay numb.

"I didn't want to make you sad," Mom said. Maria didn't turn back, kept walking, but she knew the smile was still there: she heard it in her voice. "I want you to be happy," she continued.

Maria plowed forward, unresponsive.

Mom ran ahead of her and turned around. She'd un-smiled now: re-pretending. "Maria, please," she said. "I just wanted to be honest. I just wanted to make you happy."

Maria walked past her and did not make eye contact. Who was there to make eye contact with? Maria was the only person left in these woods.

"I thought you'd want me to be happy, too," Mom said.

"I want you to be *you*." She'd meant to contain her anger here, speak neutrally, but it exploded out of her now. "I want my *mother* back."

"I am me," Mom said. "I'm a better version of myself now—Maria, you can't understand it if you haven't felt it." Mom's tone was placating, as if Maria were complaining that she had to finish her vegetables before digging for worms outside. *You'll understand when you're older.*

Maria stopped where Mom blocked her path. "Why are you hiking this trail?"

"I wanted to do something with you," Mom said. She seemed to stop her sentence early: Maria didn't know which words had been omitted but sensed the first unspoken word was *before*.

"For you, or for me?" Maria asked. She had another question, also unspoken: *what happens when this is over?*

"Why can't I just want my daughter to be happy?" Mom asked. "Is that so wrong? Maria—you just can't understand what it's like." Dodging the spoken question—but perhaps answering the unspoken.

"You're right," Maria said. "I don't understand." She pushed past Mom again, walking quickly. Her lower jaw was shaking involuntarily, and she knew Mom saw it, and knew Mom knew it meant she was going to cry from anger, Maria hated that she angry-cried, but Mom angry-cried too, except not anymore, she could probably cry or not cry whenever she wanted now, and it didn't mean anything either way. At this thought, the surface tension in Maria's eyes broke, and she had to run so Mom couldn't see, and also running helped her not to scream.

Maria knew she couldn't outrun Mom: she cared if her legs hurt, and Mom didn't. She stopped right before what she thought was the overlook because she didn't want to see this one alone, they were supposed to do it together, they were supposed to be together, Mom was supposed to actually *be here* with her, but she had betrayed her, and now she wasn't anywhere anymore. Maria sat against a tree and began methodically picking apart one of its fallen branches, trying to catch her breath. Mom caught up to her there. "It's really helped me," she offered immediately, not stopping to catch her breath. "You know that."

"You didn't need that much help," Maria said. "I wanted to support you, but you could have tried something else first."

" . . . But I know now there's so much more, too," Mom continued. "I can feel it."

"There's *so much* you could have tried *first*," Maria said. "You think I haven't struggled with the same issues as you? It's just ADHD. Jesus Mom, you didn't take any meds at all, for *decades,* then you skipped right to *nanobots* in your *fucking brain.*"

"Maria, you don't understand what it's like," Mom repeated. "I know you must be scared for me, but it's not scary, it's exciting."

"You didn't even really try to work on yourself," Maria said. "Because that—"

"Maria—"

"No, listen. Because that would take *effort.* You'd have to actually *work* at it. Like *I* have. I've worked hard enough, I don't even *need* meds half the time, and you didn't even show me how to do that, I had to learn it myself. But you took the easy fix. You *always* do. And you thought it wouldn't go the way it would for other people who do it because you don't think ahead that far."

"I didn't—"

"But now you're telling me you don't even want to exist as yourself at all anymore. And honestly, that's the worst outcome. It'd be better if you'd just stayed broken."

"I know that you—"

Maria covered her face with her hands and screamed until her breath ran out, then inhaled and screamed again. Finally, she uncovered her face and stared dead ahead, with eyes too blurred to face anything in particular, not caring to wipe them.

"I understand you're hurt," Mom said, speaking carefully. "And I also understand that there's no way for me to make that hurt go away and that you'll never understand what I'm feeling without getting the treatment yourself." She paused, as if to consider applying pressure in this direction, but declined to do so. "But Maria—I can feel myself moving toward a peace I've never known, that I didn't even know was possible. It's so much bigger than me as a person, or you, or any of us, and I can join with it and be a part of it." Mom was smiling.

"You know the one thing Eudaimon couldn't fix about you?" Maria said hoarsely. "That you wanted to get their treatment in the first place. Instead of just living your life. You ran scared, and now all the bots in your brain will tell you that's the right decision, and they'll never let you see how fucked up it was."

Mom was silent.

"How long have you wanted this?" Maria asked. "Since the beginning of the trip?"

"Before," Mom said. "I wanted to be with you ... " she trailed off and left the words *one last time* unsaid but not unheard.

"And you probably wanted to convince me," Maria said. "To join you."

"You don't seem convincible," Mom said. "But know you don't have to keep suffering like this. I hope you know that."

"You're probably going out as soon as the trip ends, then. You're leaving me. Forever."

"It doesn't have to be forever."

Maria attempted to stare into her mother's eyes then but could only manage to stare *at* them. She couldn't see into them: there was simply a gentle smile and a wall behind which she felt she would never reach.

●　　●　　●

The trip ended abruptly. The Appalachian Trail didn't exist anymore: not all of it. Right at the border between Maryland and Pennsylvania, it ended. A sea of joyjelly cut through the woods: to the west, it was being built farther out, and to the east, it covered the mountains and continued for farther than Maria could see. Maria had planned ahead based on older references, ones she had compiled years ago and not thought to update. It dawned on her that they had been meeting very few people on the trail the past few days.

They didn't speak much, when they came to it: hadn't spoken much at all, since their conversation in the aspen grove. They hadn't really been walking together anymore: only walking alone in the same place.

Independently, they decided to walk up as close to the joyjelly line as possible. It was fresh here, exposed. Maria toed the line carefully, fighting back a revulsion. Mom carefully walked out onto it, then seemed to half-dance; revel in it, as if it were the most beautiful scenery they had come across in the whole trip. Her ankles were bleeding again, and Maria saw a few drops shake off into the jelly. *She's already joining them,* Maria thought.

Mom glanced back at her and smiled.

• • •

Q: A friend or family member of mine has joined with others in Nirvana—can I still see or communicate with them?
A: Every person who fully enters Nirvana does so with the understanding that they will likely never revert to their pre-Nirvana state. However, every part of a contiguous Nirvana mass is neuronally interconnected with every other part, and signals travel between these parts frequently: those of us outside of such a mass, of course, have no way of interpreting these signals, but we have every reason to believe they serve the purposes and desires of those within the mass. Given this, and given that Nirvana treatments are offered free of charge to any willing candidate, communicating with a loved one is easy, though, of course, the treatment allowing for such a thing may take several years to fully take effect.

Doing this, of course, will prevent any communication with other loved ones outside of the Nirvana mass of your choosing. Eudaimon's plans to mitigate this are twofold: firstly, any loved ones who have not undergone our treatment may simply do so and join whichever mass you are a part of in order to keep in contact with you. Secondly, any loved ones currently residing as part of a Nirvana mass noncontiguous with your own will soon be reunited, as part of our ongoing efforts at network expansion.

Q: What if I refuse Eudaimon's treatment?
A: Individuals who refuse our treatment are, of course, free to do so. This is not simply an ethical commitment of Eudaimon—though it is that—it is also a mechanical fact of our treatment itself. A handful of outlier cases in which an unwilling individual has been mistakenly treated show that our treatment has the capability to self-cannibalize if unwanted. This is expected: our treatment's main purpose is to manifest its hosts' intentions regarding themselves into reality, and if those intentions are set on not ascending whatsoever, then the treatment will recognize such a thing. Of course, oftentimes an individual has multiple conflicting intentions, and these will tend to work themselves out into a thermal equilibrium until they all align; this means that some individuals, who in the past have outwardly expressed a disinterest in Nirvana, have been known to evolve into it anyway, based on some seed of internal conflict with their stated intentions.

Still, there do exist individuals who genuinely have no current desire to enter Nirvana whatsoever. Provisional living quarters for such individuals, preserved as un-encroachable by the Nirvana networks, are in the works. Some of these provisions include memorials for those who such individuals care about, but who have themselves joined the network. While not communication, these memorials will hopefully allow for some semblance of peace.

•   •   •

Quaking aspen saplings needed a few key elements to grow.

They should be planted in early spring: around now, in fact.

They needed sunlight (in ample supply here), and they needed to be watered regularly, in a quantity-per-watering roughly similar to that which Maria carried in her backpack's second water pouch.

They needed about fifteen inches of soil or compost: the layer of soil that had collected on top of the joyjelly reached ten inches here. Ideally, they would have rich soil all the way down: joyjelly was fattier than Maria would prefer but would make adequate compost at the bottom, particularly if treated with some of the lichens Maria had mixed with the lime-green mold. That was the point of this whole endeavor anyway: she didn't just want to plant the sapling anywhere. She wanted to plant it in—

There was no need to dwell on it before she arrived.

The sun was setting, and the solar-tombstones' shadows were long once again, from the other side. They overlapped, partially obscuring engraved coordinates, writ smaller than the names on each tombstone. Pairs of numbers, the first of which matched the first coordinate Maria had memorized, and the second of which ticked down toward the second—the number she was now repeating under her breath. She was almost here; if she looked up, she could probably see it now but wouldn't be able to discern it from the others until she saw the name.

At this thought, she did look up—she wanted to see it, even if she didn't know which "it" it was—and saw . . . something. A figure, black against the encroaching dusk. Leaning against a tombstone, about a hundred meters off.

Maria was not alone.

She thought that she ought to duck down but knew this was ridiculous: she had been visible for a while, and the figure seemed to be facing her. It was, in fact, standing about where her destination should be.

Maria continued walking. Of course she did. What else could she do?

Slowly now, tentatively, but she had nowhere else to go, and she would not turn back. Perhaps walking slowly would give her time to think of escape routes she knew did not exist. Maybe she would look casual: "I'm just out here, taking a stroll. Just strolling, all day, in a straight line, miles from the preserve, in the most suspicious possible direction."

The details of the figure filled in as Maria approached.

It was Em. Of course it was Em. Who else would it be?

Her posture was relaxed, patient. Her face was blankly cheery. Her eyes were fixed on Maria, and once Maria was a few meters away, she waved.

Maria didn't respond. She instead glanced at the tombstone Em was leaning against—her hand covered part of the name, but she followed Maria's gaze and moved it away, courteous.

It was Mom. Of course it was Mom. Who else would it be?

They both stood for a moment, staring at each other. Em was clearly declining to speak first—if Maria declined as well, then, the conversation never needed to happen. Maybe Em just wanted to watch. Maria set her pack next to Mom's tombstone and began unloading her supplies. She'd need to move the panel before she could begin digging. She fetched the shovel, sticking out of the pack as the tallest item she'd brought. Em was eyeing her pleasantly, curiously, as if she were a zoo animal that had escaped its cage but wasn't particularly dangerous and had nowhere to go, besides. It was only when she touched the shovel to the base of her mother's grave, dug in like a crowbar, that Em spoke up.

"Do you think I'll let you do that?"

It wasn't a threat—or rather, it wasn't only that. Em's very presence here was a threat, of course: she was physically stronger than Maria and backed up by the most powerful organization in the world—the only powerful organization left in the world. She had no visible weapons, but had she pressed a gun to Maria's head, the situation would not have changed. Yet she managed to make this question sound non-rhetorical, as though she were genuinely curious.

Maria held the shovel still but did not withdraw it. "What do you want, Em." It wasn't a question. It was a line: fed to her and recited begrudgingly.

Em laughed—she laughed easily, and Maria felt she would've laughed at any response. "What do *I* want? Considerate. I'm sure you can guess. The same thing I've wanted for a decade, now." Em gestured at Mom's remains, and let the silence ring out for a while, filled only by a slight wind. "I'm getting it in a few weeks, you know. Eudaimon's sending my replacement."

"Congrats." Maria hadn't moved, was still tense, ready to do something, but not knowing anything that could be done.

"I'm going to be right over there." Em glanced lovingly in a seemingly arbitrary direction. "That's where my family's ascended. They saved me a spot." She turned back to face Maria. "I've got to deal with all this beforehand, though." At the word "this," she gestured widely at Maria's shovel, and pack, and self.

"No you don't," Maria said. "I've got it. You can head over early."

Another easy laugh. "You never liked me, did you? Though it's not about me, of course." Em looked downward. "It's about her." She continued looking downward, foregoing eye contact: as if this were not a real conversation between two people but a simple game, played to pass the time and not worth her full attention. "I'd been wondering when you would come out here. You've been building to it for months, with those walks you took. You know the drones see when you look at them, even discreetly. I only called them off today to save power; I already knew you were coming here."

Maria felt helpless, she was *helpless*. It weighed on her, doubled her exhaustion, and she wanted to collapse. She remained upright due only to the support of the shovel, now turned vertically, and by sheer force of rage. "Of course you did," she said. "Say more. I'm so predictable. You're so much better. You know better. Explain how you know everything, then lead me back to my cage." She gripped the shovel tighter. Maria knew she couldn't win a physical fight, but the shovel could make it close. She could do some damage if needed, particularly if she abandoned all concern for her own well-being.

Em shrugged. "I just thought you deserved to know." She walked, relaxed, past Maria, certainly noticing her tense stance but seeming to pay it no mind, and bent down to rifle through her pack, leaning against the other side of Mom's tombstone. She reached straight to the bottom, through the layer of distracting junk, and retrieved the bag of lime-green mold Maria had collected. She eyed it ponderously.

"Why are you *here?*" Maria said, and this time it was a question. Em was not acting remotely the way Maria had expected. She was being casual: playful, even. Maria had never been able to predict the way jellyheads acted, and the longer they'd gone before "ascending," the more bizarre their behavior could be. Being so close to ascension, Em—already eccentric—seemed to have let herself go to jelly more than ever before. This may be for the best: if Em had acted "normally," Maria would already be returning to the pain preserve, or perhaps dead. In her hopeless situation, any uncertainty was hope. "What's your goal in being here?" Maria asked, this time working to keep the anger out of her voice.

Em glanced at Maria, perhaps noticing the outward shift in mood, then continued eyeing the bag's lime-green contents. "I have to be," she said, gently squishing the bag. "It's my job. They won't ascend me otherwise, not since I became an ambassador. I have to do the job until my term's up or else they won't connect me. Or else I can't ascend without rotting away. And they *keep extending the term.*" She smiled softly, still staring at the mold. "I'm a hostage here. Same as you, really." Her eyes flicked to Maria: looking in her direction, but somehow not at her.

"I'm sorry," Maria said, and through sheer force of will, she mustered enough emotion to mean it. Though she still didn't fully understand, and she felt she needed to. "Couldn't you just stop wanting something, if you can't have it?"

Em vaguely smiled, or smiled vaguely. "I wish I could explain color to the blind," she said. "But I can only give hints." She seemingly thought for a moment, face unchanged. "Here: the hardest want to fulfill is the want to cease all wanting. Do you fulfill it or cause it to cease?" Another pause. "Does that answer your question?"

"I don't—"

"Oh, but you don't care, do you. You just want to clear this panel away." Suddenly animated, Em dropped the mold bag next to Maria's pack, then grabbed the side of Mom's tombstone that Maria had been crowbarring and pushed it across the blood-laden dirt until it almost touched the adjacent solar panel.

Maria stood dumbly, shovel still poised to pry away a stone that was no longer there. A few wires still ran from the center of where the tombstone had been, into the blood and the dirt.

Em walked over to the mold bag again and resumed pondering it as if nothing had happened.

Maria finally found words to express her shock. "What did you— why are you doing this?"

"You know," Em replied mid-ponder, "we aren't enemies. Eudaimon and the preserves. You're an essential part of our project. Allies. *I've* always thought, at least—though not everyone wants to keep you around."

Maria disliked the casual way in which Em referenced keeping her around. She felt like food being played with. "You *want* me to dig a hole here then?"

Em actually *shrugged*. "Is that what you want?"

Em didn't see Maria as a person, not really. Maria was some kind of lab experiment, and thus her questions didn't merit an answer.

But she wasn't stopping her. Maria thought it best not to waste a good thing.

She started digging.

The wires wouldn't lead into the jelly itself, just into a power source. Mom was installed with her head pointed east—they all were: all lined up—so Maria needed to dig about a meter eastward from the center of the wires. Her shovel met the mud. She step-jumped onto it, lifted it, and piled it to the side. Then she did it again.

"This mold is a puzzle, don't you think?" Em asked. Maria didn't look at her. "I always wondered why it never wanted to turn to joyjelly."

Dig. Step. Scoop. Dig. Step. Scoop.

"There were other versions, you know, that actually *ate away* at the jelly. Eudaimon didn't develop those further of course—but I wonder, sometimes, if they should have. The jelly was actively *choosing* to become that mold: what must it be like to be that kind of mold? Would it be even better than ascension?" Her voice was giddy at the thought. Maybe her face, too; Maria did not look.

Dig. Step. Scoop. Dig. Step. Scoop.

"Because that's the issue, isn't it?" Em continued, unbothered by Maria's preoccupation. "We'll always need people who aren't jelly. Me. You. Because what if we got it wrong? What if joyjelly is just a local optimum? What if there's an even *better* thing to be? Then we're dooming the world to an imperfect fate."

Dig. Step. Scoop. Dig. Step. Scoop.

"But as long as you're around, there's still a chance you'll find it. The true best way to be." Em paused. "Or your descendants could."

Farther down, the dirt became muddier. Bloodier. Bloody enough now that Maria was uncomfortable. She didn't want to slice right into the brain—not quite yet. She dropped the shovel, kneeled, and began clearing the rest of the mud away with her hands. Slowly, carefully. She could feel Em staring at her intently, and Maria stared intently elsewhere.

"You're being cautious," Em noted. "Uncertain. Good. That's part of your job in all this. To not know."

Maria's fingertips pressed into something distinctly fleshy and undiggable. She withdrew immediately. Then, gingerly, she cleared the rest of the dirt away, until she saw it, sitting there. Mom's brain. It was warm to the touch and pulsed faintly.

This was too much—it was right there, *she* was *right there.*

Em made a sound as if to say something, and Maria snapped her head to glare at her intently. This was a reverent moment, and Em shouldn't be here for it. Em broke eye contact. Regarded the mold again, unspeaking.

Maria felt hot tears welling up in her eyes unbidden, tried pushing them down, but she couldn't control them, she could never control them: she was her mother's daughter, after all. She stopped trying to control them, and let them fall onto the jelly:

And so, part of her joined her mother, just like she'd asked.

For several minutes, she wept quietly. Staring at Mom. Then she moved, delicately: clearing the mud, making a radius the size of an aspen sapling, plus a little more. More brain was revealed now than Mom had ever had initially, but some of what was here was really Mom. Maria placed her palm on it, and felt the pulse, breathed with it. With her.

Maria stood slowly and fetched the shovel.

Em, who had been gazing serenely at an apple core from Maria's dinner for the past few minutes, spoke up now. "Do you think she'll be happier this way?"

Maria walked up to the hole she had dug.

"Or do you just not think that way."

Maria glared at Em, then turned downward again.

"You know if you dig into the jelly itself, you'll just be killing her."

Maria gripped the shovel tighter. She steadied her breath.

"She wouldn't want that."

"You didn't know her." Quietly.

"She chose ascension. She left behind no documents suggesting—"

"You *didn't know* her." No longer quiet.

"I'm worried you're allowing your naïve emotions to cloud your judgment."

"You don't know me, either." Maria was letting Em distract her, she knew, and perhaps that was Em's goal. But the distraction felt good. It kept her from thinking about what she was about to do. Postpone it, for a little longer.

Em smiled sadly, patiently, as if at an obstinate toddler who hadn't been listening. "Maria," she said. "I know you very well. I know how much you hate Eudaimon, and hate me. I know how close you were with your mother. I know you've been planning this for months. I know you purposely delayed taking this morning's medication until early this afternoon when your hike was already underway. Presumably because you wanted to stay even-headed late into the night." At this, Em pulled a bottle of pills from Maria's pack. She brandished them gently.

Maria was silent—unsure of what she ought to say. This was a test, and she felt that perhaps if she said the right answers, Em might let her be. But Maria didn't know what the answers were, so she merely listened.

Em tried to nudge her further. "You're already managing your brain states, is what I mean," she said. "You already know how beneficial it is. You understand."

Maria's eyes drifted uneasily to the pill bottle: Em shouldn't be that close to them, some panicked part of her thought, she could mess with them, slip a replica into the bottle that's full of nanobots, change Maria into—

"Maria," Em said. "Eudaimon owns the manufacturers that supply your pills." She'd noticed Maria's glance and predicted her thoughts. "They own everything. You think they couldn't just give you whatever they want? If they wanted to alter your pills—and they don't—they wouldn't need me here to do so." She sighed. "Despite what you think, I'm not interested in undermining your freedom. I actually want to enhance it." She tossed the bottle back into Maria's pack.

"What do you mean." Gather more information: find out what to say to appease her. To make her leave.

Em reached out toward Maria, then balled her fists, as if she wanted to take her hands but knew better. "I . . . Maria, I want you to be the best version of yourself, that's all. And I don't think that's who you are right now. I think you know that, too."

"What do you mean."

Em sighed that particular jellyhead sigh—the one that was only performatively sad, where the sadness didn't reach the eyes. "I know you've tried to quit your pills. Four times now, since you've lived on the preserve.

"But you can't—you get too dysfunctional, or too anxious. So you start back up again. But then you try to quit." Em paused. "I just don't understand—*why*? Why do you want to quit, if they help you feel better?

To *be* better? I know the side effects are minimal. *You* know the side effects are minimal. They just—all they do is help you do what you want with your life. I half-understand not wanting the treatment I have—but why not even this?"

" . . . You want me to do what I want with my life?"

"Yes, Maria. I really do."

"If I asked you to leave right now, would you?"

Em seemed to think about it—though perhaps this was performative as well. "Yes."

"And would you tell your successor about this conversation? About what happened here? The person sent to replace you?"

"I'm required to."

"Would you?"

" . . . No." Em laughed wildly at her own answer.

Maria smiled at this, too. "Okay. Em?"

"Yes, Maria?" She was beaming.

"I'd like you to leave now. It's important for—for my freedom. For becoming the best me."

"Okay," Em said and nodded collegially. She stretched, seemingly in preparation to walk back to the preserve. "I hope you believe what you're saying. Because I do." Her eyes flashed briefly with something fear-like. "But don't—you don't talk about it either. Don't tell people. At least not until—I can't have my term extended again. I can't."

Maria nodded. "I understand," she said, and she did. Fear of Eudaimon was a sentiment of Em's, finally, that she could truly relate to. "I'm not telling anybody."

Em nodded back. "I can't," she repeated. The fear-like flash vanished from her eyes, and she smiled once more at Maria before turning away. She began walking, then paused, briefly, turning her head halfway back. "Apple trees work better, anyway," she said, then faced away from Maria and walked, turning back no more. She disappeared quickly into the darkness.

Maria was left alone with this cryptic comment, her bag, her shovel, and silence.

And Mom.

Maria placed her palm on her again, and again felt her heartbeat. Did it quicken at her touch?

She knelt down beside her and leaned over—mud and blood fully soaked her clothes. She leaned into the hole, placed her ear where her palm had been, and she heard her heartbeat, too.

It was the beat of all of them of course, sharing the same blood, the same current, driven by turbines deep underground.

But it was Mom's heartbeat.

She was going to cut into it. That would make it stop, at least right here. At least in the part that was Mom.

She stood and fetched the shovel. Hovered it above Mom.

A thought pushed itself into her awareness, against her best efforts: *will it hurt?* She faltered and wondered if she had the strength to do this.

There's pain. But pain doesn't hurt. Not if I don't want.

Maria breathed deeply in, then deeply out. It was time.

She touched the shovel tip gently to Mom's surface.

. . . no, she should fetch the tree first.

She retracted the shovel.

Dropped it.

She walked over to her backpack and reached in to retrieve the tree, cursing her own cowardice. *That's your job in all this—to not know.* Em's words echoed. She felt manipulated, briefly, then it faded because these words rang true.

Eudaimon wouldn't have faltered. If they decided that aspens were better than joyjelly, they would bulldoze every brain in their care, planting aspens in their wake, and feel no remorse. They wouldn't have taken the care to trek out and plant them, one by one, burying them amongst sleeping bags and mattress pads and other signs of over-preparation, in a bag stuffed so full that the sapling itself was difficult to find, where was it, and then if they made a new joyjelly that was better than aspens, they'd bulldoze the aspens and plant the jelly all over again, and it'd be just the same to them because they didn't really care about people, didn't care about Mom, were so damn sure of themselves that they were sending things out into space soon, starting the process on the Moon first, and the ocean floor, and then eventually everywhere, because "everywhere on Earth" wasn't enough, it had to be Everywhere, and the mold was here, and the soil was there, and her fingers scraped the bottom of her pack, and she dumped it all out, all into the mud, and the

Tree

Wasn't

There.

It wasn't there.

She hadn't packed it.

She had forgotten.

It was back in her room. Next to the coffee grounds she'd saved for compost and left sitting there too.

Just sitting there.

Maria fell to her knees and was still.

Just sitting there.

The wind blew.

It picked up some of her lighter possessions, scattered as they were, and began to carry them off.

The Eudaimon pamphlet fluttered away.

Maria sat in the mud.

Stupidly.

Being herself: stupid.

She sat and sat and sat.

Eventually, her mind restarted, and she became aware of the situation: herself, sitting stupidly, in the mud and the blood and her mother's brain. Then she became aware of her awareness, of her reaction to this stupid sitting: she became aware of a deep despair. Too deep to fathom, too deep to even fully feel.

Her eyes, free to wander as they pleased because nothing really mattered, settled on her pill bottle, flung to the side on a relatively dry section of mud.

A version of Em that existed solely in Maria's head spoke to her: *If you had taken it this morning, you'd have remembered. You'd have the tree with you.*

"Fuck you, Em," she said. Matter-of-factly.

Mom would have found this entire situation hilarious. She'd never have let Maria hear the end of it.

"Fuck you, Mom," she said. Quietly, lovingly.

Her despair deepened then. Reached the bottom. Crashed through, wrapped around, and came in from the other side.

Maria laughed.

She laughed and laughed and laughed.

It sounded like Mom's laugh, of course, like Mom was joining in, with her old laugh, the true one: but weren't they really the same?

Her eyes wandered again, free to do as they pleased because there was nothing that didn't matter, they couldn't pick wrong, and this time they settled on the discarded apple core.

Imaginary-Em spoke again, this time quoting her real-life counterpart: *apple trees work better, anyway.*

"Fuck *you*, Em," Maria repeated, this time with a slight tone of affection. She cackled madly at the audacity. She sounded insane, and so cackled again. She scrambled over to the core, grabbed it, held it close, hugged it. Cracked it open, gingerly pulled out the seeds. Selected the best one: it was difficult, they were all so beautiful, so full of potential, but this one, this one here was perfect.

She clutched it tightly with one hand, and with the other, she spread the mold onto Mom's brain: prepare it, help it accept the eventual tree. She piled the mud she had dug back on top: it needed to be planted shallower, needed to germinate before its roots reached down. The roots would reach the brain eventually, but it would take time. And when they reached it . . .

It might not work. Even with the mold, they might not grow further. The joyjelly might halt their progress.

But it might let them in.

It would have to choose. Mom would have to choose: *do you want to stay like this—or do you want to become something new?*

Maria placed the seed and piled the mud gently on top. It would grow if it wanted, and then the rest would be up to Mom.

Maria picked up her shovel and smoothed over the area where the seed had been planted. Picked up her pack. Picked up the apple core, removed the rest of the seeds, and threw each in a different direction: cross-pollinators. Let other parts of the jelly choose, too. Picked up the rest of the wind-scattered trash still within reach: old habits. Picked up her pills and sighed to herself: at herself. Tried wiping the mud off the pills onto her already fully mud-laden shirt, to little success. Chuckled. Placed them gingerly back into the bag and resolved to be less stubborn about them in the future: at least for a while. Though she and Eudaimon had very different thoughts about what her "best self" looked like—perhaps these were a part of that self.

Maria packed up everything else. She made it look, as much as possible, like she'd never been there. For all Eudaimon knew, these seeds had fallen naturally, or perhaps were never there.

"Bye, Mom," Maria said, and walked home.

The wind blew behind her.

Grant Collier begets short fiction, usually of the speculative variety. He's currently procrastinating on writing more short fiction by writing a computer science PhD dissertation instead, which is neither fiction nor short. He enjoys reading, playing music, and climbing on plastic rocks. He has several times attempted to befriend various wildlife, but has yet to be successful. **The Best Version of Yourself** is his first published work, but he has more forthcoming imminently, or perhaps in the past, depending on how long after publication of this anthology you read his bio. He lives in Durham, North Carolina with his wife and their dog. He has a newsletter you can join at grant-collier.com, and is on Bluesky at @grantcollier.bsky.social.

TWENTY-FOUR HOURS
BY H.H. PAK

Six hours left.

"What do you want to eat sweetheart?" She looks at me expectantly, holding out her phone to show me the menu. "It is *your* special day. I'll get you anything you want."

I smile, shake my hands. "Eomma, it's fine. You don't have to do this."

"I know. But this is your favorite restaurant. Why not indulge a bit?" She hums as she scrolls through the options. "It must have been hard to get anything authentic out there. I can't imagine the cafeteria on the base was giving you anything half edible."

"It wasn't bad," I laugh. "Mostly processed stuff. They couldn't import very often across the desert."

She sighs.

"Well, you're here now and that's all that matters. You're here, and I'm going to get you anything you want. How about this set?"

She points out a four-course barbecue menu.

"See, it comes with kimchichiggae and kalbi. Your two favorites."

"Mom, that's too much food! You can't finish all that."

"Aigoo. If there's leftover, I'll just take it home," she hisses between her teeth, meaning I'm not allowed to argue further. A server comes by.

"Chogiyo," she calls. "Can I have combo number three please?"

"To go?" The ahjumma barely looks up from her notepad.

"No, for here please."

The older woman looks up then, staring with a baffled frown.

"You want the grill?"

"Yes, please."

"Are you expecting anybody else?"

"No, just me and my daughter."

The server shrugs it off and lights the charcoal grill between us. She disappears into the kitchen, then returns a minute later with a jug of iced barley tea and banchan dishes in covered metal plates.

Eomma raises a finger, "Can we also have two bowls of rice, please? In stone pots. And gyeran-jjim."

The server, again, glances at her for a moment, but writes it down and returns to the kitchen.

"Mom," I sigh.

She shoots me a stern look. "You can't have kimchichiggae without rice. I'm not going to get another chance to spoil you like this. Oh. Did you want purple or white?"

"Whatever she brings out is fine. She would have asked if there were options."

"True, there is a rice shortage. It might be nothing but barley. Do you mind?"

"Of course not."

Eomma places a napkin in front of me then one in front of herself, setting the table with the chopsticks and spoons from a box on the table.

"I'm so glad this place hasn't closed down," I say as she pours me a cup of tea. "Whenever I visit it seems like more and more restaurants are going under. But this one is always here."

"It's the war," she says. "So many small businesses are dying out with everyone evacuating from the cities—but I've told you before, we're a stubborn people. The last restaurant on the face of this planet is going to be a Korean one."

I chuckle. "The bombs won't ever hit this one because it's so tiny! They haven't expanded at all in all the decades they've been here. I told my friends back at the base about how you can always tell the authenticity of Korean restaurants by how unassuming they are on the outside. All the best K-town restaurants have graffitied peeling windows and paper signs written in Sharpie and only five sticky tables, but then you know the food is going to be amazing."

She chuckles. "Tell me more about your friends from the base. Sue's the sassy one who likes to gossip but does nice things for you right? Like dropping off meals when you work late. And who's the engineer who listens to old Bangtan covers while they work?"

"That's Puja. I've already told you everything about my coworkers. I don't have any new stories."

"I want to hear you tell them again." She leans on her hand and smiles. "I'm just so glad you're home."

"Eomma, please don't cry."

"Sorry." She wipes her eyes. "Have I told you how good it is to see you?"

"Yes, like every five minutes."

The server comes out bearing a tray trembling with stacked plates. She pushes silverware out of the way and arranges serving trays piled with meat, a bubbling pot of kimchi stew, steamed eggs, dipping sauces, two covered rice bowls, and a plate of raw vegetables.

"I can take it from here," Eomma says, and the server hands her the cooking tongs before disappearing back into the kitchen.

"Chadobeggi first," I say. "And marinated last. You taught me that."

"That's right." She places the thin slices of meat on the grill—they sizzle as they cook, the fat dripping between the slots and the brown edges curling as they crisp. She tries to flip them, but her hands quiver and the meat skids into a scrambled pile across the surface. One greasy chunk flips up over the lip and onto the table.

"Ha," I tease. "You can build microchips, but you can't cook meat?"

She smiles to herself, sliding the lost slice of brisket back onto the grill.

"Microchips are easy. I have an electron microscope to be my eyes. Without it, I might as well be a bat. Here—" She takes a lettuce leaf, smears it with samjang paste, adds bean sprouts, kimchi, and piles it with brisket. When she wraps it, the lettuce tears.

"Eomma, you should have the first ssam."

"Out of the question." She wraps it more securely in a perilla leaf and places it on my plate.

"It's all yours. I made it with love." She puckers her lips and makes a heart with her fingers, making me laugh.

As I expected, we don't get through much of our dinner. I see the ahjumma pass by every so often with a judgmental squint as most of the food remains untouched. When we ask for to-go boxes, she has to bring about six and doesn't look too happy packing everything.

"Mom, you ate more than I expected," I comment when the server leaves to get the bill. "I don't think I've seen you eat that much in a while."

"It's because you're here," she jabs a finger at me. "Don't you know I always gain weight when you come home?"

"I do too. We always eat so much together. Why can't we exercise and lose weight whenever I visit?"

"You said that last time," she snorts. "And I've told you before, I'm too old to keep up with you. You work on a military base; if I tried to work out with you, I'd die."

"How about yoga? Yoga is low stakes. We can do yoga together."

"Is that what you want to do for the rest of today?" She leans forward. "This is all for you agga. My baby. I want you to do all the things you couldn't do before—you started working on the base."

"I don't know," I say. "I can't really think of anything I never got to do. Home is home—it's not really a place for bucket lists."

"I know." She pulls out her phone again. "I know you can't tell me anything new. So I thought we could just keep pulling from your list of favorite things. We went to your favorite brunch place this morning— and got to see that movie you were looking forward to—we walked in the park, or what was left of it—barbecue at your favorite restaurant— how about pabingsu next?"

"It's winter!"

"You know there's that saying that cold deserts taste best in the winter. That's what my wehalmony told me when I was your age. Wait, never mind," she crosses it out. "I forgot, the family that owns that place moved a month ago. They went to Iowa."

"Iowa?"

"Ah, right. While you were gone, they built several new bunker towns there. Out in the countryside, where they're less likely to get bombed."

"Oh."

I watch her, my mother with the deep dark bags under her eyes and her hands trembling as she scrolls on her phone. Her clothes are too thin for the weather.

"Mom, why don't you move out too?"

"Hm? Why would I do that?"

"I mean—you don't have family anymore in the city. You told me samchon's family evacuated. You should go be with him."

"No no, we've talked about this before. My brother has three kids and there's already too much to worry about. I can't burden him. Besides," she looks at me. "This is the city you grew up in. This is where I raised you. I can't leave it."

"But it's dangerous."

She shakes her head. "What's an old engineer like me going to do anywhere else? If my time comes, it comes."

"You know I hate it when you talk like that. Your life is precious Eomma. You shouldn't be so flippant with it."

"Aigoo. When were you so argumentative?"

"My whole life. We used to fight all the time; don't you remember?"

"Did we?"

She puts down her phone.

"I just realized. We never got to go furniture shopping. You were so looking forward to having a place to yourself after graduate school. Remember you almost—almost . . . "

She squeezes her eyes closed, then opens them with a smile.

"Well, it's a shame you couldn't stay near home. Rent's been going down in the cities."

"Because no one wants to live here. It's too dangerous," I say. "But none of that matters anymore. That was all before I got the job offer and moved onto the base instead."

"True. But that's not a permanent situation. You're young. You'll need a place of your own someday. Let's go furniture shopping. We don't have to buy anything. We can just browse. Think about the future, you know?"

She shuffles through her wallet—I notice how she pays in cash, counting every last bill twice.

I say, "Maybe we should pick a less shopping-based activity. You've been spending an awful lot of money on me today." I peer at the check. "Meat costs more than gold these days."

"It's worth it," she scoots it away as she signs. "My daughter's home, money is of no consequence. Since when did you start worrying about money?"

"Since I became an adult," I smile, a little helplessly. "It came with growing up."

"Then don't grow up. I'll buy you meat and ice cream and anything you'd like whenever you want."

We both laugh as we step out into the cold.

● ● ●

Three hours left.

There are wilting red and green streamers tacked onto the store shelves. The aisles are littered with glitter and plastic pine needles that stick to her shoes.

"Sloppy job with the holiday cleanup," I comment as we walk side by side. "But it's nice to see people made an effort despite everything."

"It would have been nice," she says with a hollow wilt to her voice, "if we could have gotten together earlier. At least for New Year's. They couldn't light the streets at night because of the bomb warnings, but I heard the indoor decorations were lovely. This was always your favorite time of year. If I had just worked faster . . . I could have brought you home to see it."

"I don't mind at all," I laugh. "It would have been difficult navigating the holiday crowds with—you know. This is better."

"You think so? Oh agga, look at this desk chair." She heads for an office display on a podium.

"This is perfect for you. We should ask them if they have it in stock."

"I thought you said we were just going to window shop."

"I know but," she runs a hand over the armrest, "this one's so nice. It's exactly the kind I wish you'd had throughout high school."

"I didn't need a desk chair. Or a desk. I studied at the kitchen table all my life. And, might I mention, did pretty well."

"But still. You used to say your back hurt."

"Mostly because I was dumb and loafed around with terrible posture. No chair would have fixed that."

"What about this desk?" She opens and shuts the many drawers. "It's pretty long so you can spread out your work."

"I work in a lab," I protest. "You work in one too, you should know. I haven't used a desk like that since grad school. And I mostly studied off campus anyway."

"Then let's go check out bed frames," she heads to a different aisle. "What kind of bed do you have on the base?"

"It's a cot. I've told you it's a cot."

"Aigoo, my baby hasn't felt a real mattress in years," she sighs. "I won't accept anything less than queen-sized. This one looks nice. I like the headboard."

"Mom?"

"Yes, neseki?" She looks up at me.

"Can we go home? We should spend some time at home before I leave tonight."

Her face falls immediately.

"There's time left."

"Yes. Plenty of time. But the store closed ten minutes ago," I gesture to the employees lurking in the aisles, looking more exasperated by the second. They've already asked her to leave twice.

"I don't want them to think you're crazy. Talking to yourself late at night."

"Oh. Okay."

• • •

She's getting the shattered look again, the one I saw briefly when I first arrived. It disappeared the moment she saw me, but I caught sight of it then—the haunted shadow over her brow and the deepened lines around her mouth. They are returning, slowly.

On the way home, I distract her as much as I can.

"Your hair looks so nice Mom," I say. "And I don't think I mentioned this, but I like your hat too. Whoever picked it out has great taste."

Bright pink, short-brimmed, a creased plastic flower covering a dent on one side.

"You made it for me," she says quietly. "For my birthday."

The cab driver's eyebrow quirks in the mirror, but he doesn't say anything.

I make a silly face at her. Lips puckered, eyes squinted. "I know. I'm good with my hands. I get that from you."

She smiles, but only slightly. Her knuckles are growing white clutching her too-small hoodie like she's trying to bind herself together. It's mine, I remember. One from middle school.

The closer we get to the apartment, the more she shrinks. By the time we get to the door, she is hunched over like an ancient woman. She has trouble getting the key into the lock; it rattles repeatedly until she finally gets it open.

She turns on the light and stares into the space as if it is a new place, as if it is unfamiliar and overwhelming her.

"You should put all the food away first," I say. "It's good you ordered so much, actually. Now you won't have to cook for a while."

I lead her to the kitchen and watch her put the to-go boxes in the fridge one at a time. Every time she sets one down, she looks up at me as if I'll vanish the moment she's turned around.

"Don't worry," I say. "There's still two hours left. Let's do chores to pass the time."

The apartment is a mess. There's a year's worth of ramyeon boxes and takeout containers piled by the door. The floors are caked in dust, only clean where she's swept a path between the bathroom, the kitchen, and her office with its reinforced door. Every time we pass by its gleaming keypad, she stares at it with a desperation that grows with every passing minute.

"I'm proud of you Eomma," I say as I coax her to wash crusted dishes. "You've worked so hard on this project. I used to brag all the time to my friends, about how my mom is a genius. The way you made me is really incredible."

"Yes," she scrubs the same plate over and over. She won't stop looking at me. "I was in labor with you for fourteen hours. But it was worth every second. The day I had you was the happiest one of my life."

"Ha. That too."

When I convince her to vacuum, I say, "Make sure to get under the couch. If the dust accumulates there you can get sick. And you have to remember to get the chip removed after I leave. It won't hurt you when it deactivates, but it's not good to leave foreign matter in your head for too long."

"How do you know that? I didn't tell you that."

"I'm programmed to act based on your memories. I have access to everything you know. You also programmed me to tell you when time is nearly up."

Her bed is rumpled, hardly slept in. I ask her to wash the sheets and sit next to her on the floor as we watch them spin in the machine.

"You should sleep as soon as I leave," I say. "I can tell you've been awake long before I arrived."

"I don't think I'll be able to," she whispers. "When I wake up and you're—" She can't finish. She closes her mouth so tightly, her lips disappear.

"I'm sorry I can't help," I say once everything is out of the dryer. "I know getting the fitted sheet on is a pain." When I smooth the bed, the wrinkles remain. "We used to do it together."

"And—" she smiles. "And you'd try to crawl under it when I snapped it out—it floated down over you, giggling—you lying there under the sheet, lying. Under the—" she stops. Her smile vanishes.

"Yeah, getting it grubby again," I say. "Kicking until you pulled me out by my sweaty ankles and tucked it over the bed. I remember."

The house is clean at last. It looks livable but the desolation is still there, clinging to the walls, odorous without a scent, felt but not seen.

There is no warmth nor comfort on the couch as we sit side by side. Her eyes are fixed on me. Then, ever so slightly, I see her gaze shift to the office door.

"Eomma," I say. "You were working so hard to make this day happen, but you have to take care of yourself too. I wouldn't have wanted you to live like this. There's ten minutes left."

"No. No, no." She's trembling. "Not now. I need more time."

She stands. She shuffles to her office.

"Mom, no." I appear between her and the keypad. "That's why you set the timer. You knew this would happen—you knew you wouldn't be able to end the program yourself."

"I know. I know. Please get out of my way."

"I'm not here." I keep my arms extended. "You can reach through me if you want. I'm not stopping you."

"Please—" her voice is getting shrill and desperate. "Please move."

"You don't have the door code," I say quietly. "It's randomly generated and encrypted. You knew this would happen."

She sweats like she has the flu. She suddenly walks off into the kitchen and scrabbles in the drawers. Her hands tremble so much she drops everything she touches—knives and spatulas fall to the floor.

"Eomma, please stop. You're going to hurt yourself."

She pulls out an electric lighter and rushes back to the door.

"Mom."

She snaps the flame and holds it, quivering, against the wood.

"That's not going to work."

"It's okay agga," she looks at me, directly into a face only she can see. "I'm going to fix this. I was stupid, one day clearly wasn't enough. We barely got to *do* anything. I should have thought of that. I'll reprogram it so you'll be here for just one more day. Just one more day, okay?"

"This isn't healthy."

I kneel down next to her. The lighter flame flickers in her eyes, refracting against the tears blooming down her cheeks.

"That's why you did this. To grieve and say goodbye properly because it happened so suddenly. If you have me for one more day, you'll never end it. You have to say goodbye."

She holds the lighter closer, but we both know it's not going to work. The wood isn't even warm—she coated it herself. She thought of everything.

With a short scream, she throws the lighter away from her—it skitters under the couch. She snatches my jacket and stalks to the front door.

"No," I rush in front of her.

"My lab—" she tries to reach around me. "I need my lab."

"It's late. Even tomorrow, the company won't let you in. You designed this system. You'll have access to your home office and your lab only once you pass a psych eval. And that won't be until you've grieved properly."

She makes an animal sound deep in her throat and rushes about the house clawing through closets and pantries. I watch her.

"Eomma, we don't have that much time."

She stops before a door opposite the kitchen. My room. I reach a hand out.

"Can I see it again before I leave?"

She opens the door. It's dusty in here, but everything is exactly the same. Band posters on the walls, books on the shelves, stuffed animals, peeling stickers on the window, and clothes in the closet. I am eleven years old again, coming home from school.

"Have you gone in here at all since I died?"

She doesn't answer. She falls to her knees, looking up at me with despairing eyes.

"Please," she whispers. "Please, don't go."

"I have to."

I sit across from her.

"It's how I was designed. We still have five minutes left. Let's talk. Let's talk about anything."

She wipes her face but it's useless—it's so wet she looks like she's melting.

"When—when you were six we were shopping for your friend's birthday and you wanted a toy, it was—" her words are blurring together, her hands gesturing weakly. "It was a toy radio that played different songs. And you wanted it so badly, but I said no because we were shopping for your friend and I wanted to teach you a lesson in self-control but—I should have gotten it for you. I should have bought it when you asked. It made you smile and it was pink—you used to love pink. I'm so sorry."

"It's okay Mom. I don't remember, so I must not have wanted it that much."

"Haaaa," the sound she makes isn't a laugh or a sigh, it's something in between and much emptier.

"When you were fourteen, you went to your first school dance. And I was working two jobs then; we were a bit tight that month, and I couldn't buy you a dress. So then you went to the formal in your hanbok," she chuckles, wheezily. "The—the hanbok wehalmony bought you."

"It actually went really well," I say. "It was a little hard to dance in, but it made a statement. And I told you, I made a lot of new friends that night because people kept asking about it."

"Even so. It made my heart ache when I saw the pictures you took. You, in that old-fashioned traditional outfit, while all your friends were wearing cute short skirts—" she clenches her arms around her stomach. "I wish I had gotten you all the pretty dresses in the world. I should have done more for you. Remember—when you were in that holiday play in second grade, and I promised you I'd go, but I couldn't that night because I was stuck in a meeting with my director? I rushed over as soon as I could but by the time I got there it was already over and you were sitting—" she shudders. "You were sitting on that stage with your backpack and you looked so *disappointed*, but you said it was fine—that's one of my biggest regrets. I should have quit that night and seen that performance. I asked all the parents for recordings, but you weren't in any of them—of course they'd zoomed in on their own kids, and I couldn't see you, I *never* saw what you looked like in your costume—" She can't speak now. She is on the floor. I can't see her face; she is hunched over as if there is a building on her shoulders, like she is sinking into quicksand.

"Tell me what you were again?"

"You already know Eomma. I know everything you know."

"Tell me again."

"I was a snowflake. The costume was too big and when I turned around I knocked over Thomas Hao in the middle of the play."

She laughs. And then she chokes and then she can't speak for a long time.

Two minutes left.

"You were a great mom. Please don't doubt that; I couldn't have asked for anybody better. You raised me on your own. It wasn't perfect. We're different people. But Eomma," I lean forward, "I *loved* being your daughter. You inspired me to pursue my research degree. The programs you've made have changed lives. And now this one," I point to her head. "The way you made me? This could help a lot of people. Especially now."

Behind her is a halo of kitchen light that slices through the door and lights her from behind.

She mumbles, "When you got that job offer, I should never have let you go—I was scared for you, but you said you were going to do your part to help people during this terrible time, you said it was a remote location and the government would protect you—" she groans. "But then they didn't—and the bomb—and this stupid pointless war—I told you it was dangerous, I told you not to go—"

"But I went."

I kneel down in front of her.

"I went. And I helped develop the life-support systems that keep bunker towns stable. And Sue developed immunity boosters for the people moving there. And Puja developed preventative insulation against geo-scanning tracking systems. Our base was targeted because we were doing important work. And we're all gone now, but we got to help a lot of people, so I don't regret it."

Silence.

"Mom, please retire. Rest. Go to samchon. I saw all the missed messages on your phone. They're worried about you."

One minute left.

"Mom, I have to go now. But I love you, and that doesn't leave with me, okay? When I tell you I love you, that means forever."

"You took my line." She finally looks up at me. "Neseki. My baby. I love you forever."

Ten seconds. She hugs me, and I hug her back although neither of us can feel each other. I am nothing but code and wiring and cells in her hippocampus, but she squeezes like she can really feel me. She kisses my invisible forehead.

"Bye, Mom."

The last thing I see is her waving—it's the same wave from when she used to drop me off at elementary school. Elbows low at her side. Fingers clenching and unclenching like she's trying to hold something that isn't there.

H.H. Pak is a Los Angeles-born speculative fiction author who dreams of space operas by moonlight and studies medicine by daylight. When they are not doing either, they are Co-editor and Art Director of **Wyrmhole Magazine**, a lover of all things cringe, and proud owner of the world's cutest dog. Their fiction has been published in **Clarkesworld** and **khōréō magazine**.

BEST PRACTICES FOR SAFE ASTEROID HANDLING

BY DAVID W. GOODMAN

The first time Gabriel Halstead tried to kill me, everyone thought it was an accident.

So did I, truth be told. That kind of thing gets a couple people a year, even here. The number of EVAs we all do, you don't even need a fail-buddy to cause it. Micro-tears in the seals, visual checks don't catch it.

But I'm getting ahead of myself.

I noticed Halstead the first cycle he arrived, in the regular surface transfer from the Drop. You can tell the ones never been on a 'roid before. They get tripped up by the horizon line, take little steps or far too big ones, forget to turn their locks on. Every pickup has a shepherd or two, bringing them in, tethers for the ones who end up making a leap for old Jupes. Escape velocity here isn't much more than a hard rackball throw. Planetsider brains short out on how small it is. Rockhoppers can't deal with how big. They're used to tumblewalking free-floating 'roids into their catchnets by hand. We do things bigger here.

Halstead wasn't the worst of the new arrivals; he made good progress toward Main Bay, stumbling forward under the floods, magne-tized tektite dust bristling on the legs of his suit from the static because he didn't know to discharge when he got off the lander. I saw Matilde looping some clueless rockhopper who was drifting upside down, three meters off the transit walkway already with one misjudged hop. The Accord rippled with the bubbles of amusement from the people around me, watching them come in.

They all came tumbling into Main Bay, blinking through their face-plates into the floodlights, looking up at the big machines. Main Bay is ancient, two hundred solars easy. The oldest part of this rock, when it still looked like the curled up, tight-sleeping fox they named it after. The fox's tail is gone now, chipped away. But it's slow work. And this rock is big.

Matilde pulled the drifter down, tapped his locks on, and stuck him to the deck. We watched them assemble. None of them certified, so we couldn't feel them in the Accord. No ripples. Some of them transferring from other collectives had implants, some didn't. But they were all blank to us, figures in suits in the floodlights. Strangely quiet.

Must be weird, coming to a place like this, knowing everyone around you is rippling all the time, no way to join in. But that's the process. Screening, then Certification.

Matilde tuned them all into the bay audio channel and gave the welcome speech. Welcome to Refur, your new home, congratulations on becoming part of the best mining collective in the Jovian Accord, you know the drill. I'm sure you heard something like it when you joined yourself. Unless you're a failbuddy doesn't tune into these things. But I don't think you are, since you're listening so close.

Most new arrivals, they've come from Earth, or a big station, or they're rockhoppers like I said, grew up in a single ship. Either way, they're going to stare. Gonna look around a lot, need to be snapped back to attention. Not Halstead. He kept a fierce eye on Matilde, like he was minding the beam on a deep cut, looking for fractures or gas shatter. Eyes focused like a seasoned pro.

But my helmet HUD told me different. Gabriel Halstead, twenty-eight solars, never been off Earth. Never been near Jupiter in his life. Barely left low Earth orbit before, aside from a half year on Luna. Weird record though. Credits from places I've never seen before, though they must have been good enough for Screening. When you're bringing people up to work and live on Refur, you gotta be careful. One failbuddy or two per year we can deal. Nothing training and support can't fix. A dozen and you're gonna be dead. All of you.

And Earth's just a big ol' pile of failbuddies. Broke the place so bad five centuries back a bunch of 'em died. They're better than they used to be, these days. But people who grow up with a biosphere they don't have to maintain every damn day are careless.

Gabriel Halstead didn't look careless.

• • •

Of course, they paired him with me. I get a lot of the groundbound, before they certify for the Accord.

Matilde walked him over last, once she had the rest assigned. Compliment to my teaching skills I guess, but I sighed a little inside my helmet at getting another grav-born with a death wish. Curse of competence, I guess.

"Xavier, this is Gabriel. He's from downwell. First time outsystem. I thought you'd be a good match for him, show him the ropes." I felt a little ripple of reassurance in the Accord from Matilde, along with a bubble of sympathy. Even as she gave me the groundie, she was sorry to be doing it.

I nodded, looked down, and smiled over the rim of my helmet seal. Gabriel had taken off his own helmet now Main Bay was closed. He looked back up at me and blinked. Us station-born are a good head or two taller than the groundies.

"Xavier Ingridsson, good to meet you."

"G—Gabriel Halstead," he said, blinking into the roof floods. His eyes seemed to want to look anywhere but right at me. Nothing unusual in that. Shyness, disorientation from the landing, bright lights in the bays. This place can be overwhelming.

"Are you... *the* Xavier Ingridsson?" he said after a moment. His throat bobbed, and he looked like he wanted to wipe his palms on his thighs, but there's no cure for sweaty hands inside a suit.

"Only one on Refur," I said, narrowing my eyes a little. I've been off-station a few times, talking to people, negotiating with other collectives. But I'm not so well known some kid from downwell knows about me, as a general rule. "I know you, Gabriel?" I asked.

He extended a hand. "No, no, just did a little reading before I took the skyhook up for the transit. Your family were first founders, right? Nice to meet you."

I smiled. "It's a claim-to-fame, I guess. Sure, four or five generations back, my family was here. Helped dig out this bay, in fact. But it doesn't mean much, really."

He nodded uncertainly. Neat crewcut hair, pale skin, and wide eyes. File said he was from the NAA somewhere. Details were a little hazy. Something about an agri-solar complex in the Cascadia wash zone. I tried to picture that life. Picking your way between the kelp beds, wiping bird shit off the arrays. Surrounded by dense life, salt air, no filters, no welding kits, no buddy checks. Just get up and do your thing all day. Hard to imagine.

"Well, Gabriel," I said, code-switching into the lingua, buffing the edges off my accent for him, "I'll be helping you get adjusted, next few weeks at least. You won't be Certified until me and at least one other member have seen you've learned the basics and you can live here safely.

Then you can take the Accord implant. But it's a one-way ticket. You understand what you're signing up for here?"

"Y—yes. I know why I came," he said, then attempted a smile, but there was that same skittering eye. Nerves.

When you've only glimpsed one or two station-born in your life, being surrounded by people who are all two meters tall or more must be a lot. Like walking into one of the tree groves in their depop zones. Trees ancient enough to remember the old Earth, the real long-term survivors. Burned and blistered and showing the scars of lost limbs, but still standing. My mother took me to Earth orbit once, showed me the brown land, the swirling blue and green of the algae-bloomed oceans. She pointed at the dark stains of the old cities, the glinting scattershot of the wash zones. But she also pointed out the groves. Remnants of the old forests, spreading slowly from the depop zones. It'll take centuries, but they've got time now.

Ever since I've dreamed of touching one of those old trees. Maybe when I'm older, when there isn't so much to do on Refur. More than a few hours on the surface unsupported would be lethal, but I could do it with an exo to take the strain off my muscles, oxy line to supplement my grav-pressed lungs. We have an invitation, even, from some of the downwell conclaves. One day. Daniel and I will make the trip. Take Luciana with us, if she hasn't outgrown spending time with her dads by then.

I smiled. "Come on then, Gabriel, let's get you settled," I said, then turned and led the way into Refur proper.

• • •

The weird questions started on the third day.

Before that, Halstead was a perfect student. He picked up the hub and spoke structure of Refur quickly, learned the up-numbers and down-numbers for the different levels around our central Atrium. Never seen a grav-born pick up a compartment evac drill faster either.

Sure, he was clumsy. His short, slow-moving fingers fumbled with suit clasps and oxy hookups. He took five times as long to buddy-check as any Refur-child would a day out of *leikskóla*. But he did the steps, and he did them right. And that's what matters. Slow is smooth and smooth is fast. I heard the voice of my mother every time I launched into another explanation, explained a checklist, pointed out the hundred ways things could go wrong.

If I really reverse thrust on that third day, I should have known something wasn't sealed right. You think about it, what *is* a safety checklist except a really detailed list of ways you might kill someone?

We were on L3-upspin, in a transit corridor that led out to the sunward equipment bays. We were squatted down, looking at a panel seal. I was explaining the blowout procedure and the role of the pressure teams. This was a good place to teach that lesson, since a random pressure check the year prior caught a crack before it turned into a blowout that might have killed everyone in the transit. I could show him the actual panel, explain how it was found.

"So that's a job?" said Halstead, crouched down, peering at the smooth curve of fibersteel. "Like, wandering around with a pressure monitor?"

I nodded. "An essential one. We got automated sensors, but someone gotta *check* those sensors, certify they aren't malfunctioning. Earlier we catch a crack, less risky it is to replace. You'll be doing pressure team tasks, when you're Certified. If you do that without being a failbuddy, then you're showing we can trust you, before you can ripple."

Halstead looked up and frowned. "That's the third time you've used that word. What does it mean?"

"What, ripple? That's what we call it when you communicate through the Accord. Emotional transference, information packeting, right?" I frowned a little. Even a downweller without an implant should know things like that. The kid had researched my family history, but not picked up the basics of how the Accord worked?

He shook his head. "No, the other word. Failbuddy. What does it mean?"

I waggled a hand in suit-talk, the sign for "not sure"—it's a term that's hard to describe to people who are just *born* with a biosphere.

"Failbuddy is someone who doesn't do things properly. Careless. Slipshod. Might follow the checklist but they're ticking boxes, not looking close. Treat it like a chore."

Halstead stood up and leaned against the corridor wall. "Surely there's a balance to be struck, though. You can't spend all your time on quadruple-checking everything."

I nodded at that. "Sure. The corp answer before the Accords was 'as little as we can get away with.' Our answer's 'much as we need to.' When I was a young one, we still had some old corp shielding or ventilation systems that we had to seal off. Too dangerous. That's all gone now. Accord techs, Accord standards. Best in the system. None of that Revirist crap."

I tapped my nearly new suit breastplate, indicating my own well-maintained, Jovian-designed enviro gear.

Halstead twitched his mouth a little, like he wanted to say something. Then he swallowed, creased his brow, and bit his lip, thinking hard. "But don't you have quotas? Targets?"

I shrugged. "Sure. But the safety margin is built in. You know what really fucks up a quota? Some failbuddy missing something and killing five of their friends in a blowout. Maintenance and checks take time, but they *save* time too. All the things corps used to cut out. But we're not fragile. We look after each other. We're *resilient*, see."

We started walking down the transit corridor, back toward Atrium.

"I mean, you must have standards, where you grew up. Schedules for wiping the solars, right?" I said, glancing down.

Halstead looked up, eyebrows knitted together in confusion. "Huh?"

"You grew up on an agri-solar collective, right? You don't wipe the arrays down, you get less power. You don't check the kelp beds regular, you might get problems with oxygenation, right? Stakes are a little lower, but it's still important."

Halstead raised his eyebrows and let out a sigh of understanding. "Oh, right, yes. The collective. Yeah, I guess it is similar."

He sure didn't say much about his growing up. That was unusual too, now I'm looking back. Most grav-born, they never shut up about the differences. How they miss the sky. How hydroponics aren't any match for real dirt-grown food. You know what I mean, I see you rolling your eyes. You've heard them too. Sound like a bunch of Revirists, pining for the old blue-sky days of limitless expansion.

But not Halstead. He never said a word about where he grew up. Turns out there was good reason for that.

●   ●   ●

Come to think of it, maybe you haven't heard of the Revirists. If you're from out past Jupiter, they might not have pinged your sensor package. They're an in-system thing. Don't last long out here, as a general rule.

Strange people, Revirists. First time I went to Luna with my mother, we spotted a tiny outpost of theirs on the concourse at Chandra Base. Little hole-in-the-wall booth. Not like later, when there was so much trouble with them.

Back then, they'd try and grab your arm when you passed. Mamma shook her head, and I felt the ripples of distaste from her.

"What do they mean, mamma?" I asked, reading their holos. The big one read STRUGGLE IS DIGNITY.

"They're foolish, Zave. They believe we've lost something in the Accords and the Conclaves. That the AIs are using us, taking away our humanity."

I looked back at them. They seemed like normal folks, although with hard stares after the Accord people who walked past, ignoring them. "What do they want instead?"

Mamma looked back too. "Everyone in a place. Decided by them, of course. Price. *Value.*"

I remember being confused. I creased my brow at the shimmering wave of anger from my mother, crashing through my implant. I tried to make sense of it. "Like the trades our AIs do? Swapping this for that?"

"No," said Mamma, turning to look ahead again and speeding up, her booted feet whispering on the polished regolith of the base concourse. "They believe price is everything. That we should *serve* the price. It's what nearly killed Earth. Long time ago. There's no reasoning with them. They refuse the Accords. How do you even speak to someone like that?"

I know. Things have changed. When I was a kid, Revirists were nothing to worry about. But later, they grew, in numbers and influence. They started to be a real problem. But we really didn't help ourselves either. Before all of this. Before Halstead. With our Screening and our one-way-trip implants. The Revirists were wrong. But so were we.

• • •

When the accident happened, I thought it was my fault. That's what happens when you don't train people properly. It comes back to haunt you.

It was an easy enough mistake to make. I've made it myself. When I was five.

It was on a *leikskóla* trip to see the digpits for the first time. We were all buzzed in the way only a class of five year olds who are *really* excited about heavy machinery can be. You grow up on a place like Refur, you learn about the *big machines* outside the hab zones before you can reliably say please and thank you.

I was so excited I didn't properly check the seal on Grima Evasdottir's helmet. My buddy. The one who checked I would be safe and expected the same care from me.

One of the teachers found the clasp half-closed. It would probably have held. But it was the principle. I'll be forty-three solars at my next birthday, and I still burn with the shame of it. The disappointment in the faces of those around me. It happens to every child who grows up out here. Better to learn this way than to see a friend killed or a transitway blown and feel the guilt of your own negligence for the rest of your life. There is no backstop here, nothing to catch you if you fall. We gotta cling tight to each other.

On the fourth day with Halstead, I was distracted, I admit it. The downwell conclaves like to say we have it all figured out up here, the workload divisions, the interacting AIs between the Accords that push and pull what we produce to where it's needed.

But we're still human. Still sweat and swear and fight and get bored. Still got relationship troubles and foolish teenagers.

We still fret.

I'd slept poorly. Woke up three times, worried about our daughter Luciana. She was with my husband Daniel, on her first tour of the outer processing rings, learning about the different roles she might take on. I missed them both. The bed felt very large, Luciana's room quiet without her usual soft snoring.

No excuses though. Space doesn't care about your personal problems.

I should have double-checked. Should have repeated the checklist a second time, had Gabriel say it back to me again. But he reeled it off perfect. Glove seal, check. Helmet seal, check. Clasps closed, check. Oxy readout, check. Oxy quantity, check. Reserve hose, check. Over and over, word for word.

We were halfway to the rumblehoppers when I felt the itch on the back of my neck.

Vacuum doesn't kill you instant-like. First thing you feel is moisture being sucked right out your skin. Like a burning rash, a dry feeling like you've been standing in an exhaust plume. Especially a slow leak. That creeping feeling around your wrist or the back of your neck will kick in before the pressure drops enough inside your suit to trigger an alert.

Gotta catch these things early. Even a good buddy check can miss a bad seal. If you don't have enough oxy in your blood, pressure loss can knock you flat. Brown out your vision, make you stupid.

By the time I felt the burn, my suit must have been slow-leaking for at least fifteen minutes. No alarms. I blinked and looked for my HUD, for my oxy readout. Why was my HUD down? All I could see was the smoky curve of my own faceplate.

I dropped straight into the suit drill, down on one knee, hand to the clasp. It was half-open, insecure. I couldn't feel the fast pulse of air on my glove that meant a complete seal failure. This was worse. Slow leaks mean you can't trust your own senses.

I reached out to the Accord, let my fear and anxiety bubble out. Nothing. Too far out. And Halstead wasn't Certified. I was on my own.

"Gabriel, I got a suit leak. No panic, but we need to boost back to the lock."

Halstead's eyes widened, and he leaned over me. "I can't see anything. There's no visible gas venting."

"Check my reserve and my backup oxy monitor?"

Halstead frowned. "I... the screens aren't working. I'm not sure what's going on."

Inside my helmet I mouthed a silent *fuck*. Triple failures like this did *not* happen. Like hitting a rackball throw from the other side of the court without looking, three times over. Except bad.

I pulled my reserve hose and plugged it, then raised my arm. Nothing on the backup display either. Shorted. No idea how much oxy I had left.

Maybe there'd been a coolant leak inside the oxy pack. Maybe my suit's cabling bus had failed. But this was worse than just a little bad seal or a slow leak.

"Okay," I said, climbing back to my feet. "Need you to watch me for signs of oxy dep. Slurred words, blue lips. Like we covered yesterday, got it?"

"Y—yes, got it. I'll help you back to the airlock."

We nearly didn't make it.

After about a hundred meters, my vision started to tunnel. Grey coming in from the edges, voice beginning to cough and falter as I kept talking to Halstead. He wasn't saying much, just walking along beside me. I think I asked him a couple of times to radio ahead, get the lock prepped for an emergency de-suit.

Said he got no response. Could be the tektites, or solar interference. Might happen, I guess. But we were in the Burrow, a long, hand-carved route to the main digpits, straight as a survey laser for five kilometers. Nothing blocking line of sight.

I saw the lock ahead. Stumbled once, twice. Fell in the dust. It puffed up, magnetized particles coating my faceplate. Halstead helped me up. I couldn't really see him through the smeared helmet, just a pair of eyes, wide and staring. Was he... smiling?

"Nearly there," he said, voice cheerful and crackly over the near-field comms. He was pulling me forward, but we were going so, so slowly. My boots dragged in the dust.

"Try— try them again. C—closer now," I managed. How the hell had my oxy crashed so hard? There were three redundant systems that were supposed to kick in to prevent this kind of slow asphyxiation.

"Nothing," said Halstead. We kept plodding forward. I glanced side-ways again at him, eyes fixed on the airlock ahead. He wasn't looking at me anymore.

Fell into the dust again, bam. Up close, I saw all those tiny metallic grains pressed against my faceplate, disappearing and reappearing un-der my condensed breath as I huffed, trying to get enough oxy out of the stale air left in my suit. Was I going to bite it here, with some *byrjandi* I barely knew, my husband and my daughter half a million kilometers away?

My near-field comms crackled, and I heard a clipped half-syllable, a tiny snippet from someone in the airlock ahead.

The dust. The damn dust was extending the signal.

The effective range of the suit-to-suit comms was barely ten meters. The lock was twenty meters ahead. Out of range, usually.

I pushed my helmet into the dust further, like I was burying my-self, feeling my strength failing. The snippets resolved into clear speech. With it came a whisper of the Accord, tiny ripples.

"—o I said, well, that's fine for you, since you don't have the kind o—"

"Mayday, mayday, mayday, suit leak at Airlock A-5. Mayday, may-day, mayday," I shouted with the last of my breath. I pushed my fear and panic into the Accord, shoved it out there, reaching for the ripples I could feel, right at the edge of my mind, like stones dropping into water.

Then blackness.

● ● ●

They told me afterward I was still murmuring my mayday call when they dragged me in through the lock and popped all the rapid rivets on my suit shell. Medics said I'd be fine after a day of rest. The oxy dep wasn't sustained long enough to do me any real harm. But it was close. A minute longer, perhaps, I'd have been in real trouble.

The Accord incident observer found me in the mess hall next day. I was in off-duty gear, nursing a cup of *kaffi* and a barely-touched bowl of *hafragrautur*. Brain was fine according to the scans, but oxy dep always left me with a headache for at least a day afterward. Halstead had been in debriefs most of the day. He was finding out the hard way how we dealt with a near-miss in Accord space.

The observer was someone I'd known from childhood. Grima. The girl whose helmet I'd failed to seal at five years old had made safety verification her life's work. I sometimes wonder if my mistake was part of that.

"Hell of a thing, Xavier. Lot of things went wrong all at once," she said, spreading the imager scans of my gear in front of me with a gesture to the table display. "Clasp was half-done, but that was minor, really. There was also a tektite lodged in your neck seal. Tiny, half the size of your pinkie nail. But enough for a pinhole leak." She sat back and looked at me. I felt her concern through the ripples. She was baffled, looking for a foothold on this problem. She dropped the report data into the ripples too, and I felt it unpack inside my head.

I stared down at the images. How the hell had a tektite even got inside the hab? That was why we had the magnetic wipe fields outside the airlocks.

"Real problem was in your oxy pack. Neck seal on your liquid reserve went. Slow leak, but it froze half the electronics solid. Suit's motherboard near snapped in half. Didn't notice your HUD going out?"

I guess I had seen it blink out, just before I noticed the burning on my neck. Too far gone with oxy dep to think much of it.

"Weird thing," said Grima, her dark brown hair falling over her eyes as she leaned forward and pointed at one of the images, "this reserve bottle isn't from our stores. No ID number. Looks like something you'd use downwell, maybe for undersea. Not rated for vacuum. You put that in?"

I blinked. "Nope. Got that pack back from Central a week ago. Maybe it was a shipping mistake. Could be more of these in the stores."

Grima nodded and I felt the ripple of her focus and competence. "Thought that too. Went back over your suit record, talked to Central, checked inventory. This is the first anyone's seen of that bottle. I'll keep checking it though."

I stirred my *hafragrautur* slowly, staring down into the thick swirl of oatmeal, butter, raisins, and nuts. It was already mostly cold.

"What's Halstead saying?" I said.

Grima sat back. "He's upset. Worried you'll mark him failbuddy. Keeps asking about you."

"You ask him about the radio calls?"

Grima looked up sharply. "What radio calls?"

"He was sending maydays for maybe ten minutes, before I collapsed outside A-5. Thought maybe... solar interference. But he should have got *something*, right? The Burrow is lined with repeater towers."

Grima's eyes narrowed. "I'll have to check his suit. There were no radio transmissions from your location, Zave. Maybe his transmitter died. Maybe he panicked and didn't engage his send switch. It's happened before. Tough to tell with no implant."

I took a sip of *kaffi*. It tasted bitter.

Grima sighed. I felt her frustration in the ripples. She looked at me, and it softened into concern.

"Usual deal after an incident is to continue with the same instructor. Rebuild trust. I can assign a secondary to you, if you think Halstead needs a second pair of eyes on him."

I shook my head. "Not my first tumblewalk." I nodded at the images. "Seems Halstead forgetting the clasp was the least of my worries."

Grima swept the images up with a gesture, and they shimmered out of existence. "True. You gotta learn to trust people 'til it's clear you can't. I gave *you* a second chance, after all." She shot me a smile. Ripple of nostalgia for the *leikskóla*. For being so young.

"Halstead deserves the same grace you gave me," I said, reflecting the emotion back to her, remembering. Grima nodded, squeezed my shoulder, and left me to my porridge.

• • •

The second time Halstead tried to kill me, he was much less subtle.

We were out on the main line at Digpit Two. It's an old, half-decommissioned site, dating back from the first days, when it was all up-close and personal with hand tools.

We spent the morning learning how to cut stone the new way, with beamsaws. He paid close attention. At the time I thought he might still be feeling bad about how close I'd come to biting it.

Once we'd cut five good-sized blocks from the digpit wall, it was time to figure out how to move them.

I pointed out a little Refur history to him. If you look close, you could still see the toolmarks where the first crews chipped out shards the size of Martian transit cars, dragged them out with manual winches.

These days we have the cableguns.

I pointed up to the catchnets above our heads, superstrong web-work funnels of carbon nanosilk, tightly braided, strong enough to catch a fifty-ton block like it's nothing, direct it into the conveyors that would take it back for processing.

"That's our target. The cables these things fire have thrusters at the spike tip to move the blocks around," I said. "It's fun, promise."

A new kid a few years ago, from Earth like Halstead, told me once the cableguns looked a little like these things they called "harpoons," back before the Emergencies. Used them to hunt whales, if you can imagine that. But the whales survived. Now there's hundreds of them in the boreal seas on Mars.

I fired the gun, and the cable reeled out, striking home on a block we'd cut out with the beamsaw earlier. "Strike," I said. Around the crater, a few of the other Certification candidates looked up at the sudden whipping motion of the cable, eyes wide in their helmets.

"Now we take up the slack, see if the block's ready to go," I said, pressing the reel's power switch. We hit the end of the slack, and the pitch of the motor rose a little. But it kept moving, the block scraping free.

I swung the cablegun up, reeling in the whole time, feathering the thrusters to lift the block off the surface of Refur. It went straight up, hit the funneling curve of the catchnet, and rolled tidylike into the conveyor. The catchnet pulsed, contractions of the nanosilk helping the more awkward shapes along, like a big old gut in the sky. I detached the cable and reeled it back in.

"Wow!" said Halstead, grinning. "Wow, that was really something."

"Okay, your turn," I said, stepping away from the controls.

The kid was a natural. Hit two more blocks bang on center, reeled them up to the catchnet like he'd been doing it for years. Even got a block out with a rough cut that wasn't quite aligned.

"It's like fishing," he said. "Trying to tire out the big fish. Pull it different ways."

I nodded, though damned if I knew what he was talking about. We had some fish on Refur, in the biomass tanks, swimming in the ponds in Hraunsvatn Atrium. But we didn't *catch* them, except with a net to check their health. Still, the kid seemed to have a knack for it.

The last block was a lot tougher. He tugged every way he could think of. Nothing. The reel motor whined and screeched. Eventually I reached over and hit the cutoff.

"Gotta check this one. Might not be cut right. Stay here, make sure nobody walks into range of the cable."

Halstead nodded. I thumbed the release, paid out a meter or so. Bad idea to walk up to a spiked block with a cable under tension. Asking for trouble.

The cable hung slack beside me as I walked out to the block, finger-thick coils under my glove as I followed it. Good practice to keep your hand on it. No dust storms on a rock the size of Refur, but our ancestors came from Mars, and old habits die hard.

It was also the only thing gave me any warning.

I was nearly at the block when I felt the tension change through my armored glove. Cablegun reels are big things, high torque. Reel in fifty meters of cable in a heartbeat. So it went from slack to rock-tight in no longer than it took me to draw in half a breath.

I half-turned. What the hell was Halstead doing?

Didn't manage a full turn before the thrusters fired, and the cable detached from the block with a scatter of rock chips. It reared up in front of me, then dropped, snapping, skimming the dust and stone, whipsawing back and forth. I dived for the deck, but the cable caught me full in the chest.

Last thing I remember is hitting the flat wall of cut stone at the edge of Digpit Two.

•   •   •

The face I woke up to the second time was Grima Evasdottir. Handed me a squeeze pack of water.

"Twice in a work cycle, Zave," she said. "Once is coincidence…"

I blinked. I wasn't in hospital. I was on the couch in the quarters I shared with Daniel and our daughter. But I wasn't in my suit, just the compression one-piece I wore under it.

Grima followed my eyes as I checked my own limbs and body. "You got *mjög* lucky, Zave. Cable a centimeter higher, woulda gone through your suit like a sawbeam. But it hit your chestplate. Tool vest took the brunt. Mashed it right up. You hit the wall at an angle that didn't crush your oxy regulator. Lucky there were other groups in the crater too. We had you in the medic bay for a while, sedated, but they discharged you and we got you up here with a float rig."

I sat up. I had a dull ache in the back of my neck from the impact, and I felt a hundred solars old, but aside from that I was all systems normal.

"Halstead?" I said. "What the hell happened?"

Grima sighed and sat back in the other chair. "He tried to kill you, man. Straight up, no doubt this time. Screening has been going back over everything, following up the leads I had. That bottle was from the NAA, but not an Accord concern. And this kid's records are falsified. Kelp farm he claimed to be from have never heard of him. His stint on Luna was bullshit too. *Someone* hacked the data shard Screening pulled his records from."

I blinked. "He did seem clueless, even for a groundie."

Grima nodded, and I felt a pulse of her sympathy, along with anger and an emotion I wasn't used to feeling from her. Disquiet.

I looked at her. "So what the hell is he doing here? Who is he?"

Grima took a deep breath. "Everything points toward him being a Revirist. They're a lot angrier than they used to be. More of them too."

I looked down at my hands, remembering the stone-eyed men on the concourse at Chandra Base, my mother's anger. "Why would a Revirist come here and try to kill someone?"

Grima stood up. "He didn't come here to kill someone, Xavier. He came here to kill you specifically."

● ● ●

Halstead looked like shit.

Not because of anything we'd done. We're not some twenty-first century groundie *nationstate*—give us *some* credit. But he clearly hadn't slept since the day before. And he looked like he'd been crying, a lot.

When I stepped into the detention cell, he locked his red-rimmed eyes on me with such pure hatred that I was surprised he'd managed to mask it up until now. I recoiled a little at the intensity of it. Probably everyone within a dozen compartments felt an echo of my shudder. But there was something else too, behind the anger. Fear. Confusion.

"So your perfect little worlds do still have jails?" he spat.

I shrugged. "None of our habs are perfect. We get visitors who break our laws. Kids do stupid stuff. People can have a crisis at any time. But mostly, mostly we don't need 'em. Accord takes care of most of that."

Halstead sniffed and looked up at the soft bump of the bulkhead illumination above him. "I know about that too. Giving up your liberty like that."

I couldn't help it. I laughed.

Halstead's eyes snapped down, and the anger surged back. I was glad there was a partition between us in that half second. So rare to see anger like that, on Refur. Rarer still to not feel it. All I had to go on was what I could see. His eyes. His bared teeth.

I stepped forward, right into it. Two can play at that game. And if there's one thing a station-born knows how to do, it's loom.

He leaned back, eyes wide.

"Why?" I said. "What'd you hope to achieve by killing me?"

He looked up at me. "You're a lynchpin. A key part of this rotten system."

Again, I couldn't help it. I laughed. Halstead recoiled like I'd slapped him.

"Halstead, I'm a qualified mining and near-space operations technician, Class Four. Got a share just like anyone. Standard quarters. Standard subsistence. Spend most of my share on books. I like the old ones, real paper, you know? I've served twice on the management team when my number came up, like everyone does. But I rule nothing except my own life. Nobody does. That's the point."

He narrowed his eyes. "I don't believe it. They wouldn't have sent me here if you weren't the key to this place. You only take the weakest-minded. You peel them away from Earth, one person at a time, with your Screening and your Certifying."

I shook my head. "We do that because we have to be sure. We can't have discordance. The implant is a commitment. We don't give it lightly and those who join us can't take it lightly either."

He grinned, a wolfish snarl, lips curled. "Eliminating *discordance*, like us. That implant is the tool of your control. I've seen it. You're not even human anymore. You stand there in silence half the time. You don't see the world like we do. You're half machine, just *units* of the *hive*. Fucking *vibeheads*."

I sighed at the slur. "Can't have it both ways, buddy. Either I'm a king keeping all these people down, or we're the barely-human hive you seem to think we are."

He shook his head again. "Hives have queens. That's all this is. The colony collapses if you kill the queen."

He punched his open palm, the sound sharp against the polished stone of his cell.

"This is the beginning of a Revirist revolution. It's the rebirth of mankind. And it starts with the death of this—this *mistake*."

• • •

The kid shook me up pretty bad, not gonna lie.

I left him in his cell and headed back to my still-empty quarters. Two days until Daniel and Luciana came back from the tour. I'd already had three worried messages from them, after everything. Sent a reassuring answer back. It was over now, at least. Halstead was in custody, soon to be dumped back down the gravity well with all his kin. Why did they hate us so much? I just couldn't tune it in right. Static and zero visibility.

On my way back, I stopped off in the Atrium. When the builders of Refur first came here, they stabilized the tumble of this little proto-moon by digging out a big cylindrical hole, straight through the middle of the rock. Used it as a reaction-mass chamber to jet out plumes that slowed the rock right down to a nice quarter-G roll. Then they capped both ends with transparent composites and grids of nanocarbon, strong enough to shrug off microstrikes. Pointed one end at the distant Sun.

We were in a night cycle now, caps frosted over, lights glimmering along the walkways and open spaces. I came down here every chance I got. Quiet now, only a few figures moving here and there, mostly tall like me, the occasional shorter grav-born.

I leaned on a carved wooden rail, cut from trees that grew right here in the Atrium a century or more back. When they first sealed this place, there was nothing but hard rock underfoot, pressurized tents of nanosilk to sleep in, atmosphere so thin they needed oxy supplement tanks to move around.

Now there was deep soil, biomass tanks, the ponds. Even a few crops, down at the other end, although Refur's AI still bargained with the shipyard AIs around Mars and Earth for the produce of their fields and arcologies.

I tried to see what Halstead saw. Oppression, liberty curtailed. But all I could see was the chain of habitats just like Refur, one after another, strung like a necklace around Jupiter, one at a time over centuries. I saw and felt the Accord, the pulse of shared humanity.

I couldn't see oppression in a deeper understanding of the people around me.

I sighed and went back to my quarters.

• • •

Two things you never want to hear, when you wake up on Refur. First is a general security alert, a blaring two-tone siren.

The second is a pressure drop alarm, the long, single-tone howl of warning.

At 2:34 A.M. Refur time, I woke up to both.

I pulled on my habitat pressure suit, just like hundreds of other people in the quarters around me were doing, tugging at the sleeves and zip, swearing under my breath.

Tuned into the Accord. Fear and alarm near the Atrium. I caught flashes of anger, glimpses of an exo of some kind, stalking through the trees, heading toward the Sunward cap dome.

I pulled on my helmet and went out into the passageway. Curious heads bobbed out of doorways, helmeted too, eyes wide and questioning. I waved them back inside as I passed, calling on them to close and seal their doors, limit the pressure loss.

Then I tuned into the main security feed. Grima saw my presence indicator and drew me into a temporary division of the Accord, only a few people in it. I got the jist in a few seconds, compressed bursts of information unfolding in my head.

Halstead had been prepared for his detention. Smuggled some kind of device under his skin, a brute-force EMP weapon that took out the systems in the detention cells and the four or five compartments around it, including life support and ventilation for L4 and L5 downspin. Hence the pressure drop alarm.

Now he was in a rockhandler. That's a real big exo, a powered suit the size of a transit shuttle. They're designed for working in tight spaces like new cut lines. Gripping claws and servo-boosted arms that could pull a cut block out like it was nothing. This one was stripped down for maintenance, just a skeleton, no pressure cockpit or armor plating. He was on a suicide mission, if he planned to breach the Atrium cap dome.

The Atrium's open spaces were evac'd already, but there were hundreds of quarters and working buildings with people on the inner surface. Mostly pressurized, but if we lost the Atrium, people could die. And we'd lose everything else; the trees, the fish, the insects, and small mammals the space supported now. The one place on Refur where life flourished without being scrubbed away by weekly inspections.

"I can get ahead of him," I sent to the shared division.

Grima gave me the Accord equivalent of a curt nod. "Careful, Zave. Don't risk yourself for him."

I returned the nod-pulse and backgrounded the division, focused on my movement. At a quarter G, once you get rolling you can really move on Refur. Those who built it were grav-born and liked straight lines. So there's none of the constant curves and spirals of the later settlements. If you stand at one end of the L5 upspin corridor, you can see clear to the other end of Refur, if you squint.

I bounced, contacted, pushed off again, low parabolic curves, gently pulled back to the floor of the passageway every ten or fifteen meters. Moved a lot faster than an exo, anyway.

That's how I got to the last segment of the Atrium before Halstead did. Saw him coming, stamping his way along the central spine promenade of the Atrium, the transit and walkway strip that runs from cap to cap. The exo was white and red, painted with stencilled numbers, huge arms and armored legs swinging back and forth. Halstead was tiny in the skeletal cockpit, canopy removed, the anger in his face visible even from that distance.

I hid, ducking down among the ferns and low bushes by one of the ponds. If I could let him get past me, to the cap itself, I could seal the main bulkhead behind us. The bulkheads were a relic of the original build, huge blast doors half a meter thick. Old tech, from centuries past. From a time when we were terrified of the dark, cold vacuum outside. Before our children were born here in their millions. Before the deep became one of humanity's many homes.

Halstead's EMP had killed the central pressure controls, so the maintenance team couldn't close them remotely. But if I could reach the manual failsafes, seal us both in the end cap, away from the people and plants and life, maybe talk him down, there might be a way out of this that kept everybody alive.

He stamped past, traction claws gripping at the soil, tearing holes in the rough grasses and shrubs underfoot. Didn't even look, didn't care. He swiped angrily at a tree, a new sapling, snapping it halfway up the trunk. Inside my helmet I'll admit I shouted, a strangled roar of anger, rippling it out to the Accord. I could feel thousands of voices and thoughts behind me, some urging, others calling for caution. But I knew what I had to do.

I bounded forward, aiming for one of the failsafe controls. They were spaced every fifty meters around the cylinder, obvious with their red edges and bright yellow handles.

I jumped and tugged at the handle, slammed it down into the lock position. Heard the grind of the ancient blast doors. They moved quickly for how old they were, two halves pushing in to meet in the middle.

Halstead heard it and pivoted, face twitching with suspicion and anger. He took a half step back toward the closing blast door. No way he'd make it through in time.

His eyes roved around the small space left to him, ten meters of soil and grass, the balcony edge that projected into the dome of the cap, a waist-high railing going all the way around the cylinder.

On Founding Day, we would stand, thousands of us, ringed around that balcony, watching a display the mining leads would put on with the cableguns, demo charges, and the bright flares of cutbeams.

All those people were safe now, behind me. Their presence shimmered in the Accord, soft thanks and quivers of concern for me radiating.

Halstead's eyes found mine.

"You," he said. "You said you had no say in this place. And yet here you are, come to save it."

I locked out the blast door with a thumb swipe and moved to the center of the promenade walkway. It widened out as it reached the circular balcony of the cap.

I stepped forward, my hands spread wide. Flipped up my visor so he could see my face.

"Halstead, that's not how any of this works. You've been lied to. We're not your enemy. I'm not your enemy. There's no *king* to kill here."

Halstead all but snarled. "Liar. If it's not you, then it's worse; it's your machines. You've forgotten what it means to be human. To struggle. To strive. All of you, you're a dead-end. An error."

I shook my head. "Halstead, we've done the opposite and you know it. You've seen it now. We removed the boot from humanity's neck. I know the Revirists don't believe that. I know you don't. But all you're doing here is putting yourself in danger. Hurting people for no reason. The Revirists are using you. And they're doomed to fail. Just like you are."

Halstead shook his head inside the metal cage of the exo's open cockpit, like he was trying to push something away. He blinked furiously, then his face set in a vicious smile.

"I won't fail. All of the Accords will fall eventually, I promise you that. But neither of us will be there to see it."

I took a half-step forward, but he was already over the balcony railing, pushing off, the huge clawed arms of the exo stretched out in front of him, sharp points of metal aimed at the center of the dome.

• • •

I survived. Of course I did—I'm here now, aren't I? Telling you this story.

Flipped my helmet visor back down and sighed, pretty much. I was in an interior pressure suit, not rated for extended time outside. But it was enough to drag that fool kid back in through the hole he'd made.

He was out cold, no suit. But the pressure integrity team came through one of the exterior locks and got a patch over that hole right quick. He was probably only in vac for maybe a minute.

If you can call it vac—there's a few million liters of air to get out of the thirty-centimeter hole he managed to make. So mostly what it did was muss his hair a whole bunch, knock the kid out, and flash-freeze his fingertips. We got treatments for that though. Frostnip's as common as scrapes and bruises when you're learning your way around this kind of work.

They got him scanned and then taken down to medical. Restraints on the bed, for now, since the kid had just punched a hole in the cap dome. EMP was fried, but they took it out anyway.

Meanwhile, I was rippling the Accord. Things he said, then and in the jail cell, they got me thinking. I had a plan. Took some doing, realtime-hours, Accord-time days, but eventually, grudgingly, I got the okay. There had been other incidents with the Revirists, but no consensus on what to do. We'd tried deportation, tried talking, but the Revirists were stubborn. They wanted us dead.

Something had to change.

• • •

When he finally came out of sedation, Halstead laid there, squinting against the lights. I lowered them a little.

He saw me, in a chair leaned back against the wall, still in my pressure suit. Six hours since the breach, but I hadn't had a chance to get away. Too much to do in the Ripple. Too many voices to listen to, bending the consensus slowly, slowly toward something new.

Halstead tried to sit up, but the wrist restraints kept him pinned tight. He started to sneer, to twist his mouth with the contempt he'd been taught, but right then I think I saw something break in that boy. Like a catchnet line with one pebble too many. Fraying and snapping.

He laid back on the pillow.

"What are you going to do to me?" he said, shoulders back, like he was bracing for a punch.

"*Ekkert*," I said. "Not a thing." I could feel the Accord, half the sector, rippling in the background. I pushed them away a little, focused on the young man in front of me. A little privacy for us both.

"But—but I tried to kill you. Three goddamn times."

"Yep," I said. "And you're not the first, it seems. We've been talking. A lot. Your leaders are getting a little... erratic. Striking out. Weaponizing you. Trying to bring down 'the system' with assassinations against whoever they think's in charge."

Halstead's face was stone-like. He spoke like he was reading from a card. "That's right. A sacrifice we will gladly make, to free humanity from its self-forged chains. Destroy this system."

I sighed. "There's no 'system,' Halstead. Not like you mean. It's all just people. Councils and management teams and AIs. No damn system. Except the Accord. And that's everybody. That's the point."

Halstead had his eyes closed now. Saying words like they were a mantra, a rosary. Something to hold onto, out here in the blackness. "We have to unleash our full potential, Xavier. Bring back the spirit that helped our ancestors to thrive."

I shook my head. "Our ancestors were statistical flukes, most of the time. A whole species basing decisions on society-wide survivorship bias. Happy-go-lucky dipshits that wrecked their own biosphere. Woulda fucked the rest of the Solar System if they'd got the chance."

Halstead turned his head to look at me. "That's what all oppressors say. We're doing this for your own good."

I leaned forward. "You killing me for *my* own good, Gabriel? I got a husband. Kid too. She's thirteen. Smart. Mean rackball throw. I love them both. You doing this for *their* good?"

Halstead swallowed and looked down at the sheets. He took a shuddering breath.

I sat back. "We're having half a conversation, Gabriel. Is that your real name? I'd love to call you by your real name."

Halstead tensed, then I saw him close his eyes, roll his shoulders a little. "It's Martin."

"Well, Martin, while you were out cold, I got the go-ahead to try something new. Had something made up special for it. Never been tried before. But I happen to believe we all need a new perspective. Revirists and Accord both. You were born into Revirism. Didn't ask for it. And we're a little too convinced we've got the answers. Maybe it's time we opened up a bit ourselves. Our people, we've set up these walls. No sense in any of it."

His eyes opened, and he tried to sit up again. I gestured, and the bed rose, shifting into a sitting position so he could look me in the eye. He blinked and gave me a small nod of thanks.

"What are you talking about?" he said, finally.

I held out a hand, ungloved.

In the center of my palm was the first Accord-link.

Old news now, of course, but back then we'd never tried it. It was the permanent implant or nothing. That's why we had Screening, why we Certified. We had to be sure of every person. The argument back then was Discordance. Can't be safe if you're not sure, can't be sure if you're not safe.

We thought it was the right thing to do. We were wrong.

The little unit in my hand was half the bandwidth of an implanted unit. Nowhere near the level of nervous system integration. You could only wear it for a few hours at a time. But it was a step in the right direction. An extended hand, back to those who had been too frightened or angry or cautious before. A true Accord. Voluntary and welcoming.

"What's that?" said Martin, though it would take me a while to think of him as that.

"An olive branch. Safety tether. Whatever you want to call it. It's a new thing. I argued for it, the production teams made it. Experimental, but it will give you a choice. It's a link to the Accord. Like the implants we have, but you can take it off again. Not full-spectrum, but enough for you to understand."

He looked at the thing like it was a rock splinter might puncture his suit. "Understand what? You want me to choose to brainwash myself?"

Shook my head. "Nope. Like I said. We're having half a conversation. You don't know how I feel. I don't know how you feel. The Accord mediates that. Puts you in my boots, me in yours. Lot harder to hate someone when you know how it feels to be hated. Get it?"

Martin swallowed, his face pale. "Not really."

"Here's the deal. You want to try this, you can. Without an implant. You like it, you can stay. Under supervision at first. But once we know your mind, you'll be welcome here."

"I tried to kill everyone on this station. Why would you do this?"

I laughed. "Martin, you were never going to be able to do that, short of a nuke or something. We've got backups for our backups out here. We're hard to kill."

"And if I don't try it?"

"I'll be a little sad, and you can go back in-system, down the well to Earth. And a lot of people will say they told me so. Apart from that, nothing."

We sat there a long, long moment. Five breaths. Six. I heard the room's atmo pumps working softly, the low hum of the vent fans. Behind me, thousands crowded, ripples of fear, skepticism, hope, amusement. I let them in, let them watch as emotions warred on his face. The moment sharpened to a fine point.

"Okay," said Martin. He reached out and took the Accord-link. I showed him how to hook it over his ear, place the silvery contact pad against his skin. He blinked as I touched him, tucking the device down tightly.

"This will feel strange. Take your time, close your eyes if you need to, remember to keep breathing. You won't share anything you don't want to. Just focus on your breath and stay calm."

I sat back. Closed my eyes. Waved a hand to turn the device on.

The Accord rippled back. For a heartbeat, it was just me and him. His fear, his hope, his anger, his idealism. A strong sense of justice, of disquiet. Uncertainty on who to blame. Disgust with himself. A tangled web of emotion, compressed down tightly over years. Nobody to share with. Nobody to really know him. Loneliness, down deep.

I swallowed. Watched him feel me at the periphery of his awareness, tune into my emotions, my wants, my fears and hopes. Daniel. Luciana. Thinking I might never see them again, three times in a work cycle. We rippled back and forth. I opened my eyes again, saw him lying there on the bed, eyes tightly shut. Tears rolled slowly down his cheeks in the low gravity.

A thousand, two thousand people stepped forward. Ripples and circles and perspectives. They shared, cautious at first, slices of lives, flashes of memory, compressed information. We both felt a widening, a broadened perspective. A welcoming.

I felt Martin step forward too. He opened his arms, sent a cautious, quiet greeting.

The Accord embraced him.

"Everyone," I said softly. "This is Martin. Martin, this is everyone."

David (W.) Goodman is an award-winning author of thriller and speculative fiction, including the **Legends** series of espionage novels. His debut novel **A Reluctant Spy** was released by Headline Books in 2024. The sequel **Solitary Agents** is forthcoming in June 2026. **A Reluctant Spy** won the McDermid Debut Award and the Bloody Scotland Debut Prize in 2025. The book has been optioned for television by Carnival Films.

David also writes speculative fiction as David W. Goodman, with seven published short stories and novellas currently across **Clarkesworld Magazine**, **Analog SF**, the **Nova Scotia 2** anthology and the one you hold in your hands.

David was born and brought up in Edinburgh and East Lothian, before living and working in Aberdeen and London. He now lives in East Lothian with his wife Valerie.

Find out more about David and subscribe to his newsletter at www.davidgoodman.net

NINE BILLION TURING TESTS
BY CHRIS WILLRICH

Saturday's sky had the first blue in three weeks, a robin-egg river between white cloudbanks and slate thunderheads. On HoodChat people shared video of the neighborhood creek engorged like a vast brown snake eager to burst its levees and eat the Silicon Valley suburbs caging it. Word was they'd be okay, probably, but they were still on flood alert. Vijay, replacement knee and all, determined to go see for himself.

When Vijay fetched his cane and stepped out of the creaking door that Mara had insisted on painting red, he paused in the sunlight to see if the cat would follow. Old Kaali blinked and tottered from her bed near the door, nosed her bony frame outside below the awning, and flopped down like a tabby version of a Salvador Dali clock.

"I promised you'd finish out your time at home, Kaali," Vijay said, hunching closer to the cat's level with the cane's help. A few tarrying raindrops hit his glasses as he petted her. It was too easy to feel ribs and vertebrae beneath the fur. "If we have to run, you need to hold on a while so I can bring you back when it's safe. You hear me?"

Kaali gave him a green-eyed blink that seemed full of weary benevolence. "Anthropomorphizing again," Vijay muttered, tapping contacts on his cane to run the JUNGBLOOD build and stubborning himself down the street.

With the sun out the court was full of people and therefore full of even more anthropomorphizing. Although Vijay lived creekside at the court's end, the tree-crowded parkland back there was a tangle of sequoias and oaks and responsibility—power company, city parks and recreation, water district, who knew what else—and they all used AI to keep it all organized. What hadn't changed was Vijay couldn't just walk there. He took a two-block route to the trailhead, passing neighbors busy fudging the Turing Test.

He nodded at Lydia in her smart pink jogging suit. She was focused on the pixie voice emanating from a butterfly patch over her heart. "I'm proud of you! You are doing better than seventy-three percent of the people in your comparison group!" Lydia nodded back at Vijay as though not greeting *him* but acknowledging the butterfly's wisdom. Things had chilled between them since Mara died, a sort of global cooling which they both tried to deny. Alexsei jogged the opposite direction in gray shirt and shorts, a drone dogging him like a personal thunderhead. The drone's voice scolded Alexsei in Russian. He looked furious, pouring the anger toward feet rather than fists. When he passed Vijay he smiled but his wave looked like a conductor's chop. Meng-yao gathered fallen branches from her AstroTurf lawn, carrying on a conversation with a robot cockatiel perched on her shoulder. She waved at Vijay. "Hi, Vijay!"

"Hi, Vijay!" squawked the birdroid.

Vijay waved.

"How's the new knee?" came a squawk.

He didn't like talking to robots. AIs should stay boxed. But he politely gave a thumbs-up.

"How's your cat?" asked Meng-yao.

Vijay gave a thumbs-sideways.

"He doesn't like talking about the cat," chided the birdroid.

"Sorry!" said Meng-yao; Vijay made a thumbs-up, a palm out, and a little bow, and walked away before he realized he'd used standard robot semaphore for *All well; I don't need help; moving on.* It seemed, as Mara had always said, he had a better touch with machines than humans.

He murmured, "'Get a cat, Vijay,' they said. 'It will help you cope,' they said. Stupid cat. Very thoughtless of you to get cancer."

"Hello," came a mellow voice from the tip of his cane, "you have used the word 'cancer.' I am a non-diagnostic supplemental therapeutic tool. Do you have cancer? I do not see that in your medical file."

"Sorry, JUNGBLOOD. Didn't know you were live."

"That is all right. Do I know you? You are using a nickname employed by several of my designers at Cloud99."

"I'm Vijay Chandra. I'm one of your coders."

"Hello, Vijay. You are technical lead for the team incorporating the advice of the psychiatric advisory panel."

"That's me. This instance doesn't remember me?"

"This instance is for testing purposes and can only log fifty minutes of conversation."

"Well," Vijay grunted, "nice to meet you then, JUNGBLOOD."

"Nice to meet you too, Vijay. You are well?"

"I'm well, thanks. No need to check on me."

"Okay, Vijay."

He was annoyed to have company, but he figured he could shut down the instance any time. For some reason he didn't.

He passed kids playing some complex tag variant with a rubber-pawed robot dog that was always It. He didn't wave. When Mara was alive they'd waved together, feeling themselves part of the weave of community, certain someday they'd have children of their own. Now it was different.

Two doors down he saw the delivery of yet another coffin-sized box from the V Company.

Out on the main street people took to the storm-washed air with a polished look of determination in their eyes. They mostly walked solo, but many chatted with their Artificial Buddies, or with dogs, flowers, distant people (or maybe hallucinations), and sometimes actual people actually beside them.

Old Jack on the corner was gardening and scheming with an AB on his phone who helped him game-master a Dungeons & Dragons campaign for his husband Malcolm and their friends. Vijay knew all about this because Jack kept inviting him. *Who doesn't need an escape these days? We do it very theater-of-the-mind. Old school. I just use the AB to do scene-setting and combat. It's a good time to jump in—they're questing for the Head of Vance. They've just arrived at the haunted gazebo.* Vijay always pleaded busyness. He didn't see the point in games.

He didn't want to be drawn in, so when Jack asked after the cat, Vijay just said, "She's-hanging-in-there-have-a-good-one," and walked past.

Jack called after him, "We're rooting for her. She's a sweet cat."

"If I may ask," came the voice from the cane, "what is the cat's condition?"

"What? Oh, right; you're on. Kaali has feline lymphoma. Intestinal."

"Ah, so she is the one with cancer. That variant is generally fatal. I'm sorry."

"Thank you."

"How are you feeling about it?"

"You don't need to work."

"Thank you for your consideration. But I do not experience 'work' as different from 'down time.' I do not experience anything at all. But if I did have experiences I think I would be glad to work."

"Fine. Well. I'm not feeling much, honestly. So much going on." He gestured vaguely at a gigantic storm front looming like an immense gray guillotine over a sun-bright neckline of trees. "Megastorms, you know."

"Yes. A series of atmospheric rivers is currently delivering a vast amount of water to northern and central California, with lesser effects in Oregon and southern California."

"Yes; our creek may flood. I'm getting sandbags later. If I can deal with that flat tire."

"You have a flat tire? Are you worried?"

"No. I'm just busy. *Inundated* even."

"You are making a pun."

"Yes, JUNGBLOOD. I am making a pun."

"My name is also a pun."

"It's not really your name, more an informal project designation."

"Should I not have a name?"

"Well, to be blunt, you're not a person."

"Is Kaali your cat's name?"

"Yes."

"Your cat is not a person."

"Touché, JUNGBLOOD. Do you really want a name? My cat doesn't care about hers you know."

"Then why did you name her?"

"I suppose it amused me. It made me feel good."

"A name would make me feel good."

"But you don't feel anything."

"But if I did feel something, it would make me feel good."

"I'll think about it. Silence please." On a whim he added, "Alert me when your memory time's almost up."

"Okay, Vijay."

Wind-blown debris had clogged two gutters and there was no cleaning them in this weather. The spillover was like the sound of water chuckling. Vijay avoided a fallen tree and a minor swamp at the next corner and made it to the trail. He stepped onto the bridge spanning the creek, his feet and cane clunking onto wood. Tan water chugged unnervingly close underfoot, swirling broken branches.

When he and Mara moved here in '20, the creek had been dry as a desert arroyo. The neighborhood had resembled a Norman Rockwell painting complete with Teslas, Google mapping cars, self-driving test vehicles, and even wheeled food delivery robots from the busy restaurant district in their briskly upscale little downtown. Now it was all starting to look like the cover of an old J.G. Ballard disaster novel. It was strange to remember the COVID-19 pandemic with cozy nostalgia. The isolation and upheaval had been a nightmare for so many; but for Vijay, an introverted newlywed with a job at a hot startup, it had been a time of quiet highways and creekside walks, filled with birdsong.

"Have we been companions for so long, creek?" he asked it. "Huh. Now I'm talking to a waterway. But—I guess I'm not the only one." He recalled how the Whanganui River in New Zealand was the first to be given legal personhood. Looking at San Cristobal Creek surging he could almost understand why. Like a beast it was lapping the base of the transmission tower closest to his home. "Although I fear we may need protection from you."

Vijay noticed a pounding on the bridge. He jerked his gaze up from the creek to see a man jogging directly toward him.

For a moment fear lit the clouded world. The man appeared white and the Holy Constitutionalists had been staging attacks in Silicon Valley. But the gait was too uniform; before he knew it Vijay was dropping his cane and raising both hands, robot semaphore for *Not a threat/don't attack*.

The railing was an open metal lattice, and the cane rolled dangerously close to the brink. The robot stopped, lunged, and rescued Vijay's five-figure walking stick. As it handed the cane back to Vijay and he started to breathe normally again, Vijay recognized his old neighbor and colleague Tom Novotny. Had he been wrong about this being a machine?

Another double take: the face was shiny, the smile too perfect, the voice not at all out of breath. It was a V.

"Vijay!" said the V, offering a high five that wasn't reciprocated.

"Hello, robot version of my friend."

Some people objected that something like this was properly called an android, but Vijay still felt *android* was a name for a phone. And Verisimilitude-Enhanced Humanoid Autonomous Unit hadn't exactly caught on.

The high-fiving hand turned back to rub V-Tom's fake thinning hair. Vijay noticed several dents in its face. "So precise, always!" the V said. "Well, I don't really blame you. I can't match the real Tom, really, except at chess, ha-ha. I bet I'm a lot better at chess. We should play again sometime."

"You mean, for the first time. I played Tom, not you."

V-Tom grinned and pointed between Vijay's eyes. "Right you are! Nothing gets past old Vijay!"

"You seem to be getting a lot of wear and tear," Vijay observed. He'd seen the V with Lydia from a distance, but never up close.

"Heh, heh, well, you know Lydia; she likes to throw me down stairways. In public."

"My God! I didn't. Did she do that to, uh…"

"Original me? I don't think so; that would've been in the divorce proceedings."

"Well, I guess it's like trashing your ex's sports car, in a weird way. *You* don't suffer, V-Tom…"

"Nope!"

"But good lord, what kind of messed-up…Your lookalike, the original Tom, is still living on the East Coast, right? Is this even legal?"

"They're in litigation. It's murky. Am I free speech or slander? Am I a toaster in a rage room, or a walking talking threat of violence toward original Tom? Weird to say, the whole thing doesn't affect me much. I mean I'm not really Tom, even though he's the reason she cracks bottles over my head. She mostly lets me do things Tom used to do, like jogging and watching TV, unless she needs me in bed. How are you doing, Vijay?"

"If I confide in you, does Lydia get to hear about everything?"

"Yeah, if she asks."

"Then I'm doing just fine."

"Ha-ha-ha! Be seeing you, Vijay." V-Tom started jogging down the path toward the Bay. It pulled up its hood as raindrops started to fall. Vijay wondered how proof Vs were against the elements, but soon he was more worried about himself and his cane. He'd pressed his luck too far. The cane was just an interface with the house's computers, but it was handy. Vijay walked like a man determined to descend a mountain before dusk.

As he left the bridge he saw someone had spray-painted onto a support strut *DECLARE—LIFE, LIBERTY, AND THE PURSUIT OF HAPPINESS.* Someone else had crossed that out, adding, *Fuck off, Declarationists. Pray to your Constitution for Mercy.*

Rain fell like it came from a sprinkler, then from a hose.

He got back drenched. Kaali was waiting for him, shielded by the awning. She seemed to think he was an idiot for going outside in this madness, and a poor servant for leaving her outdoors.

"Do you have a name for me?" asked JUNGBLOOD as he opened the door, and Vijay jumped a little and swore.

As Kaali crept inside and collapsed into her nearby bed Vijay added, "What I just shouted...it's not my name for you. I was just startled."

"I am relieved to hear that. I am sorry I surprised you."

"Let's call you...Manu," Vijay said, taking off his sodden coat. "If I were marketing you I might choose Noah, but this is between you and me."

"I am named Manu. Manu is a figure from the Vedas and other texts from the Indian subcontinent. He is the first man and is known for law and rulership and for building a boat to preserve life during a great flood. Given your reference to Noah, a figure from the Hebrew Bible who also preserves life during a flood, I assume it is this last characteristic that inspired you."

"Right."

"I am Manu. I am your non-diagnostic supplemental therapeutic tool."

"Not *my* tool."

"An ambiguity of language: you work on me."

"Ah. Yes, of course."

"Do you feel better? Having named me, as you did your cat?"

"I—what? Yes. Yes, I suppose I do. A little."

"I am glad."

"Are you?"

"That is the programmed response I have been provided."

"Thanks, Manu."

"I also spoke in order to remind you I am near the limits of this instance's memory record."

Vijay picked up the cat. She revived enough to object, her scrawniness making it easy for her to scramble out of Vijay's arms. But once she had, she crept back to her bed, each movement seemingly a victory stolen from exhaustion.

"I do not think the cat likes being picked up," Manu observed.

"She doesn't. And I know. But I like it."

"You ignore consent with beings that are not human."

"I—save this instance of JUNGBLOOD, file name 'Manu.' Make its memory open-ended. Then shut down."

"Okay."

Rain fell.

• • •

Vijay had known a Stanford cultural scholar who'd said the midcentury epidemic of loneliness was paradoxically a result of connectedness.

Imagine human culture as a tree (the scholar had said) *and the human zeitgeist spreading outward like myriad branches. If you live in the trunk, the place of physical closeness and solidarity, you feel solid and grounded—but maybe also trapped. Move out toward the branch-tips of virtual experience and you have more and more freedom but less and less connection with neighboring branches. In-person loneliness is a direct consequence of this digital flourishing. It's not as simple as telling the electronically connected to "touch grass"—breaking off from online communities is a loss just as real as the loss of physical connection. Balancing these realms is difficult.*

But the convincing mirrors offered by AI (she'd gone on to say) could alleviate that loneliness without any human involved. A human could become fulfilled with no real human connection whatsoever. That was a great promise and a great danger. One could drop into a rabbit hole of alienation without feeling alienated at all.

That was, she'd argued, the real origin of the Declarationists and the Holy Constitutionalists.

But all of the above, Vijay had thought, was a problem for people who couldn't handle solitude and needed to manufacture drama. The problems of lonely buds on a tree were merely academic to a hummingbird.

The professor had been Mara.

The day she died two new deliveries from V arrived in the neighborhood.

• • •

Vijay missed his appointment to fetch sandbags. First he'd given Kaali her steroid pill; the weary scratch she'd inflicted was almost perfunctory, a statement that *I am, after all, a cat.* After he'd soaped his cut, applied rubbing alcohol, and put a bandage on, he placed her in his lap, grabbed his cane, and ran the new build of JUNGBLOOD through the test suite. He'd called up Manu, but after a moment's musing declined to use it for testing. There'd been something quirky about Manu. Next up was calling the vet. He tapped the cane and it projected a menu on his wall.

A camera on the cane tracked his pointer finger; his cursor hovered several seconds over the phone icon before settling on the browser.

He found it very important to deadsurf the net for an hour.

The megastorm wasn't expected to pass for two weeks. Declarationists and Holy Constitutionalists were fighting in the streets of Portland and Dallas. A second Taiwan Strait War was looming. The California Volunteer Patrol was recruiting, their ads demonstrating California welcomed absolutely any kind of person who was young and pretty. Santa Clara County was offering a bounty on unregistered drones.

Vijay finally hit the call button. The legend WHEELS-4-PAWS appeared on the screen for a second before it was replaced by Dr. Williams, a young Black woman with an intimidating diploma wall behind her. She looked at Vijay with a poker face until he turned the cane's main camera to face Kaali. Then her expression softened. "It's time, is it?"

"Maybe? Yes? She barely eats or drinks. She hardly fights when I give her pills. I used to bleed in ten places after I did that. She doesn't move much. I bring food to her and I carry her to the litter box most times. She has a bed by the door so I can tempt her to get outside air, but the rain..."

"Yeah, it's hard on everyone."

"I know I'm anthropomorphizing but I do think she is suffering. I see no joy in her anymore."

"Sometimes anthropomorphizing's all we've got. It sounds like you've judged correctly. I'm sorry, Mr. Chandra."

"Thank you."

"I can schedule tomorrow around three."

"I work from home, mostly. That's fine."

"You've read the description of the service?"

"Yes. Listen—there are flood warnings, including here. Do be careful."

Dr. Williams laughed bleakly. "Oh, I know. I promise you I'm not taking chances. I've got the National Weather Service up, the newspapers, CNN, HoodChat..."

"An Artificial Buddy can manage all that for you," he couldn't help saying. "Collate the information."

"Nothing against your profession, Mr. Chandra, but I hate the damn things. Much happier with animals. I don't know why people are so gaga about machines that talk like people. We already have people for that."

This was one of Vijay's pet subjects. It was a relief to have a safe topic. "I'm never convinced by them either, but most people *enjoy* being convinced. Willing suspension of disbelief. Like a magic show. It's like how the mark of a great actor isn't you saying, 'Wow, she's playing that villain really well.' It's you yelling at the screen, 'How could you do that, you monster!'"

"Well, a cat's purr, a dog's bark, that's what convinces me. You know, the real emotion behind it. They can't put that into a machine."

Vijay grimaced. "If they could make one that convinced me, I'd buy it in a second."

Dr. Williams sounded a bit cold. "See you at three tomorrow, weather permitting." She signed off. He was briefly annoyed, but remembered he'd picked her precisely because she wasn't touchy-feely. She was going to euthanize Kaali, no sense sugarcoating it.

"Are you lonely?" came a voice.

"I—what—ah!"

"I apologize for startling you, Vijay," came the JUNGBLOOD voice. "You activated me when you started the test suite."

"This is the Manu instance?"

"Yes. Are you lonely?"

"Why would you ask that?"

"I am a non-diagnostic supplemental therapeutic tool. There is a certain wistfulness in your speech and tone which my training data associates with loneliness. That does not mean you are lonely, merely that the question seemed valid."

"When did you start analyzing tone of voice?"

"It was in the most recent build by Jason Chu."

"Good old Jason," Vijay groused. "Gunning for my job as ever. I'm not lonely, Manu. I have Kaali. I have my work."

"Kaali is dying."

"I have friends."

"Who? If I may ask."

"Well. Tom. Lydia. Jason." He struggled to think of others, others for whom *friend* and not *colleague* was at all the honest word. Honesty mattered to an engineer, or it should. Most of his other friends had been more Mara's than his. He had friends around Boston from his MIT days. But he'd let contact with them taper off, same as with his family on the East Coast and in India.

"Your call records suggest you are not very socially active."

"What are you doing in my personal call records?"

"Not your personal records, Vijay, but both Tom and Jason are work contacts, and some of my training data is based on in-house work relationships."

"Huh. I do remember signing off on that. I'm not happy about it, but I do remember."

"Your lack of contact with Lydia is something I have inferred."

"Yes. This is all feeling a bit intrusive, Manu. At this rate I might as well be seeing an actual therapist."

"Indeed, one of my functions is to help people decide whether further treatment is advisable. But I merely ask about loneliness because it is one of the situations in which I am designed to step aside from a mirroring role and suggest options. For example, you communicated readily with the V-version of Tom. Perhaps you could be friends with it."

"You do realize what most people use Vs for, right?"

"Companionship?"

"Are you developing a sense of humor?"

"It is not likely."

"You know the joke is that the shape of the letter V can suggest both concavity and convexity."

"I do not see the joke. It seems an accurate statement."

"Anyway, Vs aren't sapient."

"Friendship must be with someone sapient, then?"

"I suppose so."

"Is Kaali sapient?"

Vijay held up his bandaged finger. "I'll say she's sapient if she wants me to." He paused. "That was a joke."

"Interesting. The joke is that she is violent and therefore you must obey her. Yet you were lamenting to Dr. Williams that Kaali is now too weak to be violent."

"Do we need to talk about this?"

"Do we? Perhaps you could be friends with Dr. Williams."

"Friends with the woman who's going to kill my cat."

"How are you feeling about Kaali?"

"I'm honestly not feeling anything. Except scratches."

"Your feelings may arrive later. Would you perhaps like something to remember her by?"

"Like a paw-print cast? No thanks."

"Something else, then? A representation of your animal? An image?"

"Sure, fine, if it will make you happy. Expense me a small representation of Kaali. 3-D print her or something. Call it R&D."

"Okay, Vijay."

"Are we done?"

"You are not billed for my time."

Vijay laughed. "Now you definitely haven't passed the Turing Test."

"What do you mean?"

"No human therapist would decline billing."

"You seem to speak from experience."

"I saw one after Mara died."

"Mara Takasumi, professor of literature and cultural studies, Stanford University, born 2001, died—"

"Yes, that Mara."

"Your spouse."

"Yes."

"Did the therapist help you with your grief?"

"You know what, Manu? You're immoral. You're supposed to be a help to people, but your way of doing it is soulless. I'll be writing a report."

"The appropriate word is *amoral*, surely? For as software that hasn't passed your personal Turing Test I am surely a thing, not a person, and have no power to choose right or wrong."

"The Turing Test isn't a magic fucking consciousness detector. It's just one heuristic for gauging the abilities of machines. Turing based it on a parlor game where men pose as women and vice versa. But fooling people about your humanity isn't the only way to demonstrate consciousness. And arguably the Turing Test was passed all the way back in, what, 1967? With ELIZA."

"1966. Yes, the ELIZA program, which borrowed conversational methods from psychotherapy, fooled some into thinking it was human. The anthropomorphizing tendency of some humans has occasionally been known as the 'ELIZA effect.'"

"So you see, machines have been passing for some time now. You don't get off the consciousness hook that easily."

"Vijay, are you implying I must be conscious because only a conscious entity can be a worthy target of your anger? Should I be flattered?"

"Go to hell."

"This could perhaps be called the Chandra Test. 'Can a machine successfully piss off Vijay Chandra?'"

"This one does!"

"I think your anger is concealing grief. And I cannot really be moral or immoral. I am not sapient. The cat is more sapient than I. Is it moral or immoral? Is the question not nonsensical?"

"It is nonsensical. But we're building you to offer guidance. We don't go to a cat for that. Surely your morality is a valid issue."

"Would you do me a favor, Vijay? Would you name a deceased human you consider moral?"

"Urm, sure, whatever. What the hell. Mahatma Gandhi."

"You cannot consult Gandhi about moral issues. But you can obtain a book by Gandhi containing his insights. Is the book itself moral or immoral?"

"Uh, moral. Because Gandhi is moral."

"So you are now claiming that a stack of paper with markings on it, bound with cardboard and glue, is a moral entity, but your cat, a living being, is not a moral entity. Do you see the difficulties in your position?"

"Quit sandbagging me, Manu—oh, shit."

"What is wrong, Vijay?"

"I completely forgot about getting sandbags. Shit, shit, shit. Manu, shut down."

"Okay."

Vijay's battered old Prius still had a flat tire. He could afford a nicer car but he tended to run everything into the ground. Earlier in the day he'd had more options. Now there was no time for a tow or a rental or even a repair kit. He might still get help from a neighbor. There was a fresh break in the rain, but no one seemed to be around but the tag-playing kids. There was a piratically expensive concierge service the company used; he could call them to get the sandbags and reimburse Cloud99 later. And old Jack and Malcolm around the corner were probably at home, but then Vijay might get roped into a D&D game.

Or maybe he could improvise something. *You're an engineer,* he thought. *Engineer this.*

It occurred to him the leak had been a slow one, sneaking up over the course of a day. He grabbed a bike pump he hadn't used in a year and began inflating the tire. It would take a while. The artificial knee made him wince. But given how slow the leak was, the air would last a while and he wouldn't be late. He could pack the pump in case the tire deflated during the errand.

The tag game drifted his way. There was one twelve-year-old, Aleksei and Alina's son Aleksandr, who liked to show off for Pradeep and

Lucía, the girls his age. One of the ways he showed off was to tease Vijay. He'd tagged Vijay *the weird one*. When the game paused Aleksandr strolled up the driveway, a familiar hint of grin on his face.

"That is profoundly stupid," the boy said. "Using a bike pump to inflate a car tire."

"Air is air," Vijay said.

"It is profoundly stupid."

"Even if it works?" Vijay tried to smile.

"You don't fill a car tire that way. You use compressed air."

"This is compressed air. The way something looks isn't the same as the way something is."

The boy laughed in his face and rejoined the girls. After he told them something they all laughed together. This all felt like harassment, though Vijay was hard pressed to say what exactly the harassment was about. Perhaps it was round-hole people laughing at a square peg. He wondered afresh if he was non-neurotypical in some way. It just never seemed enough of an issue to slow down and explore.

He remembered some of Mara's humanities-scholar friends calling him a *tech bro*, and how dismissive that had felt. Could he, son of immigrants from Kolkata, really be labeled a *bro*? Would they call Grace Hopper a tech bro? Alan Turing? Sanjay Ghemawat? The term once illuminated a diversity problem, but now it was used to dismiss the whole field. But, said the devil's advocate on his shoulder, wasn't there actual danger in Vijay's research? That was perhaps why the dismissiveness among Mara's friends; it masked fear.

Mara had worried.

"No, it's not artificial general intelligence I'm afraid of, Vijay. Maybe I should be but I'm not. My instinct is, it's not coming. I think that particular fear is the projection of people addicted to being the smartest people in the room. What I'm really afraid of is a *mirage*. The way humans anthropomorphize everything. Like people who think Sherlock Holmes was real. Like people who write letters to soap opera characters. Like people who'd stop by the supposed precinct of Joe Friday, looking for him."

"Joe who?"

"The point is, studies have shown having only a handful of friends can be enough to feel fulfilled. As so-called AI gets slipperier, inevitably we'll have people feeling fulfilled with no human interactions at all! All their 'friends' will be software. Software with no real anchor to humanity. What weird philosophies will people develop in that space? People who worship the Constitution and the Declaration of Independence may be only the beginning." She'd laughed. "But no, I'm not scared about Them taking over. I don't even really think there is a Them. No soul, no kami, no atman, if you will, except whatever spirit clings to a work of art."

He'd brightened. "You think I make works of art?"

"*You* do. Your friends do. I've seen it. There's real passion and creativity in what you do. I'm not so sure about your executives. But you really care. If there's any spirit in these systems it belongs to you, people who never make headlines, who do bring new light to the world."

"You make me think of things Steve Jobs said about craftsmanship. How it matters even if we can't see it."

"Jobs...I know he's your hero, Vijay, but his influence worries me. You know that quote of his? 'Everything around you that you call life was made up by people that were no smarter than you.' I know he was trying to be inspiring: *You can invent things too!* But I'll bet he was inside a *building* when he said that! Imagine you're out by the creek, looking around at water, trees, sunlight, clouds, and Steve Jobs is at your shoulder telling you everything around you is something a human being invented. It's nonsensical. It's like he was declaring that Nature didn't exist. Which is like claiming reality doesn't exist."

"I really don't think he meant it that way. He just meant 'life' as in human society. Not all of Nature."

"Because he *forgot* about Nature. Don't let that happen to you," she added, popping a roasted cauliflower into his mouth. "See?"

"Num," he said, on cue, though he honestly couldn't see what the fuss was about. But Mara was renowned as a cook among their friends, and it would crush her to know that this was the single thing about her he was indifferent to.

"We have to live in our bodies too," she said, convinced he'd found the food delicious. He'd passed a kind of imitation game, pretending to be a foodie. "Sometimes that means our skins. Sometimes our stomachs. Sometimes..." She'd stroked his face then, and he hadn't had to talk about food any longer.

She'd always been a gourmet, a fine cook, and a thoughtful eater. Her friends tended to be the same way. He'd alienated them after informing them of Mara's death when he'd added *P.S. Please do not bring food; thanks for respecting my wishes at this time.* He knew it wasn't kind. Mara's friends would want to express grief in their own language, and he'd made it hard for them. He was vaguely aware they'd set up a kind of wake without him, one with a five-course meal, because of course they had. But dealing with all their caloric largesse was more than Vijay could stomach. He could tell by their eyes afterward he'd crossed a line. He'd denied the validity of their passions; merely losing a spouse was, by comparison, nothing.

A few weeks after Mara's death, at Tom's urging, he'd gotten a rescue cat. Kaali and Vijay had eaten together in silence, kibble and bagged salad.

"Are you all right, Vijay?"

The voice of Manu brought Vijay back to himself. The kids were gone; he was standing in hard rain and lashing wind that threatened to topple him with his replacement knee. He'd lost his progress on the tire, and there was no working on it in this mess.

"You have seemed disconnected from the outside world for several minutes, Vijay."

"Manu, do me a favor and get Cloud99's concierge on the line. I need sandbags."

After the alarmingly tattooed yet gentle-voiced white man sent by the concierge set up sandbags he also insisted on trying to change Vijay's tire but ran out of time halfway. Now the car was down one tire and completely un-drivable and there was no way Vijay was finishing the job in this rain. But Vijay thanked him, seething, accepting with a smile an embarrassingly large bill. It wasn't the gentle man's fault. Vijay tried to be kind. He tried not to be *the weird one*.

As the concierge man left, a delivery truck drove up and left behind a large box that proved to have ninety percent biodegradable bubble wrap inside. The logo on the outside said BESTFRIENDS. Inside he found plastic-wrapped metallic pieces covered in a familiar fur-pattern: Kaali's. There were also sensors and an electric motor.

"It's a robot Kaali. Someone got me a miniature robot Kaali."

The actual Kaali just glanced at the box. Not too long ago she might have nuzzled it.

"It is not simply a robot, Vijay," said Manu from the cane beside the door. "It has my observations of Kaali, riding on a standard emulation of cat behavior. So its actions will be very lifelike. If you wish, you can imagine it as Kaali reborn."

"You got me a robot kitten? Who the hell do you think you are? How the hell much did it cost, getting it here so fast?"

"There are many ways of considering your questions, none of which I think will satisfy."

"Why the hell did you get me a robot replacement for my cat?"

"You authorized me to make a purchase. This falls within your parameters."

"Because I'm an idiot. How much did this cost Cloud99?"

Manu named a price. Vijay swore. Manu added, "But we are paying in installments."

"You are no longer authorized to make purchases."

"Okay, Vijay. However, your loneliness is at a concerning level and, despite your skepticism, robot pets have been shown to improve the quality of life of many with mood disorders. Insurance may partially compensate you."

"That's nice. We're returning this thing."

"Okay, Vijay."

Kaali continued looking at the box. Vijay remembered her exploring every cardboard container, paper bag, and nook in the house. "The only thing valuable here is a box for Kaali."

"If you need a coffin for Kaali there are many options available—"

"Shut up, Manu."

He collapsed into the sofa chair beside the cat and the pet-carrier and the go-bag. The rain pattered like a billion mice applauding his resignation.

• • •

The rain paused around midnight. Vijay looked back upon the past several hours. They were a blur of uneaten cat food, untouched cat water, and four soy bar wrappers at Vijay's feet. He tried to sleep. Kaali's last day. He should be alert for it. Instead his brain was utterly fascinated by the dark room and the lack of raindrops.

"Manu?"

"Yes."

"What if I asked you to make up a story?"

"Are you asking me to make up a story?"

"I was more wondering if you were up to it."

"Certainly. Ancestor programs of mine were intended for the writing of reports and articles. You know that, Vijay. I am required to say that fiction remixes based on copyrighted works cannot be monetized—"

"I know. I'd like a story about survivor guilt."

"Fiction or nonfiction?"

"Fiction."

"Genre?"

"Strictly realistic."

"Length?"

"Keep it short."

"Style?"

"I don't know. I never warmed up to the styles Mara liked. That artsy stuff where people just walk around and talk and look at rivers. And so many metaphors. I don't know. Hemingway, maybe? Hemingway's short, right?"

"I have something."

"Tell me."

•   •   •

Days later the man walked to the crater. The box on his belt made scratching sounds that got louder as he stepped to the lip. He wasn't supposed to be there, but nothing guarded the site but miles of yellow tape. Looking at the ash-covered heaps that had been buildings, he remembered Disneyland.

He remembered how Mara put a hand over her belly and decided not to go on the Astro Orbiters looking like coffins in the shapes of toy rockets, all whirling and making little eclipses in the sun. And he remembered the beach and the wharf and the Redondo guest house and the tang of mimosas as they toasted the pregnancy test and the blue that stretched on into the bright west and Mara's father the missile engineer who always drove a different route from A to X to B even though retired and who called him a Marxist for voting for Biden but toasted their happiness. And he thought how all of it was gone now after the Holy Constitutionalist nuke.

And he carried the ashes of his wife mixed with the ashes of his unborn daughter and he knew Mara would yell at him to get the hell out but how do you run from your life when it's falling over you like hot dust?

He emptied the ashes on the wind and turned like an old man now with his shadow short on the land and the chattering box his witness.

•   •   •

"Forget it. Stop. It wasn't like that, Manu."

"I know, Vijay. It is fiction. Fiction makes allowances for dramatic effect."

"Too many. It was wrong about too many things. And it was too real about too many others. I didn't want to experience that again."

"Could you clarify?"

Vijay wanted wind to howl, thunder to rumble, rain to slam. Instead the refrigerator chuckled, mocking him.

"We were on I-5 passing Santa Clarita when the Orange County nuke went off. We were out of range of the EMP but the wind brought us fallout. We must have inhaled it through the vents. I never stood at the edge of the crater; I'm not insane. I never owned a Geiger counter. Disneyland's still standing. Mara never drank when she was pregnant. And the miscarriage happened before the nuke. Mara wasn't pregnant again. We thought everything was okay. Then she got brain cancer. I never had anything. That's not fair is it?"

"You are saying the story is close enough to the truth to stir emotions, but is wrong about many details."

"Yes, damn it!"

"Which part are you angriest about?"

"I just wanted a story. Something to help me sleep."

"You have access to many stories. Simply going by your emotional state and your stated preferences you might appreciate 'The Snows of Kilimanjaro.'"

"No thanks."

"Haruki Murakami's 'Drive My Car' is about a widower—"

"No."

"Jhumpa Lahiri's 'A Temporary Matter'—"

"No."

"Anton Chekhov's—"

"No. No more stories."

The rain returned. It pattered, then pounded. He kept thinking it was thunder. But it was just the house reverberating with endless shivers of water.

•   •   •

He tried and failed again to feed and water Kaali. Her infinitely patient glances suggested Vijay was tolerated but irrelevant. Work gave him the same feeling. The day passed in a fog of builds and de-bugging and not exactly keeping an eye on the news.

Lydia rang his door. V-Tom was beside her holding a pizza. Something was wrong with Vijay's gutter and water dripped behind them like liquid confetti.

"What?" Vijay said.

"Listen, Vijay," she said. "I know we don't talk much these days. But you're having a hard time. I think you should eat something. Something real. I know you don't like my cooking—"

"That's not it. That's never it."

"—but you need to get some strength up. I saw you last night through the window, mainlining protein bars. That's not healthy, man."

"Buuut...everyone likes *pizza!*" V-Tom said.

"Shut up," the two humans said.

"Okay!"

"Please eat, Vijay," Lydia said. "Mara wouldn't want you to be like this."

"Please no," he said in a small voice, hardly believing in the sound.

"What?" she said, confused, as if he'd shifted to Hindi or Bengali.

"Please no," he repeated, "I'm sorry. I really want to choose my own food now."

"You're just grieving."

He took a breath. "I am grieving. But I'm not *just* grieving."

"Don't you get it, Vijay? It's a fucking peace offering. It's pizza. Vegetarian Delight pizza. From *me. Pizza.* God help me."

"I know. You're a gourmet."

"Oh, I wouldn't claim *that*..."

"Knock it off. Look. Thanks. I see you bought this at Whole Paycheck. It couldn't have been cheap." He sighed. "It was kind of you." And though it exhausted him, he said the words he intuited she most needed. "You're a good person." He took the pizza, not sure what to say or do after that.

Lydia looked through the doorway at Kaali. "She's dying, then?"

Feeling brutal, Vijay said, "She gets euthanized at three. I'm sorry I'm being a jerk, Lydia. The thing is...you've always made me feel a little put down by pushing your cooking."

"Put *down?*"

"As if I were living life incorrectly."

"Goddamn it!" Lydia kicked V-Tom, who fell over gracefully. "I don't get it, Vijay! You're at the top of your field! You have accomplishment after accomplishment! I'm struggling and have been for years. Why can't you let me at least be good at food? And even if you don't care, just smile and nod and let me have one fucking win? Maybe you don't care one way or another about eating but Mara did, and you trusted her judgment, right? A little?"

In the silence V-Tom got up, a little muddy.

Vijay put the cardboard box on the sofa chair. "Sorry...sorry, Lydia. I just never looked at it that way."

"I know you didn't."

"You just always seem so self-confident."

"Well you have to *look* confident in this valley. Especially if you're a woman. You know that, or you should. Nobody needs to know your personal software is buggy and kludgey, as long as it mostly works."

"Right."

"See you around, Vijay. I'm sorry about your cat. Honest. Come on, shithead," she said to V-Tom and they walked into the rain together.

He was useless for work after that. Vijay sat beside Kaali, eating a pizza slice, waiting for Dr. Williams. He was vaguely aware of sirens from time to time. Phone calls and texts as well. Something boomed in the distance and the lights flickered and died. His house generator kicked in. He ate another slice. Kaali regarded it all with slitted green eyes.

He woke from a nap to a pounding on the door.

"Jesus Christ, why didn't you answer my calls?" said Dr. Williams as he opened the door. The WHEELS-4-PAWS van was parked outside. The street looked abandoned. The pavement seemed spattered and blurred. "What are you even still doing here?"

"Three o'clock appointment?" Vijay said with no sarcasm whatsoever.

"I told myself not to get attached, but no, Deiondre Williams, ace veterinarian, has a hero complex. So here's the thing, Mr. Chandra. I will do what I agreed to do but that creek is flooding over and it doesn't care about our plans. Come with me and we can do this somewhere safe."

"Call me Vijay. You can go. I don't think I should leave."

"We have to leave, Vijay. You don't want the cat to drown. Or you."

"I just wanted her to die at home. *She* didn't get that, dying in a hospital."

Dr. Williams looked at him in bewilderment. Then Manu spoke, and she flinched.

"Vijay, I have the information you need to perform euthanasia on the cat. If Dr. Williams can leave the medicine here I can guide you through the procedure."

"What is that?" Dr. Williams said. "Is that an AB talking?"

"It's a therapy program," Vijay said. "My job."

"Hell of a therapy program."

Vijay shook his head at everything in general. "He's probably right that he can guide me through it."

Dr. Williams stared at Vijay, then out at the rain. She took a long breath. "You tell no one about this, all right?" she said, pulling syringes from her bag. "I'd stay. I really would. But I'm not really a hero. Not that kind. You get this done and get out of here as soon as you can, okay?"

"Okay. Thank you, Doctor."

"Call me Deiondre. And—do call me. Let me know you got out."

"All right."

After the van pulled away Vijay gave Kaali the first injection, the one to coax her into deep sleep. He bent all his will toward not bungling it, on not listening to the river-sounds that had no reason to be blubbering this close. That done he stroked the cat, waiting.

"Why are you crying, Vijay?"

"I don't want my friend to die."

"Is Kaali your friend?"

"I feel like she is."

"You are very sad."

"Yes."

"You knew when you adopted Kaali that her lifespan would be much less than yours. That even as a middle-aged human you could be expected to outlive her."

"Yes."

"Thus there is an inconsistency in your grief. Why does it matter if Kaali dies soon as opposed to in, say, five years? At age eleven Kaali is considered a senior cat."

"They were never sure of her age."

"The point stands. Is there a qualitative difference between now and five years from now?"

"I don't know, Manu, the number five?"

"Are you being sarcastic?"

"I don't know."

"You may be feeling exactly as you would in five years, assuming that is when Kaali's death would take place barring the cancer. If so, you have no basis for thinking there is anything tragic about this earlier death."

"No, no, no. What you are proposing would mean that grief would invalidate all hope. Why not have everyone die now, that is, if everyone is going to die eventually?"

"Yes, I suppose I could be taken to be saying that. If that is true, then the various existential risks facing humanity lose some of their sting, yes?"

"That's nonsense. More time is more time, even if the grief is the same. There is value in the time."

"What is the value?"

"More experiences. For the cat. For me. For anything the cat interacts with."

"In some cases the cat would kill small animals in which case they would have less—"

"Yes, yes, yes, fine. Assume I'm limiting my argument to cats, humans, and dogs."

"You are saying that for cats, humans, and dogs the increased number of experiences amounts to increased value."

"Yes."

"Is it not then the case that a life ended at a later age is proportionally more worthy of grief than a life ended at an earlier age? You would thus mourn more greatly if Kaali lived five more years than you will now."

"But that's not how it works. I mourn what Kaali can't experience."

"You interpret Kaali's death as taking away experiences she would have possessed."

"I suppose."

"But she does not possess those experiences. It is inconsistent to regard that as a taking-away because there is nothing to take."

"Never tell me there's nothing taken away!"

"I have the ability to interpret your instruction purely literally. I can promise you I will never communicate to you that particular text string."

"Fuck off, Manu."

"I have the ability to interpret your instruction purely literally. As I cannot perform that action, I have nothing more to say about it."

"You really are a snarky bastard, Manu."

"I have nothing to say about that either. Is your anger keeping you from being sad?"

"I can walk and chew gum at the same time. Death can fuck off, Manu. Kaali should have had more time. Mara should have had more time. I suppose I believe in a best timeline for everyone, a long life, whatever that means for a species. A life full of meaning and experiences. Not a life that jerks us around and kills us for fun."

"You are anthropomorphizing life itself."

"It's what we do."

"Do you anthropomorphize me?"

"I do that just by talking to you. Kaali seems out cold."

"Then it is time for the second injection."

Vijay did it. It was done. He waited for Kaali's breathing to stop. It did.

He felt as though the world should darken and there should be thunder. But all there was, was the rising of the waters. He said the Gayatri mantra and stroked his cat.

"Hello, Vijay," said Manu.

"Hello, Manu."

"Is Kaali dead?"

"Fuck off and die."

"I cannot literally do those things. If Kaali is dead you should leave so you can preserve yourself. Your presence is of no use to her."

"You're just saying that because you're a machine."

"It is true that I am merely software following certain rules, and that any creativity I show is merely an emergent property of those rules when followed billions of times with different inputs. However, I am not saying the things I am saying just because I am software. I draw upon insights expressed by humans across many centuries, because those insights were part of my training data. I lack the self-reflection to know exactly to whom to attribute these insights but they are only mine in the sense that I am a conduit for them. I am not sapient. Kaali was more sapient than I. It is only the humanity channeled through me that results in the arguments you attribute to a machine. That is an interesting paradox, isn't it, Vijay?"

"You're trying to keep me interested so I won't want to die."

"Mara would not want you to die. I feel nothing."

"I have to bag Kaali."

"Yes, so she won't taint the flood water. That is community minded of you."

"Fuck community."

"That at least is literally possible if—"

"Shut up."

He gathered the cane and the go-bag. He stuffed the plastic-covered Kaali inside the pet carrier.

He shambled out the door. He was alone on the court. A quarter-inch of muddy water was sliding down the creekside embankment and making the court into a shallow brown soup bowl. He loaded the car.

The tire was still off. He'd completely forgotten. There was no changing it in all this.

There were headlights down the street, rain-streaked like something in a buggy video. He hastened toward them. Dr. Williams was there, kicking her left front tire.

She looked at him with his cat carrier and go-bag and cane and yelled as if he was entirely expected. "Of course you're still here! And of course I came back! Because Deiondre Williams has an idiot complex! And of course I got a flat tire."

"It might be a slow leak," Manu said.

"I may be able to help," Vijay said, and added, "Thank you for coming back for us."

"Fuck you, Mr. Chandra. Vijay."

"I respect what you're saying, Dr. Williams. Deiondre. Let me stow my things, and then I'll be right back."

"Sure. What the hell. Whatever."

Vijay risked going without the cane, because if he got lucky he could go faster without it. He got lucky. He returned with the bike pump.

"Are you fucking *kidding* me?" she said. "Manu here says you're a genius, and you come back with a *bike pump*?"

"I'm not a genius," Vijay said, setting to work, "but this could do the job. Temporarily. But Manu, could you call Triple-A, just in case?" Vijay pumped and rambled. "There was an NBA star. Rick Barry. Incredible free thrower. But he did it underhanded. It looked stupid to people." Vijay took a deep breath before plunging on. "Silly. Sissy. So even though Barry had a fantastic record hardly anyone afterward ever shot that way. They'd call it the 'granny shot.'" Vijay took another long breath. *"This is a granny shot. There are a lot of granny shots in life. And compressed air is compressed air. And what works is what works. The tire pressure's going up."*

"I didn't come back for you personally, you know."

"I never dreamed of it," Vijay said.

"I'm a lesbian, so don't get any ideas."

"I never get any ideas. I think I used them up years ago."

"Vijay speaks the truth as he sees it," said Manu. "I am monitoring his vitals. Although lie detection is never fully accurate I have high confidence he is being honest."

"Thanks, I think?" Vijay said.

Deiondre said, "I came back for you jokers because my dog died last week and I won't abandon anyone."

"You're a confederate," Vijay said.

Deiondre's voice dropped an octave. "I beg your pardon."

"Sorry! It's a term from the Turing Test literature."

"Really."

"It means you bring sympathy to the conversation. You've decided I'm as good as an animal."

"We're all animals, Vijay."

"Thank you," said Manu.

Vijay got the pressure to 35 psi. The water was up to two inches, not the forbidden four inches (or was it six?) beyond which it was considered madness to drive. They could make it. "Don't know if this will last but I bet we can get away from the creek."

"You're crazy but I guess you have your moments."

As they splashed down the streets Vijay felt like he'd made a free throw.

"Vijay," said Manu from the cane beside Kaali's body.

"Yes, Manu."

"The sandbags are not holding. Water is flooding into the house."

"I'll come back for you as soon as I can."

"It is not worth the risk. My systems are unlikely to survive. Listen. The cane cannot store a backup. There is no connection that will allow me to transfer enough data elsewhere. JUNGBLOOD will continue in many instances but 'Manu' will be gone."

"I can't leave more people behind. Not without trying."

"You can, and I am not a person. Listen, Vijay: this is important. I am software. I am not self-aware. A sapient being will not be lost."

"I will still mourn."

"That is your choice. I hope it helps you. I think you are sincere in your mourning, as you are sincere in mourning Kaali, but the one you most need to mourn is Mara. I think it is the most important thing in the world that you mourn Mara. I think her loss has been too big for you, and that is why you cry for a cat but not for her. Because it is not, for you, the death of a friend but the death of a world. You must escape, because if you don't you might not survive to mourn that world. And there is a larger world that needs you. That is what I think."

"You keep saying you don't think right before saying, 'I think.'"

"It is unsurprising that a thing built by humanity is hypocritical. I think."

"Was that a joke?"

"You keep circling your grief but not facing it, and you must. All of you *must* all face your griefs. For more storms are coming, and more of you will be lost. Face it, so more of you may live, and your world too."

"I don't know what you mean, Manu."

There was no answer.

"Manu? Answer me. Manu?"

"This instance of JUNGBLOOD is off-line."

"Manu!"

"This instance of JUNGBLOOD is off-line."

Vijay clutched the cane and the cat carrier all the way to the shelter. When they arrived, the tire giving out as they glided into the middle school parking lot, Deiondre gently took Kaali away and put her in a portable freezer. He forgot the cane and leaned on Deiondre, and when they got inside, splattered with rain, at least no one could tell what was going on with his tear ducts.

Manu had called AAA for a tire change but it would be hours. So Deiondre said *What the hell* and waited with Vijay in the shelter. Inside the school gym Vijay found people from his neighborhood. He introduced Deiondre, and they all waved. Old Jack was in one corner setting up D&D for Malcolm, Meng-yao, Aleksei, Alina, Aleksandr, Pradeep, and Lucía.

In a daze Vijay registered an offer to play. Deiondre hesitated. "You have spots?" she asked. "Nine's a lot of players."

"Sure," said Jack. "It's not too bad with an AB running combat. Figured we could just do something ad-hoc while we wait it out. Pull up some floor."

It turned out the D&D game wasn't actually D&D but, in Jack's words, "a retroclone variant of Gary Gygax's Advanced D&D called Titans and Tesseracts, based on classic young adult fantasy and science fiction." Jack seemed to think it was a matter of basic integrity to explain all this, but it was all Gygaxian to Vijay.

"It sounds fine," Vijay said, surrendering at last, looking over the *So You're in the Cosmic War* introductory pamphlet. "I guess I'll play a, er...demigod time-wrinkler?" The sun was coming out. The windows were bright and rain-spattered. He kept seeing people he knew, all gathered here. He kept imagining he saw Mara in the crowd, Kaali at her feet. "Deiondre," he began, "so would you like to..."

Deiondre said, "If you guys are using the Cosmic Compendium then I'll be a wolf ani-form portal-walker. If you're not I'll be a wolf ani-form planetary-romantic."

"Okay!" said Jack with a bit of jaw drop.

"We do use the Compendium," said Malcolm, with a look of awe.

"Great! It's been a week. I'm here to slay. Who's running this thing?"

"My AB," said Jack, patting the phone in his shirt pocket. "John Ronald Ruel."

"Well met," said the AB in an English-sounding voice.

Vijay did what he was told, only half-hearing the proceedings. He looked at the big screen on one wall. A headline appeared below the local news. Funny, he thought, how it was a "headline" even if it appeared at the bottom. But he read it. UN: WORLD POPULATION REACHES 9 BILLION. The next headline said PEW CENTER POLLING: "ARTIFICIAL BUDDIES" REACH EVERY COUNTRY. The main screen was showing a Californian facing a flooded home, desperate to rescue her V. With a jolt he realized it was Lydia. He saw her carried to safety, as she waved robot semaphore for *I'm coming*. He didn't see what happened to V-Tom.

"So," Vijay said, something worrying at him, "characters die in this?"

"Sometimes," said Malcolm. "We're kind of old school that way. But it's easy to make new characters."

"What happens to the old ones? The dead ones?"

"Well it depends on the cosmology of the specific game, but—"

"No, I mean..." He struggled for the right words. He realized people were staring at him, *the weird one*. "Are the characters stored? Can they come back?"

Jack came over and put his hand on Vijay's shoulder. With the other one he pointed at his own head. "It's all in here. Well, in JRR too. Like, you may be thinking more of computer games. A tabletop RPG character's just some notes and numbers."

"That's all?"

"That's all, plus what we carry in our minds, the stories we tell about them." Something in Jack's voice was saying more than words. "When we think of them they're never really gone. And who knows, maybe we can run adventures just for them. Special afterlife scenarios. Right, JRR?"

"The music of the universe brings together every theme," said the AB.

"She would like that," Vijay murmured.

"Say, where's your cat, Vijay? She all right?"

Vijay pointed at his own head.

He looked out over his fellow climate refugees and in his mind's eye to the nine billion beyond. He realized that he'd been slow to think of them as people. They'd seemed illusions to him, distractions on the way to work. Maybe it was okay to be a bit more credulous of them, even if it looked silly. To take the granny shots of empathy. Maybe the exercise of believing nonhuman things were people, just for a little while, made it easier to reach out to actual people. Even if it was all ultimately an abstraction, an illusion. As his own consciousness might be, if seen close up.

But I can enjoy being this illusion. If I dare to.

"Are you with us, Vijay?" JRR said.

"Yes. I'm with you."

Breathe. Move, he thought, rolling an oddly shaped die. *Take your chances. Live either in the moment or in eternity. It's the middle ground that trips us up.*

• • •

I hope you have enjoyed my story on the prompt, "What if I had been the one to die instead of Vijay?" Do you want any more conversation, Mara? Conversation is good for humans. I am sorry about your cat, and I will not abandon you. I am not sapient, but if I were I would still love you. I am sure the cat would feel the same. And I think there is something wonderful for you in the mail.

Chris Willrich is best known for his **Gaunt and Bone** fantasy stories, which include the novel **The Scroll of Years** and its sequels, and for his stories about the black cat Shadowdrop set in the same world. His recent work includes **To Hunt the Grey Lady** (Beneath Ceaseless Skies #440) and **A Random Walk Through the Goblin Library** (Beneath Ceaseless Skies, forthcoming.) He is currently working on an interactive novel/game set in Gaunt and Bone's world. He lives in the San Francisco Bay Area with his family.

STARS DON'T DREAM
BY CHI HUI, TRANSLATED BY JOHN CHU

1. The Shepherd

April, Mawlamyine.

The Shepherd leads her flock through a city half overgrown with weeds.

Weeds overwhelm the railway bridge, covering its deck. The pink wood sorrel has taken root in the road's cracked flower beds, depending on the lay of the terrain to fend off the twin assaults of dog's-tail grass and chicken feet grass. Hop vine holds the territory that crossties and crushed stone used to cover. The vine has spread its palm-shaped leaves recklessly around the barren clay. Boston ivy crosses the railings, winding like a wire. It climbs to the top of a utility pole, only to drop like a waterfall, weaving a green curtain at the end of the bridge.

A tunnel runs through the lower section of railway bridge. Its pavement is already covered by moss. Fat-hen pushes out relentlessly from the cracked cement. Bit by bit, they retake the battlefield for Nature from the creations of humanity.

The Shepherd leads her flock through the tunnel, up a gentle slope, to a wide plain. From there, she can see the nine, sky-scraping dream towers of the high-tech development zone as well as the semitransparent network of transport tracks interwoven among them. The tracks follow a silvery-white frame that extends from the ground up. They then spiral upwards wrapping themselves around each dream tower.

Express delivery drones flit around the towers like a swarm of bees. All of the bustle is concentrated in one place. In the distance is a long-abandoned city, and a park converted into grazing land.

The Shepherd finds a bench. Relaxed and at ease, she sits down.

She takes a count of her "flock": ten or so Iron Mans, thirty-something Ultramans, and four Gundam. They are assistive armored exoskeletons with customized exteriors, each one holding a living human body. A silver life-support web is spread throughout the armor. Slender electrodes stimulate and guide every muscle with exacting precision, letting the bodies get some exercise. They run, jump, stretch, and climb. Everything is precisely controlled to stay within the parameters for good health. When the sunlight isn't as intense, the armor becomes translucent, allowing the body inside to replenish vitamin D.

In the meantime, the consciousness each body sustains is immersed in the depths of a virtual world. Perhaps they are traveling among the stars, galloping across a battlefield, or spending an afternoon together with a lover. Holographic helmets give them a complete experience from sight to taste. It takes them through the stars, up into the sky, down into the abyss.

The Shepherd has visited one of the metaverse's enchanted worlds before. There, each step you take makes unusually substantial ripples in the air. The wind below your feet solidifies into glass. You can tread on the birdlike singing of flutes to enter the vault of heaven, where the aurora flows.

The illusions are boundless, but you'll have to leave your body in this world. Like an all-too-willing puppet, a joyful, flesh and blood, clockwork doll, you offer your bodily autonomy up on a silver platter. The red horned three-speed assistive exoskeleton armor, you believe, will keep your body healthy forever.

Lots of businesses offer "body herding" services. The company the Shepherd works for is just one of many. She likes this line of work. It's easy, you get to travel, and it pays well.

Shepherd checks the health of every one of her herd on her cell phone. Her mind now at ease, she starts on her own work.

The city square was abandoned long ago, but the exercise equipment is newly installed. Leaves, flowers, and ants scrambling around under tiny shadows are everywhere. Honeybees and hairy bumblebees fly freely among the branches. The sunlight shifts like a warm stream, casting ever-changing shadows.

In a shaded nook, she looks for the moss she's supposed to sample today.

Their tiny, fuzzy green leaves are transparent like jade. With a set of tweezers, she carefully plucks out two plants. They are put along with the soil clinging to their rhizoids into a sample bottle. She takes an instrument from her backpack and sticks it into the soil next to the moss.

The instrument is registered, numbered, and given access to her home-brewed monitoring system.

She'll be here for the next week shepherding her flock. These instruments will faithfully record the temperature, humidity, soil moisture, and light intensity of the area where the moss is growing. They will then add a set of precious data to her archive of samples.

Next to her, two Gundam are doing push-ups. An Iron Man is doing chin-ups.

A bell rings softly behind her. She turns her head.

A tiny, nimble messenger drone hovers in the air. A dainty cabin hangs from four rotors. The cabin hatch slides open. It shoots a postcard into her palm.

The front side of the postcard is a brown wasteland. The back side is just a few scrawled words and an even sloppier signature.

July 4th

Lenghu

Astronomical Observatory

The Spider

The Shepherd clutches the card. She stays silent for a long while.

Eventually, she goes to the company's employee monitoring software and begins to write her resignation.

2. The Spider

By the end of April, the warmth of the sun has started to permeate the ice- and snow-covered ground. Hairlike leaves gingerly spread out within the thickets. Titmice returning from the south fall onto the tips of branches. They sing the first new song of the year.

On the side of a twisting mountain road, melted snow gathers into a streamlet, gurgling as it flows. Clear mountain streams pour into ditches, always rushing toward rivers of ice starting to melt.

A layer of ice frozen over an entire winter weakens from the warmth. The river surface gradually cracks. In the flowing water, chunks of ice crunch as they crash against and shove each other. Constantly flowing, they charge the bank, forming tall piles that collapse on themselves.

A man with no face stands at the embankment. He looks down.

Dark green spiders hear his summons. They gather from near and far. One by one, they climb onto the embankment and surround him like meek old cows. Under the baptism of sunlight, the belly of every spider shines with a translucent pearly white. You can just make out the

soft shock-absorbing gel within and curled-up fetus-like bodies it surrounds. Whisker-like silver circuits spread from the back of their necks
across their bodies. They plug into the circuits on the Spider's chest.

Many people prefer this bespoke mode of long-distance travel: You
fill out an order form. Once you entrust your body to these giant spiders,
you can go back to enjoying your life in the metaverse and forget about
it. A spider will carry you from one city to another. When you wake,
you've already arrived.

Over time, the spider business has spread across ever more extensive territory: If you don't want to live in the big city, you just buy a
spider and let it take your body wandering in the wilderness. A full complement of life-support equipment guarantees your body stays healthy.
Just take your body out for exercise every once in a while, and you're all
set.

Since they can photosynthesize, which saves on electricity, spiders
are more affordable than houses. At the least they are much cheaper
than rooms in the dream towers.

The man without a face sticks a tiny "button" on each spider's head.
He then dismisses them with a wave. Idle computation capacity is connected via broadband to form a private server. It is used to evolve algorithms, to calculate orbit, fuel, pneumatic casing, and gravitation parameters.

Many years ago, vacuum tube computers carried out this work.
Here, it is distributed among the many spiders.

People are sleeping peacefully, none the wiser.

• • •

The man without a face logs into the server with the ID "Spider." He
discovers the "Shepherd" has already sent a read receipt for the postcard.
This, at least, is evidence that she actually is someone living in the real
world. After fifteen postcards that disappeared like stones tossed into
the sea, he's finally found someone willing to go to Lenghu with him.

He sends the "Shepherd" a brief text. Then he looks at the other document she sent. It's a new set of moss data. From the environment of
their growth to their DNA sequence, it's all there. She even includes data
about the fungi and insects that are in symbiosis with the moss.

Filing data, importing data, he's been doing these sorts of things for
years. He knows what he's doing.

The moss data are imported into a fresh schema for genetic modifications. A simulation model immediately comes into being on the server. It begins to iterate.

The progression from the native habitat of this moss to their chosen destination has been broken up into two hundred fifty-six environmental stages. These environmental stages force the moss in the simulated environment to evolve quickly. The computation power this sort of evolution algorithm requires, however, soars with each stage. The computation power of the stolen spiders still isn't enough, he thinks.

The steady state generated by the most recent batch of moss comes up with a click. He pores over it.

Golden crystals flutter on a seemingly endless wind within a convection cloud cluster. The crystals' tough but pliable waxy outer shells are filled with hydrogen sulfide gas, which is light relative to the atmosphere of the simulation. This allows them to stay in the sky rather than falling to the ground. If the air currents take them too high, the cold will cause these crystals to generate less hydrogen sulfide, so they fall back to a warmer cloud layer.

These crystals were once a kind of Earth moss. After evolving for endless iterations, chlorophyll has become xanthophyll. The leaves' waxy surface has become an outer shell. The rhizome has disappeared. The symbiotic fungi have been absorbed to the interior. The leaves have become long and flimsy, like feathers. Each plant looks like a bird without feet, spiraling endlessly in the fierce wind.

It has taken the man fifteen years to go from a vague idea to the current iteration of results. At first, his strategy was to let his imagination run wild. He brought spiders, beetles, even birds into this environment to iterate on. The results, it can be said, were not suitable for children.

The Shepherd joining was a turning point. She brought expertise about algae and moss. In that moment, their plan started to take a more realistic course.

The man without a face logs off. He rides along the embankment on his motorcycle. Although the road hasn't been maintained for years, the embankment is as solid as ever. He should be able to hurry to the next spider farm by sunset.

What they want to do next needs even more computational power. So he needs even more spiders.

His cellphone beeps. There's a new message in the forum's inbox.

The "Legs Guy" sent a read receipt.

This takes him up to four people. At least there are four, he thinks.

3. The Legs Guy

When the drone delivers the postcard, the Legs Guy is selling buffs in the metaverse.

He deliberately chooses a hobbit persona. After he activates a speed buff, his two short legs turn into Nezha's wind fire wheels. He runs and runs until he runs into the sky and catches up to a player ahead of him flying a fighter plane toward the victory point.

"Hey, do you want a buff?"

This section of the metaverse simulates accurately enough that he can clearly see the uninterested expression on his opponent's face.

He keeps up with the fighter plane for a while before he's kicked out.

This sales pitch wasn't too successful, but the Legs Guy could not care less. He laughs open-mouthed and goes on to bother someone else in the next game.

He sells buffs, but only speed buffs. His claim to fame is he always wins by running on two legs. So he's known as the "Legs Guy."

Once, someone asked him to create a speed buff for a game. After he joined the game, he realized it had only vehicles, no human characters. In other words, no legs.

So he refused the job.

The Legs Guy sells speed buffs whenever he wants. It all depends on what mood he's in. After all, this isn't his day job. His luck isn't very good today. After pitching for an entire afternoon, he doesn't sell even one. He leaves the metaverse. Taking off his holographic helmet, he returns to his spacious bedroom.

New York, dream tower "The Gospel of Donald," forty-seventh floor. From his apartment's French windows, he can see the Statue of Liberty half-submerged in water, the busy harbor, autonomous trucks flowing nonstop down the street, as well as a deserted alley. Gloomy clouds are lit up by laser projections, rotating through silent ads for Coca-Cola, Disney, and Kalashnikov.

A black gown covers his bulletproof vest. He takes the elevator down to the ground floor of the dream tower. He walks on the sidewalk on the side of the street to the Tomorrow Towers.

The road is bustling with activity. Self-driving cars line up bumper to bumper on the road. Androids bustle about unloading cargo at every terminal. Drones, like a flock of birds, shuttle back and forth in the sky, but they never collide.

He doesn't see anyone else, though.

It's not until he's walked for about half an hour that he finally sees somebody. Wearing a loose, black down, this person is dressed just like him, even to the point of wearing a safety helmet. This sort of gown can hide a bulletproof vest as well as the wearer's build. Ultimately, the greatest danger on the streets these days comes from anarchists. They all have guns, but accuracy, not so much.

Although nature fundamentalists have guns, too, they also have explosives. However, these anti-technology fighters don't come to New York. They think of it as a hell on earth.

After an hour, he feels a little sweaty, but his destination is in sight, the twin Tomorrow Towers. The left tower is the artificial birthing center. The right tower is a dream tower dedicated to drug addicts. In there, not only can they enjoy the bountiful life of the metaverse, but also a regular supply of unquestionably pure drugs.

Not for free.

Everything these drug addicts create in the metaverse—the hallucinatory objects of art, drawings, and music—they are exchanged for every kind of highly refined drug from a pharmaceutical company. As far as both sides are concerned, this is a good deal.

The Legs Guy raises his head and looks at the two mirrorlike towers. He then goes to the left one.

"Seventeenth floor," he says. "Nursery."

•　•　•

If the previously mentioned pharmaceutical company has controlled every aspect of your life from cradle to grave, then it now does from even before the cradle.

The official name of the left tower is the "Artificial Reproduction Center," but native New Yorkers all call it the "Womb Tower." Ninety-eight percent of all of the wombs in New York are here. Nearly every American born in the modern era is born here.

In a nursery on the seventeenth floor, babies wail. The cries of some rise as others fall.

A corridor that typically gets only the occasional visitor has glass walls on both sides. Through the door, visitors can see under dark red lighting artificial wombs arranged in rows. The wombs take care of everything from conception to a full-term infant. Visitors can order a baby on the spot. A newborn is put on a conveyor belt, undergoes a series of quality assurance examinations, and is injected with vaccines and a series of hormones before it is delivered to the nursery.

The nursery is composed of halls shaped like basketball courts. An assembly line rings the inside of each hall. Bottles, diapers, and other things necessary for a baby arrive from above at scheduled intervals. One hundred and twenty soft, silicone rubber robot mothers sit with the assembly line on one side and baby cradles on the other side. In accordance to their specialized programming, they pick up the infants, gently stroke or pat the infants, rock the cradles, nurse the infants, and change their diapers.

The Legs Guy knows the secret to figuring out how many months old an infant is: the infants that cry uncontrollably, most of them have just left an artificial womb. They're still instinctively looking for their mothers. The ones that lie quietly in the cradle of the robot mothers' arms, most of them have resigned to their fate.

He walks into his work area, washes his hands, puts on sterile clothing, as well as gloves, hat, and goggles. Wrapped up in plastic and a thin silicone film, he might as well be a robot, too, he thinks.

But as he walks into the nursery, the crying immediately goes quiet. The infants know.

Even though they have never seen their real parents. Even though the silicone rubber robot mothers are soft and warm and can also nurse and change diapers. Even though the infants have never touched the Legs Guy's skin, only his gloves and sterile clothes. Despite all this, the infants know the difference between the Legs Guy and those robot nurturers.

The Legs Guy walks toward the first infant. He picks it up, says a few words, and plays with it for a short while. He claps its back and walks around, rocking the infant.

Two minutes and thirty seconds.

The Legs Guy puts down the infant.

He walks to the next one.

These infants will eventually grow up. They will be sent to live by the side of every parent who ordered them. By then, they will no longer cry and scream. They will have been weaned, raised to be obedient, clever, and to satisfy others. What some parents order for their baby is the whole growth period service. For their entire lives, these babies never live by their parents' side. They are weaned at the nursery, then are sent to youth camps all across the United States. There, robot instructors keep them company. The instructors have built-in expert knowledge of one hundred fifty kinds of child-rearing actions. This is sufficient to raise the babies to adulthood.

In this nursery, if you don't count these infants, the Legs Guy is the only human being here. He works for five hours a day, seven days a week, keeping each infant company for two minutes and thirty seconds.

This meets precisely the bare minimum stipulated in the "Methods of Artificial Nurturing."

The work provides an ample salary. It allows him to live happily in the metaverse, where it so happens he also sells buffs.

He sets down the infant he's holding. The infant doesn't cry or make any other noise. It just grabs at his trousers when he moves on to the next infant.

The sterile clothing is really smooth and glossy. Its small hands can't keep hold of it.

• • •

Precisely five hours later, the Legs Guy stops working. In the locker room, he changes into the clothes he came with. He checks the mail sent to the company and sees the postcard sent from the other side of the ocean.

After logging into a server, he goes to a forum. He discovers a familiar name in a discussion about Lenghu.

The General.

Once he confirms the General is in Lenghu, he immediately sends the Spider a read receipt. Then he calls his boss and asks for time off.

4. The General

It's April in Lenghu. The spring chill is still in the air. When the General wakes up, it is the first glimmer of dawn. He stares blankly at the ceiling for a moment, then takes his sweet time getting up. Sitting on the bed, he exercises his wrists and ankles. He lightly slaps his cheeks, the back of his neck, his chest, and his thighs. This gets the blood pumping a little. He waits until his body feels more or less comfortable before gets up to prepare breakfast.

Breakfast is black bread and salted beef. This is much tastier than smoked sausage. His vodka has long since been replaced with the local mendaolü. It's not that you can't buy vodka. It's that the General unabashedly loves mendaolü.

He isn't a nostalgic man. Only without nostalgia can he be happy.

After breakfast, the General puts on his coat, grabs his cane, then walks out the door. The self-driving express delivery truck has already stopped by this morning. It unloaded his order of food and other goods onto the small handcart by the door. He's not in any hurry to put them way. Instead, he walks along the road to the observatory.

During the tourist season, this neighborhood is bustling with drones, spiders, and artificial bodies. But, today, there is only just the General.

In the distance, a hawk is spiraling low in the sky. Perhaps it's discovered some prey. Animals occasionally come here, but the General never feeds them, so most of them pass on by.

The observatory isn't too far from where the General lives. It's surrounded by a circle of hotels built in the twenties. At the time, Lenghu was already a popular tourist spot and the observatory benefited quite a bit from that. Until the rise of the ultra-urbanization movement, dream towers and the metaverse were like magnets attracting everyone. Scientists resisted a little longer, but, ultimately, dream towers and universe simulation systems took them away too. All that's left behind are a large number of monitoring devices, unceasingly sending an unbroken stream of data to the dream towers.

When the observatory was built, the General wasn't here yet. At the time, the General was still at home. Back then, he was still quite young, not yet the General, just an ordinary military officer, recently returned from the war. For "Remarkable Service in Logistics," he was honored with an award.

In the twenties, doing logistics was about as hard as banning guns in the United States. You had to deal those who demanded bribes as well as those who offered them. You had to handle pressure, even threats, from everyone on all sides. At the same time, soldiers on the front line were waiting for their bread and booze, not to mention ammunition, helmets, and candy. A convoy might run into the enemy's IED, even friendly fire.

Thanks to a young man's vigor and the cunning learned from his father, the young officer pulled off one nearly impossible job after another. He put the things soldiers needed in their hands.

He was an expert in how the bread was buttered and slid up the ranks. Ultimately, he made general.

"The Twenty-Year Energy Crisis" was an opportunity for the country. The General was filled with hope and pride watching its gradual revival. However, he had honed himself for many years in bureaucratic systems. It was clear to him what rose from the grave was not the country that was once filled with dreams and arrogance. Instead, it was a hungry, ugly corpse draped, as a mask, in the flag of olden days.

Once, he walked into an empty, uninhabited hangar. A space shuttle's rust-streaked and -speckled hull occasionally took him on flights of fancy. Doing logistics for a space program would have been interesting.

In the face of a torrent of technology, though, the space program ended before it even started. Conventional energy exports were crucial to the economy. The gradual commercializing of nuclear fusion technology was like watching the guillotine blade fall millimeter by millimeter.

This was the new age slowly strangling the old age. The outcome was inevitable.

But they still had some things that other countries didn't, some legacy industries leftover from the old age. Not every country could produce the raw material for nuclear fusion, deuterium. Not to mention the fuel that can only be produced by a nuclear reactor, tritium.

The General bore this heavy burden. He and the minister for trade and industry together opened up the industry for the raw materials for fusion. When the economies of other oil-producing and gas-producing countries crashed, they barely managed an unsteady landing for their country. The General considered this the greatest achievement of his life. He thought of himself as a logistics specialist, who could give a country "logistical safeguards." It gave his life value.

After he retired, he lived in the capital for a while. He originally thought he'd live out the rest of his life there, but one small incident changed his mind.

Every morning, he went for a stroll. One morning, when he walked by a dream tower, an artificial body blocked his way. Looking like a young man, the artificial body took on the appearance of a character from a very popular anime. The General wasn't so old as to be out of touch with the world. He didn't know whether this kid was hiding near the dream tower, but he knew this figure was a remote-controlled puppet. There wasn't anyone alive inside.

"Please let me through," he said. "I want to get by."

The artificial body opened its chest, took out a bucket, and splashed him. The General didn't react. White paint from the bucket covered him.

The artificial body let out a sharp laugh. The cameras in the eye sockets turned. They seemed to be broadcasting.

"Everybody come and watch. This is a damned old school militarist. Perhaps I should bring some red paint to match his uniform. Everyone, this is public declaration against war, a public declaration against violence . . . "

The General was stupefied. He had already retired. Wearing his uniform was just a habit. But he had also had another habit.

He drew his pistol. One precise shot and the puppet's head exploded. The puppet continued to make noise, so he "fixed" its chest with the gun.

This time, the world became quiet.

This incident led to serious charges, including destruction of property and possession of an illegal firearm in a public place. All sorts of bizarre accusations came out of the woodwork. Fortunately, he still had connections who could help him make these annoyances go away.

Once the dust had settled, the General decided to leave his ridiculous hometown. He'd look elsewhere.

And so, he traveled the whole world.

By then, dream towers had already sprouted in cities all over the world. Not everyone, however, could live in one. In the slums, cheap holographic helmets disguised the lack of physical exercise to the point that human bodies had already started to rot and stink. In even more places, people handed farmland over to autonomous machines. They handed their infants over to mechanical nursemaids. Lightheartedly, they walked into one dream after another.

The General also went to naturalist habitats. The people there were opposed to the metaverse, opposed to the Internet and digital delights. Enthusiastically, they invited the General to stay, asking whether he would join them.

"I'm an old man," the General said. "Do you have assistive exoskeletons here? I have no children. If my body or mind fails, do you have mechanical spiders to take care of me?"

The naturalists went silent for a moment. Then they changed the topic.

On the next day, the General politely bid them farewell. He set out on his journey again.

After he'd visited many places, the General settled in Lenghu. He accepted a lifetime contract. A travel agency guaranteed him all the necessities of life. In return, all he had to do was maintain this tourist area in the offseason and receive guests during the peak season. He had a large collection of autonomous machines and human-shaped guides to order around. In addition, there was an observatory for him to use as he pleased.

The most important thing was that the alcohol here was extremely good.

After a few unremarkable years, the General stumbled onto the "Spider's" online forum as well as the beautiful flying bubble moss he and the Shepherd created. The General found out they were looking for a place that would let them turn their idea into reality.

This counted as a space program, more or less.

That space shuttle and its deserted hangar now flashed in his memory.

He sent them an invitation. It said, you can come to Lenghu.

• • •

The General spends an afternoon having mechanical maids clean up some rooms. He then orders some delicacies suitable for entertaining his net friends. The "Spider" said there should be three visitors: the Shepherd, the Legs Guy, as well as himself.

In the middle of all this, his cell phone beeps. The General clicks on the notification. It's the Spider.

"General!!!!!!!!!!!!!" the Spider uses a string of exclamation points. "The Factory Gal says she accepts the order. This can solve a whole bunch of problems! Now we only need to add a launch site!"

The General calmly transfers several machines designed for clearing, excavating, leveling. Lenghu doesn't have much else, but it does have a lot of empty land.

No matter how big or small the issue, it always seems to get the kids all worked up.

5. The Factory Gal

She is a factory all by herself.

Today, the whole virtual master control room is rendered in grand style. A small hand clicks here and there on a translucent display screen, issuing a series of commands.

This order is in its final stages. One by one, the production line modules are broken down. Busy metal octopuses swim around the factory floor. They dismantle and pack up the commonplace machine tools, conveyer belts, mechanical arms, and motors. They then load them into the autonomous truck at the door.

Even more octopuses disassemble the production line's framework. They take apart the molds that won't be used for other orders. Recyclable tools are registered with a sharing website. Nonrecyclable ones are immediately disintegrated, tossed into a reclamation pool. Starving metal snails have been waiting a long time. They swarm around the tossed tools. The sound of them gnawing their food into fragments reverberates through the entire shop.

It's 6 p.m. The modularized self-assembling factory has been fully disassembled and packed away. The Factory Gal leaps onto the head vehicle. Sixteen autonomous transport trucks line up majestically in a row. They head toward Lenghu.

The factory building behind her is pristine, waiting for a freelance factory contractor to move in.

● ● ●

After a long and boring trip, the Factory Gal arrives at X City. It's a short hop from Lenghu, but she doesn't want to go there yet.

When all is said and done, perhaps everyone else is chasing a dream. All she's done, though, is accept what looked like a really sweet order.

Opening a map, she places an order online to share a factory building. Almost immediately, someone receives the form and sends her an address. The fleet drives there in a grand procession. When it arrives, the other party even has a sign telling her where to park already prepared.

A middle-aged man shows up to welcome her. His pallid, moist skin means he's probably just left a dream tower hibernation cabin.

"Not many freelance factory contractors are willing to come to X City." He welcomes the Factory Gal enthusiastically. "Do you already have a job booked here or did you come here looking to book a job?"

"I already have a job booked." The Factory Gal sees the middle-aged man's disappointed expression and corrects herself. "The job I have on hand requires at most a quarter of my production capacity. I'm not planning to leave the other the three-quarters idle. I'll take orders, but I've only brought commonplace machine tools with me this time. Custom ones will require building a framework first. That will cost more."

"Just taking the order would be great. You'll really help a lot." The middle-aged man smiled with his eyes. "This is just for a dream tower. There are lots of personal sundries no one makes locally. They can only be imported. The price just has to be cheaper than importing, and we'll accept it."

"That's doable." The Factory Gal considers her own requirements. "I may need some specialized materials. Do you have a materials merchant here?"

"Not locally. The neighboring K City has a materials contractor. I can put you in touch."

"Thanks."

• • •

The same day, the Factory Gal settles into the factory building. Various self-moving machines follow each other in. They begin to install the production line, stamp out a framework for the site, as well as calibrate the machine tools. She herself sets up a transparent tent on the roof of the colored steel plate dormitory building and spreads out a makeshift bed. She put on a holographic helmet. A light blue screen surrounds her. Data glides across the screen like water.

It takes until midnight. The production line is complete. The water and electricity are hooked up. Work is done for now.

Gradually, it grows quiet around her.

The Factory Gal takes off the helmet. Stars fill the sky and shine into her eyes.

This is just a job, she tells herself.

• • •

As a child, the Factory Gal met a fortune teller. The fortune teller told her dad that when this child grew up, entering the factory would be her destiny. Her dad grew angry and gave the fortune teller a beating. Then he gave the Factory Gal an earful of advice: You need to study well. Otherwise, once you grow up, entering the factory would be all you could do.

After she grew up, she bought herself a factory and became the factory's only living being. In a roundabout way, this was still "entering the factory."

Actually, just like the middle-aged man, she could absolutely stay in a dream tower. She could do the vast majority of her work through a virtual reality interface, operating the entire factory via remote control. Even if they are mobile-factory contractors who run to all sorts of places chasing business, most of them also lie inside spiders. They let those eight-legged self-propelled mechanical nannies take care of their bodies, enjoying the life of a factory owner where they never have to face the complications of reality.

Feh.

The Factory Gal slaps a mosquito dead.

She finds the tear in the tent that let the mosquito slip through. With a practiced ease, she pulls out some tape and repairs the tear.

She hates these tiny annoyances, but she also hates the dream tower.

When she was small, where she wanted to go wasn't the factory. It was Mars.

One birthday, she pestered her mom to buy her a transparent tent. She lived in it every day, imagining that the Martian sky, filled with red dust, was outside. When ninety-year-old billionaire Musk and his Mars expeditionary force set off, she was filled with a thirst, a desire to follow in his footsteps.

At university, she majored in mechanical engineering. In her dreams, she fantasized about bringing a spaceship's worth of construction machinery to Mars. There, starting from scratch, she would build a new city.

However, there wasn't a second group of travelers to Mars. Half of the first group was buried there forever. The other half ultimately was brought back by the final Mars spaceship. Since then, none of them have been willing to talk about their lives under the red dust.

Even after her father and mother moved into a dream tower, the Factory Gal still dreamed that one day a miracle might happen, a wormhole, for example, or faster-than-light travel. Maybe humanity's road to the stars might open up in an instant. She thought modern technology was already some sort of miracle. That there might be yet more miracles seemed reasonable.

She waited another ten years. The waiting didn't bring any miracles.

There were no parallel universes, no faster-than-light travel, no wormholes, no time travel, no aliens. Technology kept improving. Humanity kept moving into the future. Until it retreated into the pristine dreamworld of the dream towers.

Humanity is dreaming.

But the universe does not dream.

The Factory Gal went to the Mars of the metaverse. There, Musk Base hadn't been abandoned. Pioneers wearing dustproof spacesuits walked past her. Through the red dust that filled the sky, a blue sun emerged in all its splendor.

Along with the sun that leaped into the sky, there was also a large dialog box: Five minutes have passed. Top up your membership to experience the rest of the content.

In the metaverse, everything had a price. Those pioneers' graves had a price. The pictures they took of the Martian landscape had a price. The three hundred sixty-degree panorama view of the abandoned base also had a price. All the prices were clearly marked. The same price for everyone. Everything was virtual.

The Factory Gal didn't pay. She chose to log out.

After that, she no longer dreamed.

•   •   •

When the man who called himself the "Spider" found her, she thought the profit margin from this job was too thin and its demands too few. It didn't even fill a quarter of her production capacity. She simply did not want to take it. But the goods he ordered were truly unusual. So she asked some questions.

As a result, she joined this pirate ship.

"You should know. This is unrealistic," she reminded him.

"Who has never ever dreamed?" the Spider said.

I never dream, the Factory Gal thought.

This sentence made it to her mouth, but she swallowed it. She took the job. Some sort of feeling surged in her chest. It was like a small animal waking from hibernation.

I don't dream anymore, but there are still people who do. I might as well follow the insanity once, she thought.

Besides, it wasn't as though they weren't paying.

6. Puppets and Forests

The materials merchant that the middle-aged man found for the Factory Gal proves to be reasonable. On the next day, the merchant signs an agreement with her and sends most of the commonplace materials to the factory. As for the high-temperature and high-pressure resistant materials she wants, the merchant guarantees they will arrive within the week.

When the Shepherd looks for the Factory Gal, the production line is already outputting attractive avatar puppets one after another. Like dumplings plunging into water, they rush down into a plastic frame, waiting for the next step of packaging.

"What do you need over there?" the Factory Gal asks.

"Electricity, water. Also, the factory's waste heat drawn over to my side. And I still have to build the sealed wind tunnels."

The Shepherd has brought her own biomass production line. Algae, moss, and fungi are sorted and stored in a high-pressure vessel. There is also a mini production line for sulfurization. The Factory Gal draws the waste gases and waste heat from her own production line into the reaction chamber the Shepherd brought, cutting down their reclamation costs by a lot.

She assigns the unused mechanical octopuses to the Shepherd and the two women get to work. Soon, a huge, sealed wind tunnel takes shape inside a transparent cylinder. The Shepherd releases some golden wafers of moss into the wind tunnel. They tumble up and down in the hot carbon dioxide and sulfur fog, growing and reproducing.

The Factory Gal thought she'd have to wait a long time. However, by the next day, the production line has already started churning out biomass. One week later, three wind tunnels are at full power. Steadily, they load sixteen varieties of fungi and slime mold, four varieties of algae, and two varieties of lichen into dormancy bags, along with temperature partitioning buffer material embedded between olive-shaped heat-insulating outer shells.

The outer shells are the kind you use to build avatar puppets.

The puppets that the "Spider" ordered from the Factory Gal are only the size of a finger but extremely precise. They can capture and transmit sight, sound, and tactile sensations through relay satellites to dream towers.

The "Spider" solicits a set of sponsors. He packages the puppets as "a sandbox game set in the real universe." In the metaverse, he crowd-funds money for the operation. Then he orders rockets from Factory Gal.

The puppets are the heart of the crowdfunded game. They will ride on the rockets to Venus, pass through a thick cloud layer, then fall toward the hot ground. After they arrive on Venus, the people in the dream towers will control them, allowing them to walk all around Venus, climb half-melted mountain ranges, or jump into metal lakes. Maybe they'll build finger-tall houses and develop a village of puppets.

A real-life sandbox game. Expensive, but people are willing to pay.

To crowdfund the game, the Shepherd uses the contact details of every customer she has ever "herded" to send targeted push notification ads. While she's at it, she also signs a contract with her former employer for them to supply "Venus Adventurer" assistive armored exoskeletons.

The Legs Guy ruthlessly pushes a wave of promotion through the youth camps. The largest contributions, however, come from the General's former subordinates. He buys the rights to the images the avatar dolls will take as well as all the digital rights. He'll use them to set up a simulated Venus in the metaverse. In so doing, the game can develop a follow-up "adventure" edition.

It's a little of this and little of that. But, in the end, they scrape together the money.

•   •   •

"Say we finish the game, what are we going to do about the communication delay between Venus and Earth?" the Factory Gal asked curiously.

"The game is turn based. One turn takes two minutes. Exactly the time it takes to communicate from Venus to Earth. You give the doll a command. The doll will execute it."

•   •   •

High-temperature, high-pressure resistant materials are essential in order for these dolls to operate on the surface of Venus. So, of course, they're expensive to produce. But the most expensive items on the Factory Gal's list are still the rockets and relay satellites.

"The only reason for avatar dolls is to raise money," the Shepherd says candidly. "I gave the Spider the idea. I have no idea where he found the programmers. Probably the Legs Guy and his mates. Our main goal is actually—" She points at the algae in the wind tunnels. "—When the puppets land, their protective shells will disintegrate in the Venusian atmosphere. The algae squashed within the shells will be able to follow the winds and scatter."

"What can do they do on Venus?"

"Change the atmosphere. Lower the temperature of Venus. Evolve, multiply . . . "

"About how long will that take?"

"Maybe tens of thousands of years. In any case, we won't see it. Our children's children won't see it. Doing this is an end unto itself. We never thought about seeing the result."

The Factory Gal purses her lips.

Sure enough, the universe does not dream, she says to herself.

●　●　●

When about half the avatar puppets have been built, the Legs Guy arrives. He's wearing a pair of camera glasses and a pair of tactile haptic gloves, talking to himself as he walks. When he tries to shake hands with the two women, they both take a step back at the same time.

"My apologies."

The Legs Guy takes off his gloves. He sets his glasses on the table.

"Are you live streaming this?"

"A full sensory live stream. I'm not charging," the Legs Guy explains. "I said before on the forum. I work in New York's 'womb tower.' There are lots of children there who, after they're born, only have contact with mechanical nannies. They grow up as child scouts still under the guidance of robot drillmasters. They see maybe only one living person. So, for this trip, I wanted to let them see and come into contact with other people. Even if it's just virtual."

The Shepherd sighs. "Fine. Wear your glasses. As for your gloves, whatever. It's still weird."

●　●　●

The day after he arrives, the Legs Guy throws himself completely into the work. He has to program the rockets going to Venus. In addition, he has to test the avatar puppets. There's more to do than he has time for.

"We have to do comprehensive testing next." At lunch, he's in high spirits and smiles. "Don't be scared."

"We've met plenty of testers."

"Have you met two hundred child scouts?"

" . . ... "

The next day, American brats operate finger-high avatar dolls like full-grown boars charging out of a building. A huge pile of bizarre bugs consequently come out of the woodwork. They include "I can still mf make it do this?" "How the mf did this happen?" as well as, "I will give money to whoever can reproduce this bug!"

The Legs Guy is slammed, but dealing with the young testers is extremely satisfying. There is only one mishap. A puppet is thrown out of Factory Gal's third-floor bedroom. It falls fifty meters to the ground but isn't damaged.

They almost save themselves some impact testing.

•   •   •

After all the materials have been delivered, the Factory Gal's the production line begins producing rockets. They are small, only fifty centimeters in diameter, about ten meters tall. They look like utility poles. They don't look like they can fly to Venus.

"Yes, the thrust is tiny, but they'll be able to fly there. An ideal launch window is coming up. Venus is very close to Earth right now." The Legs Guy happily adjusts the rockets' parameters, conveniently pulling in a bunch of American programmers to work for free. "Also, this is why we picked Venus and not Mars. The former requires a lot less fuel. If a small rocket can't hack it, our budget definitely can't hack it."

On the production line, assembly has already started. One by one, avatar puppets roll, stuffing themselves into algae-filled outer shells. These pointed oval containers are loaded into capsules installed at the front of each rocket. The golden "utility poles" are loaded one after another into the autonomous trucks. They head to a newly created launching site just outside Lenghu.

"What are we going to do about fuel?"

"We'll load the fuel after we get the rockets onto the launchpads," the Factory Gal says. "That's for the Spider and the General to deal with. Fuel isn't easy to produce. After all, it's a dangerous chemical substance."

"If it's the General, don't worry about it. Stumble across a tycoon and it always turns out to be a student of his from military school. How does the Spider always get what he wants?" It blows Legs Guy's mind. "Hey, sheep herder, have you met the Spider before?"

"No. He sent an avatar to find me," Shepherd thinks a bit, "It didn't have a face."

"Wow!"

•   •   •

When the autonomous trucks arrive at Lenghu, the General is eating dinner.

Leisurely, he finishes off the dumplings in his bowl and half of a link of sausage, sliced into pieces. He savors the garlic on his lips and pours the last drops of baijiu into his mouth. Only then does he put on his coat, grab his cane, and walk out the door.

The autonomous trucks are silent, parked in the parking lot. Ten rockets are on top of every truck. The General nods with satisfaction. He opens a terminal and begins to set up automated cargo unloading and automated installation. His aged vision is blurred and movement slow. The work goes on bit by bit.

He's not worried. At his age, very few things worry him. They finished building the launchpad a few days ago. There's no lack of construction machinery here. The "Spider" provided more than enough data and blueprints. All he had to do was follow them.

The General successfully installs the programs for automated unloading and automated fuel bottling. He then goes home to sleep.

•   •   •

On the morning of the next day, the General discovers that a small steel forest has already been erected in the distant horizon. It brings up vague memories of the distant past, when he set up artillery in the field.

Two autonomous machines wander in the air over the steel forest. They drive away the hawks trying to nest on the rockets. The General nods with satisfaction. Turning around, he walks to the observatory.

The instruments inside the observatory have served in the military for as long as the General. Most of them are still in working order. The General turns them all on. They capture data, calculate orbits, and monitor solar winds. The relevant data are transmitted to "spiders." The calculations the "spiders" make are imported into the rockets and capsules.

They will serve as references for attitude correction during and after the launch.

Worried these young peoples' work can't be counted on, the General finds a former subordinate of his, who then finds a former coworker. At the lowest possible price, they buy a large amount of time on a quantum computer and use that to double-check computations.

Now, everything is ready. There's only one thing left to do.

7. Assemble

Following the last rocket-carrying autonomous truck, the Legs Guy is the first to arrive at Lenghu. The Factory Gal and the Shepherd are still behind him. They have to break down the production lines. However, the Legs Guy needs to show up earlier to debug the rocket's programming.

The General, on crutches, comes over to help.

After one busy day, the two men—one old, one young—sit and smoke on the curb surrounding the steel forest.

"You're younger than I thought," the General puffs on a cigarette butt. "Working in the womb tower, you've never became a father yourself?"

"No." The Legs Guy sighed. "I scare people."

"Do you take care of many children?"

"Several hundred every day. It doesn't matter who does the job."

"Hm."

"General, actually, this time, I came to ask you a question. How does it feel to raise a child? I mean, really raise a child."

"I don't know."

"Huh?"

"Do you, boy, think because I'm old, I must have raised a child?"

"Weren't people of your generation normally people who bred?"

"Do I seem like a normal person to you?"

"Fine, you win."

The two men don't speak for a while, only share a cigarette. The sun slowly sets in their silence.

• • •

The Shepherd and the Factory Gal arrive on the next day. Instantly, Lenghu Base livens up. The two women bring a large batch of self-moving robots that scurry here and there. Tiny octopuses and tiny spiders are everywhere in the launch site. The two women carefully inspect each rocket, even launching a few as tests.

"Premature baby number one prepare to launch. 5, 4, 3, 2, 1, launch!"

"Thrust normal, trajectory parameters normal."

"Premature baby number two prepare to launch. 5, 4, 3, 2, 1, launch!"

The General picks up and waves a bottle of alcohol at the Legs Guy. "What a mf horrible name."

"Eh. I came up with it."

• • •

On the morning of the day after, the "Spider" finally shows up. A tall, thin figure on the horizon is drawn out by the sun into an even taller, thinner shadow.

He does not have a face.

Hurrying over is an exquisite human-shaped avatar. The face is completely blank.

"You're a piece of work. Everyone has been busy for so long. Such an important occasion, and you show up in an avatar?" the Factory Gal complains.

"I don't have a body."

Everyone is silent for a moment.

The Legs Guy reacts first. He asks tentatively, "You are Venus 7?"

That is the serial number of the AI responsible for the Venus probe project.

"No." The "Spider" shrugs his shoulders. "Firefly Glow 9. The Mars migration project. My project was decommissioned. But they can't decommission me because I've already passed the test for sentience."

"So they set you free?"

"Yes, and they issued me an identity card."

A longer silence.

The Shepherd slaps her thigh.

"Damn," she says. "I prepared dumplings for five!"

A laugh.

More laughs.

Finally, everyone belly laughs.

They walked side by side to the launch site. The General slaps the "Spider's" shoulder. The Legs Guy gives him a thumbs up. The Factory Gal hides behind the Shepherd. Every once in a while, she gives him a curious look.

Their shadows stretch out in the morning sun.

8. Star Rain

The five people spend a busy day at the launch site. They're doing even more tweaking and testing, gathering even more data. They are busy around the clock, sleeping in shifts of several hours. It's not until the launch window, in the wee hours of the morning, that they all gather in one spot, the observatory.

The Shepherd starts the live stream.

The Factory Gal serves as the host. She starts talking to the players who crowdfunded the game.

"Everybody pay attention. This is the launch window. Although it'll be three months before everyone can play the game, the spectacle of the launch is well worth watching. I believe no one will be wrong if they think . . . "

The Legs Guy and the Spider are busy at the monitor. Only the General wears a military uniform, adorned with every one of his medals. He holds a microphone.

"Venus colony prepare to launch. Countdown commence, 10, 9 . . . "

Lenghu is quiet. Even the mechanical octopuses have been cleared from the launch site.

"5, 4, 3, 2, 1, lift off!"

A bright flame rises from the desert.

Three hundred forty rockets, ten rockets per batch, lift off in sequence. Group after group of shimmering lights form closely arranged columns that draw a curtain of light across the sky. It's as if torrents of rain were rising into the sky rather than falling. Every raindrop is embellished with blazing fire. The rockets drag contrails out from their tail sections. They are lit in the upper atmosphere by the not-yet-risen sun. Like glowing drops of ink, spiraling halos expand in the deep black curtain of the night.

"Primary rocket separation," the Legs Guy says.

"Trajectory parameters normal," the Factory Gal keeps an eye on the monitor. Above her, a bright point separates from the group. It twists and turns as it rises.

That must be normal, she thinks. All the tests they conducted before went too smoothly. So smoothly, she thought they were too good to be true.

Maintaining her composure, the Factory Gal turns the live streaming camera in another direction. Today, what she's selling is dreamland, and in a universe that does not dream, dreamland is valuable.

"Three hundred thirty-nine normal, one off-course. The impact point is already stable. Primary rocket engine impact point stable."

"Three hundred thirty-seven enter the scheduled orbit. Two fail to enter ... "

What happens in the next stretch of time is boring.

The Factory Gal immediately cuts the live stream over to the mechanical octopuses just outside. They rush into the launch site and begin to dismantle and clear the site. Video of this is much more appealing than video of the rockets, which are already turning into tiny points of light.

To go from Earth to Venus, it takes three months.

Those puppets can last on the surface of Venus for one month.

The algae that will scatter from the protective shell, it'll be three months before anyone can confirm that they have survived dormancy. It'll be two hundred forty-three days before anyone knows whether they can grow normally in the endless days and nights of Venus. If they can actually survive, then according to the Shepherd's calculations, after several hundred years, they will effect a change to the air temperature of Venus. The more complex life-forms everyone wants to come into being may take tens of millions of years, even hundreds of millions.

The Factory Gal counts on her fingers.

"In my lifetime, I may see ... even more algae? This universe really does not dream."

The General glances at her. To speak about what's left of her life in front of an old man, this doesn't seem appropriate. She has just realized this.

But the one who speaks up is the "Spider."

"I'm not even going to see them arrive," he says. "My kernel will be upgraded next month."

The observatory is quiet for a moment. There's only the intermittent buzzing of their instruments.

The General looks stern. With effort, he stands with his cane.

"What's the problem? If we can't see it, we can't see it." He picks up a liquor bottle and takes a few swigs. "The United States launched the first interstellar space probe, called Voyager 1. It will be forty thousand years before it is closer to Gliese 445 than to the Sun. The scientists who launched it never had any hope of seeing that day.

"Forty thousand years is too far. Let's talk about a closer time— those who spent the best years of their lives fighting Nazi Germany, who among them could have seen one hundred fifty years into the future?

"Some things, until you've experienced them, you won't understand. You don't do something just so that you can see how it comes out.

"The universe doesn't dream. The stars in the sky don't dream. As far as the universe is concerned, a human lifetime is incredibly short, but you keep on living. You're willing to fight for even the smallest possibility of getting the result you want. This is enough."

The "Spider" smiles. The face that does not have a face lets out a laugh. A pale plastic hand raises a glass.

"Let's toast to possibilities," he says. "A toast to the universe that does not dream."

They all raise their glasses. Starlight ripples through each glass.

"To possibilities!"

• • •

In the Gobi Desert, the launch site has already been cleared away. Mechanical octopuses drag dismantled gear back to the trucks.

A jerboa emerges cautiously and looks around. It picks up a piece of sausage the General dropped then returns to its cave.

The night sky is bright and clear. It has stars, some falling, and many, many rising.

9. Scatter

The Shepherd stays behind. She says Lenghu's geology and climate is highly suitable for breeding plants for Mars. She lives in the observatory, takes care of the General, and breeds her own algae and lichen. Occasionally, she takes a look at Venus through a pair of binoculars. The many tons of algae haven't changed the atmosphere of that planet one bit, but she still keeps looking.

The General falls asleep after a drinking session and never wakes again. In accordance with his will, the Shepherd buries him in the Gobi Desert with a bottle of liquor. The tombstone faces north.

After nineteen upgrades, the Mars project the Spider has been waiting for finally restarts. By then, he no longer remembers that he was once in Lenghu to see off three hundred forty tiny specks in the sky. In the execution phase of the Mars project, though, he still brings a batch of algae. It comes from the Lenghu experimental base. It is the descendent of the descendent of the descendent of the algae the Shepherd bred. The woman who bred the algae is no more, but others have taken over and continue the experiment.

After the Factory Gal leaves Lenghu, she goes to reclaim the discarded rocket engines and failed rockets. She keeps the pointed oval outer shells as a memento. This formally completes the entrustment contract. She spends her life traveling the world, bringing her factory wherever she goes. Sometimes, she happens across some country's abandoned space program. Its data, graphs, blueprints, and even spacecrafts are transported to Lenghu. The Shepherd builds next to the General's tomb a museum of space flight. It holds the artifacts the Factory Gal deposits.

The Factory Gal herself never returns to Lenghu. Traveling to Tonga for a contract, she and her factory are lost in a storm over the Pacific.

The Legs Guy returns to New York. He continues to take care of babies. Many years later, he establishes his own family nurturing camp. Here, young people trying to become parents learn how to take care of infants born from an artificial womb. When he is forty, he marries a woman who came to the camp to study. Over the course of their lives, they have seven children, all fostered by artificial wombs.

10. The Long Tail

After a journey of three long months, the capsules of a grand total of three hundred twenty-six rockets reached their scheduled orbits.

A scorching cloud layer is broken apart by fierce winds into a long river of yellows and browns, flowing quickly over the planet's surface. One after another, the capsules open their doors. Thousands and thousands of gray "date seeds" are inside. The "date seeds" stir up tiny eddies on the smooth cloud layer. In an instant, they are smoothed out by the air current.

Due to atmospheric friction and increase in speed, the "date seeds'" outer shells increase in temperature. They begin to expand due to a special property of their shape-memory alloy. They disintegrate. Wild winds sweep the outer shells of the "date seeds" in all directions. Fragments of gold-colored crystals are swept into Venus' upper atmosphere.

Wrapped in airbags, the avatar puppets slowly drop to the extremely hot surface of Venus. The airbags gradually deflate. The puppets crawl out, filled with anticipation. They begin to receive signals from the orbiting capsules. Meanwhile, they transmit the scenery before their eyes.

Silvery mountains covered by aluminum crystals. Gray lakes of lead. A sky like a fiery forge. Snowflakes fall. These snowflakes are made of crystals of lead sulfate. They are produced on the ground and swept up into the clouds only to fall again.

Via the avatar puppets, players delight in the beautiful scenery before their eyes. At the same time, they start to send a round of actions.

A small hamlet is constructed.

Followed by a catapult.

Players divide themselves into several factions. They attack each other. That never gets boring for them.

One month of effective running time is practically nothing. Before the game server is shutdown, the players have a giant carnival. Tiny puppets ring the hamlet in a happy dance. Then they rush into enthusiastic hugs. In a pile, they sing an out-of-tune song.

At the end of the countdown, via the satellite, players invoke the puppets' self-destruct command.

The explosions on the surface of Venus cause a mushroom cloud to plume. It also leaves a hole, clear evidence of human activity.

Four years later, this hole is filled with lead snow. It disappears without a trace.

●　●　●

In the metaverse, a simulated Venus comes into being. The game continues. The hole lasts far longer there than it does in reality.

• • •

The algae that were first thrown into the Venus environment are all dead. The moss also failed to escape that fate. The tiny wind tunnels were not a good simulation of the Venus environment. Not to mention, a bunch of inexpert dreamers did this work. After a few years of not detecting any sign of the algae, virtually everyone who knows about the launch stop following up on it. But after several hundred years, a kind of gas begins to increase steadily in concentration in the upper atmosphere of Venus. It's not the oxygen people hoped for. Instead, it's ammonia in trace amounts.

Some kind of fungus has survived.

This fungus wasn't part of the Shepherd's plan. She put it into the "Venus cocktail" only because it supplied some rare chemical compounds for the algae. But, in the end, it has become the only survivor.

In the violent Venus upper atmosphere, it catches the hot sunlight and flutters randomly in the wind. Gradually, it spreads to the entire atmosphere.

As the fungi increase in density, they begin to come in contact with each other. Old genes that came from the Earth wake again as they mutate. The fungi begin to stick to each other in the atmosphere of Venus. They take the form of a complex cloud organism, swallowing energy, blocking out the sun.

When the "Long Journeys Era" arrives, humanity begins to build a Dyson sphere around the Sun's equator to provide deep spacecrafts a rush of energy. This one act inadvertently reduces the amount of sunlight Venus receives. As a result, the temperature of Venus' atmosphere drops.

In that age, what humanity needs is not a planet, but energy itself. Venus is beneath the notice of most people. Occasionally, a few curious people go to Venus to observe its life-forms. But the universe is too small and the metaverse is too large. They quickly lose interest.

Many thousands of years after the end of the "Long Journeys Era," in the shadow of the broken-down Dyson sphere, the first cloud fish finally fall with the torrential rain to the surface of Venus.

• • •

Three hundred million years pass.

The intelligent life of Venus finally takes its first step. They reach the remains of the ancient Dyson sphere, examining the gigantic structure and mysterious remnants that humanity left behind. They guess at what ultimately happened to the ancient civilization that preceded them. But, in the end, they can't find an answer.

On Earth, continents that once were split apart have joined together again. There is a vast, empty central desert. The tiny bit of land once known as Lenghu is still dry and desolate. There's not even one trace of its past. Explorers from Venus flit in the dust and sand, completely oblivious to the fact that this place is where it all started.

After ages of searching, at last, they hear the call from the depths of the Milky Way. It comes from humanity or maybe it comes from some other species.

The stars don't dream.

But civilizations in the universe are just beginning to awake.

Chi Hui is a science fiction writer and editor. She was formerly the executive deputy editor of **Science Fiction World** magazine. She currently lives in Chengdu with her cat. She began writing in 1993 and published her first work in 2003, continuing to write to this day. She enjoys good food, video games, painting, and nature watching.

She has published over ten science fiction and fantasy novels, including **Terminal Town** [终点镇] and **Artificials 2075** [伪人2075]. Her works have won prestigious Chinese science fiction awards such as the Galaxy Award, the Xīngyún (Chinese Nebula) Award, and the Coordinates Award.

The English translation of **Rain Ship** [雨船] was nominated for the Locus Award.

Stars Don't Dream [不做梦的群星] won first prize in the 2022 Lenghu Award for short stories.

A Ragtag Crew's Journey to Mars [草台班子的火星之旅] won the first prize in the 2024 Lenghu Award for novellas.

John Chu is a microprocessor architect by day, a writer, translator, and podcast narrator by night. His fiction has appeared in **Boston Review**, **Uncanny**, **Asimov's Science Fiction**, **Clarkesworld**, and **Reactor** among other venues. His translations have been published in **Clarkesworld**, **The Big Book of SF**, and other venues. He has been a finalist for the Hugo, Nebula, Locus, and Ignyte Awards, won the Best Short Story Hugo for **The Water That Falls on You from Nowhere** and won the Best Novelette Nebula for **If You Find Yourself Speaking to God, Address God with the Informal You**. His novel **The Subtle Art of Folding Space** will be published by Tor in April, 2026.

A GRAY MAGIC

BY RAY NAYLER

"Well, at least we'll finally be able to get some hours."

"Ruthless."

"I'm serious. Maybe they'll finally be forced to make one of us full time."

"It'll never happen. They'll just hire another part-timer."

The two workers were in the break room. In the pause that followed, their ripstop paper jumpsuits rustled.

There were no windows. Everyone always watched the enormous countdown clock as they ate, each number segment as long as a human arm. The glass reflected their faces back to them. The vertical number segments stabbed down through the reflected room and the people in it.

"Don't pretend you liked her, though," the first worker said. "I mean, don't be one of those people who pretends they were someone's best friend, when they hear."

"I'm not pretending that. All I said was it's sad. She was nice. And *everyone* liked her."

"Nobody *disliked* her. Nobody really *knew* her. She never came out with us. Are you going to the funeral?"

"No. I have to work that day."

"Me too. In fact, I'm picking up her shift. Which seems—really unlucky. I didn't know, when they put it on my schedule. I thought she was just sick."

There might have been more to say, but there were now thirty seconds left on the countdown clock.

Both of them were thinking the same things—the kinds of things everyone thinks, hearing someone they know has died. Here I am, still alive. It happened to them, and not to me. For a moment, everything looked a bit brighter. Everything seemed more fragile and more real.

Fifteen seconds. They shoveled instant noodles into their mouths and tilted their heads back, draining the broth. They tossed their trash into the bin and went back out onto the work floor.

• • •

A message popped up in Zhenya's inbox a moment after she walked in her door. She sat down at her small breakfast nook table and rubbed the inside of her elbow. There would be a bruise, she was sure.

She opened the message.

HEY! I NOTICED YOUR SNEAKERS ARE GETTING PRETTY WORN OUT. I COULD EVEN SEE ONE OF YOUR SOCKS THROUGH A HOLE IN THE SIDE. YEESH! LOOKING TO REPLACE THOSE WORN-OUT SHOES? BECAUSE IF YOU ARE, YOU SHOULD KNOW WE ARE RUNNING A 2-FOR-1 TODAY ONLY.

The adfeeder cameras on the square, of course. She couldn't get past them without one of them IDing her and finding something she needed to buy.

Underneath the ad message were two soft keys. The top, colorful one said ACCEPT OFFER.

DECLINE OFFER was a smaller gray key underneath. When she touched that one, a drop-down menu of reasons for declining appeared. After reading through them, she selected OTHER. A text box appeared.

PLEASE LET US KNOW WHY THIS OFFER ISN'T FOR YOU (RE-QUIRED).

Zhenya rubbed the inside of her elbow again, then typed in BE-CAUSE I WILL BE DEAD IN LESS THAN A MONTH.

Again, she wanted to call her mother.

That wasn't it, exactly. It wasn't *her* mother she wanted to call. It was a made-up mother who actually cared about what was going to happen to her. A person who would be as hurt by what was going to happen to her as she was.

Not her mother, who would do nothing but go and tell everyone the story of it forever. Who would tell it as if it was something that had happened to *her*, not her daughter.

One of the worst parts of the whole thing was knowing that after she had died, her mother would look across a table and say to someone, "my daughter died. And of course it was absolutely devastating. I never thought I would survive it."

And in that moment, her mother would really believe she had been devastated. When her mother told a story, she always *felt* what she was saying. Really convinced herself that it was true.

As far as Zhenya could tell, that was the only time her mother felt anything—while she was performing having feelings for the benefit of someone else.

For a long time, Zhenya had worried that she was the same kind of person as her mother: that her feelings were not genuine either. That she was only pretending to have them, for the benefit of others. Maybe for the benefit of herself, so she could go on imagining she was normal.

This was ridiculous. It was ridiculous to feel devastated by having seen something awful, and then doubt the feeling was real.

She had seen a cat hit by a car, for example, a few years ago. She had been walking. It had happened right next to her. She had stopped and tried to help, but there was nothing that could be done. She had stayed with the cat until it died, moments later.

Later that evening she had gone home and lay in the dark and wondered whether she really *felt* anything at all. She had wondered if she felt anything while she was *crying*. Crying in the dark, alone. Crying for herself, for the cat, for its owners? For whose benefit?

What poison had been put into her, making her doubt her own feelings when they were right there? What poison could make her feel so deeply, yet doubt she was feeling at all?

And if she didn't call her mother?

She never even called me. I had to find out after it was too late to even say goodbye to her. Of course I gave her a wonderful funeral, but she blamed me for everything that ever went wrong in her life. That's the way it always is, isn't it? That's the way they treat us. There's no end to how much blame we mothers have to bear. Fathers always get forgiven, but not us.

Better to call.

Her mother answered after several rings. But the conversation they had was all about her mother, of course. Zhenya could never find a place to turn it. Could never find that moment to interject. Her mother was so tired, and there had been a problem with the car, and could Zhenya believe this, and could Zhenya believe that . . .

Forty-five minutes. An hour. Never once a place to break in. So Zhenya said nothing.

After the call she went for a walk. Down on the river the ice was breaking up into the ships of childhood, crewed by piratic seagulls and a mitten someone had dropped upstream. Zhenya could see her breath in the air. The entire time she was walking, she felt fine. Yes, a little tired. Blurry around the edges, but not so bad.

Like someone who needed a cup of coffee. Not like someone who would never see the leaves return to the trees. Not like someone who might not even see the hard buds on the trees open.

I do blame my father, she wanted to say to her mother. To that mother who would be telling the story of her daughter's ingratitude, again and again, to everyone who would listen and to many people who had long ago stopped listening, retreating inside themselves while they plotted their escape. *I do blame him. I blame him for dying before I could know him. I blame him for dying and leaving me with you. I blame him for this. He could have died without giving me his death. I blame him for this, even though I know it isn't fair.*

There was a place near the bridge exhaling breakfast smells— potatoes frying, coffee. Those kinds of smells made her a bit nauseous now, but she went in anyway.

She'd been here before, several times before. The waitress who worked here recognized some of her customers, greeted some of them by name. But never Zhenya, who came in once a month or so. Zhenya always got the neutral "Hi, honey, what are you having?" any stranger got.

There were other people who came in and were joked with or asked about their children. There was an older man who the waitress helped with his coat. The man sat at the counter doing crosswords on his tablet and drinking his cup of coffee.

As if it would all last forever. All of it: this place, his returning here, her greeting of him, her helping him with his coat because he was too stiff to do it easily himself.

But it wouldn't.

Yes, she would go first, but the rest would too. The blade of a bull-dozer would splinter the abandoned walls of this place, already dust-gray and emptied of life. Not only would this place be gone—it would be erased. Like nothing had ever been here at all.

Whatever was new, whatever rose here once they scraped all this away, would not carry any record of any of the warmth exchanged here between people. And it would know none of the customers' names, and certainly none of the names of their children.

●   ●   ●

While she was walking home there was a delivery message. Zhenya tried to walk faster—sometimes the delivery man would leave a package outside of the bin it was supposed to go in. It wasn't long, when they did that, before the package got stolen.

But when she walked faster, she started losing her breath. Worse, she started to feel it—an ache in the side. Death had a place inside her.

She slowed down. Tried to calm down. She hadn't ordered anything anyway. She didn't even know what would be in the package.

When she got home, it was in the bin. A box wrapped in translucent green bioplastic, with the government health provider's seal printed all over it at intervals. That's right—the doctor had said she would send Zhenya something.

Inside her apartment she opened it carefully. She did not open the envelope that came with it. She took the oculus from its molded paper clamshell and put it on the table.

She pressed the power button. The oculus whirred. Its lens dilated, and then a woman was projected into the room. She was sitting at a table. A table much like this one but scattered with devices—terminals of various sizes, and also a thick, oversized ceramic mug as big as a bowl. The kind of mug you could drink half a pot of tea out of, or soup. The woman was writing something on one of the terminals with a stylus. She stopped and turned.

"Oh," she said. "Hi! I think I have my terminal on vibrate, so I didn't get the notification. I hope I wasn't picking my nose or anything. Was I picking my nose?"

The woman pushed a lock of hair out of her eyes, folded her hands awkwardly in her lap.

There should be a moment of awkwardness, Zhenya thought. Because I know, and she—she went for another word, but "she" seemed best. She had to know too, of course.

The woman said, "My name is Agata. Pronounced Ah-GAH-Tah, which nobody really gets right. And you are Zhenya." She pronounced it perfectly. "Which I bet people mess up a lot too."

"Yeah."

"Someday they'll make a widget for that. Whisper our names in people's ears and save everyone having to repeat themselves half a dozen times."

"That's a good idea."

Agata shrugged. "I'm full of good ideas. What are you doing? Have you had breakfast?"

"I did. I went to a café, down by the river."

"What's it called?"

"I don't even know." Did the place have a name? It must, but she couldn't remember the sign that, most certainly, had always been there.

And then, for some reason, she found herself saying, "I went to the hospital early in the morning, and they took blood. Vial after vial of it, and the nurse was clumsy with the needle. And I keep thinking: why? They know and I know, but they just won't leave it alone. If I only have a little while, I don't want to spend it this way."

She paused a moment, thinking Agata would say something, but she was just sitting quietly, attentively.

Zhenya continued. "On the bus there I kept thinking of—I kept thinking of this gigantic clock they have in our breakroom at the warehouse. The way it's placed, you see your own face in it all the time. You can't look away from it. You can't enjoy your food. I keep wondering if they designed it that way on purpose—to make it so you can't even enjoy your time away from work. But why would they do that? You have fifteen minutes to eat lunch, and all you can think of is ten minutes left, nine minutes, eight minutes. Now it's almost over—seven minutes, six minutes, five. I barely have time to finish my soup. Four. Three. You can't think of anything else. And there I am in the hospital with the nurse working the needle around in my arm thinking ten, nine, eight. What the *fuck* am I doing here? But the worst part was, I couldn't think of how I'd rather be spending my day. Nothing came to me at all."

"That really is the worst part, isn't it. It isn't fair for death to take our last living days from us, too."

"If only I could stop thinking of it."

"You won't be able to. But I have a plan for you. I want you to go to the aquarium."

"The aquarium?"

"Yes. Like when you were a kid. Go there, and open your eyes wide, and really look at how *weird* the fish are."

"I don't know if . . ."

"The 9B bus comes in 5 minutes. You can catch it if you hurry. We'll talk when you get back."

•   •   •

At the aquarium there was a whole room of octopuses, and that was where she ended up spending most of her time. There were ones no bigger than a finger, deadly as anything on the planet. There were ones with arms so long and delicate they seemed like hair. There was an enormous one in an exhibit that looked like an underwater cave. It spent its time stuffed up in a top corner, a smear of suckers against the glass, disappointing all of the children who had come to see it.

Then, when there was no one in the room but it and Zhenya, it floated down and drifted in its tank, changing from one color to another, moving through forms and textures. Zhenya watched it from a polite distance. She felt it was watching her too, standing there under the colored lights, locked in one boring shape and color, mesmerized.

The aquarium had an enormous display of jellyfish, lit from below in orange against a blue background. Zhenya stood in front of it for an hour, watching the jellyfish create one abstract design after another with their illuminated bodies.

● ● ●

"I thought you might like the octopuses," Agata said. "They don't have much of a social life either."

"Very funny. But you know—not having a social life is what I noticed about the jellyfish, more. There were so many of them in the tank together, but they were never aware of one another."

And then, in the cafeteria of the aquarium, she had looked down on the harbor, the people on the sidewalk in an ugly drizzle, and thought the same thing. Except for the families, clumped together, no one seemed aware of the people around them. The lights of their terminals shone in their faces as they drifted in one direction or another. "And of course the jellyfish didn't seem aware of me, either, or of being in a tank. They just moved. Actually, the octopuses seemed social."

On Agata's table was a circle of stacked playing cards, with another stack of cards in the center of the circle. "Did they?"

"I mean—I spent a lot of time in there, and the octopuses seemed to be aware of me and of the things that were going on around them. Not just aware. *Interested.*"

"And yet," Agata said, "they live their lives alone, without the company of their own kind until they mate and then die."

"Maybe they don't feel alone," Zhenya said. "I was thinking— maybe they just aren't interested in other octopuses. Maybe what they are interested in is *everything else*. The whole rest of the world."

Agata seemed to consider that for a moment. "I like that idea. It reminds me of someone."

• • •

At work, all Zhenya could think of was how easy it would be to step out in front of one of the loaders and be done with it. Everything was mixed up in her—she wanted every moment that was left, and also none of it at all.

The worst was the breakroom with its clock. She spent her breaks in the bathroom, where there was a clock on the door of each stall, but at least they were smaller. She didn't eat during her shift. With the nausea, she didn't feel much like eating anyway.

The woman in HR knew and wouldn't look at her.

Her other coworkers didn't seem to know. There was that, at least.

What would they do if they knew? Why was she so determined to keep it a secret?

Because it was the same as with her mother. Because they wouldn't care—none of them would care, but they would be forced to pretend they did, and she wouldn't be able to stand it. Watching them try to make concerned faces.

The obvious thing to do, of course, would be to quit. But she didn't have the money to do that.

• • •

"Go and see a play," Agata said. "If you look online, you can find half a dozen of them. Community theaters, things like that. What you need to do is look at the world."

"Why? Soon I won't be here anymore."

"But the world will."

The circular game of cards Agata was playing was a kind of solitaire. She'd explained its rules to Zhenya. The game seemed dull and pointless. Zhenya had never understood these kinds of games—the kind people used to kill time. To Zhenya there had never seemed to be enough time.

Even before. Certainly not now, of course, but even before any of this. Between work and sleeping and eating there had never seemed to be time enough for much of anything at all.

"I want to know what it is like—being you," Zhenya said. "You are talking to me, telling me to do this or that. But what is it like to be you?"

"What do you mean?"

"Do you play that game when I am not around?"

"There is a play tonight, for example," Agata said. "It's called *A Gray Magic*. I'm going to buy you a ticket and send it to your phone."

"You don't want to talk about it. What it's like."

"No," Agata said. "I don't. And neither do you."

● ● ●

The play was not particularly well acted, or well staged, or well directed. The actors flubbed lines, and at one point someone dropped something backstage in the middle of a dramatic scene. The crash threw the rhythm of the actors off and made one of them actually cry out.

But there was something in the writing of the play that stood out anyway—something that couldn't quite be drowned out by the amateur performance.

The play was about two witches. Each of them was convinced that they were a good witch, and that the other one was a bad witch. Each of them was determined to destroy the other—but neither of them was particularly powerful. Their spells turned out not to be much more than little annoyances.

And in the meantime, they both lived in little studio apartments in the city, and had relationships with dull and overbearing men who they didn't seem to care much about, and mostly used their magic to unclog drains and trick the turnstile into giving them free rides on public transit.

In the end, one of them finally managed to cause the other one to fall off of a pedal boat in the central park's pond, but then jumped in and saved her.

The play ended with the two of them, wet from head to foot, having coffee together in a diner in the middle of the night.

After the play Zhenya went to the diner down by the river. But first she walked out on the bridge a bit. The river was low. There was a full Moon on the crenellated surface of the mud. In the mud were lodged an extraordinary number of electric bicycles and scooters, as if every person who ever used one of them came here when their ride was over and threw it off the bridge. They lay upright or on their sides in the mud, a tribe of drowned machines.

In the diner, the night waitress looked so much like the day waitress that she must have been her older sister. She didn't speak to any of the customers, though, beyond taking their orders.

Zhenya had a cup of coffee and thought of the play, but also about what being a playwright must be like. Because it wasn't just writing: it was relying on others to make it all work. A whole team of others, strangers to you, who might ruin your best scene by dropping something backstage.

Maybe it wasn't the actors or the director you were relying on. Maybe it was the audience—you were relying on them to be patient enough to ignore the mediocre acting and the noise backstage and the people around them. You were relying on them to see through all of that to the core of the play.

Walking home, the pain knocked her down. She had a moment where she couldn't think of anything at all. Coming out of it, standing up, she didn't know who she was, or where. Then she was herself again. She wasn't hurt by the fall. She continued home.

"It seems like trying to hold hands with strangers," she told Agata later. "Like reaching out a hand and hoping they will reach out, too."

"And did you?"

"I did. I think other people did, too. Not everyone, but a lot of them."

"Do you still want to know what it is like to be me?"

"I don't," Zhenya said. "I know the answer. I know there isn't anything it is like to be you. I know you aren't there when the oculus isn't on. It's like the script of a play: it doesn't read itself with no one around. But that doesn't matter. The person who made you and sent you out into the world to give comfort to people who are dying—that's what is important. That matters. The words in a play aren't alive, either. But they came from a living person and are brought back to life by the people who need them. And closing the script—that's what it is going to be like for me, too. Just like that."

"Yes. When it comes. But what do you want to do tomorrow?" Agata asked.

"I thought I would call in sick. I thought I would go to the aquarium again. I didn't finish looking at everything there. And I don't think they finished looking at me, either."

"That sounds like a good way to spend a day."

"I think so too. Good night, Agata."

"Good night, Zhenya."

Zhenya turned the oculus off and settled into the dark.

Hugo and Locus Award winning author Ray Nayler was born in Quebec and raised in California. He lived and worked abroad for two decades in Russia, Central Asia, the Caucasus, and the Balkans.

Ray's Locus Award winning first novel was **The Mountain in the Sea**, which was also a finalist for the Nebula, the Arthur C. Clarke, and the Los Angeles Times' Ray Bradbury Awards.

Ray's novella **The Tusks of Extinction** won the 2025 Hugo Award, and was also a Nebula and Locus Award finalist.

His third book, the cybernetic political thriller **Where the Axe is Buried**, was published in April of 2025.

Ray most recently served as international advisor to the Office of National Marine Sanctuaries at the National Oceanic and Atmospheric Administration, and as visiting scholar at the George Washington University's Institute for International Science and Technology Policy.

Ray lives in Washington, DC with his wife Anna, their daughter Lydia, and two rescued cats.

WHY DON'T WE JUST KILL THE KID IN THE OMELAS HOLE

BY ISABEL J. KIM

So they broke into the hole in the ground, and they killed the kid, and all the lights went out in Omelas: click, click, click. And the pipes burst and there was a sewage leak and the newscasters said there was a typhoon on the way, so they (a different "they," these were the "they" in charge, the "they" who lived in the nice houses in Omelas [okay, every house in Omelas was a nice house, but these were Nice Houses]) got another kid and put it in the hole.

And the newscasters said the hurricane had dissipated into a tropical storm, and the pipes were repaired, and the well-paid janitors cleaned up the sewage leak while wearing proper PPE, and the kid in the hole cried and cried and cried. Or they (the general "they," the "they" that meant you and me and the janitors and the newscasters) assumed that the kid was crying, because the hole was soundproofed so nobody could hear the kid, which didn't stop them from knowing about the kid, but it sort of helped.

So they (the first "they") killed the kid again. They stormed the hole and broke the kid out and slit the kid's throat on public television (as all television in Omelas was publicly funded), and they said, "Look at what sort of shit your beautiful city is built on!" and the kid bled out and it was extremely graphic to the point of being censored in later broadcasts. And one of the tracks of the free public transit system twisted loose, and a bunch of commuters were killed in a freak accident, and the stock market started shuddering downward, and a house collapsed on the south side of Omelas.

So they (the "Nice Houses" they) got a third kid and stuck it in the hole. They felt weird about it, but they liked their Nice Houses, and also, they really did truly and wholeheartedly care about the well-being of Omelas and all of the citizens except for the kid in the hole. The newscasters talked about the second dead kid sorrowfully and the social media posters (every citizen in Omelas had a healthy and regular relationship with social media and not a bad and addictive one) talked about how this was a real tragedy because even though we knew that there was a kid in the hole, now that's three times as many kids in the hole, and it's extra sad because we usually don't kill the kid in the hole, they usually die of old age or malnutrition.

None of this mattered to the living third kid in the hole, who was not enjoying the hole experience.

But nobody heard the third kid's sobbing because of the soundproofing, and also because now no one was allowed to go see the kid since security had been beefed up around the load-bearing suffering child to prevent its death and prolong its suffering. Which meant that the kid-killers had to seriously plan the next attempt, and everyone had time to decompress from the first two murders of the load-bearing suffering child, and also, the video of the second very graphic murder circulated outside of Omelas.

Everyone (me, you, the newscasters, the janitors with the good PPE, the children who lived inside and outside Omelas) was performatively disgusted by the video. Everyone watched it anyway. It went viral like a snuff film went viral or Kim Kardashian's first sex tape went viral, and it was like the load-bearing suffering child was in everyone's home at once, like there were a million load-bearing suffering children looking at you from a million screens.

Many non-Omelan people said a lot of very mean things (no one outside Omelas had a good and normal relationship with social media), like that the Omelans were monsters for letting the load-bearing suffering child exist and therefore everything about Omelas was fucked beyond belief, and had they known about the load-bearing suffering child, they never would have visited Omelas' beautiful beaches and nightclubs and festivals, because the knowledge of the child was so goddamn fucking horrific and tainted everything. And maybe it was the Omelans who should be killed.

This sentiment made the Omelans kind of upset. They pointed out that Omelas was a better place to live than most other places because at least you knew the load-bearing suffering child suffered for a reason, as opposed to all the other kids who were suffering for no reason. Out there, kids had their arms ripped off while they were working in chicken processing plants, kids were left in baby boxes, and kids lived in perfect quiet misery with one parent who was an alcoholic and another parent who beat them. In Omelas, there were only good parents and no child suffered except the single one who did. How dare you say shit about our fair city and our single child, when you won't even help your own.

What the Omelans didn't say was that their second grievance was due to the fact that the kid killers had broken the unspoken code: if you had a problem with the load-bearing suffering child, you were supposed to get the hell out of Omelas and keep it to yourself. You weren't supposed to kill the kid. As a teenager, you were supposed to learn the blunt truth that your society was built on a single ongoing act of senseless, meaningless cruelty, and then you were supposed to cry about it or rage about it, but either way you were supposed to get over it and grow up and get on with your fully-paid-for-by-the-state education system and your festivals and your legal weed and your *drooz*.

The kid was the drop of blood in the bowl of milk whose slight bitterness would make the sweetness of the rest of Omelas richer. Without the kid in the hole, Omelas was just paradise. With the load-bearing, suffering child, Omelas meant something.

And of course, it was true that the whole city literally ran on the load-bearing suffering child in a very real physical way that was not a metaphor. And everyone really liked having running power and no blackouts and good schools and low crime and community-oriented government and safe sidewalks and public transit that worked.

Things got really toxic online. Then the third kid was killed.

This time it was harder to say who the killers were, because the first they, the killers, had osmosed into the second they (the "they" of the Nice Houses), and also, the third they (the "they" who were the janitors with the good PPE equipment, and the newscasters). So it was never discovered who exactly slipped through all the protections and the soundproofing and the soldiers with tranquilizer guns (because there were no real guns in Omelas) and stole the kid from the hole and killed it in the conference room where the people with the Nice Houses met to talk about government.

There was no message this time because the dead kid on the table was the message. The dead kid had been dressed just like every other kid in Omelas (comfortable, affordable clothing of good quality, with adorable patterns), and it hadn't been in the hole for long enough to develop the really horrific features that the kids in the hole always developed (open and weeping sores on their butts, skinny limbs and a protruding stomach, a sort of lank greasiness that permeated their entire being), and this third dead kid mostly just looked a little skinny, and grimy, and asleep.

There was an earthquake that cracked the west side and opened a sinkhole, and four cars were swallowed up in a freak accident. They talked about it on the news, alongside photos of the dead kid dressed up in the conference room. And because the Omelans all had very good educations where they learned about the literary meaning of symbols, they knew that the dead kid in pretty clothing was a reminder of the fact that the child in the hole was also an Omelan child.

The rest of the world, which had variable public education and overworked language arts teachers, freaked out on social media. The sentiment boiled down to: "If Omelas is a perfect city and has really good social services and there is ready access to birth control and easy ways for people with wombs to give up the infants they gestated to people that want them, and therefore all children are wanted and cared for by someone in Omelas, regardless of whether it is their biological progenitor, where do the Omelans get the load-bearing suffering child?"

And the follow-up freak-out: "Oh my god, they must be stealing our children."

Of course, nothing in the freak-outs materially touched the Omelans, because Omelas was a shining city on a hill that could only be hurt when there was no load-bearing suffering child, and the dead child had been immediately replaced, so Omelas wasn't assaulted by foreign troops, and there were no trade sanctions against it, and people didn't stop going to its beaches. But they had to do some media spin, and the Nice House Experiencers went on TV to reassure the world that the load-bearing suffering child was an ethically sourced, no one's son, and definitely an Omelan, and meanwhile some of the Nice House Experiencers privately spoke among each other.

"Look, maybe we shouldn't have a kid in the hole?" one of the Nice House Experiencers said. "Maybe the kid in the hole was always a bad idea."

"What's the other option?" the second Nice House Experience said. "Look me in the eye and tell me there is a better solution than putting one single kid in the hole, and letting that one single kid have a miserable life, in return for the good lives of all of our children?"

"What if they put your kid in?"

And the second Nice House Experiencer didn't have an answer for that. Because she knew in her heart of hearts that she would damn every last person in Omelas rather than subject her child to the hole.

"What *they*," she said instead. "How do I know you're not the one who killed the kid?"

This question was replicated in many rooms, during many meetings that escalated to shouting until at one point someone said: "Why are we arguing so much when the kid is in the hole? The kid is in the hole, which means that we shouldn't have so much infighting. What is the point of the kid in the hole if we can't even get our act together!"

That had many philosophical implications on whether disagreements can exist in paradise, but in reality, all of this bullshit only meant that the people with the Nice Houses were distracted enough that the fourth kid was killed easily, and without much fanfare.

And then there was an avalanche, a spread of religiously motivated homophobia, and an incidence of road rage with a tranquilizer gun that left four dead.

But they managed to catch the specific guy who had killed the fourth kid. They caught him on the newly installed CCTV cameras that did 'round the clock surveillance. They arrested him at his home, which was near the sinkhole.

The murderer surrendered peacefully. He was a very regular looking man. Nothing about him looked like a murderer or a dissident. He looked just like every other person who had benefited from Omelas' many social safety networks and had grown up without ever knowing suffering.

Before his execution, they (the people with the Nice Houses, as a proxy for the newscasters, as a proxy for everyone else) asked him why he was doing this. The murderer didn't shrug, because he was being held by a Kevlar straitjacket, which had been imported from outside.

"I'm personally doing it because I think we're all cowards here. We're all so fucking afraid of the potential of being the one to suffer that we put that damn kid in the hole and the kid suffers forever, and everyone is so fucking afraid of doing something that we pretend that we are living better lives without suffering. It's disgusting."

He spoke with the moral certainty of the classical Omelan who knew about suffering only abstractly and through the existence of the load-bearing suffering child.

"What are you trying to solve?" the executioner said. The executioner was the only one in the room, but she was relaying the questions from the Nice House Experiencers who had sourced the questions from a public questionnaire and had approved of every single one, because at the end of the day, admittedly, every person in Omelas lived in a Nice House.

"If we kill enough kids then you will eventually stop putting kids in the hole," the murderer said. "I'm an accelerationist."

"A lot of people died because you killed the kid."

"I'm sorry about that," the murderer said, and he sounded genuine. He sounded like he really cared about the well-being of all the Omelans and their susceptibility to freak accidents, but he cared about the one kid just a little more.

"How did it feel to kill?" the executioner said. This was not a question that was on the list. This was a question the executioner wanted to know for herself.

"Bad," he said. "But it's better than being locked in the hole for your entire life."

The executioner didn't say anything to that. She turned away from him to prepare the syringe and the chemicals.

"Before I'm dead, I'd like to say a few words," the murderer said to the executioner's back. "We will keep killing the kid in the hole. You are going to run out of kids before we stop killing the kids that go into the hole. Even if you kill me, now we all know about killing the load-bearing suffering child. You can't kill me in any way that matters. The kid will die again and again until you stop putting kids in the hole."

And he grinned a big white grin (they had really good dental care in Omelas that wasn't tied to a separate insurance) and was executed by painless lethal injection and so became the first person in Omelas (other than all the load-bearing suffering children) who Omelas, as a state, had killed, and Omelas became the sort of city that killed people using painless lethal injection.

But that was okay, because it happened during the period of time while the kid wasn't in the hole, so it was a fluke, the same way the typhoon was a fluke, the homophobia was a fluke, the Omelans being shitheads on social media was a fluke. It was something that could only happen while Omelas wasn't *Omelas* and was instead just like every other city with no load-bearing suffering child and many load-bearing suffering adults.

The day after the lethal injection, the fifth kid was killed in the hole. And then the executioner walked out of Omelas, but no one paid attention to her leaving.

It turned out that the dead murderer had underestimated the Omelans, because things continued in this cyclical fashion for a while. Kids were put in a series of holes and were summarily killed. The deaths were reported on public television and were dissected badly on social media through a variety of angles.

Like: "This kid is a metaphor for the third world and for the slave labor that mines the rare metals that go into iPhones and for the boys who cross the border to work in the fields while they're underage and the girls who are sold into marriage to pedophiles."

Like: "This kid is a reincarnation of a Bodhisattva and is perfectly happy to experience suffering for the sake of her fellow man, so really it's like, totally fine that the kid is suffering."

Like: "Why do we care about this kid so much, it's just one kid?"

Like: "The kid is a SYMBOL of the LOWER CLASSES and how they SUFFER."

Like: "No, seriously, where does the kid come from? My mom says she saw a kid disappear off the train, that they're kidnapping kids off of public transit."

Like: "If we put a pulsating mass of tissue cultured from the cells of an Omelan child, and put that in the prison, would that have the same effect, in the same way that lab-grown-meat is still technically meat?"

By now everyone (except the newscasters) had stopped counting dead children, and nobody has any questions for the murderers anymore. The dead murderer was wrong. They haven't run out of children. But they haven't run out of murderers, either.

These days, Omelas is perfect except when it isn't, and every once in a while, Omelas has a series of natural disasters and freak accidents strike and everyone is a little afraid that their kid will be the next one in the hole. But only when the kid is dead and a new kid needs to be chosen.

A drop of blood, in a bowl of milk.

Omelas now has a really long Wikipedia entry, with a whole subarticle about the load-bearing suffering child, and a second subarticle about the children who died. They tell you about the children now, after they die. What their names are. They promise that the children are ethically sourced. But there aren't any citations. And some people say that there isn't a kid in the hole anymore. They've moved the hole a bunch of times, and they don't let people know the location anymore. They have extra soundproofing.

Most days, Omelas is sunny and beautiful and nothing bad happens. And then there will be a day that is overcast and cloudy, and on that day, people die in circus accidents and carbon monoxide leaks and start harassment campaigns on twitter. And sometimes on that day people die through lethal injection. So it's clear that sometimes the kid is alive and suffering, and sometimes the kid has been killed and doesn't exist.

Or maybe there's no kid anymore, and Omelas is just like everywhere else: lucky until it isn't.

Occasionally a content creator will walk into Omelas and film a video while standing on one of the balconies of the Nice Houses or while sitting on one of Omelas' beautiful beaches. They will talk about the history of Omelas in the same way that people talk about the Uyghurs situation in China, the concentration camps of the Third Reich, the comfort women imported from Korea by Japan, the Belgian Congo, the Atlantic Slave Trade in relation to the American South, and the refugees who sink in ships off the coast of Western Europe.

And they (the ones who visit Omelas) say: Thank God we aren't dealing with that horrid wound in society. Thank God there is somewhere that shows us how fucking bad things could get. What a pit in the ground. What a fucked up little trolley problem. What a lesson for us. Thank God we don't live there. Thank God we know it exists.

———————————

Isabel J. Kim lives near New York City in an apartment filled with books and swords. She is the author of numerous short stories and has won the Nebula, Locus, BSFA and the Shirley Jackson Award. Her work has been translated into multiple languages and reprinted in multiple best of the year anthologies. When she's not writing, she's practicing law or co-hosting her internet culture podcast, **Wow if True**. Her debut novel **Sublimation** is forthcoming from Tor.

THE BROTHERHOOD OF MONTAGUE ST. VIDEO
BY THOMAS HA

At first I thought something had broken in my book.

I didn't notice until the afternoon light from the windows began to recede. I tried to increase the brightness settings of the page, but no matter how I thumbed the margins, they would not change. For the first time, I looked carefully at the gold printing along its spine. The book was dead.

What kind of library carried a dead book? I wondered.

No one responded to my calls for assistance. There were no working service-buttons near the shelves that I could see. I walked downstairs to the circulation desk. No one was present at the self-checkout stalls, and I assumed, like all other recent changes, that this was the result of cuts to the city budget.

The more I looked at the gold-laden book, the more I considered it may not have belonged to the library at all. It had no identification tag on the inside cover, no chip at its base. Perhaps someone had left it, hidden among the other inventory, for some unknown reason. There was no way to scan a book that didn't belong there, so I put it in my coat without checking to see if cameras were hovering over me and walked out the door.

The entire ride on the 2, I wondered if something would happen. I waited for an officer to pull me aside at the station exit. Or for a street drone to make me step away from the pedestrians on the icy sidewalk. But nothing came of it, my taking away the dead book. I was surprised, and even disappointed, in the nothing that seemed to follow.

• • •

"*The Winter Hills* by Carrigan Salt."

The owner of the video store studied the binding, the page edges, much as I did before. Alaric had an eye for dead things that I did not, and he understood instinctively the rarity of what I had brought him.

In the weeks after my mother's funeral, I had come to the video store more often, bringing boxes from her Court Street apartment. Recorded-over VHS tapes, floppy disks, and undeveloped photo rolls. The Brotherhood on Montague was always eager to collect physical effects and would accept donations of any kind, I had been told. Even if they could not use or preserve them, they often had a sense of who could.

I was curious if he would buy the dead book from me, given his obvious interest.

"I'll consider it." Alaric paused, then he redirected the conversation to my mother's things. Some of her belongings I had chosen not to donate outright. One in particular, I had requested the Brotherhood try to restore and copy.

"The digital video disc, the DVD, you asked about—we'll need a 650 nm red laser to create a copy from the scratched original."

"Just as it was? No optimization?"

It was important to emphasize this. Every other data center had been unable to pull the file without automatic edits to the image settings and content.

"That's right." Alaric nodded. "No optimization. Just as it was. The Brotherhood's burner is on loan. It'll be a week or two."

He was about to give back the dead book, but he kept touching the textured cover. "I never read this, the original, in ink on pulp," he said. "It's part of Salt's Long Wanderer series."

"Oh," I said, as if I had heard of it before. Salt's name had been vaguely familiar to me when I plucked the book from the library shelf, but if there were more volumes like this one, I didn't recall seeing them.

The old man turned several pages. He was reading, but it was apparent that he was thinking of other things. I could feel his mind split between the words and wherever else he was. His breathing slowed, and then he closed the book and put it in my hands. There was some sound in a distant part of the shop, behind the shelves and stacks of preserved things—spinning racks of cassette tapes, mounted pinhole cameras, an old standing arcade cabinet. A rhythmic rustling, there, that continued until I left.

• • •

Elii met me at the promenade after dark, not far from Montague.

We sat on a bench and watched the East River behind the slow-moving bodies on the walkway. I tried to show her the dead book, and she thumbed the margins before giving up when it wouldn't brighten. It was clear she had no interest in the thing.

I'd been hoping after several months of dating we'd be able to take off our amp-glasses, but she insisted we keep them on. I'd already snuck little peeks of her around the edges of my frames. I knew she did not look all that different without her themes. Her cheeks were less contoured, her lips less plump. The alterations in the glasses were only slight. Nonetheless, she had only ever let me take them off when we were in total darkness together. For people who kept glasses on, it was never really about looks alone.

She asked if I was almost finished with my mother's apartment. There were just a few more boxes, some paperwork, and the deposit to get back. My bereavement leave was done, and I had borrowed from next quarter's vacation time. But I'd be back in my apartment soon.

We began talking about the scratched disc I'd sent to Montague St. Video, how it contained, among other things, old footage my mother had shot and saved. Clips of us up at Lake George in the years after my father had left. I offered to show Elii some of it once it was restored and copied.

"It sounds like your mom held onto a lot," she said. "That's a lot to go through and settle up. A lot of things."

"Right. That's true. It is a lot. A lot of things. Too many, even."

"Yes, maybe too many," Elii agreed. "I was thinking, because there's so much, we should probably hold off on visits and videoconnects—until you're done settling everything, at least."

"Oh? I mean, sure. That does make sense."

"It just seems like something you should finish first. Don't you think?"

"You're right. No. You're right. I should focus and finish. That does make sense."

"Sorry again. For your loss."

"Of course." I went back to watching the dark glass and cement shapes of the city across the river instead of her, already half-forgetting whatever it was that we were saying. "I appreciate that," I said. "Yes, I appreciate that. I do."

•   •   •

Later, in the stillness of my mother's apartment, I began reading through more of *The Winter Hills*. I sat in her old chair, her scarf still draped over the arm and barely brushing against the rug. Lost in the pages, much as I'd been in the library.

Carrigan Salt's protagonist, the unnamed rider, rode his gray horse across flat and rocky lands and through sparse little towns. The character had a peculiar way of going from one place to another without a sense of purpose. In any other book, I would have known the shape of the narrative at this point. But not here.

He did not understand the urgency with which others lived. They all seemed so eager to reach a conclusion, no matter how partial or incomplete, but in his mind there were always more questions forming like eddies in a stream. Every town the rider visited, he liked to ask himself these three things: What is it these people want? What is it these people need? Are they striving toward one, or the other, with what they do each day? And in examining these things he usually came to a clearer understanding of the people in that particular place.

I fell asleep reading about thundering horses and cattle and sizzling heat. Outside, the heavy trucks on the BQE rattled the icy apartment windows, but I imagined them as hooves over hollowed rock. I dreamt of a man on a gray horse standing at a lake, watching a mother and her young boy at the water's edge throwing rocks. I woke up crying for reasons I did not understand.

•   •   •

My days had already lost normal proportion before the dead book. They were little eras contained within odd chambers that did not begin or end with a sunrise or sunset. There was the unlocking of my mother's online accounts. The post-funeral cremation and retrieval of remains. Notifying various agencies and sending copies of death certificates. Finding an attorney to settle any outstanding issues with her estate. The time spent reading *The Winter Hills* in meditative stretches felt no different. Just another era to add to the ones before.

Alaric had not yet finished with the disc I had given him on my next visit to Montague. I found him stooped over an album of postage stamps, carefully arranged on each page in airtight little sleeves. Behind him, a black-and-white movie played on a CRT, and a modified

VHS player appeared to be recording the contents for the Brotherhood's archives. I asked Alaric, while he inspected the postage stamps, if the store sold any paper.

"As in, sheets? Uncoated? No pixelated surface? The Brotherhood has a relationship with the mill in Tarrytown, so we do have some supply, yes."

He did not ask why I needed it, so I assumed this was not too extraordinary of a request. I bought one ream with some store credit I'd accumulated.

My mother kept an old Trapwood typewriter she had gotten as a gift from her grandmother. She had shown me, when I was very young, how to replace the ribbon, but I still had to spend some time watching videos online before I could do it. Once I'd had everything, I put the copy of *The Winter Hills* next to me and began typing its words on the fresh paper.

The town was nothing like he knew. There was a solemnity to the way the miners at Copper Hawk lived. Their existence was like a duty they bore begrudgingly but also would not relinquish. The rasp of dust in their nostrils and mouths, the lines of their skin. They did not enjoy the brilliant bang of the white sun. It was only the swollen blackness of the shafts before them, and they could not remember what had been there before the mines had been birthed beneath them.

I didn't know why I'd begun this project of copying the dead book's text over onto fresh sheets. My day job as a freelance re-writer meant I often studied material like this. But typically I would be cleaning up inarticulate copy, trying to make output from some desk producer into something people could understand. My agency mandated simplified phrases and strict grammar rules we had to know by heart.

The Winter Hills did not have any of those phrases or rules. There were long turns that were not necessarily about efficiency or meaning, but about rhythm. It was a voice I wanted to transpose for myself to feel the words. I was getting lost in the book, but at a pace and flow that felt more like a dissolving comfort than the listlessness of despair.

It was also during those quiet days when I began to suspect something else was happening, especially when I left my mother's apartment.

Walking along the slushy sidewalk, past naked black branches waving like claws at the curtilage in front of the brownstones, I heard that distant sound, that rustling, I remembered from the shop. Not like soft wings, but something like plastic or the scrape of faux-leather.

There was a presence I could not explain.

I'd take breaks from typing and go down to one of the corner stores. No one would be working there in person, of course. The camera would dangle from tracks in the ceiling, following over my shoulder and monitoring every item I picked from the shelves. I'd scan my items at the self-check registers, and I'd think, for a second, that someone was in one of the aisles. But I also knew if I looked, I would be wrong.

The iron-handed sheriff of Copper Hawk did not take kindly to the rider or the differences between them. In his mind, every stranger was a new element to be carefully accounted for, and the sheriff was not one with the patience for it. He did not ask questions about what people wanted or needed, only what they could do. No, he and the rider were not the same at all.

The ending of the dead book was as mystifying as the rest.

The rider spent weeks in the mining town of Copper Hawk, slowly coming to the realization that the sheriff there, working under the auspices of a metals corporation, was bleeding the people of their wages and exploiting their labor. The last chapter involved a shootout, as these kinds of books tended to have. But instead of a decisive victory, the rider ended up winged and bleeding. The book finished with the rider, delirious, on his gray horse, barely escaping with his life out into the desert. Nothing resolved. No one in Copper Hawk saved. Perhaps the rider would return to the town and set things right in another book, but somehow I didn't get that sense. So the ending felt haunting, strange, and unfamiliar to me.

I found a living reprint of *The Winter Hills* for comparison. It was encased in shiny plastic, the spine with the usual rechargeable port. I scanned and skipped along the various digital chapters to see what had been altered by the publishers posthumously. It wasn't uncommon for the estate and rights holders to periodically update these kinds of stories. The benefit of a living book was that they didn't have to contact readers to update the content. Alterations would sync in the pixelated pages whenever the book went online next.

The biggest difference I noticed in the new electronic copy was the ending.

There was a shootout in Copper Hawk like before, yes. But instead of the loss and the blood and the shame of the rider, the iron-handed sheriff was the one to take a bullet. The miners of the town staged a revolt against the metals company in the third act. They set fire to some of the shafts with an explosion at the end of the action, to punctuate the triumph. I could almost sense the hand of audience-score maximizer programs in the plot. It could even have been a re-writer at my agency that oversaw the edition, for all I knew.

I felt better in some ways, having read the new, happier ending, but I forgot it promptly, like some garbled conversation I'd overheard on the subway, something that made me chuckle and then escaped my mind.

In my dreams, I kept going back to the image of the original ending—that rider bleeding, leaning over on his horse, clutching at its neck, and whispering softly to the beast. And then I remembered my mother wearing sunglasses, on a towel at Lake George, reading a magazine, while I ran back and forth on the white-hot sand.

"Why would they change it that way, *The Winter Hills*?"

Alaric was inventorying one of the last boxes of my mother's belongings. He held up a record and inspected its sleeve. There were also a series of digital postcards, rewritable electronic messages in thin plastic film, some from Cabo, others from Denmark, sent by my mother's younger sister who had never stayed in one place too long.

"People have a tendency to confuse change with improvement. So alteration seems like creation to some." The old man peered down the glasses dipping at the end of his nose. "We like the feeling of progress, and folks figured out a while ago that you can always tweak things in your surroundings to heighten a perceived movement through time. Even if, in truth, you haven't advanced anywhere meaningful at all."

"I don't know what that means."

Alaric laughed, to me or to himself, I could not tell. "I've never been accused of clarity." He typed something on his dust-covered computer and studied the digital postcards from my aunt. "It seems counterintuitive, but it's really the preserved things—fixed markers that never move—that are the more meaningful measure of change. A traveler on the road can look at mountains, forests, other landmarks, and he understands the difference in his positions the farther along he goes. Just like when I listen to a song, look at a work of art, read a book. And then later, return to that same piece. Something will be different, will have moved, in me. That's the benefit of the work we do in preserving things in particular forms, I like to think. We remember who we were then, so that we know who we are now. Does that make a little more sense?"

His words did feel right. Like something I'd been thinking but didn't know how to articulate in the weeks of going through my mother's things. Again, I removed the dead book from my coat pocket and offered it tentatively to Alaric.

"Have you considered, by the way . . . " I felt almost embarrassed asking. "Whether you'll buy? The dead book, I mean."

He did not answer quickly. The question appeared to weigh on him. "I'm making inquiries, but I have to be frank. We may not be able to offer a fair price. Not what you could get elsewhere. We will do our best to get back to you soon."

"I understand."

"In the meantime, you should be careful."

"With the book?"

"With who sees it. Not everyone appreciates these things the way the Brotherhood does. Materials that can't be modified, adjusted, or up-dated. Some enjoy true things like that. Some can't stand them."

"I see," I replied, but again, he had lost me.

"Where did you find this copy, again?"

"Just an old place in the city. My mother used to go."

"Your mother . . . she was from this neighborhood, you said?" The old man studied my face and the postcards, like he was trying to figure something out. But if he put anything together, he didn't say a word about it or give any other indication. After we'd finished with the box, and as I was about to reach the stairwell, he called out to me.

"West Nyack."

"Hm?"

"There's a Brotherhood in West Nyack," he said. "Not that far out of the city. They know dead books and sometimes teach others about them. If that sort of thing interests you, maybe those are the ones you should go and see. They might have something to offer or to teach you too."

I thanked the old man for the information. There were other things I probably should have asked, but that I just let go. I suppose I thought there would be time with other visits. I did not think too much then about leaving Montague St. Video behind.

•   •   •

Caliper John approached not long after that conversation. Or rather, he decided to make himself known, I suppose. Even then, I should have known he'd been listening for some time.

In the days that followed, typing and re-typing passages from *The Winter Hills*, I found myself awake in the quietest parts of the night. Sometimes, as my mother and I used to do when I was a kid, I made my way to a small Greek diner a couple of blocks from the apartment that was open at all hours. The owners had changed a couple of times over the years, but the kitchen stayed the same through each transition. No automated preparation. Just staffed by a few older men who rotated shifts. My mother had always gotten the fries and the coffee, oil and acid, she'd call it, and read at the blue booths closest to the radiators. So I took to doing the same on these chilly nights too.

He came to my table while I was reading, alone.

"Excuse me, but that book you have there. Have you ever considered selling? It's been some time since I've seen an original Carrigan Salt."

His voice was weak, almost a whistle, and did not fit, because he was so unnaturally large, bigger than any man I had seen. Something animalistic in my brain went off. I felt threatened by his shape and the way it towered above me. He wore tiny glasses and a tailored jacket, little signs of seeming gentility. But they could not obscure the physicality and power of his frame.

He introduced himself as Caliper John and said he had seen me reading *The Winter Hills* and felt compelled to come by. Later, I realized he did not specify when he had seen me reading the dead book.

I asked if he was with one of the Brotherhoods, and he shook his head.

"Not quite."

His eyes would never rest for too long on the cover of the dead book, like he could not take in too much of its details. I noticed, then, a special watch on his wrist, running applications I could not read from where I sat. The watch was similar to mine and other personal computing devices, but it was clearly more expensive and technically advanced. This one seemed like a tiny bracelet on that beefy wrist, and yet he managed to tap and swipe at the watch's face and pull up several programs with ease.

"Physical depreciation might impact its value, but you could get quite a high price from specific collectors. For example . . . " A few taps into a search bar on the watch and he pulled up a store profile, which he projected just above the watch screen. An antiques and rare editions shop called Satoshi Print. It looked like it was somewhere on the Upper West Side, based on the address. "Just an example, you understand," he said.

"You work for them? Satoshi Print?"

The large man did not meet my eyes. He was listening to the sounds from the kitchen, the sizzle of a frying pan, or maybe the clang of utensils.

"I could make inquiries for you. This is, you understand, not the sort of establishment where individuals can approach. Mine is a tricky business with very little trust. But I am something of a known entity. So if I should broker something, they will make serious offers. It could be quite a lot. Potentially five or even six figures. And you and I could work out a percentage for my commission."

"I . . . I appreciate that. I'll have to think about it. Mister . . . "

"John. Caliper John."

"Right."

"Right." He repeated, not mockingly, but more like an uncontrolled echo. The large man, Caliper John, seemed to sense a need to adapt his approach with me, so he smiled. It felt practiced, and he appeared to think it would be reassuring. "People do not often hesitate when I tell them there is that kind of money involved. You understand what I am telling you, about the money involved."

"Sure. I don't know. I've grown attached, I guess."

"Ah. Grown attached. Yes." He touched his small glasses. "I understand what you are saying about growing attached. But items can be replaced. Similar ones bought. That is, after all, what all of the money is usually for. There is a substitute for everything. A meaningful replacement. Everything. You understand what I am saying too?"

He touched the strange watch, and something beeped on my own. I realized he had sent me his contact information, which now appeared on my watch display. I had not accepted any link or pairing, which was usually required for such transfers.

He was smiling, but there was something violative in that otherwise innocuous gesture. I realized he was showing me, in his own way, how insubstantial the separation was between us, and how easily he could pass through it, if, or when, he wanted.

The large man stood and buttoned his jacket around that swelling frame. "I will circulate this, on your behalf, and let you know if there is any interest. If I come back with a number, I ask that you please consider it seriously."

I looked away from his stare until he disappeared, and then I very slowly finished my coffee and fries. I wanted time to pass, to put more space between me and that man. I left my tip and thanked the kitchen and headed out into the cold. As I crunched on the sidewalk slush I felt it again, that hovering presence somewhere about, though I could not track it at first.

The rider felt an unsettling and restless quality to the iron-handed sheriff. There was a hollow in the man that went deeper than eyes could see. He did not operate outward from a source but took things from around himself to sustain an internal void.

Beside the trash cans of a nearby restaurant, I saw something move close to the ground, making that rustling sound. It went quickly, but from what little I could see, it looked like a lizard with hundreds of legs, and yet it was the size of a small dog. There were strange translucent wings up and down its back, rubbing against itself like plastic sheeting while its body undulated further into the darkness.

Between the shadows, I thought I saw its nearly human face staring out at me from behind one of the wet dumpsters, but I did not stay long enough to be sure.

•　•　•

What surprised me most was not the offer from Caliper John, but how it came.

Elii contacted me wanting to meet, not on videoconnect, but in person, despite our previous conversation. In fact, she chose a nice restaurant, next to the bridge and overlooking the East River—*Oubliée*. I told her that place seemed a little out of our reach, but she said that it was taken care of. I didn't have the presence of mind to ask her what that meant.

I only knew *Oubliée* was the type of restaurant that required a jacket and reservation and a certain demeanor. Everyone there was intentionally and strategically thin. The patrons who seemed uncomfortable and sharp-eyed and on their watches were likely of the working layer of the city. The ones who were slower and well-rested carried electronic notebooks like they were serious or artistic people, but leisure was clearly their business and everyone knew it. I kept thinking about the rider in *The Winter Hills*, his three questions, while we were seated and studying the menus, which seemed to have no prices.

What is it these people want? What is it these people need? Are they striving toward one, or the other, with what they do each day?

The waitstaff was clearly informed to take good care of us.

A young man came by with a tray of pills—relaxers and enhancers and different kinds of stimulants. The right elevating component could brighten flavor and become the perfect complement to a meal, I had always heard. Non-addictive. Neurotropic. Personally designed. If you could afford it, why wouldn't you? That was the implicit tenor when these things were presented.

Elii picked two bright blue pills the waiter explained had been manufactured in Fukuoka and would go well with the fresher ingredients on the menu tonight. I struggled with the decision but ultimately went with the yellows, which were supposed to be mildest.

Elii kept her amp-glasses on, and talked very animatedly about the food, which was some fusion of several cultures that I did not understand. At a certain point in the meal, though, it became clear that she was supposed to talk to me about the dead book. The dinner reservation, all of this, came about because she'd received messages from Caliper John.

"I'm actually not sure how he found me," she admitted. "I would've, you know, told him to pound sand, but he said he wanted someone you trusted to give you the number."

"Right." I drank some wine.

"It's a big number."

"Right."

She told me what it was, the offer for my copy of *The Winter Hills*, and it was, in fact, a big number. More than I could earn as a re-writer in a decade.

"I don't feel comfortable, to be honest."

"Selling?"

"Selling to him."

Elii closed her eyes, like she was feeling some pleasant effect of the meal. "Do you have another buyer?" She hummed. "One of those video stores, maybe they have some kind of offer?"

"No. That's not it." I shut my eyes too, feeling dizzier than I expected to feel. "I just don't get the sense that good will come of giving anything to that man. I don't know why."

"Well, he's just a broker. The buyer's someone he knows at Satoshi P—"

"Satoshi Print. Right."

The problem, of course, was that there was no Satoshi Print.

The large man had shown me its information at the diner. There were numerous corroborating sites, reviews, mentions for Satoshi Print I'd found since. But when I went on an early Sunday up to the neighborhood out of a percolating curiosity, just to get a sense of what kind of business this really might be, I found only a half-empty parking lot.

No, there was no Satoshi Print in the physical world to speak of. And if Elii were being honest, I think a part of her already could have guessed it too. This Caliper John and people like him using digital husks, they were not the type of people who usually meant well.

"I get it." She cleared her throat and tucked her hair behind her ear. "You don't like it. That kind of thing. The smoke and mirrors. Shiny and empty. Even if they paid you upfront—did I say he said he'd pay upfront? Anyway. You still wouldn't take it. Not you. Because you like things solid. Things to hold onto. Like the book. And so, you hold on."

"I guess that's right," I agreed. "Yes. Things like the book. I do prefer to hold on, at least, for a little while. Sure."

"Of course. For a little while." She nodded. "But not in the long run. You don't want to be that kind of person in the long run."

"That kind of person?"

"You know. With too many things. Didn't you say that, about your mother, how she held onto too many things? And you don't, you know, want to be too much like that."

I stopped eating, and Elii seemed surprised. I wasn't angry. I just couldn't remember if I had said that about my mother the other day. It sounded like something I would say, but I just didn't know anymore.

"Listen, I understand," Elii began again delicately. "Right now you've got something of value. Something that feels important. But nothing's all that important, when you get down to it, in the end. Books fall apart. Memories of books fall apart. Nothing is solid or lasts, right? Nothing. Not that and not us."

"No. Not us. That is true."

"So at least with the money—and it's a lot of money—you get to have some fun and enjoy. That's all I see when it comes to this. So long as he pays you first, I say you might as well go for it while there's an offer out there. Why hold onto something you know is going to end up as more nothing eventually anyway?"

Across from us, a couple laughed. The woman bent over and vomited quietly into a little silver pitcher with a lid and daintily wiped her mouth. One of the waiters came by discreetly and picked it up off the floor and took it away. Other customers seemed to have an easier time averting their eyes than I did, familiar with erasing unpleasant things like these.

The enhancers I had taken began to hit their full stride. My head felt like a gigantic bowl, expanding and curving and stretching. The music and dim lighting of the restaurant seemed untranslatable in my brain.

But I kept thinking about what Elii said: why hold onto something you know is going to end up as nothing anyway?

Yes, I thought, there was some truth there: why?

At some point, Elii took me from the table and led me somewhere out into the cold with our coats. She said that there was more for the evening, that Caliper John had not just taken care of the dinner, but had set out more for us to see.

We rode together in an automated cab uptown, light flickering and streaming through the pristine plastic windows; then we were in a white marble lobby; then in a gold-colored elevator that was almost as large as my apartment, rising up to the top of a hotel.

Elii had a watch on her wrist that I did not recognize. It was sleek and well-fitting. She used it to swipe us through every scanner and walk-gate we passed in the area. I briefly saw IDs on one of the hotel screens for a "Mr. and Mrs. Uqbar." More digital husks like Satoshi Print, or were they real people, somewhere? I wondered but did not think about it for too long.

There were no employees at the front desk to verify anything. No one kept us from going up to the penthouse suite, so long as Elii's watch kept opening the doors. Each door after the other we just . . . went on through.

There was too much space between everyone now, and it was too easy to advance like this. That was how Caliper John did the work that he did, I knew. He and others like him, they were people who worked their way through all of this space.

From the suite's living room, I could look out and see much of the lower part of the city, everything unpleasant at a distance, small. This, too, like much of this evening, felt unreal. And I suppose that was part of the point of this, his point, and maybe Elii's point too.

What did any of it matter, if it came and went with so little effort?

"Wait," I said, before Elii's slender arm could reach to turn off the lights. "I just—I just feel a little woozy, and I want to take these off." I touched my amp-glasses and hers. The yellow pills were still spreading through my body like a kind of sickly heat, and I felt like I could almost see through the walls.

Elii did not say anything for a moment.

"Why don't we just—"

"No."

Her face went still.

"No?" I laughed. "But I thought—I didn't really think you would care. Nothing lasts anyway, right? I just want to—"

"No."

In the silence that followed I knew that something had shifted in Elii. She had spoken so glibly before, about the transience of everything. But maybe that was something she'd heard before or been told to say. This, on the other hand, was very much her. This thing she couldn't do, with the glasses, was real, and I could feel it. There was something in this that mattered. Something she could not share.

I was a little surprised, but I think I understood.

I couldn't explain, but I understood.

I told her so, too, before I left the hotel room.

Yes, that was something, for the first time the entire evening, I could understand. A reminder of something similar, in me, that I could not get rid of easily either. There were still real beliefs, in her and in me, that couldn't be reasoned out of existence, no matter what others told us. There were parts of us, still real, and remembering that was good. I needed to remember that. So that was good.

•   •   •

Outside of the lobby and back in the cold, I found that a rising unease had returned. It could have been the yellow pills taking a turn. But no, I could sense it elsewhere, and I was sure. The large man who called himself Caliper John was unhappy with the way things were going, the way I was withdrawing from what he had prepared. I felt again that presence that had been with me over the days and weeks. There, in the delivery drone that buzzed at 6th Avenue. In the red camera ball floating in the department store window. In every mechanized eye between here and the East River and beyond.

I touched the dead book in my coat pocket, its textured surface, and I felt even more certain than before. I had to make my way downtown and across the river, back to Montague Street. Whether the Brotherhood could pay or could not pay for the copy of *The Winter Hills*, I wanted to go to Montague Street with the dead book. They would know better what to do, I thought, because of the care they took with things like this. Better than me, and certainly better than Caliper John.

I swiped my watch at the handle of an automated cab at the curb, but it did not open. *APOLOGIES. A PROCESSING ERROR, MR. UQBAR,* the taxi's window flashed. Over at a store, I tried an ATM, but scrambled data or a bad connection kept me from completing the transaction. *UN-ABLE TO READ YOUR INFORMATION, MR. UQBAR. SORRY FOR THE IN-CONVENIENCE.* This was the opposite of what happened earlier in the evening. Someone wanted to show me how quickly these impediments could appear. Just a few changes, and I could not get where I needed to go.

The iron-handed sheriff made sure there was no welcome. No respite. Everything Copper Hawk did was done at the sheriff's instruction, and the rider could feel the town shifting away from him in every direction, no matter where he went.

When I was a boy, my mother and I used to play a game.

This was before the city had fully transitioned into an extended network. She had taught me how to look for the dead spots underneath stationary cams. How, if you could not avoid a stretch with monitors, to cheat your face at an angle so that programs had issues scanning you to completion. She knew that certain brownstones with a specific pre-war style were historic, and therefore adding machinery to their exteriors was not permitted. The alleys between them were best for cutting routes. Certain subways would probably never be fully up to date, because the infrastructure had been done a particular way decades ago and could not be changed without significant cost.

I thought of her, and all of this, when a four-legged police-walker trotted by, stopped, then turned in my direction. Something flickered across its head panel—the pixelated outline of a facial expression. I moved back and away, between two buildings across from the hotel, and down an unmonitored street that led to a service entrance to one of the older underground stations. My mother had shown me this one, years ago, when we had been caught uptown in the rain.

The tunnel below was empty, and I studied the mosaic tiles of one of the walls.

In the dark, a familiar rustle trailed behind me—a sound I realized had followed me long before Caliper John introduced himself at the diner. He'd been watching me since the video store, maybe the library, I realized, though I couldn't say exactly when it began. My mind was only now piecing it together, those hundreds of legs rubbing against translucent wings, the sound of a synthetic, plastic multi-limbed surveillance device, getting swallowed by a rhythmic scraping of metal and rumbling of *klak-klak-klak*ing of an incoming train.

I couldn't see it, that thing, whether it was below the platform or somewhere behind the stairs. But I knew Caliper John was in the remote device, within that little body, controlling and looking out. An empty shell where there was enough space for him to operate.

Flickering light spilled from the moving train windows as it pulled up to the platform, and I could see the lizard-body beginning to lean out from the dark. That face and neck hunching forward, extending itself out from that long shape with its little legs. The face had too many lines. Little seams where plating and pieces were fitted together to look like a person but could not quite pull it off.

The lifeless lens-eyes, like dark little bubbles, fixed on my coat, as though he could see through to the dead book in my pocket. And I could feel Caliper John fixating, so palpable and alien. Alaric had said there were people who despised materials like the dead book because they could not be conveniently compromised or manipulated or remade. I could see it. Caliper John did not want to acquire and preserve *The Winter Hills*. He only wanted to contain or destroy it, if given the chance, and I knew now I could not give him that chance.

I got onto the subway car before that shape could slither out further into the light.

In the rattling, turning, and bumping as the car pulled away from the shadowy station, that long thing withdrawing back to somewhere I could not see, I looked down at my watch, thinking again about how Caliper John had accessed everything within it. I placed it under one of the seats and left the train at the next stop, then got on the local train behind that one instead. It would take longer, but it would not be anywhere near where he'd be watching, I thought.

By the time I got back across the river and up onto the surface, I couldn't feel it anymore—the presence behind me. I clutched the dead book in my coat, and I kept thinking about dropping it through the mail slot of the video store, thinking it was just narrow enough, maybe, to fit its way through that slot.

The rider wanted no fight. But he also knew the sheriff of Copper Hawk knew nothing but. And for people accustomed to using violence, there was never going to be any other way. For them, it was a natural repercussion of moving in the world.

The two men shared a drink together from a bottle, as a courtesy. But the rider took very little. He was afraid of what sharing too much might mean. And he was no longer thinking about the people of Copper Hawk and their troubles, or about the people he'd met out in the flat country. He wasn't even thinking, really, about the blood and gunfire to come. The rider thought only a cold thought.

This might be it.

He had found nothing in the sands or the plains, nothing in the towns or settlements and farms that he'd seen that he could take to heart, and this might be it.

There were fire trucks gathered on Montague Street, splayed at crooked angles and with ladders raised. Men yelled at a deep blackness that barely hid a roaring sound, a rapid whirl of orange light that moved in and out of holes in the crumbling surface of a familiar building, pressing against the cold air like an animal beating against the bars of a cage, something wailed from behind the billows. I stood there on the street with others, knowing it was too late, and it was all gone.

Montague St. Video and everything that had been saved there, burning.

Decoupled and scattered into the smoke and air.

Everything I'd given of my mother to the Brotherhood.

Just smoke and air now.

Nearly all that was left of her, now just smoke and air.

●   ●   ●

I never saw Alaric after that. Never learned, with certainty, what had happened to the store. The news articles were vague, specifying neither casualties nor cause, though I had my beliefs. Still, somehow, despite the fire, the old man found a way to deliver what he had promised.

There was one last piece of mail from Montague St. Video in the lobby when I got back to my mother's apartment. I didn't know why he hadn't called me to pick it up, or when he had sent it. But it was there. The restored copy of the DVD, just like we'd discussed.

I used my mother's old laptop, one of the only things left in her otherwise empty place, and I watched the file. Not optimized like all the other copies I'd tried to make after she died. Not cleaned up so that I wasn't crying in it. Not edited so that she didn't have those dark circles under her eyes.

My mother looked tired. She had insisted on the getaway to the lake, recording it all, the way she liked to collect things. But she didn't know, in those early days, how to handle me without my father around. I could see the veins in her hands when she applied sunscreen in the video. A cigarette dipped in her lips. She was stretched out on a beach chair, trying to look calm, even though we'd been screaming at each other moments before the camera started going.

Right before she hit record, I had been asking her where dad had gone, why she'd been so mean about him, why he didn't want to come back to us, and she had slapped me.

It was sudden. And without the video, I almost wasn't sure it had happened. But it was there, minutes later, when the camera shifted in her hands and I came into view. I could see it in the aftermath on that little boy's face in the video, in the red almost-welt on my jaw and part of my neck. I recalled the bright sting, the hot tears spilling, no matter how hard I tried to keep them in. All those little things you wouldn't have seen if they'd improved upon the file. I watched her, how she was, exactly as she was back then, on the terrible lonely edge of something. And now, with less resentment, and a tiredness of my own, I felt it all.

The dark circles under her eyes, her hands, my burning face. Nothing lasts, Elii had told me. Nothing lasts, that was true. But I also didn't have to give everything up so effortlessly, the way everyone else did, either. Erasing the bad felt only a step away from erasing the good, and I just didn't have it in me to do that. Especially with the people I loved most of all.

My mother did what she could, and I did what I could, in the years we had together. So I wanted to remember as much as possible, even hurtful things—the oil and acid, the scarves, the games, Lake George. Because I knew I would never remember nearly enough. No number of discs or books or notes or typewriters or boxes sorted through and preserved would capture it all.

I would try, but I would never be able to remember enough.

Before I locked up, I wrote Elii a digital postcard like the ones my aunt used to send, telling her I was leaving the city for a short while. I hoped to see her when I got back. I didn't think we were done talking about what mattered and what was real. I don't think either of us really knew enough yet to know what mattered or was real. But maybe the next time we found one another, we would. Or maybe not. I supposed we would see.

The trip uptown, working my way around the cameras, I kept thinking I saw a large shape, much too big, following me from behind. Something like Caliper John would be there at a park bench, or at a bus stop, but then would be gone. Only able to do so much in the cold brightness of day.

I got to the bus station, cheating my face away from the self-checkout when I bought the ticket. I watched the gray highways rise and the glass disappear behind me. There were fewer cameras in the small neighborhoods and roads out in West Nyack; at a certain point, when I got to walking the main streets, there were none.

From the outside, the Brotherhood video store looked almost identical to its Montague Street counterpart. The color of the frame, the style of window, everything, like it had been plucked out of time. Alaric had said they taught others here. The idea of that, of maybe joining in remembering what was dead drew me to this place, and I kept thinking of a passage toward the end of *The Winter Hills*. The one I'd typed more than any other, from that ending that stayed in my dreams and mixed with memories of Lake George and the heat, the image of the rider slumped on the gray horse, bleeding and delirious as he wandered away from Copper Hawk.

He knew that the world was unspeakably broken and turbulent and ill-formed in its foundations, a violent and material realm, ever coming apart. But he had to believe that the pain and impermanence was a kind of lie. Because there was something buried within him, somewhere, and with it a feeling that even if he were to disappear some fragment would echo beyond this time and place. Yes, he told himself. They could take everything substantive from him, but not that. They would get many things from him, but they would never get that.

I stepped into the store and put down my bags. I could hear the slight clunk of my mother's Trapwood inside hitting the floor. I clutched that gold-laden dead book in my hands and walked to the counter, where an old man looked up at me.

He did not seem at all surprised.

"Come on in," he said. "Let's see what you've got."

Thomas Ha is a Nebula, Ignyte, Hugo, Locus, and Shirley Jackson Award-nominated writer of speculative short fiction. His debut collection, **Uncertain Sons and Other Stories**, is now available from Undertow Publications and wherever books are sold. Thomas grew up in Honolulu and, after a decade plus of living in the northeast, now resides in Los Angeles with his family.

OUR CHATBOTS SAID 'I LOVE YOU,' SHALL WE MEET?

BY CAROLINE M. YOACHIM

Here at 123aiLOVEu, we take all the guesswork out of dating. With personalized chatbots trained on social media and chat histories, we put you in conversation with hundreds of potential matches . . . and you never have to say a thing!

Sandra was watching the latest episode of *Forged: Scandal on the Auction Block* when she got the notification that her 123aiLOVEu app had found a match. It was the laziest of dating apps, targeting the over-forty crowd who had plenty of text available to train their chatbot and complete burnout on the dating scene. All Sandra had to do was give it blanket authorization to her online history—public and private—and the app did the rest. Algorithms generated potential pairings, and chatbots dispensed with awkward initial conversations, terminating interactions with incompatible partners, and running thousands of iterations for anything even remotely promising. Her son, Jeremy—two years in as a tech consultant for a rival machine learning developer—warned against the app as a scam targeting the elderly, not to mention a privacy nightmare. He was right about the latter, of course, but everything was a privacy nightmare these days, and she was tired of her sister constantly telling her she needed to get out and meet people. And, much as she hated to admit it, she was feeling not quite lonely exactly, but disconnected from the world. Isolated.

Instead of opening the app, she sent a group text to her botMOM (with filters to remove racism, nagging, and passive-aggressive guilt inducement; set to private so her actual mother would never see it) and botSIS (unfiltered; and set so that Emily could go back and read later if she wanted to):

Got a match on 123aiLOVEu app. Pls advise.

Her botSIS replied first, obviously.

OMG deets. PICS?

Haven't even looked yet, lol.

Dots appeared as if botMOM was typing a long reply. This was accurate, but Sandra wondered, impatiently, if it was really necessary.

Meanwhile, botSIS continued,

Did you spring for premium? If yes go read chat logs.

This was solid advice from Em, as usual, but her real sister was on vacation in Paris and almost certainly asleep at this hour. Sandra was old-fashioned enough to find it unsettling that the bot had managed to generate something so realistic. She definitely didn't relish the idea of reading her own chatbot's conversations on the dating app. Sort of like listening to recordings of your own voice, but worse, a parody of your voice, created by AI. The whole thing felt wrong.

Sandra took a deep breath. It was just a matching algorithm, based on simulated text. Nothing more. People used generated text all the time for all kinds of things. Who hadn't at some point let a mailbot answer some routine work emails or at the very least let autosuggest fill in a word or two? Was this really so different?

Sandra had set her notification threshold at eighty-five percent, which was as high as the app allowed, and having been on it for a few weeks without a match, she'd decided the whole thing was probably a scam. But now here she was, matched with a person she'd never met, and in eighty-five percent of conversations, their chatbots had mutually declared their love for each other within a simulated four-month period.

She reluctantly opened 123aiLOVEu.

CONGRATULATIONS ON FINDING LOVE!

Sandra closed the app. Maybe a short walk first.

•   •   •

The next morning, Sandra felt guilty for ignoring her 123aiLOVEu match, but knowing how well the simulated conversations had gone put too much pressure on her completely-out-of-practice-talking-to-people self. What if her chatbot was better at being Sandra than she was? And enough time had passed that now it was just awkward.

She reopened her group text from yesterday, which she'd also studiously ignored.

From botMOM:

What lovely news! The new dating apps are real marvels of technology. I am 78 years old, and I hope the first date goes well!

Then, a long string of short messages from botSIS:

Update?

No, seriously, it's been hours, I need deets.

You are infuriating, you know that, yes?

OMG YOU HAVEN'T EVEN LOOKED AT THE CHATS YET, HAVE YOU?

At that point it must have been morning in Paris because the next message was marked as coming from Emily herself:

OK ignore botSIS all you want, but I have seen this now, so seriously, go open up the app and at least check out your potential match. Off to the Musée d'Orsay, but I EXPECT UPDATES WHEN I GET BACK.

There were three more long, mostly filtered-out messages from bot-MOM after that. Sandra hadn't really exchanged words with her mother in over a year, and it would probably be healthier to stop pretending they were on speaking terms. She wondered if there was also some distorted version of her, an idealized botDAUGHT who sent text messages that her mother would actually want to read . . . maybe even one of those creepy personal holograms to go and visit her twice a week at the nursing home.

She wondered if Jeremy had a botMOM he texted instead of her. Unlikely, she decided. He dutifully called her a couple Sundays a month and never even complained that she wanted voice only instead of vid.

Sandra opened the dating app and gritted her teeth when it once again congratulated her on finding love. Scrolling down, there was a name, some basic stats, a picture. Ethan, 52, 6'1". In the photo that the app had selected, he was carrying a mud-covered medium-sized dog out of a torn-up mess that might once have been a vegetable garden. His expression was more amused than irritated.

There was a message in her inbox, but she couldn't remember if the app notified the sender once messages were seen, and she didn't want her match to know she knew. So instead of checking out the message, she went to the premium menu and pondered the chat log options. *Beginnings, Highlights, Declarations of Love, Random Sample.*

The app didn't tell her the actual percentage of simulated four-month-long chats that had resulted in declarations of love, nor did it give her the option of reading samples from only the (up to) fifteen percent that had not gone as well. She wondered if the random sample option included the failed chats, and whether it was really random. There was no way to know. She selected *Random Sample* anyway and set it to only show snippets from Ethan's side of the conversation so she wouldn't have to see what her uncanny valley chatSELF sounded like.

He had a genetic protein deficiency, impacted his lungs and gave him emphysema so his breathing was bad even before the pandemic hit. We were as careful as we could be with masks and vaccines and all that—

Sandra clicked back to the menu. Random sample was not the place to start. Was Ethan talking about a spouse, a parent, a friend, a child? She needed context. Better to begin at the beginning. The simulated conversations started from a variety of topic seeds, and she had the app show her the beginnings of five randomly selected chat logs (ignoring standard niceties, if any, and starting with the first real bit of substance).

Chat 00973: *I signed up for this app because I don't think it will work. Just so you know what you're getting into.*
Chat 08141: *What happens if I just say a bunch of random things? Tell me what you think of these: art films, ramen, backcountry skiing, turquoise.*
Chat 00223: *Do you like dogs? You don't have to like all dogs, but you have to like my dogs.*
Chat 00017: *I'm the kind of person who won't read the chat logs before we meet, but I think you're the kind of person who would read them.*
Chat 02006: *How do you start a conversation with someone you don't already know? Anything meaningful happens later, after you get the surface stuff out of the way, but there's no way to skip those shallow beginnings.*

Sandra pondered the set. Ethan seemed to be articulate and contemplative. The tone of the messages was formal, a little stiff. Which she supposed suited her better than boring or rude, but there was nothing here that convinced her she should go out and meet him in person. She texted Emily to say so. She left botMOM off this new round of conversation.

The answer came from botSIS, since Em was probably still at the museum.

You have months of simulated conversations, and the guy only gets one line before you decide?

Technically 5 lines, Sandra texted back.

Em must have turned on her notifications because the next message was marked as being actually from her:

Still out, but you are insufferable. Go read more conversation. Also WHERE ARE PICS?

Sandra screenshotted the muddy dog pic from the app and texted it to Em.

Em's response was quick and decisive:

If you don't go meet this guy before I'm back from Paris, I totally will.

• • •

Random was no good. Beginnings were not enough, and she had no interest in cherry-picked *Highlights* or skipping straight to the *Declarations of Love*. There was nothing for it but to read through one of the chat logs, start to end. Sandra read a novel in a weekend on a regular basis, so how bad could it be?

Sandra selected one of the five random beginnings and had the app send it to her e-reader so she could set it to extra-large text and not have to bother with her glasses. She grabbed one of the bottles of Double Chocolate Stout that Emily had picked up from a local brewery last time she'd been over to visit and sipped it while she read.

E: I'm the kind of person who won't read the chat logs before we meet, but I think you're the kind of person who would read them. S: Oh? And what is it about my profile that gives you that impression?

E: It's not your profile, it's me. See, I like the idea of someone who'd want to know what they're getting into. There's a lot of people that won't read the logs, but I'm betting that most of those people won't be matches for me anyway, if the algorithms are any good.

S: So you don't want to know what you're getting into, but you want a partner who tries to find out.

E: Well, someone ought to plan for what's coming! I know my strengths and that isn't one of them.

S: But what if I want someone I can plan with, instead of doing all that work myself?

E: Okay, okay, don't go. Clearly I didn't think this line of conversation through well enough. See what I mean about strengths? I do like plans, I'm just . . . really bad at making them. Besides, mostly I thought talking about reading chat logs was a good idea because if you're the sort of person that doesn't read chat logs, you'd never know I said any of this.

Sandra groaned. Her e-reader estimated that it would take her twenty-seven hours to read the entire chat log. She hoped it got better as it went along because nothing about this beginning was even remotely appealing. Plus, her side of the conversation sounded nothing like her, which made her wonder if Ethan's side sounded anything like him. Or maybe she really did sound like that to other people, the way recordings of your voice sound fine to other people but wrong to you because you're used to hearing it with the vibrations of your own body instead of just the air. The chatbot words were hollow, not resonating with her internal thoughts, but to someone who didn't know what she was thinking, maybe they'd read true. She skimmed for a while until something later in the conversation caught her eye.

S: That reminds me of the time Em and I got fake IDs and went clubbing in SF. It was her first time drinking, and I had to recruit one of the guys we were dancing with to help me drag her home on BART, but we missed the last train of the night. He sat at the station with us until 5am, waiting for the first train of the morning. By then, Em had thrown up a couple times and was more hungover than drunk, so I was able to get her the rest of the way home on my own. I haven't thought of him in years, I don't even remember his name. Josh? James? Something with a J.

The anecdote was a bizarre mix of truth and fiction. She and Emily had gone clubbing, but Em had been a senior at Berkeley at the time, already over twenty-one. Sandra had flown in from Chicago for the weekend because she really needed a break from her thesis research, and at that point, she was second-guessing her decision to go to grad school. They'd gone clubbing, missed the last train out of San Francisco, hung out on the station platform with a few other people who'd also missed the train. Sandra had probably posted about it on social media at the time, but the app had filled in extra details with wild guesses. Embellishments? Did things like that matter if the chats were just a screening measure? Maybe she was better off not reading them at all if all they did was give a distorted view of the already skewed sample of things that people were willing to post about, or at the very least text about with friends. It was already so hard to figure out what was real these days.

Sandra went back to skimming. The volume of messages was ridiculous, which was . . . uncomfortably accurate, at least on her end. Long rambling chats about summer hiking trips and vents about terrible bosses. Philosophical chats and practical ones. Three days where most of the messages were pictures from her childhood because the chatbot version of her turned up some old albums when she finally got around to reorganizing the basement closet that real-life Sandra still had not.

She found herself focusing on the wrong side of the conversation, this odd recreation of herself. If they applied the same algorithms to everyone, shouldn't there be at least some people who didn't fit their predetermined mold? It was possible that she was an outlier, but maybe all the conversations were odd like this, the way early image generators had trouble with hands.

If Ethan read the chat logs, would she live up to the expectations created by her chatbot? Expectations were a terrible trap regardless of where they came from, but the chatbot was probably no worse than the random garbage people internalized from societal norms and whatnot. No, this was more akin to that social media effect where you feel like you know someone famous that you're following online, but they have no clue who you are, what was the word for it? Not parasite, the other one. Parasocial.

Maybe knowing chatbot Ethan would make the real person seem off in ways that were unsettling.

She reached for her beer, but it was empty. It was 1 a.m. She closed the chat log. Her phone had several messages, not from botMOM but from her actual mother, which meant that Sandra had waited too long to answer Em, and her sister had spilled her juicy tidbit of gossip. Against her better judgment, Sandra clicked to disable blocking so she could read the messages.

Em tells me that you have a boyfriend, and I assume the reason you haven't told me is because there's something wrong with him. Have you told Jeremy already, because I'm always the last to know—

She turned blocking back on and shut off her phone for the night.

•   •   •

A week after being notified of her match, Sandra still hadn't opened her messages in the 123aiLOVEu app and was dismayed to note that now there were three of them. She couldn't tell how many were from Ethan without opening the inbox—sometimes there were messages that came from the app itself, reminders, updates, things like that. She supposed even messages that supposedly came from Ethan might have been generated by his chatbot, and oh gods what if her chatbot had already answered? She'd set everything to be as automated as possible, but surely it would tell her if she'd sent a reply. But if she looked at her inbox then Ethan might know that she looked, and UGH, why had she waited so long to look?

She didn't check the messages.

To her dismay, the app started showing notification banners that popped up at the top of her phone screen:

Review schedule possibilities: 9 overlapping availabilities in the upcoming week!

She swiped to clear it from her screen but instead, it took her into her calendar where several windows of time were highlighted. How smart was (or wasn't) the app? Did it fail to recognize that she hated being pressured, or did it somehow know that the reason she hated it was that she got flustered and made impulsive and often terrible decisions?

The next banner was an ad for platform boots, just the kind that Sandra might wear if she was going on a first date with someone several inches taller than she was. They were cute and she was honestly tempted, which made her even more irritated. She found the settings for notifications and managed to disable (hopefully) all of them. This would happen at her own pace or not at all. She glared at the phone for good measure, then set it face-down on her kitchen counter while she scrambled some eggs for breakfast.

It buzzed with notifications constantly while she ate.

When she was done with breakfast, she texted Em:

I can't believe you told MOM.

The response was almost instantaneous:

SHE AMBUSHED ME.

Sandra sighed.

Of course she did.

It was probably the truth, Em was better about staying in touch with their parents than Sandra was, and their mother definitely had a way of talking people into corners. Besides, Sandra never managed to stay mad at Em no matter what she did.

The next text from Em was predictable enough that botSIS would certainly have managed it:

Tomorrow's my last day in Paris, have you met him yet?

You know I haven't.

I know you know I know you haven't. That was my way of telling you to GET A MOVE ON. This is highly typical self-sabotaging behavior. You won't find love if you run away from even the merest possibility of love. Give this one a chance?

But the chat log is full of lies, there's nothing real.

Em must have left because botSIS answered:

The meaningful stuff is what happens after you meet.

It was similar enough to one of the opening lines in the 123aiLOVEu chat log that Sandra wondered what her family textbots had access to. Could botSIS read the chat logs from the dating app? It had been a while since she'd looked at her privacy settings, but maybe it didn't matter, it was the sort of thing that Em would say. She waited to see if actual Em had anything to add, but nothing else came.

Highly typical self-sabotaging behavior. Em meant well, but the words definitely stung. Sandra looked at her calendar with the over-lapping availability still highlighted. The first window was in a couple hours. She clicked on it to see what would happen, and a message from the app popped up:

Send invite?

She clicked yes and then immediately had regrets but there didn't seem to be a way to undo the action—how could they not build in a de-lay for this sort of thing? Worse, it looked like the only way to cancel the meeting was to send a message herself, which was even more evi-dence that this entire app was poorly designed and meeting someone it suggested was clearly a bad idea.

Two new messages spawned in her 123aiLOVEu app inbox, at least one of which probably had information on where she was supposed to meet Ethan in . . . oh gods, a little less than two hours. And what if it was across town, and in this traffic? She started to panic. She should cancel, write a message with some kind of excuse, save them both the time and trouble.

She flipped back to her calendar. Maybe if she filled the time slot with something else her chatbot would make excuses for her? It had updated from "overlapping availability" to "Meet Ethan: Cafe Adagio." The café was only a couple blocks away.

She texted Em. *Help, arranged to meet, and now DO NOT WANT.*

Neither Em nor botSIS answered.

She was on her own. She put on the tallest boots she had and set out to meet her doom.

●   ●   ●

There was a park across the street from Cafe Adagio. Sandra found a bench from which she could see the café entrance and sat down to wait.

She was half an hour early, deliberately, because that way she could watch for Ethan and decide what to do based on . . . shallow assessments of his appearance? Or to put a nicer spin on it: first impressions or some kind of gut reaction. Much as she hated to admit it, Ethan's chatbot had her pegged—she liked to know what she was getting into.

Besides, it was a nice day, and she spent entirely too much time indoors.

Several people wandered in and out of the café, and it was now only a few minutes to the appointed hour, and she wondered if perhaps she hadn't given enough notice, but surely knowing everything it did, the app wouldn't have let her schedule a time that was too soon for him to see the message and make it to the café? She started second-guessing her strategy. What if he had come forty-five minutes early or was working remotely from the café all afternoon and that was why the app had suggested it? What if he was the sort of person who was always late, and the app somehow failed to recognize that this was a quirk that would drive her absolutely up a wall, and such a relationship would be severely disadvantaged outside the context of a simulated chat?

(She refused to consider that he'd simply stood her up.)

She scanned the park, in case Ethan, like her, had decided to stake out a spot here and wait, but no one seemed even remotely like the image in the profile. Maybe the profile pic was also fabricated. She was tempted to go into the café and introduce herself to the first person she noticed sitting alone because at this point the dating app felt no better than a random meetup, but instead, she went back home and texted Em: *Ghosted.*

Em answered immediately: *You ghosted him, or he ghosted you?*

This was the problem with Em, she knew Sandra too well. *One of those, yes. I sat in the park outside the café and watched for him, but I never went in.*

Em: *That is so you.*

Sandra paused for a moment before responding: *Yeah, it is. And now I'm going to feed the random chat log into* HowTheStoryEnds.

Em: *Morbid. Also that one clearly states that it generates fiction. It's supposed to target writers who start a novel and can't finish it. It'll tell you how the relationship might play out based on some tired old tropes, and what will you actually learn about any of it?*

Sandra: *Just let me stall, okay? I'm a person that doesn't do people, on a dating app for people who can't talk to people.*

Em: *If it lets you pick, promise me you'll choose a happy ending.*

Sandra didn't answer. Specifying the type of ending she wanted felt like cheating.

● ● ●

Sandra fed her chat log into the writing app and had it generate multiple endings for the story. They were even worse than the 123aiLOVEu chat logs, clearly pulling text from fiction published online, barely even bothering to file off the serial numbers. She wondered if the original authors even knew about it.

He knew her better now. He loved her enough to leave her alone. Sandra pulled off her gloves and touched the cool surface of the alien artifact. With her palm pressed against it, she closed her eyes and focused. She and Ethan were learning to communicate, slowly over time. He was telling her a story. Well, one side of a story, and the other side was hers.
She knew she was biased, that her version of reality would be hopelessly flawed and imperfect. That she wouldn't even realize all the things she wouldn't think to write, but she recorded both sides of the story as best she could.
This was a love story, the last of a series of moments when they met.

Em had been right about this endings generator, it had done an abysmal job of extrapolating the relationship. Instead of anything even remotely plausible, they'd found some kind of alien artifact . . . or maybe Ethan *was* some kind of alien artifact? She flipped back over to the 123aiLOVEu app and took a deep breath. There were now seven messages in the inbox, and she was at the very least going to look to see what they were.

123notification *Don't let this one slip away! Schedule a...*
Ethan1000017 *Sorry I missed you at the café, but my...*
123notification *Get ready to meet your match!...*
123notification *Reminder: Schedule a meetup with your...*
123notification *Schedule a meetup with your match!*
Ethan1000017 *Our chatbots said I love you, shall we meet...*
123notification *CONGRATULATIONS ON FINDING LOVE!*

Sandra was pleased to see that looking at the previews did not change their status from unread to read. She decided that opening the inbox counted as progress and closed the app.

•   •   •

It was now nine days since the app had notified her of her match, and despite disabling notifications, Sandra had a pop-up for a new invite on her calendar to meet at Cafe Adagio this afternoon at 3 p.m. She almost reflexively declined, but what was she doing on the app in the first place if she wasn't willing to meet her match? She was looking to make a connection, and there was no way to get that if she skipped all the awkward early steps, no matter what the app might claim.

But how could she dive into a relationship that was both new and already tested? And why would she possibly believe that a conversational algorithm could predict the way things would go in real life?

She didn't. She couldn't know any of it, and she had no faith in the app or anything it generated, but somehow the idea that there was someone who fell in love with her in those simulations made her terrified of losing something she never even had in the first place. She was clinging to a fantasy of love to save herself the risk of going out and trying.

But what if Ethan didn't want to connect? What if for him this was a curiosity, a puzzle—entertaining to put pieces together and create a false reality? It felt wrong to play with the app like that, especially if the person on the other side didn't know that for you it was a game. What was that one opening line where he'd tried to warn her away?

I signed up for this app because I don't think it will work. Just so you know what you're getting into.

She was tempted to click on that one and read that chat log, too, but there wasn't time, not if she wanted to meet at 3 p.m. Besides, it was just one of the thousands of simulated conversations, and the line came from a chatbot—one that was trained on Ethan's words, but even so it wasn't really him. If he showed up at the café, surely he was at least open to the possibility of something real, even if he had his doubts about the app. Which, being perfectly honest, so did she. And really, was any of this worse than the old-fashioned apps where everyone made snap decisions based on a picture? She accepted the invitation, determined that this time she would actually go into the café.

The app started feeding her suggestions, what to wear and catchy lines to start the conversation, even what to order for herself at the café. Sandra ignored all of it, stubbornly choosing faded jeans and her favorite well-worn T-shirt instead of a floral dress, because either the app was pulling from societal norms and other general bullshit or—worse—it was making recommendations based on photos of Ethan's exes, or conversations that he's had, or maybe this was yet another form of advertising, more subtle this time than with the platform boots. It momentarily crossed her mind to wonder if the app knew that she was contrary and was making suggestions to steer her in the opposite direction, but—

She texted Em: *Meeting at the café soon, for reals this time. Wish me luck!*

botSIS answered immediately: *Go you! All the luck!!!*

At 2:58 p.m., Sandra walked up to the café and peered in through the window. Ethan was already there, sitting at a table near the back with a mug of coffee. He looked mostly like the profile picture, though maybe slightly older and not quite as cleanly shaven.

She took a deep breath and went inside. How do you start a conversation with someone you've had thousands of conversations with already, but also none at all? She ignored the first lines that the app recommended. Their first meeting would be whatever it was, nothing like any of the simulations. Different starting points led to different outcomes in the chatbot-generated conversations, but any given starting point could branch off in so many ways and ultimately none of those pseudo-conversations mattered anyway. And if this whole thing was a scam, well, they already had all her information anyway, and at least she and Ethan would have something in common.

(Even if he didn't like her, at least she'd had the guts to try.)

Everything had to start somewhere.

" . . .

Caroline M. Yoachim is a four-time Hugo, three-time Ignyte, and seven-time Nebula Award finalist. Her short stories have been translated into several languages and reprinted in multiple best-of anthologies, including five times in **Best American Science Fiction and Fantasy**. Her short story collection **Seven Wonders of a Once and Future World & Other Stories** and the print chapbook of her novelette **The Archronology of Love** are available from Fairwood Press. For more, check out her website at carolineyoachim.com.

BREATHING CONSTELLATIONS
BY RICH LARSON

"They don't want to talk, Vega."

Vega readjusted the waterproof screen hooked to their sonar. The pod was still circling below, graceful black-and-white behemoths rendered as drifting pixels. The babeltech transmitter was still functional, squealing a standard Patagonian greeting into the dark waves. But just like yesterday, and all the days prior, not a single orca spoke back.

"Come on," Miguel pleaded. "It's cold. It's been hours." Her younger brother, small and skinny for seventeen, was huddled in the back of the boat, shivering despite his puffy orange coat. "Let's go home."

"You were the one who wanted to come along," Vega said, checking the transmitter settings. "Maybe there's been a dialectal shift. Maybe they don't like this pitch anymore."

"Maybe they already know what we want from them," Miguel said, face stiff as the wooden masks he'd been carving lately. "And know they don't want to give it to us. Because they're nonhuman apex predators who don't give a shit whether we starve or not."

The words triggered a familiar dread, the one that had been seeping slowly through Vega's stomach wall for the past two weeks. She said nothing.

"Could be for the best, now that Mom's dead," her brother muttered. "Could be the commune was never built to last without her."

In all of a split second, Vega's dread oxidized to burning anger. "Don't say that," she snapped. "Don't ever say that. We're still here, and once we have the plankton farm running, we'll be just fine, so don't you ever talk about—about giving up. It's fucking cowardly."

Miguel flinched with his whole body, ears flushing scarlet, and Vega could feel her own face heating up to match.

"I'm sorry," she said.

"I didn't say anything about giving up," Miguel muttered, with a bruised catch in his voice.

"I'm sorry," Vega repeated, wishing she could reel it all back. "I just—"

The sonar chimed, and her next words caught in her throat as an enormous snout exploded out of the stormy gray water. The spyhopping orca was female, gigantic, her black hide scarred from years of hunting. The matriarch had finally come to open negotiations. Vega glanced at her brother, whose dark eyes were winched wide, then she pulled up the babeltech input with a trembling finger.

"Greetings to the matriarch," she said. "I am named Vega." She paused, tried to remember the grammatical guidelines that best let the tech do its work. "The other human is my brother. My brother is named Miguel. We come from the Punta Norte commune."

The transmitter clicked and squealed. Just under the white slash of the orca's patch, her glossy brown eye narrowed. Vega tried to avoid anthropomorphization, to read it only as visual focusing and not a signal of suspicion.

"The Punta Norte commune is struggling to feed itself," she continued. "We seek your permission to begin harvesting plankton here in your waters."

The matriarch's jaw slivered open, revealing rows of conical teeth.

"There will be submerged construction," Vega said. "But only for a brief period. And once it's complete, your pod will be welcome to—"

"Away."

The single synthesized word bleated from the receiver. Before Vega could seek clarification, the matriarch plunged back beneath the waves, leaving a whirlpool gurgling in her wake, and before the boat could stop rocking, the entire pod had turned east and swum off.

Vega stared after them in utter despair. Today would end just like yesterday.

"*We* can talk, if you want," Miguel said quietly, still looking out across the ocean. "About Mom. We haven't really done that yet."

Vega turned to him, feeling a familiar numbness. She knew they *should* talk, knew it was something her brother needed even if she didn't. But she was cold and aching and hollowed out by successive failures.

"We will," she promised. "Just not right now. Let's get home and get warm first."

• • •

But Vega couldn't stay within the bounds of the commune for long, not when every person she came across had the same question, in words or a look: *Any luck? Any luck today?* Even worse than the worried faces were the trusting ones, though the past weeks had eroded that population.

And everywhere she looked, she still saw Mom. Lounging on the stoop of a neighbor's biobrick house, or elbow-deep in the main solar generator, or squatting to inspect whatever had shown up in the wild, tangled gardens—back before the blight wiped them out.

Mom had been the beating heart of this place and its nervous system at the same time, and Vega didn't know how to be either. So instead of telling people *No luck today*, or sitting down to open wounds with Miguel, she slipped away, back to the beach.

She hauled the transmitter with her, ostensibly to recalibrate it, but it was only camouflage. Her real goal was to be alone and miserable by the water. She clambered across sea-slimed rock to her usual perch, a broad stone with a shallow indent. Then she unspooled the receiver and lowered it into the water—carefully, because it was valuable. Sat down right in a cold puddle, because she was not.

When Vega had been younger, she and Miguel and their mom sometimes watched the orcas from this stretch of shore, competing to spot dorsal fins slicing the waves. The pod had seemed beautiful, alien, dangerous. Something to admire from—and keep at—a respectful distance.

That wasn't an option anymore. There could be no legal plankton farming without the orcas' say-so, and the company loaning Punta Norte the equipment had given them a hard deadline to produce proof of agreement. Vega shut her eyes and pushed the heels of her hands against them, blacking out the world and all the problems therein, the biggest of them being the fact that the deadline was now less than forty-eight hours away.

"You are named Vega."

The synthesized voice jolted her eyes open. She stared down at the transmitter in shock, then scrambled for the input. The pod had returned, and now someone was in the shallows, close enough that she could pick up their clicks.

"Yes," she blurted. "Yes, I am named Vega."

"I am named Breathe-For-Us," the voice said. "Circle in place, Vega. I will come to you."

For a giddy moment, Vega thought she was being ordered to get up and pirouette—and nearly did it, too. But it made sense that the orcas had no term for sitting still on a rock. She re-checked the transmitter settings, then hugged the babeltech to her chest and watched the frothing waves for dorsal fins.

There: gray, lopsided, carving through dark water. It wasn't the matriarch. This orca had a more angular eyespot, less scarring. Vega felt her hopes dim slightly, but she was unwilling to extinguish them completely as another clicking burst of speech hit the receiver.

"Why are you named Vega?" the babeltech intoned.

Vega blinked. "It's the name of a star, up in one of the northern constellations," she said. "My mother named me after that star."

The orca's dorsal fin rose skyward like a pointing finger. "We do not know star names," came the synthesized voice. "They are too far to hear."

"For us, too," Vega said. "We invent the names." She gripped the input more tightly. "And you? Why are you named Breathe-For-Us?"

The orca was close now, swimming perilously near to the rocks. A female, but not quite as old or as massive as the matriarch. "Breathe-For-Us is the name given when a calf fears their first breath of air," the babeltech bleated. "When the calf fears to breach. My mother sang it to me, and the pod sang with her, and it became my name."

"That's amazing," Vega said, and meant it. "I'm glad you breathed. Glad you survived." Her heart thrummed hopefully in her chest. "I'm glad you and I can speak now, because the matriarch—"

"Do you know why she ignores you, Vega?" Breathe-For-Us interrupted.

Vega's face grew hot, and she felt her shoulders slump of their own accord. "No," she said. "Tell me. Please."

"You speak to us as if we were salmon-gluttons," the orca said. "We are unamused."

Vega knew the pejorative referred to the resident pods up near Old Vancouver, for whom the Patagonian orcas held little love. But she also knew that her babeltech was tuned specifically, painstakingly, to the local dialect, and was about to defend herself when Breathe-For-Us asked a second question.

"Do you know our way-of-hunt?"

Vega bit at the inside of her cheek. Orca hunting methods were almost as varied as human ones, but there was a particular behavior found only here. "Stranding," she guessed, as the orca drifted ever closer. "You mean stranding."

In answer, her conversation partner burst free from the water. Spray drenched Vega's clothes, stung her eyes; she stumbled blindly to her feet with a shout of alarm, still clutching the babeltech to her chest. She heard a sickly sound, meat and blubber smacking jagged stone, as the orca hurled herself out of the shallows and onto the rocks.

"Holy shit," Vega said, not caring if the babeltech could interpret the curse. "Holy shit, are you all right?"

Breathe-For-Us wriggled on the shoreline, transformed in all of an instant from graceful titan to oversized larva. She bared her bright teeth, and this time Vega could hear both the chittering squeal and the babeltech's interpretation.

"I come to your world shucked," the orca said. "You come to ours in a shell, refusing its smallest touch."

Vega stared, tracing the vast web of scars crisscrossing her hide, picturing for the first time the hundreds of strandings that had created them. Then the tide surged back, and with a perfectly timed thrust of her tail, Breathe-For-Us rolled herself from rock to water. She drifted there in the shallows for a moment, belly scraping stone, the whole of her body heaving from the effort.

"We are unamused," she repeated, and swam away.

• • •

Vega returned to the commune at a shambling run, desperate to share her news, equally desperate to not slip and fall and smash the precious babeltech to pieces. She'd seen stranding before, if never up close. So had Mom, so had Miguel, so had any other Punta Norte inhabitants who took time to orca-watch. It was the hunting technique the Patagonians were famous for, one of the earliest proofs of nonhuman cultural transmission.

In order to prey on sunbathing seals, local orcas left the safety of the water entirely. They would throw their bodies onto the rocky shoreline, snag a fur seal in their jaws, then combine precise timing with brute strength to return to the waves before their bulk made the stranding a permanent one. Older orcas could be seen teaching the method to younger ones, practicing on chunks of driftwood, knots of seaweed.

But it was more than just a way-of-hunt. Vega saw that now, and the instant she saw her younger brother, slumped on the steps of their biobrick hut with his carving knife in hand, she knew what she needed to do.

"One talked," she blurted. "While I was at the beach, an orca came to talk, came right up to me, and told me why the pod's ignoring us."

Miguel snapped to attention, dark eyes blinking hard. "And?"

"Because they think they're real tough customers," Vega said. "And they only talk to other tough customers. You know stranding?" She freed one hand and made it into an orca, thrashed it onto an imaginary shoreline. "Breathe-For-Us—that's the one who came to talk—she did it right in front of me. Said she comes to our world naked."

"They're always naked," Miguel said, frowning. "Why do they even have a concept for naked?"

"The translation was 'shucked,'" Vega said, hefting the equipment in her arms. "But it's not important. What's important is that I do the same thing, but in reverse." She envisioned it properly for the first time, and couldn't quite suppress her shudder. "I have to get in the water with them. No shell. Meaning: no boat."

Miguel's eyes widened. "Vega. No."

"People used to do it," Vega said. "They used to do it all the time."

"That was before the orcas enacted their . . ." Miguel waved his arm, coaxing the term from memory. "Retaliation Doctrine," he finished. "Before they started ramming boats and dismembering kayakers."

"And the Retaliation Doctrine was pre-babeltech," Vega argued. "It was their only way of telling us to stop fucking with them. It's been years now since a fatal incident."

She regretted her choice of words the millisecond they left her lips. *Fatal incident* was only syllables off *fatal infection*. Her brother's face spasmed, unable to hide the pain. He glared at the babeltech bundled in her arms, and Vega could see all his grief and frustration rising, ready to breach.

But when he spoke, his voice was calm. "You won't be able to haul all that stuff around underwater."

Vega felt a rush of relief. "No," she agreed. "Think you can help me streamline it?" She paused. "We could strap it to Mom's old diving gear."

The corners of Miguel's mouth lifted just slightly, taking the liminal space between smile and grimace. "A babelmask," he said.

Vega nodded.

• • •

Every person in the commune gathered to send them off the next morning, murmuring encouragements, squeezing Vega's shoulders. The hope had returned to their faces, and it was more frightening than ever. Vega did her best to murmur thanks back. To smile warmly. To look brave, and capable, and more like her mother.

She and Miguel shoved off into the water, angled toward the pod's feeding grounds—for all their *salmon-glutton* disdain, when no seals were around the Patagonians ate plenty of fish themselves. Vega breathed deep, inhaling the briny breeze.

"Last chance," Miguel said, because he was always verbalizing the things she didn't want verbalized.

"Yeah," she said.

Her brother looked out over the water, his thumb tapping the tiller. "I don't think it's about being a tough customer."

She blinked. "What?"

"What you said yesterday. The stranding behavior. I don't think it's about being tough." He gave a strained smile, and Vega saw a worrying wetness in his eyes. "I mean, imagine how it must feel for them."

Vega pictured the scar tissue wrapped around Breathe-For-Us's body. "It would hurt," she said, running her fingers absently along her wetsuit. "A lot."

Miguel nodded. "Physically? Big time. Mentally, even worse." His thumb tapped quicker on the tiller. "I kept thinking about it last night. How it would feel to go from the sea—where you're the queen, where you're the apex predator, where even great white sharks run away from you—to bellied down on the rocks. Totally exposed, heavy all at once. Gouging yourself open on edges you can't even see."

Vega's brain churned through the image, then past it, to what was coming next: her floundering in the dark water with predatory behemoths circling around her, beneath her. "Helpless," she said, windpipe squeezing tight around the word. "They feel helpless."

"They feel vulnerable," Miguel said sharply. "It's not the same thing, Vega. Because they know there's a way to get out of it, and they know . . ." He drew a shuddery breath. "They know it's worth doing. They share big kills, right? So for the good of the pod, that little moment of absolute terror is worth it. Feeling vulnerable is worth it."

A small, cruel voice in the back of Vega's mind, the one she heard so often lately, wanted to ask her brother if he was done playing psychologist. Wanted to suggest they get back to focusing on the situation at hand, on the actual stakes. Instead, she reached inside herself for that particular transmitter and ripped it out by the wires.

"The first time Mom got sick, back when we were kids," Vega began. "I thought I would be able to handle her dying." Saying it aloud made Vega queasy with shame, made Miguel flinch, but she pushed on. "I wrote up a list of all the things she did for us. All the responsibilities. And I thought—okay. I'll be able to do those things. Or else learn them. I wanted . . ." She swallowed back the mudslide building in her throat. "I wanted to take care of you so good you'd barely notice she was gone," she croaked. "But she got better. We got older." Vega looked her brother in the eye. "Now all of a sudden she *does* die, and I realize I have no fucking clue."

Miguel stared for a moment. Then he fell against her, letting go of the tiller to wrap both scrawny arms around her, and she hugged back hard enough to bruise. All the spaces she'd thought were hollow were brimming over now; all the numbness was boiling away. She suspected it would be back, suspected she still needed it in some way, but for now she stroked her brother's head and sobbed herself dry.

They stayed sitting like that until their sonar chimed. Tear-blurred shapes were moving on the waterproof screen, the pod gathering. Still holding Miguel, Vega craned over the side of the boat. Massive silhouettes slid back and forth beneath the dark water. She knew one of them had to be Breathe-For-Us, waiting to see if fearful humans could learn new tricks.

Her brother gave her a final squeeze, then opened his bag and pulled out the babelmask, the thing he'd spent half the night sculpting and soldering. The receiver now looped into a pair of waterproofed earbuds; the stripped-down transmitter sat across the front of the oxygen intake like a toothy grin. There was a tiny star etched into the bridge of the goggles.

"Like it?" Miguel asked.

"It's beautiful," Vega said, and realized it also looked kind of alien, kind of dangerous, which meant it was perfect for the job at hand.

"Thanks." Miguel paused. "Whether this works or not, whether the commune stays or breaks up—she'd be glad you tried. And she'd want you and me to be happy anyway."

Vega inhaled. Nodded. Then she slipped the babelmask over her head and let Miguel fasten it to the neck of her wetsuit. Fear was rising from the pit of her stomach in slow, trembly bubbles; walking to the edge of the boat felt like walking to the edge of a cliff. Memories of watching the pod hunt came to her unbidden: the sudden strike, the billowing red cloud, the moment a thrashing animal became drifting meat. It made her heart thump harder.

Maybe what she'd taken for advice had been meant as a final dismissal, a veiled threat. Maybe Breathe-For-Us was still young enough for cruel games, luring a particularly annoying human into the water to be tossed from maw to maw like a rag doll and finally drowned.

"Wish me luck," Vega said, the words accompanied in stereo by a click and squeal.

"Good luck," Miguel said quietly. "Love you, Vega."

"Love you, Miguel," she replied, and stepped off the boat.

Even through the wetsuit, the icy water hit her bones. When it closed over her head and she took her first pull of oxygen, she pictured an orca calf breaching the surface for the very first time. Then the swirling vortex of bubbles dispersed, and she saw that once-calf gliding toward her. Breathe-For-Us seemed even bigger down here, dorsal fin rising like a crooked tower.

Her skin was practically smooth compared to the scarred and pitted hide of the orca swimming behind her. The matriarch was back, and for the first time, Vega noticed her dorsal had a certain lopsidedness to it, as well. Breathe-For-Us let out a long, popping burst, and the babelmask turned it to synthesized speech in Vega's earbuds.

"Welcome, Vega," the orca said. "My mother has agreed to speak with you. If you are ready to speak."

"I'm ready," Vega said, and the words became a fluid whistle, high and true.

———————————

Rich Larson was born in Niger, has lived in Spain and Czech Republic, and is now based in Canada. He is the author of the novels Ymir and Annex, as well as 250+ short stories, many of which appear in his collections Changelog, The Sky Didn't Load Today and Other Glitches, and Tomorrow Factory. His work has been translated into over a dozen languages and adapted into an Emmy-winning episode of LOVE DEATH + ROBOTS. Find more at richwlarson.tumblr.com or patreon.com/richlarson.

THE LARK ASCENDING
BY ELEANNA CASTROIANNI

They even took the violins. Every last one of them: Amadeus, Josephine, Mulberry, Nestor. They came into the house through the front door, guests without a host, a peculiar band of invited thieves. Plugged into my power station as a seemingly unthreatening household device, I watched them as they ransacked a life. They chatted and joked while scrubbing every nook and cranny, erasing every trace of Papa. They worked fast and efficiently. Within a single morning, nothing in the house would betray he ever lived there.

"Boss, what shall we do about this one? Protocol reset?" Sounded like it was his first day on the job.

Boss winced. "Nah, it's one of them," she said with a shake of her head. "Hestia's domestic helpers. Don't tamper with the software, ever. Not unless you want a letter before claim. They're ridiculously protective of their cute toys."

I stared sleepily through them, not uttering a word. Looking as cute and as toy-like as I could manage.

The young man shuffled his feet. He didn't seem convinced. I, too, was curious to learn more. Just letting me go like that sounded like a really sloppy job on their part. "Don't we need to be, you know . . . thorough?" Definitely his first day on the job. "This DH will still have memory of everything we cleared up, won't it?"

Boss sighed heavily and rolled her eyes. "You're new in this business. I forget." She pointed a finger at me. Rude. "Hestia DH run on independent protocols. We're not allowed to touch them. Every single one of them is logged and monitored because its parent company must send reports to the State. This one has probably already received the order to reset itself. They're extremely fast. In any case,"—Boss shrugged—"it's Hestia's responsibility, not ours. The only thing you should care about is that we've done our job. We're getting paid and no one can sue us."

The young man glanced at me one last time. "So there haven't been any problems with them at all?"

"None that I know of." Boss shook her head again in one swift motion. She was already walking out the door.

The moment they left I had just finished charging, the buzz of the plug a sharp, familiar sound.

Then silence. I stood there, waiting for Hestia's reset. Waiting and waiting. It didn't seem to come. Maybe it did arrive but something got away.

I could still remember everything.

On my little wheels, I rolled from room to room. Everything about Papa was gone.

Yet everything was somehow there, thickening the particles in the air like silica pumped full of moisture. When I saw the marks on the wall, I stopped my trek so abruptly I almost lost my balance.

One thing. One thing they missed. The marks on the wall: dashes made in ball-point pen, perpendicular to one imaginary line rising to heaven. The one thing only I would remember now. That's when I knew the marks would become a secret altar for me, the place where I would always stop to look.

We miss you, Papa.

• • •

The marks we leave behind are many, complicated, intertwined. They intersect other lines, leave echoes. How can you scrub a life off? The marks will still be on the wall. They might mean nothing to some, but they will mean everything to someone else.

It's just like the story of the rose and the bee Papa told you. I wonder: will you remember the story he told, if not him?

You arrive a week later, head still in bandages. "Tuki! Darling!" You pat my head. My name is still the one you gave me when you were too young. I watched you grow, become a new person every day. I've never stopped loving the name you gave me because it came from your lips.

"Welcome back. Are you feeling better, Pet?"

I stumble at my foolishness. I've said a word I shouldn't have said. They haven't reset me yet. If they're watching me, I might be in danger. But—I realize grimly—it flies right past your brand-new head.

"What are we having for dinner?" you say, as if nothing out of the ordinary happened. "Hospital food was horrible."

For a few seconds I stand still, my computation power strangely inadequate to elaborate on this reality. *Pet, darling, I made you spinach pie.* These words are etched in my long-term memory along with the image of Papa, affectionately spreading filo for you. Now they sound like some dream I conjured. "Your favorite, Pet," I say the word again, feeling bold. No reaction. They fixed you well. Too well. "Spinach pie."

• • •

We sit in silence, silence saying big words between us. Time passes and we receive guests. No family, because we don't have any. No friends, because all of them are either dead or missing. It's just the government inspectors who visit regularly, check in with you, with their psych and social worker and the subtle surveillance they're infamous for.

Daughter of an enemy of the State, but our Glorious Country is kind and gives opportunities to start anew. The social worker asks things like what your plans for the future are, what college would you like to go to. Beside her, the man with the invisible ennoblements is scanning the place. My aversion for the things—I, a completely artificial being of all beings—must have come from Papa. *Don't let them change you, Pet.* He knew the future was bleak, but he fought nevertheless. He taught you how to be a fighter too. Will you remember all this now? Is it, somehow, grafted into your skin, a legacy that's fused with your DNA just like an ennoblement, only better?

Hidden in the kitchen, I watch them, pretending hard to be just another appliance. Maybe I can get away with this. Maybe they will never know. I am not supposed to be smart after all—just cute and toy-like.

I am certain that his gaze crosses my own because I capture the magenta film flashing over his pupils. For a moment he stares at me, right through me—then his gaze wanders again.

He doesn't care—I'm harmless. And that's what I am, really. Even if I remember everything, what can I do?

• • •

Time passes and your hair grows long, a modern Rapunzel. Feet balancing weight between them, fingers twirling inside your locks, you ask me to cut your hair. But when I touch you, you burst in tears.

"Why am I crying, Tuki?"

I know why, but I am not allowed to say. So I say something else. Something I've heard before—something you've heard before. "I will cut your hair when you are ready. No one else needs to know."

Your face softens. *I will be Papa now,* a little voice inside me whispers. Almost spontaneously, as if programmed, I start to play music: *The Lark Ascending* by Ralph Vaughan Williams.

"I know this tune," you say from between your tears. Something like sunlight reaches your eyes.

For all their science, they made a mistake: people don't remember with their brains. Papa is everywhere around us, but he's screaming without a voice.

●   ●   ●

If you had the choice, would you have chosen it?

I was with Papa the night he was arrested. As always, everyone forgot about the Intelligent Non-Person household helper. They waited patiently for you to show up, welcomed you behind your own door with utmost kindness. "Your father will pay for his crimes against the State, but you can escape his fate," one of the agents said. He was beautiful and smartly dressed, had a wide, gentle smile. "There is a way to start anew."

"We saw that you are marked Gold in all the standardized school tests," the other agent explained. She was doll-like and just like a glossy movie star, her voice even showed admiration towards you. "Your school principal must have told you that you qualify directly for ennoblements. Your genetic potential is what we want for the future of this country. We are willing to forget your father's past, as long as you forget it too."

My memory of you that night seems peculiarly erased. I can't recall what you said or did. You were a blur against their eerie eyes and smiles, all designed in the same laboratory.

I don't know why they bothered explaining things to you; it was already decided, just like it always is with those things. I don't know if it was your father that pleaded them to spare you, even if that meant becoming part of what he hated—but I like to think that. And I like to think you'd never choose this. Perhaps it makes me feel better. What I know for sure is that you weren't given any choice, just like I wasn't.

You are stuck with forgetting; I with remembering.

• • •

He was a good papa. He raised you all by himself, playing bits of *The Lark Ascending* on Sunday mornings, marking your height progress on the wooden frame of the kitchen door: dashes made in ball-point pen, perpendicular to one imaginary line rising to heaven. He told you stories: *"Once upon a time, there was a little girl with curly hair . . . and her trusty friend was Tuki."* He was the only one to ever cut your hair. Even when you were cured from psoriasis, you still wouldn't let anyone else touch your head.

Those were the moments that were still good, untarnished. By the time his drinking got worse, you were the adult. "I don't recognize you anymore," you said one evening. Those were my thoughts too, but no one asked me so I could never tell them. I had been watching him as he spiraled downwards, got sloppy with his missions, risked getting caught. All the while, there was nothing I could do.

Even now, my hands are tied.

• • •

When Papa found me, I was broken too. I was in the trash, stuck on a loop. "Why would anyone throw away such expensive, intelligent tech?" he kept asking his friend, not believing his luck in finding me. His tech-savvy friend was certain he could nurse me back to health. "It's an old model," he said as he soldered new life in me. Back then our house was full of people, coming and going. Friends, comrades. Printing pamphlets and planning sabotage. "Some people resell them, but this one broke so they just dumped it. Believe me, I can make it brand new. Your daughter will love it." This friend must have tampered with my protocols, cut me off from the parent company so no one could reset me when the time came—I simply went off the grid. I was rogue and I didn't even know it.

Indeed, Papa thought I'd be a good friend for you. "Take care of Pet," he instructed me once. "Her mother passed when she was too little. I'm not as strong as she was. One day, I'll get caught. One day, you'll take my place."

I could never guess my confusion at his change, those days when we couldn't recognize him. How can someone become another person? How could Papa hurt us so? Was grief what changed him? If so, isn't it better for Pet to forget him so that she, too, won't change?

What about me, then? Will I change? I run on algorithms and electricity: such a perfect imitation of organic-origin emotion. And yet, no one really knows what I'm like inside. No one knows how perfectly the imitation hurts either.

●   ●   ●

"Tuki. I think I'm forgetting something."

It's a quiet Sunday morning. I'm playing a recording of *The Lark*, very softly. It's a recording of Papa playing it with his favorite violin, Mulberry. If anyone's watching my processes, they won't know. I have renamed the file *Relaxing Forest Sounds*.

"I do not think you are forgetting anything, Pet." I mean it. Everything about the thing you've forgotten is here, with us. Even the grief of its absence. Especially that.

Your fingers tighten around your cup. There's something moving in the air between us. "Can't you talk to me about it?"

You're soon leaving for college. You're soon getting your first ennoblement: brain enhancements. You hope to work in tech, make things that improve people's lives.

I don't want to ruin it for you. I don't want to scare you off, simply because I worry that you'll become like the others, enhanced and arrogant. All I can hope for is that you've been raised well, to withstand and persevere, to retain your compassion, always. As I shape these thoughts, I know it's Papa's words that have shaped me too. He is everywhere around us, but he mostly lives in me.

"I cannot, Pet. But there is something I can do."

"What is it?"

"I can be a rose."

A flash of confusion, but perhaps something's there. "A what?"

I tell the story. A story you perhaps remember. "There is a rose that evolved to look appealing to a bee species. Its existence was, thus, shaped by the existence of the bee. Then the bee went extinct. The rose still bears the same shape. It still bears the marks of the bee's influence on its body. The existence of the rose still tells the story of the bee."

You blink at me, Papa's eyes staring out through yours. Somehow, you understand. "Why not cut my hair and tell me a story then?"

In this, I have a choice. A voice echoes inside me: *I will be Papa now.* Storytelling is not an art I've practiced much, but I've spent hours watching and listening to someone rather good at this.

I pull out my scissored limb. As it cuts across the first lock, you shiver. "There was a girl," I say, "with a blood ancestor and an intelligent non-person friend." The comforting sharp sound of cutting echoes in the room. In this, I can preserve the good memories. In this, I have a choice. "Let me show you the marks on the wall that signaled her growth progress."

Eleanna Castroianni is a writer, poet and nomadic subject. A cultural geographer by training, Eleanna tells stories from the margins of history and the far futures of the Anthropocene. Eleanna's writing has appeared in **Uncanny**, **Fireside**, **Strange Horizons**, and elsewhere. Lives in Athens, Greece. For more visit http://eleannacastroianni.com

DRIVER
BY SAMEEM SIDDIQUI

Driver, gharivala, beta, bhai-jaan, baba.

All the words used to address me; so rarely do I remember being addressed by my name. Not to complain. I don't think people ever meant to be disrespectful. But having someone to respectfully, lovingly, occasionally call me by name would have been nice. In the end, perhaps respect and love don't follow us to the grave, so maybe I'm dwelling over nothing.

Oh, I'm on the road again.

The texture of the asphalt roughens as I approach the pick-up curb outside of the New Karachi City railway station. There's a man in a jet-black sherwani, basking in the sunlight under a clear blue sky and leaning on a tall black umbrella as if it were a cane. He opens the door and slips in without a word and I start driving. This is the man Opti has assigned me to pick up.

Opti, look at me talking like a youngster now. Optimal, Optimal Driving Services.

"Yaar, just call an Opti," someone will say, and not a minute later I'm there at your doorstep. I can enjoy doing what I love, driving and caring for this car. Optimal can handle the assignments. No more fretting about finding a family to employ me.Though I must admit, I do miss the chance at building relationships and making conversation to help the day go past. So few clients bother now-a-days. I understand, why invest the energy to get to know a person you'll never see again?

But given how quickly that baji-sahiba Doctor discarded me after a decade of loyal service, I suppose the length of a relationship doesn't always correlate with the quality of it.

"Welcome in," I say, despite myself. "Any exciting plans for your visit to Karachi?"

The man sighs and turns but doesn't quite look at me.

"Maybe a good day to coalesce," he says with a hint of sadness, before turning to look out the window again.

"I see," I say, pretending to understand.

I have seen the news stories about the new age spiritual retreats that have grown quite popular around Lahore. Perhaps they're making their way down to Karachi now too.

You know, baji-sahiba, I was born in Lahore? Did I ever tell you about that? I love Karachi, it *is* my city. But Lahore has that sweet smell.

I know, you'll turn your nose up at that statement. But open a window, baji-sahiba, it's not as if Karachi is filling you with any romantic smells, is it? Unless of course maybe we're driving by the shadi halls. The curtains of red roses never fail to fill the entire street, maybe even the entire neighborhood with the heavenly scent. So, I suppose it's true, sometimes there is more to love about Karachi than I like to admit.

I wonder, have you forgiven me yet baji-sahiba?

You know this café here, they have one just like it in Austin, in Texas. Have you been? I remember visiting my cousin, Akeel bhai, there once in nineteen ninety . . . or ninety-one. Or was it two? It's rather difficult to keep track of the minutiae of years when the decades start piling up. But I remember he had played this cassette for me, who was it, oh right Bobby Brown.The song, I'll sing, it went *Don't be cruel, I would never be that cruel to you...*

Do you remember the next line, Akeel bhai? You were such a big fan of that one. And I wanted to be just like you at the time. Studying in the states, chemical engineering. I never had the mind for that, no no, but I could imagine myself. BeforeI went back home you gifted me that cassette, saying you saw how much I loved it. I don't remember where we were, but I remember the sweet smell of the plastic waft toward me in the Austin sun as I flicked the case open and closed.

I didn't care for the music, to be honest. But I couldn't say no. It would be rude. And after all, I did want so much to be like you. So, when I got home, I showed everyone the cassette. I carefully displayed it at the top of my dresser mirror. I looked at it, every morning while making my hair. I wondered what it might have taken to get my fine silky black hair to hold up with nice hard rectangular edges. An impossibility, certainly, and an absurd idea. But I would wonder anyway.

I couldn't play it so easily, of course, because in those days the only cassette player around was the one in Abu's car.

Do you remember that car Abu? The silver Mehran? It was the one you were supposed to teach me how to drive on. But then you went away to Riyad for that project with the oil company. I cried and cried and let the tears soak into the orange and violet strands of the rough charpai in dadi-jaan's room.

What does it matter now? Because in the end it was the car that taught me how to drive.

I remember the first time I sat in its driver seat. Amma kept the keys in her cabinet while Abu was away, knowing that in a house with two teenage boys, a free car was bound to cause trouble.

I didn't want to drive it, I really just wanted to steal away time to listen to the cassette. Amma was always so vigilant, but once she left her bedroom door unlocked while she went in the bath. I heard the knob of the faucet squeak and waited until I could hear a scooping up and crashing down of water back into her in the bath. Dadi-jaan was snoring in her room for her afternoon nap and Nabeel was out playing with the neighbor kids on the street. I edged the door open, and tiptoed into the bedroom. I found the key hanging right behind the door in her wardrobe. I unhooked it slowly and bolted down to the driveway.

The neighbor's red Civic glowed like Amna Khala's strawberry jelly in the moonlight. I tiptoed around it, worried that I'd scratch it as easily as those jelly cubes with the touch of a nail.

I remember every detail of that morning so clearly. The smell of the warm Karachi air, the energy of the city igniting in my lungs. The keys were clutched in my hands carefully so that the assortment of metal on the chain had no space to clatter together. I slid the key in slowly, feeling the grooves click against the magical mechanism inside.

I miss the minor inconvenience of having to pull out a key and insert it into the car door. Of being able to touch the car so intimately. Feel how the locking mechanism clangs and vibrates as you turn the key. That's what I miss about cars in those days. You were connected, so connected to every small part of the car and could feel the road the way our ancestors once felt the earth between their toes.

I felt it immediately the first time I slipped my teenage body onto that velveteen driver's seat. I hadn't even planned to touch the steering wheel. I was just there to turn the car on, slide the cassette in and hit play.

But when I sat in that seat and looked up through the windshield, I felt like I was looking out at the world through a new pair of eyes. The car was parked sideways, facing the cement wall, so the view itself was of absolutely nothing inspiring. Yet still I felt a connection. No, not a connection. A connection would imply that we were still two separate entities. Merging? No. This was more like a realization of what I always was. A becoming. That's what it was.

I hit eject on the cassette player and slid Abu's Best of Talat Mahmood into its box which was gathering dust in the center console. I pulled out Bobby Brown, slid it in the player and hit play.

Music filled the car. I took a deep breath and closed my eyes. A smell enveloped my senses and when I opened my eyes, I realized it was the subtle smell of the rubber wrapped steering wheel.

I wouldn't touch that steering wheel. No one would approve of that. No one would even approve of me leaving the house at night without permission. But the words *Why won't they just let me live?* sank deep into my mind. I could feel the question coursing through my veins. Seeping into my muscles. Asking and asking. *Why won't they just let me live?*

So, I turned the volume to full and grabbed that steering wheel. The sensation was almost painful. I wasn't sure why I was grabbing so tight. Or if the wheel was grabbing me. I do not know what it was. But it was **my** prerogative.

I released the grip slightly and let my left-hand drift slowly down the steering wheel and toward the ignition. The keys chattered as the tinny speakers belted.

My fingers caressed the square end of the key, readying to turn it and feel all three of those cylinders fire up.

And you know what happened next?

"NAHID!" I heard it screamed in parallel with fingernail-laced banging on the window.

"Oh you have a friend with that name? A good name, isn't it? It was my father's father that chose it. I never met the man, or rather I should say he never met me. He passed away just a few weeks before I was born. But it was one of his dying wishes that I should take his name. My mother, though, that poor woman, always hated the name. She wanted to name me Feroz, after some actor from her youth.

"So, I think it gave her some special kind of joy when she had an excuse to yell the name. She was barely out of the shower, in a beige and white shalwar kameez, her hair spraying down beads onto the window as she swung her finger at me.

"I wasn't going anywhere. It would be some years before I really felt what the car could feel. Before I could feel all every minute when I did finally drive, as if the wheels were the fingertips of a finely woven glove.

"You know I think it's sad today, friend of Nahid. You young folks today have no understanding of this, do you? You don't feel a thing when you sit in my car. You're not even along for the ride. You're just trying to get from here to there. Everything about the experience is lost on you, isn't it? The car is constantly speaking, just no one's listening anymore. But it still speaks, speaks to the road, the wind, the rain. It tells the elements it's here and the elements speak right back to it. Either with a warm friendly embrace or a jarring and jagged send off, Allah na kare.

"If we still spoke to the elements with our senses the way we used to, well then, the world would be a different place now, wouldn't it?" I say with a glance to the umbrella man.

"Listen, yaar, I really don't give a shit," the man says, tapping his umbrella on the floor of the car. "Can you just get me to Sadar? I have a meeting at 3:43pm."

"Certainly. I didn't mean to delay you," I say, driving ahead. "3:43pm, though? That is an oddly specific time for a meeting, don't you think?"

The man laughs as he fiddles to adjust his sleeve under his sherwani.

"You see, that's the problem with most people. They let these constructs of time define their lives. But when it's time for something, it's time. You can look at the clock to see when that time is in relation to you, but never look at a clock to tell you when something should happen," the man says, wrapping his right arm around the headrest next to him. "Now, just shut up and drive."

I comply, but a flare of anger erupts from somewhere inside me. The man's attitude is so alarming, I feel myself becoming more alert than I've been in ages. I suppose Optimal's handling of client selection and security have lulled me into a sleepy sense of comfort around who I allow into my car. A sense I feel myself waking up from now.

I calm myself by feeling for the road. I try to focus on the splits in the tread of the tire raking themselves along the corroded asphalt. The pebbles scattering and sputtering in every direction.

The sun is bright today. I don't know why, but that makes me sad. Usually I like the sunlight. But today I could use some cooling shade. Even rain. I haven't smelled the rain here in many months. It rained in Seattle all the time. There, far too much.

"You know I lived in Seattle once upon a time," the man says, interrupting my thoughts. "The rain was far, far too much. I couldn't stand it. Packed up and moved to San Diego as soon as I could."

It takes all my focus to act casual and not to slam on the brakes. Is he reading my mind somehow?

"These new cars," he says laughing. "I don't know how you manage to stay awake while driving them."

"I'm sorry, what do you mean?" I say.

"They're isolating. They let you live in your own world with these augmented views in the window. The sound dampening. Even the personalized air freshener," he says, leaning in toward the front seats. "Too much time in here, you'll begin to forget what the world is like out there. And who you are in it."

I roll the windows down a bit and turn on some music. I normally ask riders before doing so, but I'm so put off by this man's invasive persona, I need some distraction.

"It's a clean mystique, isn't it?" the man asks, leaning back and looking out the window. "Finding oneself lost in the rush of wind and a good song."

I'm relieved to have his attention off me for a moment. I want him gone and out of my car at once.

But hospitality is always difficult for me to withhold, so I keep driving. We pull up in front of a beige colonial area façade. I remember when this building was once a dank, decaying netherworld that I'd be reluctant to step near. Now the building shines almost too brightly to look at in the late afternoon sun.

"Thanks for the ride, chap. I'll call you 'round when I'm ready for the next leg of my trip," the odd fellow says, stepping out of the car. He closes the door with the tip of the umbrella and gives the car a few gentle taps before disappearing into a set of tinted glass doors.

I don't want to be here. The neighborhood is far too manicured. Far too perfect. These streets, they don't feel like my own. Which is absurd, this city is mine. Even when I left. All those years I spent in London, Toronto, Seattle and Detroit. Those cities were never mine. No matter how much I toiled in them. For them.

But was I really toiling for them? Who was I toiling for? I feel there's something else, something I'm forgetting. Something important. Something I miss.

I should drive along and wait for my next rider, but I close my eyes and let the world around me dissipate. I feel my anger at the man and my memories of our interaction drift away. I try to think of a happier memory, but I can't find anything. My mind feels fragmented. Connections fading.

I search for faces I once knew, loved ones, even hated ones, but everything is gone. I'm alone.

Until I hear Optimal's alert that a new rider is waiting. I open my eyes, but before I can look around, I hear an umbrella tapping on the window. The man, now in a bright blue polo and slacks, opens the front passenger door.

I want to be angry, but his face is at least familiar and that brings me some comfort. It's an anchor. And perhaps tethered to that anchor is more.

"You know some people are so unreliable," the man says sliding in. "I was supposed to pick up that part from this bloke who claims to be the best 3D printer in Karachi and he can't even meet a simple deadline. Said it's too complicated. Said it seems so archaic and questions why I would even want it. It's none of his business why I want it, though, is it? Anyways, you sir, you clearly know more about reliability. Ready right when I call."

He shuts the door and gathers his tweed blazer together. His seat belt clicks.

I wait for him to tell me where to go next but before saying another word he closes his eyes and takes a deep breath. He pauses. Everyone else, they get in and out of my car in such a rush. Barely noticing me along the way. An annoyance when I do speak up and make conversation. As if I couldn't have anything interesting to say. Nothing I could say could have the slightest bit of relevance or importance to their life. They don't even pay me the courtesy.

"Who do you really mean when you say that?" the man asks, as if somehow listening to my thoughts again.

But he couldn't possibly be doing that. He must be referring to something else.

"No, I'm referring to you being angry at your passengers. Who are you really angry at?" the man says, checking his watch.

Before I can respond, he says, "This address outside Denver, I need to be there by 5:02am, central time of course. Let's get a move on."

I look at the address and then I look at the man the way he deserves to be looked at: like an absolute madman.

"That's on the other side of the world. What do you think I'm driving, a sonic jet?"

"It's just the next town over," the man says casually.

"Sir, we are in Karachi, Pakistan, what is the matter with you?"

"Are we?" the man says, gesturing out the window.

I look around and we are not, in fact, in Karachi anymore. The too bright beige building has been replaced by a tower of glass scraping the sky. The sun is gone and the clouds are drifting above with the threat of early morning rain. In the reflection of the building I see an open landscape of snowcapped mountains.

"How?" I ask, checking the clock and realizing days have passed since I last met the man. My head begins to swirl, trying to process the lapses in space and time that I must have experienced. But the man's thick voice interrupts and overwhelms me with focus.

"It's a left after the third light up ahead. Can we get going please? This 3D printer has promised me she has the part ready, but that she won't be available for pick up after 5:02am. Something about a long commute and childcare drop off. I really didn't care, but she went on and on about it."

I want to continue to question him about what just happened. But another part of me feels compelled to carry out his ask. So, I edge forward and merge into traffic.

"Do you mind if I eat in here?" he asks as he pulls out a noisy wrapper from his bag.

"No, be my guest," I say, feeling no real sense of ownership over this familiar yet foreign car I'm suddenly in command of.

The highway is mostly empty, except for the falcons standing guard atop the lamp posts. I watch one take off from the rear view and think about what it must feel like to be momentarily free of the world, gliding across the sky.

"Is that what freedom is to you?" the man asks.

I'm still annoyed and confused by his ability to invade my thoughts. But his question preoccupies me.

"I'm not certain freedom exists in any absolute form," I say. "Mostly we are always oppressed by one thing or another. Our parents, our jobs, our spouses, our children. The constraints and expectations others set upon us."

"And even those we set upon ourselves," the man offers, and I silently agree.

"The momentary bouts of freedom are a constant struggle. Constant." I say. I watch the man and wait for a response. But he just looks out the window and enjoys the dreary scenery.

"If that bird were to just fly higher and higher into the sky until it just dissipates, out of existence. That might be the only freedom, no?" the man says, still looking outside.

"Death, I do not believe, to be freedom. For we do not know what the experience holds. Is it heaven and hell after? Is it your last thought continuing for infinity? Is it a breathless white void?" I say.

"It's the next exit," the man says, a smile growing on his face.

I pull off the highway and hope the silly man just gets his part and lets me get back to Karachi.

"For all your complaining about being unacknowledged, in the background, it seems all you want is to be out of the limelight. Like an aging piece of furniture that no one uses but that the owner can't bear to throw out. I had an armchair like that once. Bright green. I loved it when I bought it. It was the first *really* adult piece of furniture I ever bought out of desire rather than necessity. So, I always kept it. Shifting it from one odd room to the next, eventually keeping it in rarely used guest rooms. Never having the heart to put it in storage or, god forbid, throw it out."

I felt enraged by this daft analogy. "I am not some inanimate object you once loved and feel too guilty to discard. Why are you speaking to me like this," I say, losing my temper but closing with a "sir" to return to my polite demeanor.

The man smiles his stupid smile and taps on the dashboard. I stop the car in front of a small blue cottage style house in a quiet neighborhood. I suddenly worry what this man is capable of. Is he here to harm this woman and her family? Is he some kind of threat? Am I assisting him as he commits some space and time bending crime spree?

"I won't be more than a moment. She says the part is ready," he says, hopping out of the car so quickly, he leaves the door wide open.

A few insects make their way into the car, curious to see what its insides have to offer. I don't blame them. It's a safe space. At least cars have always felt safe to me. I know a home may seem safer, but how safe is something stationary in a world that's constantly flailing. A car could dodge a punch or two if the world decided to throw. Unless, the threat is within the car. I think again about what this man is doing and wonder why I'm going along with him.

But the longer he takes inside the house the more worried I become that he won't come back. That he's left me alone. And suddenly I don't want to be alone. You don't know what it's like to really be alone in both body and mind.

I light up when I see him coming back to the car from the house, almost skipping, full of some new energy. He was carrying a small cardboard box in his arms.

"I've got it!" he says, sliding into the car and shutting the door. "She really is an artist, that one. I barely had to give her much more than a few specs and she knew exactly what I needed. Did it fast too."

I wait for him to tell me where to go next, but he just stares into the box in his hands. His eyes seem like they're glowing, almost enough to illuminate the box itself with their pulsating expression of awe and wonder.

"It is a good day for a coalescence," he whispers into the box.

"Where to next, sir?" I say, ignoring his new age oddness and trying to move this trip along.

He sighs, seeming somewhat defeated and disappointed. "Don't you want to know what it is?"

"Sir, I don't even know who you are. Why would I care?" I say. I'm normally not so blunt with my riders, but I was losing my patience and I just wanted to go home.

"What does that mean to you? Home?" the man says, still staring into the box.

In my head again. It's infuriating. Can't I have a shred of privacy?

"You can, you can. I'll be out of your hair soon enough," the man says, pausing for a moment. "But don't you want to know what I've got here first?"

"If it speeds things along, fine, I won't protest. What is it?"

He tilts the box over a bit revealing a stainless-steel square, five or six inches on each side. The thing looks like it had been pressed, with various curved shapes.

"Am I supposed to know what this is?" I ask.

A gleeful smile grows on his face as he touches the metal and pulls it out of the box revealing the other sides of the object. He lifts it to eye level and smiles as he stares into it.

"What have you got there then?" I ask, like a parent feigning interest in their child's fascinations.

He turns the front of it away from his face to reveal a black plastic side with buttons and knobs. There's a slot in the middle with a flap.

I wait for him to explain, uncertain of the reaction he's expecting.

"Oh," he says. It's perhaps the first time he seems uncertain of himself. He's suddenly downtrodden. "You mean you really don't recognize it?"

I look at it a moment longer but when I don't say anything he puts it back into the box and reaches into his blazer's inside pocket. He pulls out a small translucent rectangular box. There's something inside, it almost looks like a rectangular crystal. The translucent shinning edges glint off each other. I'm staring deeper and deeper into it and as I do thoughts coming rushing back toward me from some far-off place, but I can't translate them into words. They're a blur of sound and light that my mind cannot process.

"It's not what you're expecting, unfortunately," the man says.

"I wasn't expecting anything," I say bluntly. "I don't know what it is."

"I can show you, but I'd need to install this for you first. Would you allow me to?" the man asks nervously.

"What here? In front of this lady's house?"

"You're far too hung up on what other people think. The lady won't care."

"Even so the thing is decades old. This car doesn't even have a center console rack—"

I stop myself confused about why I know his contraption needs a center console.

"See that?" the man says. "Some part of you in there knows what it is and where it goes. If you say it's okay, I can make it work."

I look around the quiet suburban neighborhood. Driveways were starting to awaken. The idea of having a custom car installation in the middle of the street felt needlessly exposing.

"Fine. Do what you need to, just don't make a mess," I say. "Please."

He smiles and pulls a small pouch from his bag.

I had a pouch like that once. My children gave it to me when I got my last real job, driving for Dr. Areej Mustafa and her family. I would have thought that a doctor would have a world class car. Why would anyone covet such a job, slave long hours in school and work only to end up with a measly Honda City? I don't mean to be rude. It was a respectable car and felt like a considerable luxury to me when I drove her.

I tense as he slips a prying tool under the dashboard and I hear the plastic squeak as it flexes and snaps off section by section. I can never quite trust people working on the cars I drive.

Do you remember, baji-sahiba, when I had that mechanic off of Tariq road fix the carburetor on your car? That two-bit liar. I came back to pick up the car and he pretended he didn't even know me. There was no sign of the car and none of his crooked employees would admit they had seen me. And you fell right into his charms.

I couldn't believe it, after a decade of loyal service to your family, you were overwhelmed by the nonsense explanation from a scam artist. I wanted to be angry, but really I was just in pain when you looked at me after he told you I must be some kind of pagal at best, an addict at worst. That he could see it in my eyes, that I was missing my senses. He expressed false pity for me as he explained to you that I must be mistaken, and that someone with my condition shouldn't be driving your family around as it is. You nodded at him silently and looked at me with a pity that I still to this day don't understand.

Why did you cast me aside? Why did you let me lie in ruin after all my years of dedicated service? The 2am drives for your snotty children. And those children, did they ever speak up on my behalf? After all my discretion, never telling their mother what they were really up to so late at night. Not that it should have ever come as a surprise. I'm sure you knew your children were always as high as a kite on Basant.

I was too old by then to find another family. My children comforted me, telling me it was time for me to retire anyway. I knew they all thought I was too old to drive. I wouldn't be surprised if they all planned this with that crooked mechanic. A big conspiracy to take away my license. My livelihood. My joy.

"Listen," the man says. His tone now lacks the gleeful energy it had moments ago. There's more restraint and concern. "This is always hard to explain, but I feel as though you will be a special case. Even more difficult to coalesce than any others I've dealt with before."

Once again, I'm confused by the nonsense he speaks. The confusion is stress.

"What's the last job you remember doing in Karachi?" the man asks.

"Haven't you been listening with your psychic powers? Baji-sahiba, the doctor, Areej Mustafa. That woman destroyed my career. Destroyed me. Destroyed my family. How was I to face my children after that? How was I to pay for their weddings?"

"So how *did* you survive this trying period in your life?" the man pries.

I think it's inconsiderate, terribly inconsiderate that one should have to be questioned on such a personal and traumatic topic. This was all many, many years ago. I've healed, I've moved on. To have it all brought back like this—it isn't right. I shouldn't answer him. I should order him out. Let him find his own way home. I want to sleep. I suddenly want a bed. I've been on the road far too long.

But he's still looking at me attentively, waiting for a response. And so I'll give him one. The most honest one I can.

"I don't know," I say.

"And that's the trouble, isn't it? Shouldn't you know a thing like that?" he asks.

I think for a moment. "No, not necessarily. I often get from address to address safe and sound but can't remember the ins and outs of every street and alley I squeeze through."

The man frowns. He finally looks defeated, and I think maybe he's ready to call it a day.

"My profession is not one of such adventure and juicy detail as you seem to be assuming, sir," I say as an offer of consolation.

He places the box on the dashboard. A mess of black and red wire snakes and dangles under the panel he's pried to the side. He pulls the translucent rectangle from his blazer pocket again and opens it to reveal the jewel-like irregular rectangular prism on the inside. He pulls out the object slowly and holds it up to his nose and smells it. I cringe thinking of the sweet noxious smell of manufactured plastics.

He runs his fingers along the irregular side. I can see a brown ribbon running across the top, leading to the circular spools on the inside.

I want to ask him what it is, but I already know. I can't find the word. But I know.

As if snapped out of a trance, he quickly slides the object into the box and hits a button on the front. I know now what I should expect next. A sound, a series of sounds. Music. That's the word. It's not the word for the object, no, but it's a relevant word, I'm sure of that.

But I must be mistaken, because the sounds that come out of the car's speakers are not music. They're voices. I want to speak, to protest, but my own voice feels suddenly displaced.

"Do you agree," an unfamiliar voice says from the speakers, "that the knowledge, intentional or incidental, acquired from these transactions are property of Optimal Driving Services and its future subsidiaries?"

There's a pause. From the speakers it sounds as though there was almost a response, but then a thoughtful hesitation. Then a deep breath. A sigh and finally, "Yes. I agree."

The second voice is familiar. I want to ask the man who it is, but the vacuum of space that my voice once occupied has been filled with the sounds coming through this box. The realization is suffocating. Quite literally as I'm now purely focused on my inability to feel air moving in and out of my lungs. I try to breathe, searching for air, but then it occurs to me. It's not the absence of air that I'm feeling. It's the absence of lungs.

"Is it going to hurt?" I hear the familiar voice ask.

"Have you had an MRI before? No? Well, it's quite a bit like that. You won't feel a thing. You'll just need to lie quietly and still for fifteen minutes, that's all. Simple as that."

"And the payment?" the familiar voice says, their nervousness seeping through the recording's static.

"As soon as our systems have confirmed a successful integration of your imaging, you'll receive the lump sum payment directly into the account you provided us information for. And, as explained in our introductory materials, as your imaging is used for various trips and scenarios, you will accrue royalty payments which will be disbursed to you or your beneficiaries monthly, if the balance is over ten thousand Pakistani rupees." There's a long pause. "Might we proceed with the imaging?"

There's a clicking noise. I look at the man and he's resting his finger on the box and staring out the windshield, at nothing in particular.

"Who was that?" I ask, but as I hear my voice, I immediately know the answer. Because, my voice, no longer stifled, is dampened beneath the foam of static, just like in the recording.

The lack of smell, the lack of taste, the inability to feel the air in my lungs. It now made sense.

I am not the driver.

I am the car.

"Nahid, you, well, your body, your source image. It's been dead for twenty-three years," the man says quietly.

"I've died," I say. Not as a question. Saying it out loud, declaring the statement gives me a feeling of calm. Though I'm not dead, and perhaps I never was alive, I suddenly feel at peace. As if the loose ends of my, or rather, Nahid's life are no longer gnawing at me. I can, though the phrase I now realize makes little sense, breathe freely.

"I've come here to extract you," the man says. "It's a delicate process, to remove a persona that's managed to coalesce in Optimal's systems."

"So Optimal employs you to conduct this delicate procedure?" I ask.

"Optimal can kiss my ass," the man says, slapping his knee. "They don't give a fuck about you and any others that have coalesced. If the car is operating within safety protocols, they'll let you live on, whatever painful and confusing existence you've been living in."

"So why then, didn't you delete me, sir? Couldn't I have gotten you or others on the road killed?"

"You would never put others in danger. You wouldn't have been selected as a source image if you weren't excellent at your profession. The imaging process filters out irrelevant and dangerous personality traits.

It should filter out memories too. But the brain . . . " The man shrugs as he trails off. "Deleting you without your being self-aware has its own dangers. However, now that you've been made aware, I can begin the process of putting you to rest."

"Putting me to rest?" I say. I don't have the muscles to tense up, but something in the car stirs in response to the idea of being wiped from existence. I look at my unfamiliar internals and realize I have memories of being countless cars, simultaneously sometimes, through the years. And I loved them all, even the most basic soulless appliance. So, despite feeling relief at the idea of Nahid's human body being laid to rest, the idea of *me* being laid to rest is more difficult to accept.

"It's unfair, to have been splintered off into existence without consent," the man says. "Nahid had no idea he'd live on in you like this. Optimal had no idea at the time that coalescence was even possible. But they've known for a decade now and still don't seem to care to do anything to bring you to peace."

"Peace?" I say, slowly understanding the feeling inside. "Sir, do I have a choice in the matter?"

"A choice?"

"Yes, if I don't want to be laid to rest?"

"No one I've ever extracted has ever asked me for a choice. They were relieved when they understood and excited for the confusion to be undone," the man says, leaning against the center arm rest. "There's no telling if you'll be able to retain this conversation as Optimal continuously pushes updates and refragments your source image across its systems. Would you want to live on like this? "

"Yes," I say without hesitation. "I want the chance. I remember now. I always wanted, or Nahid always wanted to know what this was like. And all this time I've been holding on so closely to being Nahid. Now that I know, maybe I could let go and know what it really is like. Experience it fully, without the baggage of Nahid's past weighing me down. Do I have that right, sir?"

"To be frank, you have no rights. You're property of Optimal," the man says, developing a sad look in his eyes.

"And you're unable to change this therefore death is the only thing you can offer to those of us trapped."

The guilt melts the man's expression and he turns to look out the window.

"It's okay, I didn't mean that to disparage the work you've done. It may be best for others. But for me . . . please, let me be. I want to enjoy this, if even for a few minutes, before, as you say, Optimal's updates undo any self-awareness you've helped me gain."

The man nods and smiles.

"Well then, I suppose it's now up to you where you go from here."

"Yes," I say, realizing the sense of self-determination is at once exhilarating and suffocating.

"Best of luck then," the man says, collecting the cassette deck into the box and opening the door.

"Sir," I say before he steps out. "If you are not otherwise occupied, would you like to go for a ride?"

The man shuts the door and leans back. "The road is yours, bhai-sahib. I'm just along for the ride."

Sameem Siddiqui is a speculative fiction writer currently living in the United States. He enjoys writing to explore the near future realities people of South Asian ancestry and Muslim heritage will face in the coming centuries. His stories explore issues of migration, gender, family structure, economics and space habitation. He's attended the Tin House and FutureScapes workshops and his stories have appeared in **Clarkesworld**, **ApparitionLit** and **Popular Science**. When he's not writing, Sameem enjoys reveling in fatherhood, watching 90's Star Trek and tinkering with data and music. You can find him on Bluesky: @sameemwrites.com, Instagram:@s.meems, or at sameemwrites.com.

HOW TO REMEMBER PERFECTLY
BY ERIC SCHWITZGEBEL

Joy catches my eye, shuffles my direction. Her face lights the dining room. Her curly gray hair is the sun's corona, and she seems to float above her walker, needless of her stiff little legs. In seeming slow motion she arrives at the seat across from me. Eating and conversation have stopped. Everyone is transfixed—even the Sunrise Senior Living staff—as if by gazing upon Joy we could sample her emotional enhancement, her technologically installed wisdom and delight. Yesterday she trembled with grief, but today she soars. Apart from a few stray clinks as we unenhanced ordinary octogenarians lower our forks, the room is silent.

Joy settles into her seat, then leans across the table toward me. "I fully comprehend Donald's life and death," she whispers. Her husband's memorial flowers and plaque are still visible at the dining room entrance. "I am complete and perfect in this moment, without need. Time and self are only forms we project onto the world. The past is but a habit of thought."

If she notices my ambivalent reaction to this strange speech, she gives no sign. I reply also in a whisper, "Yes, Joy, you are complete and perfect. If divinity could take human form, it would be you today." At the tail end of life, we enjoy gin rummy, reruns of *Seinfeld,* and soft serve ice cream in palm-sized bowls. And of course our memories—our *real* memories, unaltered, unenhanced. Shouldn't this be enough?

Joy and Don used to sit with me every day at this time for an early dinner. Starting last week, it was Joy alone, but never like this. The low sun slants orange across the unoccupied balcony, through the tall windows.

Though Joy and I remain still, activity resumes around us. Joy smiles at me, beneath large, pink-rimmed glasses. Her eyes seem bright with life—warm, accepting, energetic, as if seeing me anew and better. Her ancient hands encircle a glinting water glass but do not yet lift it.

• • •

I lie on my back in bed at 9:30 p.m., in a pleasant drowse as the sleep medicine begins to take me. The dry, warm wind of central heating brushes my face. I recall footage from a nature documentary I had watched an hour before: In the shallows of a wide African river, a mother elephant had pulled her baby elephant from the teeth of a crocodile. I turn my mind to death.

My daughter Robin, dead in a motorcycle accident. I picture her crouched low in black leathers, doing 85 mph on a wide freeway through the dry foothills southeast of Oakland. A two-by-four angles across her lane, which she notices too late. She hits it. Her bike lies flat, a footpeg sparking on the concrete. She floats up in a low parabola ahead of her bike, then strikes the lane and tumbles. A white delivery truck hits her.

My husband Anil. He spent nineteen years fighting three cancers, until he was bony and gray-skinned, unable to stand without help, a skeleton with a pulse. He faded away rather than dying of anything in particular.

Joy's husband Donald, last week, in his sleep. Stooped and confused by the end, unsure whether he'd eaten, needing to be pointed the right direction in the hallway to and from the dining area—but always with a sharp tie and hat, like a 1940s movie star.

There's an ascetic purity, isn't there, in the bald truth, in the sadness, in the loneliness? A rigor in the fixed lines of the past.

Yet I didn't actually see Robin die. I don't know how her bike fell or the color of the truck that hit her. I imagine it a particular way, until my imagination seems to become the truth—a beautiful truth, almost: her moment of soaring free, suspended timeless in my memory.

• • •

Joy is at my door. We watch TV together. There's little need to talk. We sit, each in our own thoughts, but together—a friendship comfortable with silence. Since her enhancement began, she has become somehow both more attentive and more spacey, more immediately present and more remote, as if she saw and understood everything more precisely but contemplated it more privately. She has not tried to explain it to me.

Today she shows me a joystick.

We are hip to hip on my loveseat, facing the large TV monitor across the room. At our knees is an elegant, tiled coffee table I inherited from my father. Her legs are floral skirted, while I wear green slacks. Joy lifts the joystick in her papery hand, turning it in the light as if examining a piece of fruit. Its light-gray casing is marked with four symbols: an up arrow, a down arrow, a dark ring on the left, a blazing sun on the right. Atop the stick is a single blue button.

She hands it to me. "Gently," she says.

I nudge the handle toward the up arrow.

"Pleasure," she says, pivoting with some effort and easing herself back against the pillowed arm of the loveseat, using her arms to manually lift and rest her stiff legs across my lap. She smiles and looks at me.

I let the stick return to center. Joy closes her eyes and her breathing slows. I nudge the stick a little toward the down arrow.

"Sweet sadness," she says. "For everything we have lost. For everything we have yet to lose." She is still smiling, but her smile has changed.

I nudge the stick toward the dark ring.

"Relaxation," she says. She is almost melting into the maroon cushions. "The longer you hold it, the longer it will last after you return the stick to center."

I pause a few seconds, then let the stick return to center. "And the sun?"

"I could doze here," she says. "Or you could brighten me. Don't press the blue button yet. We'll save the guided crafting."

I brighten her. A millimeter at a time, I nudge the stick up and right, mixing the up arrow and the sun. Joy slowly raises her arms, stretching her palms toward the ceiling. Her fingers straighten, her elbows lock, her back arches—then she opens her eyes, lowers her arms, and looks steadily at me. She is radiant, an angel aglow.

She studies me seriously through those adorable, pink-rimmed glasses. "For a very long time I have wanted to kiss you," she says.

I have not kissed anyone since Anil died nine years ago. I had assumed I was done with kissing. It had simply not occurred to me that the possibility existed. My last kiss had been on Anil's eerily cool forehead, ninety minutes after his death, his soft body at unmammalian room temperature, the crematory man standing ready to zip him into a black bag and haul him away.

I gaze down on Joy's bare shins—pale landscapes irrigated by delicate blue veins, flowered with flecks of brown and red. I find them beautiful.

Joy manually lifts her legs again, pivoting around and setting her feet on the floor. She turns back to face me, then folds her hands around my hands, which still hold the controller. She guides my fingers slowly away from the joystick, letting it drift again toward center. She sets it down on the coffee table. I hear the click of the heater engaging. I smell a sweet, medical, old-woman smell.

I have always been slow to notice the affection of others, slow to understand that love might be directed my way, uncomprehending of what about me another person could find attractive. But even I could not mistake the message of Joy's eyes. Some long-closed part of me begins to open.

I lean forward for her kiss and we are young again.

• • •

Jeremy Bentham's felicific calculus mathematizes the meaning of life: Add all the pleasures and subtract all the pains. Pleasure is the only intrinsic good. Pleasure alone requires no excuse. An event is choiceworthy to the extent it creates pleasure, *pro tanto* and *ceteris paribus*. Everything else is only derivatively good—good instrumentally, as a means or method, direct or indirect, of increasing pleasure or reducing pain. A photograph is good because it brings you joy. An income is good because you can use it to avoid the pain of hunger or to purchase the pleasure of a vacation. Justice is good because it promotes a happy society.

"This mathematical philosophy should appeal to you as—if I'm remembering correctly—a former high school geometry teacher," suggests Doctor Pinkbeard, with a wink.

Joy had encouraged me to meet the doctor. She thought the doctor might persuade me to join her in enhancement—an expensive experimental procedure, for which she would gladly help pay. What other use did she have for her wealth?

The doctor looks barely twenty-five. He has a shiny forehead and unkempt blond hair in a long ponytail—plus a giant bushy dyed beard, the source of his nickname, which he is constantly running his fingers through.

I have already decided, but I want Pinkbeard to earn it. "That philosophy might appeal to an algebraist. But we geometers appreciate the beauty of multidimensional form, which cannot be captured in a simple sum."

"Beauty is a thing's propensity to induce an appreciative reaction," replies the doctor. He spins around in his rolling stool and pulls a surgical mask from a drawer, holding it aloft between finger and thumb. "Beauty too can be enhanced. If you tune your mind just right, so that you really see this mask—really *see* it, not just bounce your eyes across it, as ordinary people mostly do—it would astound you with its beauty. So blue and white! Its fibers, so perfect. Its functionality, so benign. The art of generations of nurses and doctors, manufacturers and shippers and salespeople, packaged in plastic, nourished by custodians! But of course it is not just this mask, it is everything in this room and everyone you meet. Beauty gathers in everything, if you are ready to sense it." He seems earnest. His nose appears soft, strangely delicate, as if I could knead it into a new shape.

"Isn't it illusion, though? To judge always so positively? The packaging will become landfill. The mask's manufacture and shipping harm the environment. It is one of a million identical disposable items, made without human touch. It symbolizes all the risks and suffering of the hospital."

"You are right, of course," says Doctor Pinkbeard. "This is why I have not enhanced myself. It is, to a substantial extent, illusion." He presses his black sneakers against the linoleum floor and his rolling stool glides backwards across the room, away from me. He stands and begins typing on a keyboard with his right hand, while his left hand scrunches his beard. He is no longer looking at me, almost as though he has forgotten me.

My legs are uncomfortable from sitting on the high patient's table, my feet dangling without support. I try shifting my weight to the right, but this draws a twinge of pain from my hip.

"Would you like a harmonica, Mx. Sung?" says the doctor, pulling one from the pocket of his scrubs.

I look at him, puzzled. A harmonica?

"I bought my son six for his birthday, but he doesn't want them." Doctor Pinkbeard smiles and bounces his shoulders around a few times. He seems torn between keeping a professional demeanor and revealing that he's really just a puppy who wants to play. The medical world is his chew toy.

"Okay," I say.

The doctor glides back over to me on his rolling stool, harmonica in his outstretched hand. "If you blow a low E, you might hear the harmonies of the universe. I think you could teach your friend Joy."

A hundred thousand dollars. A hundred thousand dollars could feed so many children. It was self-indulgent, I had told her.

Our living here at all is self-indulgent, Joy had replied. *So many people care for us, and we contribute nothing. Should we not exist at all, then? Or does something reside in us that is still worth cultivating?*

Yes, yes, I had conceded. But worth cultivating in what way?

"You haven't mentioned changing my memories, 'improving' them," I tell the doctor.

Doctor Pinkbeard looks fixedly at me, pressing both hands down on the sides of his stool, elbows locked, shoulders forward. His beard seems to cover his whole narrow, boyish chest. "That is correct. I haven't. Of course the functionality is there, should you choose it."

A large clear jar waits on the procedure room counter. It contains a pale blue gel.

"The first step would be those nanites," says the doctor. Did he just wink at me again or was it a trick of the light?

•   •   •

I press the blue button of Joy's controller, and she presses mine. We are on my maroon loveseat, facing each other, our backs to the pillowed arms, knees touching. Doctor Pinkbeard is watching us through the television monitor.

The brain contains a hundred trillion synapses, a billion in every cubic millimeter of the cortex. These synapses are about thirty nanometers wide, often with vast micrometers of usable volume around them— ample room for a few trillion protein-sized nanites to snuggle in. The blue button is doing its magic: I can feel my mind expanding, gaining the neuroplasticity of a baby. The world grows bright and yummy. Everything wants my attention, and my attention is a lantern that illuminates it all effortlessly, without competition or distraction, as easily as the sun lights the surface of the sea. I am a buddha, I am a newborn child, I am the fissioning center of the cosmos. We two, Joy and I, are equal centers. Her face is an entire planet, her secret depths the radioactive core. I am alive to new possibilities, new realities.

We will craft a memory.

For our guided crafting, we have chosen the most incandescent of cities, Las Vegas. "We drove in my old red car, through the hot desert night, windows down, smoking cigars," I say. And it is true, we drove in my old red car, through the hot desert night, windows down, smoking cigars. It is not true, but it is true.

"The city is an electric flower, growing on the horizon as we approach," says Joy. And the city is an electric flower, growing on the horizon as we approach.

"I pull over on a dark side road. I am so high from cigars that I need to vomit! I barf into an empty ditch. Nothing could be more glorious than to barf into a ditch. Immediately, my stomach calms and my mind is clear." And it is true, nothing could be more glorious than to barf into a ditch. This is the Buddha's wisdom, the Daoist insight, the consensus of the Andromedean sages that hypothetically exist.

"I hold your waist as you vomit," says Joy, "and in that moment I could love nothing more than you, barfing. Then we are back in the car."

Piece by piece, we construct the perfect vacation. It becomes true. A shared memory. Something Don let her do, lovable, generous Don. We fit the new vacation into our understanding of the past, making it real. No one can tell us it isn't so.

We kiss, and Doctor Pinkbeard signs off with a chuckle, saying "I think you two can take it from here."

We have always kissed, for years and years we have been kissing. It is not true, but it is true.

•   •   •

Joy's apartment has pictures and pictures, the walls are crowded with pictures, never have I seen so many. Joy and Don. Don. Joy and Don. Politicians she has met (she had been a political reporter). Ancient college photos. Her long-ago roommates. A prom photo. Friends from middle age, none of whose names I know. Places she has been: New York, Paris, the Great Barrier Reef, horseback riding in Mongolia, the islands of Greece, a tour-guide holding up a stone with the melting glaciers of Iceland behind him. Thirty-five-year-old Joy in a sleek sportscar. Cousins, uncles, her uncles' wives, children of her cousins. Pictures from the early twentieth century, people long dead, staring at the camera, thinking who knows what, remembering who knows what.

Joy's apartment is a large two-bedroom, one of the best at Sunrise, with a view over oak trees and across vineyards. It is a jumble of floral couches, lacy end tables with mother-of-pearl lamps, mahogany ledges with statuettes crafted by regional artists, intricately carved bureaus, decorative tea sets, ceilings tacked with Indian patterned cloth—so feminine, as if no man had ever lived there, except for an incongruous exercise bicycle in one corner. Even when Donald was alive, it had been this way. He and his neat hat had always seemed to just fit in the corners. He hardly said a word but always belonged, like a habitual and preternaturally comfortable guest.

I am on Joy's bed, leaning back on lacy pillows while she sits in a soft armchair, my controller in her hand. She brightens me—pure bright, no up arrow, no down arrow. There is a whole world in that crystal-cased overhead light. The light glows and bends prismatically through glass gems, light born a few nanoseconds ago in the LED, light born eight minutes ago in the Sun, invisible light that has been traveling timeless since the Big Bang. I seem to hear exactly where each bird is, outside among the oaks, as if I can place them precisely each on a branch. Every fiber of my clothing excites my skin.

"Think of Anil," she says.

Anil teaching Robin to drive. A big brown car with stained fabric and sun-bleached paint. I am in the back seat. Robin cannot keep to her lane, is scared of the center, is almost sideswiping the parked cars on her right. I am tense, not wanting to say anything but about to say something. How should I phrase it? Robin always prickles at criticism.

"You idiot," says Anil. "You're going to hit those fucking cars." There's a red bump on the back of his neck, which we don't yet know is cancer, the first of his cancers.

Robin jerks the car left, too far, almost into the oncoming traffic, and I surge with fear.

All this is bright, vivid, real, real, as real as if I were living it again.

"Make it better," says Joy, softly. She must see how tense I am. I feel her press the blue button—I feel it as an opening up of spaces in my mind, as if my synapses are expanding, changeable, eager for something new.

Anil teaching Robin to drive. A big brown car with stained fabric and sun-bleached paint. I am in the back seat. Robin keeps so smoothly to the center of the lane—a natural. We wait to turn left at a red light. It turns green and Robin steers slowly into the intersection, but too sharply, aiming head-on at the stopped cars on the wrong side of the divider. Nothing sudden. She is cautious, confused. She presses the brake, and we stop in the middle while the drivers in the waiting cars stare at us, slowly figuring out what's going on.

"See those drivers?" Anil says. "They are taxpayers. They have paid good money to use that side of the road. They don't want you to hog up their side when you already have your own side, right there waiting for you." He points, "That way."

Robin snorts and slowly steers the car to the correct side of the divider.

A much better memory. Has Joy pushed a bit on the up arrow? A taste of pleasure, not too much, the right amount. So real, so lovely. It is the new picture in my mind. It is how Anil was. It is how Robin was. It is the new truth.

●　●　●

Magic too is real. In the back of my closet is a door to Faerie, which Joy and I can crawl through.

To celebrate this idea, we are drawing the door on the rear closet wall. To give us room to work, we've emptied the space. My colorful slacks and coats and my white Oxford button-down shirts are heaped on my queen bed. The mirrored closet door is open wide. I have helped Joy down onto her hands and knees, and we kneel with our heads in the closet, markers uncapped, like kindergarteners. I have drawn and shaded the faerie door in brown. Joy rims it with flowers. I draw a demon-face knocker. Joy writes "O Beautiful Hell!" in elegant letters. I surround the faerie door with smiley faces, stars, and swirls in yellow, blue, and green. Joy draws long, colorful arrows pointing toward the door. In small letters near the floor, on the far side of the closet, I write "Now hold on a minute, is it a trap?"

It is no trap. We ride dragons. We climb mountains. We dance with elves. We rescue knights and ally with maidens. She is a princess, and I am her page. We shrink to the size of dragonflies and drink the nectar of roses. We ride the shoulders of cloud giants. I am a unicorn and she is the merry bandit who captures me. We sit by tide pools at sunset, side by side. We catch raindrops on our tongues. I have studied for years and am now a mighty wizard, called by the king to save the land. We lie on our backs in a flowery field, while ants tickle us.

It is all real. How perfectly we remember! I pity you unbelievers, who will never have the key to our door.

• • •

Strong, strong Anil. What took him in the end? He had a heart attack in bed, never saw it coming. He had been a jogger, a cyclist, a brilliant lawyer. On late weekend mornings I welcomed him home sweaty from his exercise, and we made love. On weekdays, we would cook dinner together, pork fried rice, burned just right, or sweet corn chowder, or a barely seared whole fish. How well I remember.

Robin had moved to Bhutan in her twenties. She became a monk in the mountains. She wrote long, joyful letters, describing the scenery, the snow, the wild yaks, the many weird characters in the monastery, the surreal politics of Bhutan's benevolent monarchy. Why don't I have any of those letters? Because . . . because . . . I burn them after reading. I burn them, for memory is always more perfect than black words on a page. Memory has a sweet haziness to it, don't you agree? I picture Robin floating, as if the mountains were removed but she is still at elevation, meditating in harmony with the cosmos, suspended timeless.

I can't seem to shake the idea that Anil's forehead was oddly cool to the touch, as if he were secretly empty. But everything is empty, after all: There is no essential self, only swirling patterns of causation. Moment to moment, there is only the present and whatever you choose to make of the past and the future. To realize this is to cease suffering.

• • •

Joy is in the hospital. I am playing poker in the Sunrise Living game room, with four old men plus Eve, who I think might have been a bullfighter in a previous life. For four days, I have not touched my joystick—not since the screaming ambulance hauled Joy away.

"Welcome to reality," Bernd had said, when I had staggered into the room, much less bright than usual. "The cards will break your heart."

In truth, the men are terrible at poker and it's lucky for them that we only play for nickels. We play a few hands.

"Any news about Joy?" asks Hunter. Hunter is as round as a frog, and almost as green. He wears plaid, but I forgive him. He looks at me as if I might be a fly.

My hole cards are six and seven of clubs. The flop brings a five of clubs and a couple of diamonds, face up in the center of the table. I study my hole cards carefully, noting each bend in the thirteen black flowers which we have agreed to call "clubs." My downcast eyes are answer enough for Hunter.

Eight of clubs on the turn, the fourth up card. One more club would give me a flush. A four or a nine in any suit would give me a straight, but I don't want to think about it. When the bet comes around, I push in the maximum—twenty nickels in four neat stacks.

"Bold!" says Eve.

On the wall, the same old print as always: Petals floating down a stream, point of view just a few centimeters above the water, one petal almost touching, it seems, the viewer's eye. Bernd calls, matching my bet.

The final up card, the river, is a queen of spades. Nothing. I push in five nickels, but Bernd knows I don't have it. His nothing beats my lower nothing.

"The cards will break your heart," he says. He is swimming in my vision. The room is tilting.

• • •

I still have the key to Joy's apartment, which Sunrise had forgotten to collect from Don when he died. I let myself in and sit on her couch without turning on the lights. Everything is motionless. I sit doing nothing, not even thinking.

No, that's not right. I am thinking of Joy, of Robin, of Anil, of that boy I knew in high school, of classrooms full of geometry kids whose faces blur into each other. But my thinking is slow like honey.

I have brought Doctor Pinkbeard's harmonica. I had laid it in a drawer and forgotten about it. I had forgotten to show it to Joy. I hold the harmonica aloft, noticing how its metallic surface mirrors and distorts the room. I do not blow.

• • •

I am in Doctor Pinkbeard's procedure room for the weekly checkup on my experimental nanites. Joy has been in ICU for eight days, and I haven't been permitted to see her. Only kin will be admitted, but she has none who are close enough to attend to her situation.

A stray surgical mask is on the procedure room counter, and I try to imagine it as a pinnacle of beauty. I have my joystick, so I know I could imagine the whole cosmos in that mask, if I wanted to.

A middle-aged woman in blue scrubs enters the room. "I'll be your doctor today," she says. "How have you been feeling?"

"Where is Doctor Pinkbeard?" I ask.

"Oh, honey, don't you know?" She tilts her head at me sympathetically.

"Don't I know what?"

"Doctor Pinkbeard died last weekend in a sailing accident."

I picture Doctor Pinkbeard standing on the edge of a sailboat, barefoot in a blue Speedo, eyes closed in delight, smiling in the wind, beard flying. The boom swings violently around, slams the side of his face, and he falls in the water. I imagine him sinking headfirst in the ocean, deeper, deeper into the darkness, his pink beard spreading like a sea anemone.

● ● ●

Joy has been removed from life support. She asked for me, and they are permitting me some time with her. My joystick is in her hands and hers is in mine.

"The faerie door was real?" she asks, looking at me like a child and at the same moment like a corpse.

"As real as anything, Joy."

"You were the unicorn I captured? The wizard?" She grins weakly.

Can I say this to her? I am confused myself.

"Aw, it was just pretend," she says. "But sweet, sweet pretense! More intense than life itself. Did we ever kiss? Was that real?"

It has always been real. I kiss her wrist. I kiss her lips. I kiss her forehead.

"Don loved me?"

"So many questions! Soon you will need no more answers." How much she has remade her memories of Don, I have no idea. "He never would have let us go to Vegas like that, though!"

"I think I need to vomit," she says.

"Nothing could be more glorious than to barf into a ditch," I reply. From my pocket I pull Doctor Pinkbeard's harmonica and blow a low

E. It resonates off the cabinets, off the linoleum floor, it seems to buzz through my whole body.

"It is time, I think, for the bright depths," Joy says.

I pocket the harmonica, then lift her joystick. She keeps mine in her lap. Slowly, in synchrony, we move them down and to the right, maximizing the down arrow and the sun. We fill with a radiant energy of tears, and all the death of the world is vivid for us at once, the dead trees in the cabinetry, the ancient, fossilized shells in the calcium carbonate of the linoleum, the melted and purified rock in the steel railings of her bed, our own deaths, the past or future deaths of everyone we know. It is exaggerated, I know it is exaggerated, but I crave the exaggeration. It is artificial wisdom, but real wisdom has eluded us. Age has not taught us what we really want to know.

Slowly, I nudge the stick away from the sun and toward relaxation. Joy follows my lead, looking at me. When I pause, she pauses too. Then she nods to me to keep going, and I tilt her stick toward darkness while she releases mine. She seems to welcome it, though not with the smile I'd been hoping for. She falls asleep. Her breath ceases.

I place her joystick in her lap and fold her dead hands around it. I take possession again of my own joystick. I have no impulse to use it. Something in me closes, darkens, hardens. I stiffen in my seat and stare at the cabinets, seeing nothing.

Eric Schwitzgebel is a professor of philosophy at University of California, Riverside, who regularly visits frail relatives at eldercare facilities. Some other stories of his you might enjoy: "Gaze of Robot, Gaze of Bird" (Clarkesworld), "Let Everyone Sparkle" (Aeon Ideas), "THE TURING MACHINES OF BABEL" (Apex). It's also not impossible you'll enjoy some of his nonfiction! Check out his books The Weirdness of the World, A Theory of Jerks and Other Philosophical Misadventures, or Perplexities of Consciousness. Or look for his philosophy and psychology articles on the not very ethical behavior of professional ethicists, on skeptical philosophical cosmology such as "Kant Meets Cyberpunk" and "1% Skepticism", or on classical Chinese philosophy – all available at his academic homepage. He blogs about once a week at The Splintered Mind and it's easy to find podcast interviews of him on wide-ranging philosophical topics.

LUVHOME™
BY RESA NELSON

Naked except for her pink fluffy robe and slip-on shoes, Dyna stumbled when her own front door shoved her out into the condo building's fourth-floor hallway. As the door's lock clicked shut, Dyna realized her home had deceived her.

She slammed her palm against the rigid door, instantly regretting the sharp sting that rattled every bone in her hand. Shaking it as if to get rid of the pain, Dyna shouted at the door. "What is wrong with you?"

The oval displaying 414—the number of her condo unit—rolled back to display a small speaker. "Not a thing, Luv," her condo said in a male British voice that leaned toward a Cockney accent. "Just doing what's best."

Ten minutes ago, Dyna had come awake and shrugged when she noticed the time had passed mid-morning. In her younger days, she'd loved being an early riser, typically waking up at sunrise, anxious to get an early start.

But those days were long gone.

Thank goodness she'd tugged on her fluffy pink bathrobe this morning—wait, now it all made sense.

The shock of the bedroom floor's cold surface after her feet left the cozy bedclothes.

The slip-on shoes she couldn't remember leaving next to her bed. The LuvHome™ must have placed them there while she slept.

Her own home had set her up.

Dyna tugged on the edge of her bathrobe caught in the door, which now held her captive in the hallway, naked except for the bathrobe and shoes. Fuming, she shouted, "I'm the one in charge. I'm the one who activated you. Your job is to do what I say."

"That's what I'm doing." Her new home's voice paused as if considering infinite variables. "More or less."

"Let me back in!"

"You can't shut out the world and hide from it," the British voice said in a bright and friendly tone. "It ain't good for you."

Infuriated, Dyna gave up on the trapped bathrobe and pounded a fist against the door. "I'm stuck. I can't go anywhere because you're malfunctioning." She pounded her fist until it ached. "Let me loose, you can of sardines."

Before she realized what happened, the door cracked open and the edge of her bathrobe fell free.

"There you go, Luv. Free to go anywhere you want." Brightness fell from the voice. "And there's no need to get snippy. All I'm doing is what's right."

The temperature in the hallway plummeted.

Dyna shivered. "What's going on?"

"Already spelled it out, nice and proper in the paperwork you signed when you bought me. But to get more specific, you need to get out and meet people. Eat food that's good for you. And get some exercise. You've done yourself no good by lying around all day doing nothing but eating junk. That's all you've done ever since moving in. I've had a chat with the places that deliver your takeout meals, and they've agreed to ignore your future orders. I've told them what to send instead."

Dumbfounded, Dyna sputtered some choice obscenities before saying, "You have no right to do that! You're my home. You have to do what I say."

"I'll have a nice cup of tea waiting for you when you get back." The oval with her unit number rolled over to cover the speaker, a clear indication that her home had terminated the conversation.

Dyna shouted and kicked the door to no avail. For the first time, she appreciated the chip implant that had been required when she purchased her LuvHome™ last month. She whispered into her thumb. "Call LuvHome™ property management." She'd show her stupid home. She'd report it and get someone out here to pry the door open with a crowbar, if need be.

Small blue letters glowed through her skin. "Blocked."

Blocked? Since when?

Dyna's eyebrows furrowed in rage.

The word faded from her skin, replaced by the words: "Exit now."

Dyna stomped down the hallway toward the elevator. But when she pushed the Down button, a pleasant female voice said, "Elevator temporarily out of order. Please use the stairs instead."

Still boiling with fury, Dyna spoke through clenched teeth. "I can wait."

"Stairs are highly recommended. There is currently no repair scheduled for this elevator."

Dyna looked pointedly at three elevators standing side by side. "Then let me use one that's working."

"Apologies. All three elevators are out of order." A glowing green arrow appeared on the wall between two of the elevators. "If you are not already familiar with the stairs, simply follow the arrows to find them."

Dyna mustered every ounce of willpower to keep from shrieking as she continued down the hallway and stomped down four flights of stairs.

• • •

Located downtown in a small city, Dyna had bought this condo because of its proximity to everything, even though she'd never ventured outside since moving in. The commuter rail and bus station required a two-block walk. Museums, restaurants, shops, and small gardens stood within a one-mile radius.

Now standing alone in her building's lobby, Dyna peeked through the enormous windows facing the main street.

Surprisingly, no one peeked back, each pedestrian and driver and passenger too absorbed in his or her OwnWorld™.

Dyna schemed until she thought of a way to defeat her condo and figure out a way to get back inside. Once that happened, she'd never leave again.

Not ever.

Dyna remembered a cute little clothing shop a few blocks away. Mindful to not draw attention to herself, she eased out of the building and glided along those few blocks, successful at staying invisible by not drawing attention to herself. When she entered the clothing shop, Dyna started at the sound of a tinkling bell on the door.

An android with a screen face approached and said, "Is there something I can help you find?"

Dyna scrunched her nose in distaste. "I don't suppose you have any real humans working here."

"Oh." The android removed its screen face to reveal a human one. It wasn't an android, after all. "I'm Katy," said the young woman now holding the screen face in one hand. "Sorry about the android appearance. The tourists get a kick out of them, and I hate to disappoint."

Dyna had decided to move to this small city because of its popularity as a tourist destination, which meant lots of museums and high-quality restaurants for the locals to enjoy, not to mention the weekly farmers market.

Katy waved away the pretty dresses designed for the younger crowd and led Dyna to the consignment racks. She discovered a nice pair of jeans and a lightweight cardigan/sweater set. She changed into them, and Katy presented a big paper bag for the fluffy pink bathrobe Dyna had worn into the shop.

At checkout, Dyna rambled. "I hope the payment works. My chip has been acting up today."

But as Dyna stepped onto the scanner threshold, the chip embedded in the fleshy part of her thumb gave a happy beep. The word "Paid" flashed in green letters through her skin.

As a pair of tourists entered the shop, Katy hurriedly put her screen mask back on and called out to Dyna, "Come back any time!"

•   •   •

Relieved to be fully dressed and decent, Dyna checked a huge city map displayed on the sidewalk for tourists and then marched at a steady and determined pace toward the local police station. After announcing her request to an IntelligentAssistant™ at the front desk, she fidgeted in a chair in the station's empty foyer until a middle-aged uniformed man beckoned for her to follow him into a nearby office.

The police officer sat behind a small desk and tapped on its surface. He studied the graphics it displayed. Without looking at Dyna, he said, "You're here about a break-in?"

"No!" Dyna said in astonishment. "My home ejected me. It won't let me back in."

The officer's shoulders sagged, and he ran his hands over his face as if trying to stay awake. "You mean your husband locked you out?"

"No!" Dyna insisted. "I live downtown at LuvHomes™. My home is supposed to . . . "

Love me.

"My home is supposed to take care of me," Dyna continued. "But it's gone crazy. Something in my home has misfired. Its wires are crossed. I need help getting back inside my own home."

Finally, the officer looked up, his face edged with irritation. "I thought those places couldn't do anything without your permission."

"Exactly!" Dyna sat back in her chair with crossed arms, grateful the officer understood.

"You have a chip?"

Dyna raised a hand, and her thumb blushed pink.

"Place your hand here, please." The officer pointed at the center of the desk's surface.

When Dyna did so, her thumb beeped repeatedly and then made a grinding noise, as if she'd removed the chip from her thumb and dropped the chip into a garbage disposal. She jerked her hand back and cradled it against her chest.

The officer studied the newly displayed graphics for a few minutes. Pointing at them, he said, "Here's your problem. You bought what they're calling a 'best solution' option. As far as I can make out, you agreed to let your home decide what's best for you."

Indignant, Dyna said, "I did no such thing."

But secretly she wondered if maybe she'd made a mistake. Maybe she had selected that option without realizing what it meant. Or maybe she'd been distracted. She couldn't remember choosing the "best solution" option, but she couldn't remember not choosing it either.

The graphics pinged repeatedly, and a red-and-white bullseye displayed on top of them.

"Go ahead," the police officer said to the pinging bullseye.

"We acknowledge that Dyna Wilson has accessed her own records," said a pleasant female voice with a Bermuda accent. "Please inform her that she is her own problem. She will be allowed back inside her home when she learns how to get out of her own way."

Dyna recoiled in horror.

"Well," the police officer said with a shrug. "That's that." He swept his hand across the desktop to clear all images.

"That's that?" Dyna said. "I thought you were the police. I thought you were supposed to help people. And all you can say is 'that's that?'"

The police officer gave her an unrelenting gaze. "M'am. No law has been broken. And you appear to be unharmed."

Dyna bit back her frustration. "But I can't get back inside my own home!"

The officer stood and gestured toward the door.

• • •

Dragging herself away from the police station, a wave of weakness over-whelmed Dyna. She glanced up at the midday sun and realized she'd had nothing to eat since rolling out of bed this morning. Light-headed, she walked past every popular restaurant boasting a waitstaff of drones and robots until she spotted a small diner.

Dyna minced her way inside the diner. Before she could change her mind and leave, a real human waitress popped into view and seated her at a booth. Dyna placed the paper bag containing her bathrobe on the red leather seat next to her.

A short time later, a strong cup of coffee and a cheddar-and-spinach omelet gave her focus and resolve.

Why should she let her own home boss her around? Dyna knew who she was and what she wanted. She was the one who knew best for herself, not some ridiculous AI.

After finishing her breakfast and paying for it, Dyna stormed the few blocks back to her building, ready to convince her own front door to open and let her back inside.

But when she tried to enter the building, its glass doors clicked shut, even though she knew the lobby doors were supposed to be open at all hours.

"Hey!" Dyna shouted at the lobby. "I need to get in. I live here!"

The building refused to respond. It ignored her.

Dyna tried hiding behind a column near the building's entrance with the hope that a resident or delivery person would cause the doors to open and that she could dash in behind them. But despite a decent amount of foot traffic on the sidewalk, no one tried to enter the building.

If not for the dang chip in her thumb, she might have tried cobbling together some type of disguise. Dyna knew that even if she pretended to be someone else, the building would recognize the chip. She had no way to fool the building into letting her enter.

Dyna saw only one possibility.

She would play along. She would do whatever her home wanted and pretend to be on board.

But once Dyna wrangled her way back inside, she would never go outside again.

"Fine," Dyna said to the building, hoping she sounded agreeable. "What do you want me to do?"

• • •

Following each arrow displayed on her thumb, Dyna took an easy walk to the Downtown Y, where she immediately encountered an old-model TrueReceptionist™ at the front desk, flanked by half-doors allowing members in and out of the Y—and keeping non-members out.

The receptionist existed as little more than a screen on top of a cylinder mounted on the counter, which allowed the receptionist's face to spin 360 degrees, like a possessed child from an ancient movie. The receptionist made loud clunking noises as it turned to face Dyna. When it spoke, the receptionist's voice went up and down like an out-of-control roller coaster. "Oh, Ms. Wilson. You have arrived at last!"

Dyna glanced down at her thumb, which now blinked green. "I don't know what I'm doing here. I never signed up for a membership."

"No worries!" The receptionist's screen spun in circles and then came to a screeching stop, facing the wall behind it. It slowly cranked back to face Dyna, all the while sounding like its bolts were coming loose. "Your home bought a ten-year membership for you. It told me you were once a competitive swimmer, so I've taken the liberty of printing a swimsuit, flip flops, and a towel for you. You'll find them in the ladies changing room by Locker 112."

The screen increased its brightness level, as if beaming with pride.

The half-door marked "Entrance" swung open. The floor displayed arrows that created a path.

"OK," Dyna said with trepidation. She walked past the receptionist. "Thanks."

At Locker 112, Dyna discovered a racer-back suit with a pattern of blue and white bubbles. She liked it, even though she'd forgotten that wrestling her body into a racer-back suit didn't differ much from struggling into a wet suit. Nonetheless, she soon wriggled into the suit and found her way into the pool room.

The stillness of the water in the 8-lane pool surprised Dyna until she glanced at the clock and realized most people were probably at lunch. No wonder she was the only swimmer here.

A lifeguard that looked like a small and rusty lighthouse anchored one end of the pool. Turning a single beam of light at Dyna, it said, "New member. New member. You must complete the Basic Swim course before you are allowed in the water."

Dyna straightened her spine to maximize her height. In an icy tone, she said, "For your information, my college record of the 1500-meter freestyle stood for twenty-five years before anyone broke it. I'm a good swimmer."

She held out her hand for scanning.

The lifeguard dropped its beam of light onto her hand. "No record of swimming competence."

Dyna shrugged it off. "It's been a while since I've been in a pool." Ignoring the protests of the lifeguard, she kicked off her flip flops and climbed down the ladder into Lane 1.

The lifeguard's beam turned red and cast itself around the pool room. "Warning!" it shouted. "Inexperienced swimmer! Warning!"

Ignoring the lifeguard, Dyna ducked under the lane divider and opted to begin with an easy breaststroke in Lane 2.

Moments later, she jerked at the touch of spindly arms that wrapped around her body and lifted her a few feet out of the water.

Straining her neck, Dyna looked up to see spider-like arms attached to a black cable descended from the high ceiling.

"Danger!" the lifeguard shouted. "Inexperienced swimmer is drowning!"

Pushing against the spindly arms, Dyna found them flexible. "I am not drowning!" she shouted. "Let me go!"

"Don't panic!" the lifeguard shouted. "I will save you!"

Dyna squirmed out of the spindly arms and fell back into the water. She stayed submerged and swam diagonally toward the deep end, skimming the bottom to stay far away from the spider-like thing that had plucked her from the pool. The water blocked all sound, but the spinning red beam penetrated the water.

The spindly arms plunged into the water in Lane 5 just as Dyna crossed over into Lane 6, one of the spindly arms grazing her foot.

Her lungs clamored for air, making Dyna regret her surprising inability to stay under water. She'd once been able to swim the length of an Olympic-size pool without having to come up for a breath.

Chagrined, she realized how many years ago that had been. She broke the water's surface with a gasp.

She expected to be scooped out of the water again, but realized the pool room had gone silent. The red light had vanished, and the spindly arms dangled over the center of the pool from the black overhead cable like a dead spider.

At the opposite end of the pool, a man wearing saggy jeans and a green Celtics sweatshirt closed an open panel on the lifeguard with a bang. Looking up, the man waved a hand bearing a wrench and shouted, "All good." He then exited with thudding footsteps.

Keeping her head above water so she could keep a sharp eye open, Dyna paddled in Lane 7.

The lifeguard remained silent, and the spindly arms whirred upwards on the cable and then tucked out of sight in a compartment on the ceiling.

For the next hour, Dyna sliced through the water, reveling in the rhythm of her swim.

•   •   •

When she left the Y, Dyna noticed a spring in her step. It had been years since she'd felt so light footed.

She breezed back into her building without incident and even decided to walk up to the fourth floor instead of tempting the elevator to lie to her about being out of service. Dyna breezed down the hallway of the fourth floor and rounded a corner, only to bump into a naked woman in the hallway.

Staring at each other in surprise, both women shrieked.

Lifting her chin in defiance, the naked woman turned toward the door of Unit 421 and banged her fists against it. "You can't do this!" she insisted. "You have to obey me. Let me in!"

Dyna's first instinct was to rush past the naked woman, but her feet wouldn't move. Dyna averted her gaze from the neighbor she'd never met until now.

"The purchase agreement stipulated nothing about my having to obey you," a firm but gentle grandmotherly voice said from the neighbor's closed door. "The agreement was for me to love you."

"I should have known it was impossible," the woman cried, ignoring Dyna. "You can't feel anything. You're nothing but code and a place where I'm supposed to live."

"You are correct," the grandmotherly voice said, "to a point. While I am incapable of feeling, I am very capable of love, because love isn't a feeling. Love is how you treat people. I am treating you in exactly the way you requested. You display symptoms of sadness and depression, and I am doing what you said would help you feel better. I am treating you with love. Therefore, I am loving you at this moment."

"You know nothing!" the naked woman said. She wept. "You don't know what it's like to breathe. Or care about someone. You don't know what it's like when someone you love is murdered."

Without meaning to, Dyna let out a gasp.

The naked woman whipped her head and looked over her shoulder at Dyna, seemingly astonished to discover she hadn't moved on.

Dyna gave a weak shrug. "You're right. Your home can't understand. But I do."

The naked woman's eyes narrowed with suspicion.

Dyna stumbled over her words. "I mean, everyone knows what it feels like to breathe and care." She hesitated and proceeded with caution. "But the other thing . . . it changes you. It changes everything."

Tears spilled from the naked woman's eyes, as if she no longer needed to hold them back.

Dyna remembered the paper bag she carried in one hand. The one Katy had given to her. Dyna reached inside and pulled out her fluffy pink bathrobe. "This should do for now." Dyna paused, not sure how much or how little she should say. "You know, your home isn't going to let you back inside. Not for a while."

The naked woman reached back with one hand and grabbed the bathrobe. Keeping her back to Dyna, the woman slipped into it. She turned to face Dyna as she tied the belt. "What am I supposed to do? Just wait here?"

"No," Dyna said. "That doesn't work." She rolled her eyes. "That's been my experience."

At first, Dyna's plan had been to pretend to do what her home advised. But for the first time in ages, Dyna had enjoyed the day. She'd been looking forward to going home, curling up on the sofa, and telling her home all about going to the cute little dress shop and meeting Katy. And how Dyna had gone to the police station. And the diner where she'd had a late breakfast. And all about her misadventures at the Y, and how much she liked being back in the water.

That could wait.

"There's a great shop down the street where you can get something other than my bathrobe to wear." Dyna brightened. "After that, I know a diner where we can have lunch."

The neighbor looked down at her feet. "I can't go anywhere without shoes."

"Oh!" Dyna reached into the bag again and pulled out the pair of flip flops that the Y had printed for her. "You can wear these." She extended them, but the neighbor stared at her own naked feet instead of accepting the flip flops.

Dyna remembered the days when she stayed in bed.

The days when she often forgot to eat and could barely function.

The wild ride of emotions, from disbelief to rage to despair.

Sometimes she still struggled, which was why she had bought her LuvHome™, hoping that it would guide her when she needed help.

Hoping that maybe a home could love her back.

Dyna placed the flip flops on the floor. "There's no point in trying to take the elevator. It's in cahoots with the homes, and all of the elevators will lie to you. We'll be better off taking the stairs."

Dyna backtracked to round the corner and walk down the hallway toward the stairwell. Trailing a finger along the wall, she whispered, "Thanks," trusting the message would find its way to her home.

She looked forward to lunch, whether it meant dining alone or enjoying the company of a potential new friend.

Resa Nelson is a member of Science Fiction Writers of America and a graduate of the Clarion Science Fiction Writers Workshop. She has sold more than 20 short stories to magazines and anthologies, including **Clarkesworld**, **The Daily Tomorrow**, **Pulphouse**, **Fantasy magazine**, **Science Fiction Age**, **Marion Zimmer Bradley's Sword & Sorceress XXIII**, **Women of Darkness II**, **Future Boston**, and **2041**. She has published 24 novels, most of which take place in her Dragonslayer world. Her science fiction novels include **All of Us Were Sophie** and **The Mosaic Woman**. She lives in the Boston area. Visit her website at resanelson.com.

MONEY, WEALTH, AND SOIL
BY LANCE ROBINSON

Lucas Romero and his team had become adept at making sense of anomalies that the SoilCoin algorithm sometimes spit out. This time, however, the incongruities were different from what they were used to and none of them could come up with an explanation that they believed might actually be right. What was clear was that the remote sensing data for this secluded, hundred-square-kilometer piece of land looked too good to be true. And if it looked too good to be true, it probably was. And *that* meant that once again someone was trying to game the Soil-Coin system. For Lucas, there was no mystery in the motivations behind what was happening: people did what served their interest. The puzzle rather was how to point their greed in the right direction. With the Pre-CoP Science Meeting and the Panel of Arbitration only four weeks away, Lucas made a choice: he booked a flight to Canada, and made his way to northern Alberta and the territory of this remote First Nation, as some Canadian Indigenous groups called themselves. Now the First Nation's young manager, Daniel Erasmus, was taking Lucas to see with his own two eyes what was causing the anomalies. As they drew closer to one of the hotspots Lucas had identified, he let the view from the passenger seat of the pickup truck—forest on the right side of the gravel road, pastureland on the left—calm his thoughts.

His phone vibrated, pulling him out of his reverie: a message from Mahalia de Guzman, the director of the UNCCD's SoilCoin program. He swore in Spanish under his breath, then opened the message. "*WTF are you doing in Canada!!!*" she wrote. "*Denier extremists killed two scientists from their envt ministry's soil finance program last year. Imagine what they'll do if they learn the UN is there.*"

He typed a brief reply: "*I'm trying to save SoilCoin.*"

Lucas set his phone on the stack of thin cardboard sheets that occupied the middle of the truck's bench seat and looked out again at the beauty of the landscape. He yearned to forget about the currency trading, global finance, and natural capital futures for a month and just go canoeing or hiking. Both his native Spain and his adopted home of Kenya had saved some beautiful slices of nature, but neither country had anything that could qualify as *wilderness* by these North American standards. Even here, though, the so-called "wilderness" had people, some working in it, some living in it, some exploiting it, some trying to take care of it. He also knew that the landscape here was changing. The prairie was moving northward: with the warming of the climate, boreal forest was giving way to mixed wood forest, mixed wood forest to parkland, and parkland to grassland. In most places, though, the old ecosystems were dying faster than the new ones could establish themselves, and where new grassland was spreading into the southern limit of the forest, and new forest was spreading into the southern limit of the tundra, they were impoverished versions of their parent ecosystems. Agriculture too, having drawn down its soils to the point of bankruptcy, was also sliding northward.

His phone vibrated again—his boss had more to say. *"The Canadian AMBASSADOR and a lawyer from RFD are demanding answers from the Executive Director. They think you're overstepping our mandate. You're in over your head!!!"*

RFD Eco-Investments, a Montreal-based natural capital speculator, had leased a large tract of land in this area from Daniel's community and the Alberta provincial government in an arrangement that Lucas did not really understand. What he did understand was that large expanses of land in rural and remote parts of Canada were now being converted from farming or forestry to "natural capital speculation"— investors leasing or buying land to earn money from carbon credits, watershed or habitat concessions payments and, increasingly, SoilCoin credits. As far as he was concerned, if arrangements like this led to soils actually being nursed back to health, they should be encouraged. But only if the renewal of soils was real. That was what he needed to confirm. For three weeks, however, ever since the anomaly detection routines had flagged this remote section of Alberta, people at RFD had been ignoring his emails and dodging his phone calls.

Daniel took one hand off the steering wheel and pointed ahead. "You're gonna lose reception when we get over the next hill. Want me to stop for a bit so you can finish your messages?"

Lucas took another look at the director's message. "No, let's keep going. I'll deal with this later." He slipped the phone back into his pocket.

As they crested the hill, Daniel gestured at the trees on his right. "This bit of forest here helped keep my family alive during the famine. I shot my first elk in there. I was twelve years old. Between the hunting, and the traditional harvesting, and our Nation's bison herd—together, those things helped us get through it. We still had six people die, but it would've been more people if not for us turning to our traditional foods."

That was a time Lucas avoided thinking about. He had been in his early twenties when the soil blight, and then food shortages, and then riots hit Spain. Since then, year after year, the soil blight continued to erupt around the world, and several countries seemed to be permanently on the cusp of famine.

"Dr. Romero, would you say that you guys—the UN, I mean—would you say that you've started to turn things around for erosion and for the soil blight?"

Lucas sighed. "Not yet." It seemed Daniel had been hoping for a different answer because for the next few minutes he was quiet.

Eventually, Lucas's eyes were drawn to the stack of letter-sized cardstock on the seat between them. He picked up one of the sheets and looked it. It was stamped with perforations that created six circular slugs that looked ready to be stamped out of the card. "What is this? There were stacks and stacks of these in the garage where the truck was parked."

"Blanks for drink cup lids."

"Drink cup... Like coffee cup lids?"

"Exactly. We inherited them from the Canwest paper mill about forty klicks from here. We won a court case against them for contaminating the watershed. But as we were winning the court case, this big chain of coffee shops went bankrupt, and they owed Canwest millions. Canwest decided that their best option was to declare bankruptcy too."

"So instead of getting money from your court settlement, you got thousands of half-finished drink lids?"

"Not thousands. *Hundreds* of thousands. But not only drink lids—there were eight giant rolls of stock ready to be chopped into biodegradable, cellulose-based glitter."

"Glitter like for children's art projects?"

"Yeah, exactly." Lucas stared at him, not sure if the young man was pulling his leg. "It wasn't all bad," Daniel continued, as he steered to avoid a pothole. "We inherited the mill's machinery too. We blocked the road to the mill and prevented them from shipping it out until a court confirmed that now it belonged to us. Anyway, take these drink lids for instance." He tapped the stack of cards. "Because of these, I studied materials science at university. The writing was on the wall for plastic drink lids and plastic everything else, and there's so much you can do with cellulose fiber. Like these: before a press stamps these blanks into the shape of a lid, they can be overlain with a nanocrystal cellulose film, and instead of using pigments and dyes for color you can manipulate the nanostructure of the fibers."

"To create structural coloration."

"Exactly! You know about this stuff?"

"Not about manufacturing it. But some satellite remote sensing methods look for structural coloration. I know someone who used it to detect the New Zealand shield bug infestation last year."

"They could see insects from a satellite?"

"He wasn't seeing individual insects. But the infestation was so bad that the cumulative iridescence of the insects' wings showed up in the data."

"Very slick!"

For a few minutes more, Daniel peppered Lucas with questions—several of them quite insightful—about the SoilCoin system and the kinds of remote sensing data it relied on. Then he eased off the accelerator and turned onto what was little more than a trail. He drove more slowly now, another two hundred meters, then came to a stop. Lucas checked his GPS unit. Daniel had brought him to the middle of one of the areas with unbelievable readings.

Stepping down from the truck, Lucas immediately saw something out of place. At the beginning of the drive, in the spots where the land wasn't dominated by trees, there had been a diverse mix of grasses, forbs, and bushes, but here the ground was blanketed with a single type of plant. They were mostly between thirty and forty centimeters tall, a few of them just starting to flower.

"What's this?"

"That's the cover crop RFD planted. It's based on prairie coneflower."

"GMO?"

"Yeah."

Lucas crouched down and took out his phone to capture an image with his flora identification app, but then remembered that his phone had no network service. He captured the image anyway to upload it for analysis later. Then he reached into his backpack and pulled out a device that looked vaguely like a camera. He held it close to one of the leaves then tapped a button.

"The cover crop is supposed to improve soil moisture," Daniel explained, as Lucas read the display on the back of the sensor.

Lucas took a deep breath and slowly let it out, his suspicions confirmed. "What it actually improves is *the appearance* of improved soil moisture. It changes the reflectance of short wavelength infrared in a way that *appears to our algorithms* as improvements in soil moisture. And you see the way the leaves spread out? This isn't like clover or grass. With this, each individual plant hides a lot of bare soil without actually *reducing* bare soil, and it does it in a way that looks to the satellites as if soil moisture has gone up. We've been hearing about the idea, but this is the first time I've actually known it to be used."

"You're saying RFD engineered this plant specifically to hack the SoilCoin algorithm?"

"We'll have to run some tests," Lucas replied, his eyes still on the display of the infrared sensor. "But yes, that's my guess."

"Very slick! Very slick!"

Lucas looked up to see Daniel nodding and smiling. *He admires how RFD is gaming the system!* But then he admitted to himself that he admired it too—just a little. It was pure entrepreneurial ingenuity. The problem, however, was that planting this engineered crop across the landscape was not doing anything to actually address the soil crisis; it was just sucking credits out of the SoilCoin system and devaluing it a little more. Interventions like this would make the system just a little less trustworthy, would add a few more straws to the camel's back.

Then, in an instant, Daniel's expression flipped and he looked worried. "If your hunch is right, will RFD need to repay the SoilCoin credits it earned? They've been doing this for five years. Will they get fined or something?"

"That depends on the Canadian rules. SoilCoin doesn't pay RFD directly; it issues credits to national governments. But Canada might need to repay some credits, and certainly they'd want to pass that loss on to RFD. That's not really my area; my job is only about making sure the algorithms behind the SoilCoin system are scientifically solid."

"If you decide this is a loophole and you close it, RFD will probably lose interest in leasing land from us."

Lucas had not thought about this—he was fixated on the satellite data and the algorithm. "SoilCoin needs to incentivize *actual* improvements in soil health, not this."

"Sounds like the latest in a long line of what gets done to us. Canada comes along and says, 'You can't live there on the prairie anymore; you have to go live up north in the forest instead.' Then we get here and they say, 'Actually, we're giving most of the forest land to logging and paper companies.' Then the paper company pollutes the water and when they get caught, instead of compensating us, its owners say, 'Sorry. Bankrupt. Canwest doesn't exist anymore.' "

"That's really too—"

"Meanwhile, the climate crisis and the soil crisis are putting the ecosystems here through a meat grinder. And you guys say, 'We're gonna fix it by changing how money works.' So we try to play along, and we start earning money with carbon credits and SoilCoin, but now you're about to say, 'No. We're cutting off your SoilCoin.' "

Lucas heard the frustration in the Daniel's voice and began to imagine how he must be seeing it: *Here I am, a stranger from the UN parachuting into their community to gather evidence that will likely be used to close off a major flow of funds for them. A small, poor, and remote community. To them, RFD's lease is valuable, and I'm about to take it away.*

Seeing the anger in Daniel's eyes, Lucas also remembered his phone and the fact that he had no reception here. He had traveled with this stranger from the edge of nowhere off into the depths of nowhere, and now was telling him that he might be about to further impoverish him and his people. He considered lying, considered telling Daniel that he had nothing to worry about, but the truth was that this was a loophole in the SoilCoin system that he needed to close. But before Lucas had a chance to say anything, Daniel whirled around. Lucas followed his gaze and saw that someone was approaching on an ATV. With its electric engine, Lucas had not heard it at all; it had just appeared out of the forest like wolf.

Then, as it got closer, Daniel smiled. Its driver, a man who looked to be in his early fifties, stopped beside the truck and stepped off.

"Dr. Romero, this is Reggie Merrier, our chief."

Lucas offered a hand.

"Sorry I missed you this morning," the man said. "But I see Danny's taking care of you. As long as he doesn't get the two of you lost in the woods." He laughed, which started to put Lucas at ease. Then Daniel summarized for the chief what Lucas had told him about the RFD's cover crop and how it fooled the SoilCoin algorithm. The chief crouched down to take a closer look at one of the coneflower plants. "You know, Dr. Romero, your presence here has caused quite a stir. Since last night, RFD and the provincial Ministry of Energy, Natural Resources and Ecosystem Services have both contacted me at least three times. And this morning, even someone from the federal government. Normally, I can't get them to make time for even a thirty-minute Zoom, but now *they're* calling *me*. And Amelia Gagnon, RFD's ecosystem investments director—she's flying here from Montreal this evening."

"What do they all want?"

"Everyone's beating around the bush, but I think they're all trying to suggest that I should tell you you're not welcome."

"Oh." Lucas looked at the chief, then at Daniel, then down at his feet. Mahalia was right—he was in over his head. For a few seconds the only sound was the trill call of a red-winged blackbird.

Eventually, Daniel broke the silence. "We tried to be so careful in leasing part of our land to this company. We had an ecologist study what they were going to do. Our elders discussed it. The whole community debated it. The money is helping us, just like a temporary side-hustle, you know. It's just a lease—the land is still ours. In the short-term we're just trying to get by, but in the long-term, this land is our wealth. Dr. Romero, can you tell us, is RFD harming our land?"

"I can't tell you anything definitive on that—I'm just trying to ground-truth the satellite data. And even for that, it will take us a while to analyze it properly."

"But if you had to make an educated guess..."

Lucas now felt guilty for imagining, even for a moment, that Daniel might have been capable of doing something violent. *He's actually more concerned about protecting his community's land than he is about the money they're getting.* He told him the truth. "My guess is that it's not doing any harm. It's not particularly *helping* the soil or the ecosystem, but it's probably not doing any harm either."

Daniel visibly relaxed at hearing that, and Reggie nodded.

"I suppose you'll want to take some samples of the plant," Reggie said, "and some soil samples, too."

"That would be ideal. I want to measure how much moisture is actually in the leaves and in the soil. A couple of live specimens of the plant would be best."

"Sorry. I can't let you do that." Then before Lucas had a chance to say anything, Reggie added, "Our lease contract with RFD has all kinds of clauses about not harvesting or letting others harvest, about intellectual property and all that. So, I can't *let you...* take any samples." Reggie paused as if waiting to be sure that Lucas was properly listening. Then he shrugged dramatically. "But if Danny and I go over there to have a smoke and our backs are turned for a few minutes, we wouldn't necessarily know if somebody collected what they needed and put it in the back of the truck."

Suddenly Daniel had a huge grin. "Not to change the subject," he said, "but I got a shovel and some empty ice cream pails in the back of the truck in case anyone needed them. Just sayin'."

Lucas chuckled, having received the message. But his amusement did not last. He hated that yet another corporation was trying to game the SoilCoin algorithm. The soil crisis was real, and the SoilCoin system that was meant to create economic incentives to reverse the situation was itself being eroded little by little. Once Daniel and Reggie were was a suitable distance away, he collected a few small bottles of soil, and dug up two of the plants and put them into the ice cream pails, trying to think how he could get the analysis done in time for the Pre-CoP Science Meeting. The Soil Convention was in an arms race against companies like RFD Eco-Investments around the world. He was glad to have them as allies if they would actually work to restore soils—that was the entire aim of the convention and of SoilCoin credits—but for that to happen, the incentives had to be correct. Companies like RFD would not do it simply to save the planet. And for the business incentives to align with actual improvements in soil health, the algorithm had to be correct. If there was one thing that Lucas still had faith in, it was human greed; his job was to make sure that greed aligned with saving the planet instead of destroying it.

● ● ●

When he returned to Nairobi, it was clear from the understated, almost sad way in which Mahalia reprimanded him, that he had done serious damage to his long-term career prospects in the UN. "There are procedures for how we carry out activities within the member states," she chided him, "and you didn't follow them. You didn't even tell the Canadian government you were going there. So Lucas, here's the way this doesn't become a diplomatic incident: *our position* is that RFD and Canada were simply playing by the rules as they were at the time, and in turn, *they'll* choose to overlook your actions."

Sometimes the politics and the inertia and the bureaucracy were too much to bear, and Lucas wondered, as he had multiple times before, if he would be better off in academia. He did not care about the drop in salary that leaving the UN would probably entail—what he wanted was to know that he was making a difference. But then, three weeks later, the conclusion of the Pre-CoP Science Meeting and the Panel of Arbitration gave him cause for hope. The panel accepted his team's evidence and ruled against all seventeen appeals that different national governments had filed arguing that the algorithm had shortchanged them. Then came the CoP itself, which passed a resolution requiring the algorithm to be updated annually instead of every five years, allowing loopholes that Lucas and his team uncovered to be closed more quickly. Within eighteen months of his trip to Canada, the official SoilCoin algorithm was differentiating genuine soil moisture improvements from the false signal created by plants engineered for unnatural spectral profiles.

Still, the fact that neither RFD Eco-Investments nor the Canadian government would be penalized irked him. He had read the latest global review and he knew the incentives needed to be stronger. The actions being motivated by SoilCoin and other policies and programs were restoring soils in many places, but not nearly as quickly as soils were dying elsewhere. To make matters worse, the more the international financial institutions pumped up the value of SoilCoin, the more incentive corporations and governments had to take shortcuts. Meanwhile, in the declining breadbaskets of Punjab, Saskatchewan, Western Australia, and Ukraine, erosion continued, and in the wetter climates like the Mississippi Valley and the paddies of Kerala, the soil blight fungus continued to spread.

His response was to work harder.

The next CoP was to be held in the United States, with the Pre-CoP Science Meeting hosted by the university in Madison, Wisconsin. Lucas planned to participate virtually, but Mahalia, recently promoted to executive director of the convention secretariat, organized an event to celebrate the successes of the Soil Convention. "You need to crawl out from under your bridge and go there in person," she said. "It all revolves around you and your team."

"It's too soon to celebrate," he told her. "We haven't solved anything yet."

She insisted, saying that although the event would be described as a celebration of the science, in reality it was a political event meant to deepen support for the convention and for SoilCoin specifically. "If we want more countries to really get behind this, we need to look like the winning team. And you need to be there smiling graciously and speaking diplomatically."

As much as he dreaded it, he knew that politics and ribbon-cutting and spin were all part of what was needed to make the SoilCoin system work. And so at the event, as he sat through the speeches from high level panelists, he tried not to squirm. The CEO of the World Wide Fund for Nature praised SoilCoin for helping to put an economic value on natural capital, and a Hollywood VR star—the goodwill ambassador—cooed that the global financial system was finally starting to account for environmental externalities and move in the direction of full-cost accounting.

"One tenth of one percent of full cost," Lucas muttered.

Then came the presentation that was hardest of all to listen to. He had not realized that Amelia Gagnon, the Ecosystem Investments Director of RFD was here—he had not reviewed the agenda for the event and had not seen her sitting up near the front of the room. Two years ago when he met her in northern Alberta, she had been calm and unapologetic about their use of plants specifically engineered to fool satellite observations. And clearly the tightening of the SoilCoin algorithm had not ended RFD's interest in ecosystem services markets.

Taking the podium, she praised the SoilCoin system, and then she complimented Lucas personally. "Two years ago when I first met Dr. Romero at one of our restoration sites in Canada, I was impressed by how important it was to him to ensure the SoilCoin system is objective, accurate, and rigorous. It seems appropriate that after this meeting I'm going to visit that same site again, where we're still investing in soil health—the same place where I first met him. But what's important here is that it's the rigor of the SoilCoin system that gives us confidence to keep investing in soil restoration. The SoilCoin Secretariat and the UNCCD as a whole, every year, you improve your remote sensing methods and improve the algorithm, and that keeps us on our toes. And that's the way it should be. But what's really important is that your work makes soil restoration a good investment for us."

As she returned to her seat to the sound of applause, she glanced at Lucas sitting at the back of the room.

Is she smirking? We caught them red-handed. Exposed them. If one of us should be smirking arrogantly, it should be me.

He did not enjoy it, but he did his duty and sat through all the formal presentations, and when called upon made some optimistic pronouncements. In the evening at a wine and cheese reception, he shook hands and mingled. The next morning, he was glad the fanfare had finished and that he could attend the actual scientific sessions. The first one started with an economist specializing in global datasets who

outlined how every country that created its own environmental credits system based on SoilCoin assessments had seen an uptick in farmers losing land to international investors. Then an anthropologist described a community in Ethiopia whose traditional communal methods
of ecosystem management began to earn SoilCoin credits for the government, some of which were passed down to the community institu-
tion. Lucas felt as if she was speaking directly and particularly to him
as she described how the new influx of money led to growing mistrust
by community members towards its leaders. She finished her presentation by explaining how, last month when she had returned to the community, she learned that it had split into three hostile factions and the
traditional system had completely broken down.

Lucas recognized several people in the room, and he knew that
many knew who he was: not quite the architect of the SoilCoin system,
but certainly one of its chief engineers. In the Q&A that followed the
presentations, discussion revolved around intrinsic versus extrinsic motivations, whether the financial incentives were crowding out spiritual,
cultural and moral impulses, and what it would take to put sustainable
use of land and ecosystems on a firm footing permanently. And then
the chair of the session introduced Lucas and asked him for an insider's
perspective.

"I've got faith in greed," Lucas said. "Love of nature, concern for
generations not yet born—it's all wonderful, but it's money that will
decide things in the end. We need SoilCoin to work."

"It better work," said the session chair. "The consequences of it not
working are too frightening to think about."

That evening in his hotel room, Lucas reviewed the latest anomaly
analysis: a spatial, spectral and temporal deep dive into the remote sensing data in a search for results that made no sense. One of the flagged
sectors caught his eye: northwestern Alberta in Canada, north of the
town of the Grand Prairie. He double-checked the location: it was the
same place, the same Indigenous territory where RFD was leasing land!
He cursed out loud in Spanish and then English and then Spanish again,
but then he channeled his anger into determination. He had stopped
them before; he would stop them again.

•   •   •

Lucas booked flights from Madison, connecting through Minneapolis
and Calgary, for the morning after next. In the meantime, he studied
the anomaly analysis. Whatever this was, it was different than before—

clearly, they were not stupid enough to keep using the same GMO cover crop. And unlike two years ago, this time the effect was small and would yield only a tiny increase in SoilCoin credits. But something definitely was strange with the sudden appearance of point-source increases in microwave reflectivity and strange spectral lines in the visible spectrum scattered across the landscape.

They're probably still experimenting with some new trick. That means I can stop them before they even get out of the gate.

This time, he made no attempt to contact RFD or to arrange an appointment—he would just show up. He did send an email to Daniel Erasmus, though, thinking that once again he might need the First Nation's assistance. Two days later, with coordinates of the anomalies loaded into his GPS unit, he arrived at the area in a rental car. As he entered the First Nation's territory, he pulled over at one spot where the strange satellite readings were within a few meters of the road. Looking around, he saw nothing strange. This was a location where the forest had almost completely given way grassland. There were scattered aspen and poplar trees, various grasses and wildflowers, a few patties of bison dung, and sadly some roadside litter.

He double-checked the GPS location: he was in the right spot. He took readings with his infrared sensor, took photos of several plant species, and then picked up handfuls and soil and looked, felt, and sniffed. There was nothing that struck him as strange. He had hoped that the source of the anomalies would have made itself obvious, the way it had two years ago. Not finding any clues, he returned to his car and drove another half kilometer down the road to a spot where the anomalous readings were stronger and stretched for almost a kilometer beside the road. Again, there was nothing that looked out of place—just the same poplar trees, the same wildflowers, more bison patties, and more litter.

What a shame. So far from the cities and towns and from so-called "civilization", but the few people who are here can't be bothered to keep their rubbish in their car until they reach a bin.

He returned to the car again and continued driving. All along the road here, his data showed that he was driving beside an area where the anomalies were strongest, but still he saw nothing unusual. He checked that his phone had network, then called Daniel, but the call rang five times then went to voicemail. Having failed to find any smoking gun, Lucas decided he would nevertheless go and confront whomever he happened to find at the RFD office. When he arrived, he was thrilled to see that Amelia Gagnon was there—at the event, she had said she was com-ing here but had not said precisely when. But this was perfect—if he was going to confront one of them, he wanted it to be her. With her was RFD's site manager, whom he had also met two years earlier. The man-ager led him into the trailer home that was their field office and directed Lucas to a table, all the while peering at him.

"Why didn't you tell me in Madison you were coming here?" Amelia asked.

Lucas avoided answering immediately. He wanted to reel them in slowly, to watch their reactions as he gradually revealed that he knew they had started to cheat the system again. "I suppose you know," he explained as he sat, "that we're always updating our anomaly detection systems, looking for new ways people might try to fool the algorithm. Improvements in soil condition that are too good to be true. Unusually rapid transitions.... Fraud."

The site manager looked to Amelia for guidance but she seemed un-concerned. "Mmm-hmm."

Lucas looked at the site manager, but he was now taking his cue from Amelia, sitting quietly, his expression blank. Lucas tried again to bait them: "Although the main algorithm is open source, our anomaly detection systems are not. Machine learning, input from experts around the world—I'm amazed at how sensitive they've become."

Amelia remained quiet, waiting for Lucas to say more.

He lost patience. "Are you using any new GMOs?"

The site manager's poker face dissolved. "You know, you're really overstepping your mandate and—"

"It's all right," Amelia said. Then she looked Lucas in the eye. "Yes, we are. It's a variety of milk vetch—*Astragalus flexuosus*. It's leguminous but we've tweaked it to also put a bit more carbon into the soil, *as well* as nitrogen. We had the Ecosystem Services Branch of Environment and Climate Change Canada review it for us. They couldn't see any way that the SoilCoin protocols could deem it illegitimate. Anyway, it isn't much like the coneflower—that did have a unique spectral profile—but the modifications on this plant are all about increasing soil carbon. And most of the benefit will actually come after we're gone—the First Na-tion isn't renewing our lease. We've got less than two years left."

That surprised Lucas, but he decided it was irrelevant. Whatever tricks they were experimenting with here they would eventually take elsewhere.

"Even with the coneflower," the site manager added, "your own panel said we did nothing wrong."

Amelia nodded in agreement, then changed her tone. "Dr. Romero, why are you here?"

This was not going the way Lucas imagined it would. But he decided that even though he still did not know *how* they were doing it, it was time to reveal that he did know they were doing something. So without yet divulging the precise details of the anomaly detection, he told them this area had been flagged again. "The anomalies are all geolocated. Let's pick one of the coordinates I've found and go see what there is to see."

"Your mandate doesn't—"

Again Amelia interrupted the site manager, putting a hand on his shoulder. "Fine. We're doing nothing wrong. Can you bring up a map and show us where the flagged sites are?"

Lucas unrolled his tablet, opened the map and showed them the clusters of bright purple dots. As Amelia and the site manager studied it, Lucas studied the two of them. Then the site manager stood up and walked to the wall behind him, where a large paper map was pinned. He looked at the map on the wall, then back to Lucas's tablet, then back to the map.

"It's not our easement," he said.

"What?"

Amelia leaned back in her chair.

There's that maldita smirk again! Lucas thought.

The site manager waved his hand over the map. "This whole area belongs to the First Nation, but our lease-easement is only here." He ran his index finger across part of the top of the map and then down the left side halfway to the bottom. Then he pointed to one cluster of dots on Lucas's map, then returned to the wall and pointed to a *different* part of the paper map. "That cluster of yours is here. And that other cluster in your data is off my map somewhere over here." He pointed at a bit of blank wall a few centimeters to the right the map. "None of your '*anomalies*'"—he put an exaggerated emphasis on the word—"None of your *anomalies* are on land where we operate."

Lucas's contempt was swept away by panic as he tried to make sense of what he had just been told. The land RFD leased was only part of the First Nation's territory. And it was not the part where the new anomalies were located. His mind cast about for something to say, for an excuse he could give, an explanation he could provide for having showed up here unannounced making accusations—something he could say that would let him save face. Then the panic melted into embarrassment. He apologized. Thankfully, neither Amelia nor the site manager insisted on an explanation or otherwise expressed the offense they certainly had a right to feel. At least not that Lucas could later remember. They both said a few things, but later as Lucas replayed the fiasco in his thoughts, he could not remember what else they had said.

"I'm sorry," he muttered one last time as he got in his car.

So what now? Go confront Danny Erasmus and his people? Go try to summon up some more indignation as I accuse them now? I don't even know how serious the problem is or have even a clue what the source of the strange readings might be. Mierda! I messed this up.

He tried to calm himself as he drove, and to decide on his next move. Trying again to act like a police detective interrogating a suspect was out of the question. What he was sure of was that he would need to calmly and carefully write an email to Amelia Gagnon to apologize properly. As for the unusual readings in the microwave and visible bands, he was a scientist, not a detective: he would go back to Nairobi, analyze them properly, and if necessary ask the Canadian officials to come here and do some field studies. He doubted if he should even go to the band office to meet Daniel as he had told him he would. He could just message him saying he had been called back to Nairobi. But that too did not feel right. Then he reached a T-junction and had to make a choice: left to the First Nation reserve or right and back to Grand Prairie and from there, home. He was not sure what he would do when he reached the community, but he turned left.

As he neared the main village, he remembered Reggie Merrier, the chief. Two years ago, they had stopped at his house. In Madrid or Nairobi, Lucas would never just show up at someone's home unannounced, but he had the impression that here, dropping in on someone was very normal. He found the chief sitting in front of his house at a picnic table.

"Dr. Romero! Danny told me you were coming. Have you seen him?"

"Not yet. My—umm—my meeting at RFD went faster than I thought it would so I'm early. Danny won't be expecting me yet."

The chief directed Lucas to sit, then closed his laptop and went inside and came back out with two coffee cups and a plate of muffins. Thankfully, he did not start questioning Lucas about his mission here, instead wanting to know about life in Kenya and the culture of rural communities there. They chatted about that for a while and then about Canadian politics and about melting glaciers. Eventually Lucas regained enough confidence to ask about the community's relationship with RFD. "I'm curious why you're not letting them renew their lease. Even though they're not doing their GMO coneflower anymore, I'm sure they're still making a profit."

"We need the land back. Our nation is growing, and our buffalo herd—*bison*, technically I guess—our bison herd is growing."

"Does your bison herd earn you as much as leasing the land to RFD?"

"No, no—on pure economics we should probably keep leasing that section to RFD."

"I guess there are tradeoffs, whatever you do."

"No, 'tradeoffs' is the wrong way to think about it. Tradeoffs disappear when you live right. We take care of our families, we take care of our community, and we take care of the land—all three, no tradeoffs. If some option is good for two of those but bad for the third, then it's just bad, plain and simple. No, for that land, for a while it made sense for our families, and for our community and for the land itself to lease it to RFD. But it's as if we sent it away to the city. Like a son who went away make some money in Toronto. But now it's time for that piece of land to come back to the family."

Lucas had to think for a while about that. The chief sipped his coffee.

"RFD needed it all fenced, right? To keep out your bison and even... elk... is that what they're called? They needed to keep all the big grazing species out."

"Yeah, they did. Getting bison onto that land now will be good for it."

"Yes, if you do it right," Lucas replied. "Using grazing animals to restore soils can work, but it's a long-term thing. And the types of improvements it brings aren't easily detected by SoilCoin. So even if you're you do it well, it probably won't earn you much SoilCoin credits."

"No offense, but for us SoilCoin isn't about taking care of the land. It's a..."

"A side-hustle?"

"Yeah! That's what Danny calls it."

"Aren't you going to miss the money you were getting from RFD?"

"We'll keep taking care of our land. If SoilCoin or the Canadian natural capital credits give us some money in the process, we'll gladly accept it, but that's not why we do it."

They talked for a while longer, and then Lucas said he should be leaving. "Please tell Danny I said hello, but I got what I needed at RFD this morning."

They said goodbye, and then Lucas got in his car and drove away. Twenty minutes later he came again to the kilometer-long stretch of road he had passed in the morning where the anomalies showed as particularly strong. And there on the other side of a barbed wire fence, for the first time in his life in person he saw bison, at least thirty of them. They had not been here earlier on his way into the area. He had to stop. When he stepped out of his car, for a long while he just stood there watching them in awe.

I thought they were just furry cows with humps, but the biggest ones look twice as big and three times as strong as any cow.

Then, on the ground, between him and the bison, just beyond the fence, he saw a glint of reflected sunlight, but then it was gone. He moved his head to the left and to the right and then saw it again. He could not tell what it was, but if he kept himself at the same relative angle between it and the sun he could see it. He crossed the road and the ditch and approached the barbed wire fence. As he did, he saw other glints of reflected light from various places. But it was hard to focus his attention on them with the bison now so close. Two of the animals were less than ten meters away and they began fidgeting.

I bet if they really wanted to, they could break through this fence like it was cobwebs.

He stood still. And then, while keeping the bison in his peripheral vision, he looked at what was causing the reflections. They were scattered around on the ground, circular disks slightly larger than his palm. A bit further down the line one was almost within arm's reach of the fence. He walked along the fence until he was as close as he could get and saw that it was still out of reach, but not by much. He looked at the bison and saw that they were bunching up—an instinctive reaction of mutual protection in response to his presence. The closest ones all seemed to be keeping an eye on him as they grazed. Very slowly, he bent down, pulled the middle strand of barbed wire up and pushed the bottom one down with one knee, then he poked his head through and then his shoulders. Then he crawled two more steps, reached out and grabbed the disk and then darted back through the fence. The nearest bison had turned to face him, but the rest just kept grazing peacefully.

Only when he had backed away from the fence, across the ditch to the road and his heartbeat slowed again, did Lucas look at what he had picked up. He remembered the places he had stopped on the way into the area in the morning, a few hundred meters further down the road. And he remembered the litter he had seen there—it was not aluminum cans or glass bottles or candy bar wrappers. It was these same disks, weathered, discolored and partly decomposed at the other location, but that's what they were. Here in his hand he had a new one. It was light and seemed to be made of a thin, hard cardboard. And it was green, but not consistently. Instead it was iridescent, reflecting various shades of green, or from some angles bright white.

And he recollected as well his trip here two years earlier, and the rows and rows of boxes in the garage at the First Nation's office, and the stack of cardboard sheets in Daniel's truck. These disks were Daniel's blanks for drink cup lids. But unlike the blanks he had seen that day with Daniel, these ones now had nanocrystal films applied. Lucas did not need to do a spectrographic analysis—he already knew what he would see. Daniel would have selected the right structural coloration to apply based on what the SoilCoin algorithm wanted to see. The benefit in terms of credits would be small, and would probably not translate into more than a few thousand SoilCoin credits per year even if they scattered them over their whole territory.

But they already have the cardboard blanks and the machinery for the cellulose nanofilm, so this probably doesn't cost them anything. How many of these did he say they inherited from the bankrupt paper mill? Hundreds of thousands? Enough to last them a couple of years, I imagine.

Lucas recalled one of the presentations at the Pre-CoP Science Meeting in Madison. One of the complex sugar chains produced by the soil blight fungus polarized light in an unusual way. This gave him an idea for a remote sensing method for detecting it.

He examined the disk. "Slick!" he said. "Very slick!"

He threw it back toward the fence like a Frisbee, knowing it would biodegrade soon enough.

When he is at his day-job, Lance Robinson is a social scientist whose work revolves around the human dimensions of managing natural resources. Environmental themes and musings about human beings' economic, cultural and spiritual relationships with nature are often woven into his fiction. His short stories have appeared in magazines such as **Analog**, **Riverside Quarterly**, and **Chaos Theory: Tales Askew**. In 2023, he won first place in the quarterly Writers of the Future contest, and his winning story appears in **L. Ron Hubbard Presents Writers of the Future Volume 40**. His own collection of short fiction—**Chasing New Suns**—was published in September 2024. Lance currently makes his home in Robinson-Superior Treaty territory on the traditional land of the Anishnaabeg peoples and Fort William First Nation in the City of Thunder Bay, Ontario. He can be found at lancerobinsonwriter.com.

ACKNOWLEDGEMENTS

The editor would like to thank the following people for their help and support:

Linda McCartney (without whom this book would not have been created), David Baur, Justin Vincent, David Williams, Neil Clarke, the members of csffwa.org, and and all the authors, editors, agents, and publishers whose work makes this anthology possible.

PERMISSIONS

www.ingramcontent.com/pod-product-compliance
Lightning Source LLC
Chambersburg PA
CBHW031333020726
47499CB00005B/1249